CHELSEA LEACH

Riptide

Crossroads Series: Book Two

*For all those that have picked
themselves up and soldiered on:*

*"Our greatest glory is not in never falling,
but in rising every time we fall."*
— Confucius

One

Anxiety in a Box

The atrium of Indianapolis International Airport thrummed with the energy of several hundred passengers as they passed in droves—some coming, some going, and still others sitting patiently on leather couches outside the nearby Starbucks, sipping their coffee and enjoying the Christmas music chiming over the loudspeaker. Jessica Morales shifted from one foot to another uncomfortably as she stared out the floor-to-ceiling windows overlooking the eastern gates of Terminal A and western gates of Terminal B. She sighed, trying to relieve the uneasy quell of emotions rioting inside her.

Hosting her boyfriend-slash-baby daddy while they celebrated the holidays and welcomed their child into the world was a little daunting. Not because she wasn't excited to see him.

She was.

Totally.

She had known Tucker since they were children and missed him terribly, but the idea of having someone else in her space for the next six weeks when she was used to being on her own was exhausting. Were hostesses even allowed to ugly cry? Lord knew she'd done plenty of that over the past six months.

Grieving over *him* had been a process, and one she'd muddled through alone. After all, who could she tell? She was dating Tucker Montgomery, brother to her best friend and son to her pseudo-adoptive parents. It wasn't like she could pull one of them aside and tell them she was still heartsick for a man who, for all intents and purposes, was a footnote in her *Encyclopedia Britannica*-sized list of exes.

Her unborn son landed a ferocious jab to her liver that made her wince, and she gave a sharp inward push of her hand. "Cut it out in there," she grumbled, feeling his solid weight settle on her bladder. With a glance at her smartwatch, she sighed and looked around for the nearest bathroom. A young mother passed close by, hauling two small children, one of which was doing her best impression of a sack of grain while wailing hysterically.

Spectacles like that made the prospect of motherhood seem more like a jail sentence than a Hallmark special, but she was determined to go into it with optimism. Well, as much optimism as one could muster with swollen ankles, raging back pain, and the constant urge to pee. She caught sight of Tucker at the same time he saw her and gave him a shy wave from her spot by the windows. He took two huge steps toward her, let his duffle slide off his shoulder, and wrapped his arms around her, pulling her off her feet for a split second.

"Hi," she murmured as she hugged him back. His powerful, broad-shouldered frame was warm and familiar, comforting.

"Hi," he whispered back, placing a light kiss on her cheek before pulling back to get a better view. "Look at you." He tentatively rested his hand on the bulge of their child, wriggling like an excited puppy within his confines. Tucker's eyes popped open as he felt the languid heave of her stomach. "Whoa."

"Tell me about it," she muttered, looking up into Tucker's gaze. Her stomach flip-flopped, and she thought she might puke.

His eyes had the reflective quality of spring water, allowing the irises to change from a deep hunter green to the blue of sapphires, and every shade in between. Today they were as blue as the occasional peek of sky between snow-filled clouds, and her heart stuttered as she looked into their depths. Despite what had passed between them—one drunken night resulting in the creation of their son—she felt unaccountably shy. He was a beautiful man, tall with sandy blond hair, lightly tanned skin, broad cheekbones and almond-shaped eyes. The attraction was definitely there.

How could it not be?

But it wasn't the all-consuming fire she'd felt for…*him.*

She took a deep breath and pushed all intrusive thoughts aside. If she and Tucker had a shot in hell of making their "fling" into a functional relationship, she had to move on. Sure, for a little while, Tucker would be able to chalk her awkwardness up to the fact they hadn't seen each other face to face in six months. But after that, she'd either have to find a shrink or exercise her demons.

Snow flurries danced in the air as Tucker pulled out of the

parking garage and onto the main road leading off airport property. Jess shifted uncomfortably as the baby pushed into her diaphragm and leaned back in her seat to try to alleviate the pressure.

"Your sister better come back soon. If I get any bigger, I won't be able to leave the house. Kind of hard to get to the hospital if my legs can't support my weight."

"Well, that's what I'm here for. Besides, something tells me she won't be coming home for a few more days," Tucker said as he glanced over his shoulder to check his blind spot before merging onto the interstate.

"*What? Why?*" The sense of panic she felt at her best friend potentially missing the birth of little No Name was overwhelming. Her support system wasn't exactly abundant. If Alaina wasn't here, that only left four people who even cared she was about to give birth: her grandmother, Tucker, and Tucker's parents—Nate and Maura.

"I think she'll be a little busy, that's all," Tucker said with a shrug, staring fixedly at the road to avoid eye contact with his girlfriend.

Jessica smelled a rat. "Tucker," she scolded with a scowl.

"I can't. I promised!" His tone held a pleading note, begging her not to pry, but she was like a dog with a bone.

"If your sister is going to miss the birth of her nephew, she better have a damn good—" Jessica paused, observing the bright red blush creeping up her chauffeur's neck in an unflattering shade of raspberry. "Oh. My. God…"

Tucker glanced over at Jessica, panic flashing in the whites of his eyes.

"Oh my god! Grayson's going to *propose*?" A squeal of ecstatic glee escaped her lips before she could clamp a hand over her mouth. "How long have you known?"

"Not long," Tucker muttered in mortification. He was nearly as bad at keeping secrets as his sister, and he knew it.

"When? How? Oh my god. Have you seen the ring?" Questions swarmed through her mind like a busy hive of bees as she thought of all the possibilities. Alaina had called the night before to say they were leaving London for Paris.

Awww...Paris...How romantic. Ugh, why can't I find somebody like—

She choked off the thought abruptly and tried to sit up from her reclined position.

"I don't know when," Tucker admitted. "Soon. Dad and I had a video chat with Grayson a few days ago. He was supposed to be at some event on his media tour, but he managed to get away from Alaina long enough to make sure he had our blessing."

"He's so old-fashioned."

"I think it was nice of him."

"Of *course* you do." Jess's eyes rolled so far back in her head, she thought for a second they might get stuck.

"An-y-way," Tucker continued, guiding the conversation back onto the rails. "He also happened to be picking up her ring. So *yes*, I've seen it." His voice was smug, and she wanted to smack the smirk right off his face.

"Okay…" Her brow furrowed, confused. "I have questions."

Tucker snorted at her confusion, but waited patiently for her to continue.

First things first.

"Are you seriously telling me Grayson picked a ring from a random store in Paris? Because, honestly, that doesn't sound like something he would do."

Tucker opened his mouth to elaborate, but Jess cut him off. Another thought occurring to her. "And how the hell did he get away from Alaina to get said ring?"

"Well, if you'd let me get the words out of my mouth," he grumbled under his breath.

Jess caressed her belly with gentle strokes and stared at him with angelic innocence, making it clear she had finished her cross examination.

"He ordered her ring from Tiffany's three months ago. He had it shipped to the Paris store because he was afraid Alaina would find it if he carried it around for two months. We didn't really talk about the specifics, but as far as I can figure, Alaina was out working on her spread for *Travel Bug* because she thought Grayson was going to be at some event all day."

Some of Jess's frustration faded at Grayson's genius. Somehow, she didn't think Alaina would mind a little white lie if it ended with an engagement ring from Tiffany's on her finger. "I don't suppose you have pictures." She tugged at the seat belt as it inched back up toward her boobs, irritated. She had secretly hoped Grayson would ask her opinion when it got to the point where he was looking at rings.

Guess not.

"Well, I might," Tuck allowed, glancing sideways at her. His body shook with barely suppressed laughter as he eyed her clearly disgruntled posture.

Frustration at the damn seat belt that wouldn't stay situated around her bump and the sheer audacity of her boyfriend to laugh at her struggle had her temper boiling. *"What?"*

He gave a manful swallow and turned his emerging chuckle into a throat clearing before looking back out the window. "Nothing."

* * *

The midday sun gleamed through a thick layer of gray clouds to provide the only pale light in the nursery. Jess leaned back in the padded rocking chair, moving back and forth in an absent-minded rhythm. A pile of freshly laundered baby clothes sat at her feet, and the residual heat from the dryer seeped through her socks to her frozen toes in a surge of pleasant warmth.

Tita had come over to help her paint the nursery last week, and Maura and Nate had helped with the big things: moving furniture, hanging decorations, and sorting through the gifts from her baby shower. The crib had been a critical—albeit late—arrival and had thus sat in the box propped against the wall of the nursery awaiting assemblage for several weeks.

"Je-sus *Christ!*"

A clatter of wood and the musical clinking of metallic parts pinging against each other made Jessica look up from her spot in the corner where she was folding the final load of laundry. Layla, Jess's border collie, who had been sprawled near the door, sleeping, raised her head off her paws and let out a startled *wuff*.

"What's wrong?" The rocking chair creaked as Jess leaned over to pull the top drawer of the dresser open and placed a stack of newborn-sized sleepers inside. She glanced at her boyfriend, who sat in the middle of the floor surrounded by what seemed to be the remnants of a recent furniture explosion.

"I *swear* companies intentionally make crib assembly as difficult as possible just to watch new parents squirm." Tucker scowled down at the diagram and instructions spread out in front of him.

"You aren't reading it upside down again, are you?" The urge to laugh bubbled up inside her and she snorted uncontrollably.

"Ha. Ha." He grumbled and pointed a stray crib bar at her in accusation. "How about *you* put this damn thing together and *I'll* fold the laundry, hmm?" His tone was gruff, but his blue-green eyes twinkled with mischief.

"I just thought I should leave something for you to do—to help it all sink in." Jess widened her eyes in mock innocence, and Tucker's own eyes narrowed in skeptical response.

"If you think I haven't been straight-up panicking for the better part of the last six months, you're sorely mistaken. This is just anxiety in a box." He gestured at the haphazard pile of shiny brackets, glimmering screws, and wooden planks like it was a blank, thousand-piece jigsaw puzzle.

Jess scooted to the edge of the rocking chair and leaned forward to grab his arm and pull him toward her. "Come here." She laughed softly at his poorly concealed panic and wrapped her arms around his neck. "It's going to be okay."

He swallowed once, twice, and took a deep breath, looking down between them at the bulge of their child pressing lightly into his chest. "How do you know?"

She leaned forward and rested her forehead against his. "I just do."

The corner of his mouth twitched. "I didn't have the best fatherly example growing up. It's hard to model your behavior after someone who was never around."

Jess smiled at his feeble attempt at a joke and tugged on his earlobe. Tucker was not a small man, but somehow his small ears fit with his sharp jaw and high cheekbones. "I know," she whispered. Tucker's father had made a concerted effort in the past year to make up for lost time, Jess's mother, on the other hand, was drowning in a pool of self-pity a thousand leagues deep and wasn't likely to surface any time soon. "We'll do the best we can, Tuck. That's all anyone can ask."

He nodded, holding her gaze for a long moment before leaning in and kissing her on the forehead. "You're gonna be great. I know that much." He twisted back around and took a seat next to her so he faced the mountain of crib parts, but kept his shoulder pressed to her knee. Once he zeroed in on a task, it was hard to pull him away, even if it was stressing him out. Since his sister had the same laser focus, she figured it was most likely a hereditary trait.

Thinking of Alaina gave Jess a sinking feeling. Her best friend had been through a lot in the past year. Besides running their business, reuniting with her estranged father, and falling in love with an insanely gorgeous IndyCar driver, she'd also been in an accident that nearly killed her. Rehabbing had been a long, exhausting road. So, when Alaina's boyfriend, Grayson, suggested taking her with him on a two-month tour of Europe, she couldn't exactly tell her friend *not* to go, but the longer Alaina was gone, the more anxious Jess became.

What if she didn't make it back for the birth?

Jess took a deep breath and tried to shove the thought aside. Worrying about something that may never come to pass didn't do any good. She would be back. She had to be. Jess couldn't do this without her.

Well, she could, *but she sure as hell didn't* want *to.*

The soft *zzz-zzz-zzz* of a vibrating phone pulled Jess out

of her anxiety-riddled daydreams and back to the present. It was four in the afternoon, which meant it was probably Sydney calling to make it an even ten calls before her workday ended at five. The girl's simple existence relieved a lot of Jess's stress, but the plump little brunette was fresh out of college with little work experience, and her executive decision-making skills had a little less oomph than Jess preferred. It wasn't that she minded answering Sydney's questions—quite the opposite. She would rather the girl ask questions than make a critical mistake. But when she asked questions about the little things she clearly knew the answer to, Jess got irritated. She was on maternity leave. The whole point was to be out of reach of professional crises.

*Yet another reason Alaina needs to come back...*now.

"Speak of the devil," Jess mumbled, seeing her best friend's picture shimmering in and out of focus on the screen of her smartphone as it pulsed. "Hello, world traveler!" Jess beamed as her friend's glowing face came into focus. Texts were an almost hourly occurrence, but live conversation was hit-or-miss, and it had been nearly a week since they'd last spoken. "Where are you now? Rome? Amsterdam?"

"Paris!" Alaina stepped aside so Jess could see the lights of the Eiffel Tower twinkling in the background.

"Oh wow. That's gorgeous!"

"Isn't it?" Alaina drew in her bottom lip and bit down to hide a smile.

Jess arched an eyebrow. "What?" She knew by the sparkle in her friend's eyes and the flush on her cheeks it had happened. She was engaged.

Alaina raised her left hand in front of the screen to reveal a gorgeous one-and-a-half carat oval cut diamond surrounded by several smaller stones in an antique white gold setting.

Damn, Grayson… The boy had good tastes. She'd give him that.

A smile split Jess's face from ear to ear. "Oh. My. *God!* Congratulations!"

Tears of happiness welled in Alaina's eyes, and she glanced off-screen for a minute before tuning back into the video chat. "I just can't believe it." Her hazel eyes were wide with wonder, and the camera dimmed in and out of focus with the slight tremor of Alaina's hand as she held the phone. "It was so romantic, Jess, and I was so surprised. I had no idea!"

Jess curled one leg up underneath her in the cushioned rocker and settled in. "I want to hear everything! What did he say? Did he get down on one knee? Did you cry? Did *he* cry?"

Tucker smiled up at her and winked—a silent thank you for covering his indiscretion.

Alaina giggled and Grayson said loudly off-screen, "No, I did *not* cry."

"He's right. He didn't cry, but I did—once I realized what was happening. We ate dinner at Ducasse sur Seine—that restaurant on the boat that's glass all around. You remember me telling you about it?"

"So he was buttering you up," Jess jibed, hoping Grayson was listening. She loved to tease him. The guy was so good-natured, you could stab him with a dinner fork and he'd shrug it off. Testing his patience was half the fun.

"Shut up," Alaina said with a roll of her eyes. "Anyway, we were walking back across the Pont d'Iéna with the Eiffel Tower all lit up, and Grayson just stopped. I couldn't see him, so I thought his shoe was untied or something. I was just leaning back against the side of the bridge waiting on him, taking in the view when he said. 'Would you get over here? I'm trying to make a grand romantic gesture.'"

Jess shook with silent laughter and covered her mouth with her hand, trying to stifle the giggles that were bubbling out of her.

Tucker, on the other hand, had no such compunction. "Oh my god, Alaina! Seriously?"

"Thank you!" Grayson shouted, leaning over his fiancé's shoulder to come into full view.

"Well, how was I supposed to know?" Alaina asked indignantly. "I wasn't waiting for you to drop down on one knee and pull a ring out of your jacket pocket."

Grayson smiled and kissed her cheek. "Well, I'm glad I managed to surprise you—even if it wasn't as romantic as I imagined."

"It was amazing, babe. Really." She turned to kiss him, and Tucker made a gagging noise.

Alaina smiled and pulled back from Grayson to face the camera again. "Well, it's getting late here, but I just wanted to call you while we were on the way back to the hotel to tell you the news!"

Jess's heart twisted. As elated as she was for Alaina, she couldn't help but feel the smallest ache of loss in her chest. If she was being completely honest, there was a bit of jealousy there too. "Congratulations, Lainie. I'm so happy for you."

"Thanks, girl. I'll call you tomorrow." She blew her a kiss and then disconnected the call.

Jess sagged back in the chair and studied Tucker.

"What?" he asked, gazing up at her.

"I guess it's official."

"Guess so," Tuck said with a shrug. "But you know…I don't mind as much as I thought I would. Grayson's great, and he loves Alaina. That's all I have a right to ask."

Jess snorted. "Well, that's philosophical." She eased her leg out from underneath her and groaned as she stretched the muscles in her back. She took a deep breath and rocked forward to gain momentum before heaving her thirty-eight weeks pregnant frame out of the rocking chair. This baby would be here soon. She just hoped he would cook in there a little longer so Alaina could be here too.

Two

What's in a Name?

Generally speaking, it took a lot to get Jess worked up—even with pregnancy hormones thrown into the mix. But if she had to take one more call about these end-of-year tax forms from Sydney, she was going to explode. So, against her better judgment, she found herself out in the bitter cold and snow flurries, on her way to the shop to help her protégé finalize 1099s, W-2s, and any other documents that could potentially cause issues with the IRS.

The background music playing on her radio abruptly cut off with an incoming call through the speakers, and Jess clicked the answer button on her steering wheel. "Hello?"

"Hola, cariña." Her grandmother's greeting came through the speaker with a tinny echo in her warm, deep voice.

"Hola, Tita. ¿Como estas?" Jess glanced over her shoulder to check her blind spot before merging right to take her exit downtown.

"¡Tu madre esta loca!" Well, yes. Her mother was crazy, but that wasn't news to anyone. Abuela switched over to strongly accented English, as she often did when speaking to her American granddaughter, and continued the story. "I got a call from Juan Gonzalez last night. The wonderful young man who owns the bar down the street? María refused to leave, passed out on the bar. I had to go pick her up!"

Jess closed her eyes and gave a frustrated sigh, gritting her teeth to maintain her composure. "Lo siento…" Her mother had a way of inconveniencing everyone with her behavior and embarrassing those closest to her in the process.

"No te preocupes."

Don't worry. Right…

"I only called to tell you she will be staying at Recovery Centers of America for the next month or so. When she woke up, I told her she was going to get clean. She has a nieto coming, y no accepto un no por respuesta." Her grandmother had a heart of gold, but Jess couldn't help being pessimistic when it came to her mom's recovery. She'd been down this road before—about twenty times.

"Can you send me the facility's information, Tita? I'm driving, but I will call to see when they're accepting visitors."

"¡Por supuesto!"

Jess pulled into her parking spot on the street outside of Decadent Designs and put her Blazer in park. "Gracias. I have to go. I'll call you later."

"Te amo, cariña."

Jess smiled softly as she relaxed her head back against the headrest and stroked her belly. "Te amo." She'd never been close to her mother. María was not the kind to inspire undying loyalty and affection. If anything, she was one of the biggest pieces of human garbage Jess had ever met, but she held a special place in her heart for her abuela.

Her mother had been a brilliant contemporary dancer in her younger years. So talented, The Julliard School, NYU, and several other prestigious programs across the country had been considering her for scholarships. Her natural-born ability to create poetry with movement had been her ticket out of small-town life—until she turned up pregnant two months before high school graduation. Jess had been her mother's punching bag for most of her life, and as long as she lived, she would never forget the feeling she had when she'd turned around in the back seat of her grandmother's sedan and watched María's apartment building grow smaller and smaller out the back window as she left for the final time.

Tita had done her best raising her granddaughter, and Jess loved her dearly, but Alaina's family had been her point of reference when it came to "family." She'd spent more time at their house than at her own over the years, and the news of Nate and Maura's divorce had cut nearly as deeply for her as it had for her best friend. Tucker had always been the shadow in the background—a typical little brother always cracking jokes and partying it up. It wasn't until Jess had run into him nine months ago at a club in Dallas that she'd seen him as more than Alaina's little brother. He was still funny, but he was also kind, smart, and smoking hot. Even without the influence of alcohol, she would have been drawn to him. Tequila just ended up being a convenient excuse.

They say history has a tendency to repeat itself, but Jess didn't see her situation that way. She was seven years older than her mother had been with an established career and a roof over her head. While this child hadn't been planned, she didn't harbor the same resentment for him that her mother had for her. He would be loved, treasured, and adored. Every moment of his life would be a blessing, and she would be there for it, however complex the situation with his birth father might be. She watched in mild fascination as her stomach rippled and heaved with his movements. Soon he would be out in the world, and she wondered what that would feel like, to finally lay eyes on this tiny human she and Tucker had created together.

It's something a girl should be able to ask her mother.

Well, fat chance on that one.

* * *

The astringent fumes of bleach wafted around Jess in a thick cloud, burning her nostrils as she scrubbed at the soap scum on the bathroom sink. Things at the office had gone less than stellar, and she sent a scathing text to Alaina in which she demanded she return home to deal with the newbies.

Alaina had replied, "Coming home Friday."

Christmas Eve. Alaina would be home in two days.

She just had to hang in there until then. And then she could kick up her swollen feet and contemplate life in blissful peace until the baby arrived. All she had to do was make it two more fricking days. She scrubbed at the sink even more ferociously.

"If you don't take a time-out, you're going to scrub the finish right off that sink," Tucker said as he leaned against the doorjamb, arms crossed in the perfect image of nonchalance.

Jess sighed and leaned back, wiping sweat from her brow with her forearm.

"Rough day?" Tuck's dark eyes probed her silently, observing the tense set of her shoulders and blotchy cheeks.

"You could say that." Jess turned the water on and rinsed the cleaning solution off the surface and into the bowl.

"Want to talk about it?"

Jess closed the toilet lid and sat, leaning to one side to ease the tension in her lower back. She carefully peeled the yellow latex gloves from her hands and tossed them onto the sink before looking up at him, mildly annoyed that he couldn't just leave her alone. When she wanted to talk, she'd talk. But she also knew he wouldn't leave her alone until she told him what was bugging her. "María is in rehab."

"Well, that's good, right?" Tuck asked, pushing off the doorjamb to come closer.

"Until she falls off the wagon," Jessica grumbled, kicking at the fluffy white rug on the floor at her feet.

"Maybe this time she won't."

"Please. I really don't have the mental energy for that kind of optimism," she huffed as she dabbed at the sweat running down her temples.

Tucker snorted. "Well, you never know. I've seen crazier shit."

After a beat of silence, she sighed heavily and reached out for his hand to help her up. "I think it would take a minor miracle for my mother to sober up."

Something in his eyes made her stomach quiver with a sudden, powerful yearning. She wanted him so badly, she thought she might rip the clothes from his body. He felt it too. She could see it in the way his gaze lingered on her lips and his Adam's apple bobbed.

Her breathing hitched, and he leaned down, brushing his

lips tenderly against hers. It was their first kiss in months, and she'd been nervous thinking about it. At the moment, she couldn't remember why. After all, it's not as if they hadn't done much more than kiss.

Exhibit A, the bun currently residing in her oven.

Her memory of that night was cloudy, but from what she *could* recall, it was all hot, steamy—

"We can't," Tuck said, breaking away from her. Their bodies had been rubbing together in such a way that her intent was perfectly plain, and from the bulge in his pants, his body was on the exact same page.

"Why the hell not?" she moaned, wrapping her arms around his neck and pulling him back down to her.

"Because you're—"

"I swear to god if the word pregnant comes out of your mouth, I'm going to castrate you with my bare hands, Tucker Montgomery."

His sandy eyebrows shot up in astonishment and a muscle in his jaw twitched with barely suppressed amusement. "I was going to say 'upset.'"

She glared at him. "I'm trying to understand what that has to do with us having sex."

"I just wanted the next time we had sex to, I don't know… mean something?"

Jessica stepped back from him and put her hands on her hips. "And because I'm upset, it *doesn't* mean something?"

He sighed and closed his eyes. "That's not what I'm saying."

"What *are* you saying?" The blood was pulsing through her head, creating a ringing sensation in her ears, and she attempted some deep breathing exercises through her restricted diaphragm to lower her blood pressure as she waited for his answer.

"It's not that I don't want to. It's just…is it the right time?"

"Seriously, who *are* you?" She stepped back in his direction and wrapped her arms around his waist. "I didn't realize that committing to a monogamous relationship meant being celibate too, and I *really* have an itch in need of scratching."

He gazed down at her, a smile playing on his lips. His pupils were so dilated by desire, they seemed like bottomless pools of shiny black ink. "Well, no…celibacy was not the goal." He snaked his arms around her and pulled her firmly into him before slowly backing her out of the en suite bathroom and into the bedroom. "Now…about this itch…"

Her calves hit the edge of the bed and she gave him a scorching gaze before running her hands up under his shirt. He shuddered and let out a groan as her fingers trailed back down and traced the oval shapes of his nipples. Goosebumps erupted across his body and he seemed paralyzed under the onslaught of sensations. Then with a hunger akin to her own, he grabbed at her shirt and whipped it over her head.

"Come here," he growled and pulled her to him, his mouth covering hers, devouring her. She fiddled with the button of his pants, the need for him growing by the second. If she couldn't have him, she'd die trying.

His pants hit the floor. Her pants hit the floor. And somehow in the flurry of clothes and pent-up sexual frustration, they wound up on the bed.

"God, you're beautiful," he whispered, raising his hands to cup her full, tender breasts as she hovered over him. A deeply rooted instinct within her responded to the low tender croon of his voice. Male appreciation—possibly the biggest craving of her entire pregnancy. Her body was throbbing for him, for his touch. God, she *needed* him.

A devilish grin curled her lips as she swept her dark hair over her shoulder and dove in for the kill.

* * *

Boneless and jellied, Jess slowly found her way back into her body, breathing deep to take in the familiar scent of her Downy laundered sheets mixed with the unique musk of their lovemaking. Tucker tightened his arm around her midsection and fit himself behind her, spoon-fashioned. The rasp of his five o'clock shadow scraped against the soft skin of her cheek as he nuzzled her and laid a tender kiss on the side of her neck.

"We still haven't picked a name," Jess murmured with a yawn as she burrowed further into her pillow.

"Not exactly what I expected to hear after an impromptu roll in the hay." He gave a subterranean chuckle as he laid another kiss on her bare shoulder.

She rolled onto her back, placing one arm behind her head to prop herself up. "I don't know where that saying came from, but that doesn't seem at all comfortable."

"Ah, it's not so bad." Tucker shrugged and pushed himself up to lean against the headboard.

Jess's eyes widened. "You've actually *done it* in a pile of hay?" She couldn't decide whether she wanted to pry further or burst into peals of laughter.

"Definitely not the strangest place I've ever had sex, but yeah."

Jess struggled to right herself, fighting against her enlarged center of gravity until she managed to get herself into a position identical to Tucker's. "Okay, now I have to know."

"Madison Carmichael's sixteenth birthday bash. We snuck off to the barn and christened the hay loft." He shrugged again as though it wasn't a big deal. "I'd say the strangest place would probably be…in the women's restroom at Fuse Night Club. There may have been a fair amount of alcohol involved in that one."

"May have been?" Jess asked with a giggle. She wasn't a stranger to sexual exploits. She just generally chose to go home with her conquests rather than hook up with them in the establishment's darkest recesses.

"What about you? I know you have some stories."

She gave him the side eye. "Oh you do, do you? Honestly, nothing comes to mind. I did have sex in this guy's kitchen once. That was kind of different. Not sure why though…" Jess drifted off trying to remember what had prompted that particular encounter, but all she could recollect was the cold granite of the countertop creating friction with her ass. Not necessarily a pleasant experience. Chafing is a bitch.

"The kitchen? That's your weirdest spot? Man, maybe you're a little more vanilla than I thought," he teased with a gentle elbow into her side.

"Hey, I was ready to take my chances in the bathroom earlier. You're the one that moved us here."

"Oh, so it's my fault then?" His deep, throaty laugh sent echoes of their intimacy pulsing through her, and she struggled to pull herself back to a cognizant train of thought that didn't involve ravishing her boyfriend again.

"Unless we want to name our son "Sex Fiend" or "Orgasm," I think we should probably course correct this conversation."

Tucker's smile broadened. "Alright party pooper. What

are you thinking?"

"Well…I like Daniel. Jameson. Maxwell—"

"Not Maxwell. Too prep school, trust-fund for my tastes."

"Ooookaaaayyy."

Tucker drew intricate patterns down the side of her arm and across her breast with the lightest of touches before coming to rest on her voluminous belly.

"Do you have any suggestions?" she asked in an attempt to avoid distraction.

"I like William. Orrrr Landon. Maybe Chase?"

Jess made a disagreeable "Mmmm," and turned into him, shifting her weight so they were staring at each other. "How about Parker?"

His face didn't crinkle up in immediate disagreement. Instead, he internalized and then said, "Parker Montgomery. I kind of like it."

"Parker…Maxwell…Montgomery?" Jess asked hopefully.

"Not a chance." Tucker shot down her suggestion with a definitive shake of his head.

"Okay…" She stuck out her lower lip in a pouting gesture before continuing her thought. "What about Nathan? After your dad?"

Tucker shook his head. "Nah…me and Dad are on better terms than we were, but we're not close enough to name my kid after him."

"Alright. Ummmm…Elijah?"

"Too biblical."

"Well, how 'bout you give some suggestions instead of nixing all mine?" Jess asked defiantly, crossing her arms and resting them on top of her baby bump.

"I like Blane."

Jess let the name pass through and flip over in her mind. "Parker Blane Montgomery." She nodded slowly. "I think we have a winner."

"Really? You like it?" Tuck sat up from his reclined position, surprised.

"I do," she said with a smile and leaned forward to kiss him lightly on the lips.

"And you're okay with Montgomery as—"

"Of course." Jess stopped him mid-thought. "Your family was mine too growing up."

He gave her a soft smile and leaned in to give her a deeper, slower kiss that warmed her insides and made her tingle all over. "You know…" He snaked one arm behind her to pull her into him, while the other hand ventured beneath the sheets and between her legs, cupping her possessively. "Even back then, I thought you were sexy as hell." His voice was husky with want as his dexterous fingers stroked her.

She moaned, arching into him as his mouth came down on hers. If she was honest with herself, she had never noticed Tucker when they were younger. He was just Alaina's cocky little brother, but now…Well, he wasn't little anymore, and he certainly had a reason to be cocky. She let out a high-pitched gasp and dug her nails into the nape of Tucker's neck, her teeth sinking lightly into the flesh of his shoulder as she shook with waves of pleasure. "*God*." She gave a euphoric sigh and fell limply back into her pillows.

Every inch of her skin buzzed with the afterglow from Tucker's magical fingers, and she smiled as she gazed up into his sparkling eyes. She loved the translucent quality of his irises. You never quite knew what color you would see when you looked at them, but they were always somehow familiar in their intangible beauty.

They gazed at each other for a long time, the silence between them comforting rather than awkward. It was one of the best and strangest things about their relationship. While a romantic commitment was new to them, they had known each other most of their lives. In many ways, Jess had more in common with Tucker than Alaina. They had both been part of the same crowds in their small high school—though three years apart. They'd come home from parties drunk, smoked the occasional joint, and even wrecked the family car. They had tested the limits of their juvenile freedom together. Alaina had always been a goodie-two-shoes, but that's what Jess loved about her, and as they'd grown older, it was Alaina's influence that had worn off on her the most, even if she did still enjoy a good party.

"Do you think…" Jess trailed off, drawing an imaginary pattern through the dusting of hair on Tuck's chest.

"What?" he whispered as he rolled onto his back and closed his eyes.

She had been hesitant to bring it up, but curiosity was slowly killing the cat. "Do you think we'll ever have what Alaina and Grayson have?" Her voice was wobbly and lacked its normal confidence.

Tucker lay frozen for a moment, eyes still shut, but his face had tensed slightly. Eventually, he sighed and turned his head to look at her. "I don't know."

Jess nodded slightly and gazed down, entwining their hands as she thought. "I didn't think anything that perfect existed before I saw it for myself."

Tuck smiled. "But now that you know it does, you want a little piece of the action?"

"Don't you?" She gave him a questioning look. Guys couldn't be that much different from girls, could they? Didn't everyone want that perfect sense of completion?

"Well, sure. I'd love to have someone who looks at me the way they look at each other, but honestly, I think those stories are few and far between. Doesn't mean other kinds of happiness don't exist, though."

The argument made sense. Alaina and Grayson had fallen into each other's laps and their relationship had been forged in the fires of life and death experience. The couple that emerged from those fires was unbreakable and picturing them apart now was as foreign a concept as breathing underwater. For most people, it didn't happen that way. Except Jess felt like it had happened to her. She had found someone who understood her like that. But in typical Jessica Morales fashion, terrible timing and poor decision-making had led her in the opposite direction.

"Yeah…I suppose," she murmured, letting her words drift into the space between them quietly. Her mind raced with uncertainty and far-fetched scenarios as it so often did these days. In fact, it happened with such frequency she wondered if it was a possible side effect of impending motherhood. Jess sighed and glanced over at her bedmate. His hand had relaxed in hers and the regularity of his deep breathing told her all she needed to know. Tucker was fast asleep.

No rest for the wicked though.

It wasn't that she resented Tucker, or blamed him in any way for their situation. They were both adults, and they had both played a part in the choices that led them here, but she'd also be lying if she said she didn't think about *him* sometimes, late at night, lying in bed. She often wondered where he was, what he was doing.

If she called him, what would he say? Would he let her call roll to voicemail or would he answer? If he answered…

She sighed and squeezed her eyes shut. Jack Kinney had an awful habit of sneaking into her thoughts, and she couldn't help but wonder if he ever thought of her in the same way.

Three

The Night Before Life Goes On

The intimate feel of strong, masculine fingers walking over the bare flesh of her thigh made Jess smile in drowsy contentment. The fingers continued their trek over the peaks and valleys of hip and waist, before the large hand pressed into her love handle with a possessiveness that stirred a fire deep within her. She took a deep breath and turned onto her back, opening herself to the man next to her. The mattress shifted, and suddenly, she was staring up into smoldering, slate gray eyes rimmed with dark, thick lashes. She'd always thought they were beautiful. She'd even go so far as to say she was jealous. Lashes like that were lost on a man, but they made his dark irises stand out even more in their framed setting. She ran her hands through his dark hair as he bent to lay tender, warm kisses on the curve of her neck, followed by the slickness of his tongue dipping into the hollow of her clavicle. She shuddered and moaned at the waves of eroticism unleashed by his touch.

With a shallow gasp, her eyes shot open to the darkness of her bedroom. Trying to control her breathing and the racing of her heart, she looked to her left where Tucker lay on his back, bare chested, sandy blond hair sticking out in a hundred different directions, sleeping like the dead. She closed her eyes with a sigh and threw her head back into the pillows, trying to erase the sensations of naked flesh and hot, tangy kisses by sheer force of will.

A radiating pain crept through her lower back and she shifted, wincing as she tried to ease the twinge. She was in a constant state of discomfort these days, and this was only the latest in a laundry list of physical complaints. She stared up at the ceiling, replaying the dream.

God, she missed him. Tears pricked at her eyes and overflowed down her face. She swiped at them, trying to erase any evidence of her grief. She loved Tucker. She did. And there was no denying there was a physical attraction there, but…

The pain throbbed at her back again and she sniffled, wiping the rest of the tears from her face before she rolled to the side and swung her legs off the bed. If she kept heaving to and fro trying to get comfortable, she'd wake Tucker, and she sure as hell didn't feel like explaining to him why she was bawling her eyes out. Getting out of bed and waddling to the bathroom, though, that was perfectly normal for her at this time of night. Even if he woke in her absence, he'd hear the flush of the toilet and go back to sleep.

The expenditure of energy for something as simple as a trip to the bathroom was remarkable in the third trimester, and the closer her due date came, the more she welcomed it.

Not only was she anxious to have her body back to herself, but she was also anxious to meet this little person she'd been cooking inside her for the last thirty-nine weeks. She stood in front of the sink, staring at her reflection and trying to clear her head of the chaos within. She would only be able to loiter in the bathroom for so long without raising suspicion. So, she peed, flushed the toilet, and wandered out into the living room to light her favorite Christmas candle.

The sound of claws clicking on laminate greeted her as she opened the bedroom door and made her way out into the living room. Never one to leave her mistress without company, Layla pressed up to Jess's leg and stared up at her, big brown eyes gleaming in the light from the Christmas tree. She whined and pressed further into Jess's leg, as if urging her to talk, to unload her burden to her sweet little ball of black and white fluff. She hoped Layla would adjust well to the baby, but wasn't worried. The dog was small for her breed, only weighing twenty-five pounds, but she was twenty-five pounds of sugar.

Now wide awake, she knew going back to bed was a fool's errand. With one hand massaging the knot at the base of her spine, she waddled into the kitchen in search of refreshment. Satisfied with a mug of hot cocoa and a few pretzels, she lowered herself onto the couch with a groan and gazed meditatively at the Christmas tree. The tree's cherry red globes glinted in the glow of its white twinkle lights, and she smiled thinking about how, next year, she could watch the wonder of Christmas through her baby boy's eyes for the first time.

She caught her breath as the knot expanded into the worst muscle spasm she had ever experienced. It gripped her lower back like a vice and sent radiating pain down through her legs. Maybe it was a pinched nerve. With how swollen she felt, it wouldn't surprise her if all sorts of things were getting squished into abnormal positions. She let out a breath and leaned forward, pulling her legs out from underneath her so she sat on the couch with one hand on the source of the pain and the other gripping the arm of the couch.

"Can't sleep?" Tucker's raspy voice startled her, and she jumped. "Sorry," he whispered, a smile in his voice.

She turned toward him as he made his way around the couch to face her. "It's a little hard to get comfortable these days, and every time I do, I have to pee again."

Tuck leaned down and ran his fingers along her cheek, moving a piece of hair gently behind her ear. "How about a foot rub?"

"How about a back rub?" It wasn't that she didn't appreciate the sentiment, but this pinched nerve was driving her nuts.

"Your back's still bothering you?" Tucker asked, sitting down on the coffee table opposite her. A deep pink line from his pillow was imprinted down the side of his face with a boyish charm that made her smile.

Jess let out a deep breath and rolled her neck from side to side to stretch her cramped muscles. "Yeah. I've tried everything."

"Have you tried timing the pain?"

Jess stared deep into the shadow of his dark eyes, lost. And then it dawned. "I'm not in labor."

He raised a skeptical eyebrow as she hissed and bowed her head, letting out a cleansing breath. When she looked up again, he was taking note of the time on his G-shock. As the pain passed, she rocked herself on the edge of the couch, hoping to gain enough momentum to propel herself up out of the cushions. She'd only made it two paces past the coffee table when she froze at a popping sensation followed by a gush of fluid that soaked her black tights before trickling onto the hardwood laminate flooring.

She froze, unable to breathe, as reality smacked her in the face. She glanced at Tucker, who likewise sat frozen, his Adam's apple bobbing precariously in his throat as he swallowed.

"Tell me again you're not in labor?"

* * *

Jess turned onto her side, trying to get comfortable in the awkward hospital bed. She felt another contraction coming on and took a deep breath, trying to breathe through it. After her water broke, Tucker had jumped into emergency mode, calmly collecting their hospital bags and taking them out to the car while she changed out of her sopping wet pants and took a quick shower. Two hours later, checked into the maternity ward, clothed in a hospital gown, and hooked up to what felt like a million different monitors, panic began to take hold.

"I don't think I can do this," Jess hissed through the pain. Her stomach felt so tight if you pricked it with a pin, it would pop like a balloon.

Tucker rubbed the small of her back in a soothing circular motion as Jess hunched over her pillow. "Yes, you can. You can do this. It's going to be okay."

"I want Tita." Jess sobbed, burying her face in her pillow.

"She's on her way. Take a deep breath. Just breathe."

Her body relented its rhythmic spasm, and she let out the rest of her breath in a loud whoosh. "Why are you so calm?" Jess asked, half irritated at her boyfriend's demeanor.

"Who says I'm calm?" he asked, raising a brow at her before checking his phone for the thousandth time since they'd arrived at the hospital.

"If this is you freaking out, then you have no emotional range."

Tucker's lip twitched, and he glanced at her. "I'm just…" He rubbed his hand slowly over his eyes and sighed. "I'm trying to keep it together. The last thing you need is me losing my shit, and…"

"And?" Jess leaned over to grab her cup of ice chips off the bedside table and tip a few into her mouth, crunching loudly as she waited for Tucker's reply.

"I can't reach Alaina."

Jess paused as she tipped the cup up to release more ice and slowly lowered it back down. "What?"

"I tried calling her. She's not answering. Neither is Grayson. I think they might be on a flight home, but they didn't send me their flight info."

Jess nodded calmly, despite the utter terror that had its hand around her throat. "She said they would be home on Christmas Eve. That's today, right? I mean, it's technically eleven in the morning in Paris. They could be somewhere over the Atlantic."

Tucker nodded and rolled his shoulders back to release some of the tension in his neck. "You're right. I know. I just—"

"Can't help panicking after what happened?" Jess finished his thought with a small smile. She knew how he felt. When the worst happened, it was hard to keep your mind from jumping to that same conclusion every time someone didn't answer your texts. "It'll be fine," Jess continued, shifting her weight to get comfortable. "Besides, I think we have bigger fish to fry at the moment."

Tucker snorted, dodging around machines and wires to lean in and give her a quick peck on the lips. "I suppose so."

The curtain partitioning their birthing suite from the entrance to the labor and delivery ward zinged back on its track and a nurse entered, pausing to place her hand under the hand sanitizer dispenser, before rubbing her palms together furiously. "How are we doing, Mom?" she asked in a sweet contralto voice as she wrote "Madeleine" on the dry-erase board near the door in bubbly scrawl.

"I'm okay." Jess inhaled deeply, bracing herself for the contraction she could feel stirring in her lower back.

The young woman, roughly Jess's age, eyed her patient before stepping over to the monitor and examining the output of the fetal monitor. The thin black line began its slow ascent up the screen, and they all stared at it like it held the secrets to the universe. "Your contractions are becoming more regular. Baby's heart rate looks good. Are you still wanting an epidural?"

"God, yes," Jess groaned, feeling beads of sweat forming on her brow as she pursed her lips and tried not to moan at the vice grip around her abdomen.

Madeleine gave an amused chuckle. "I'll page the anesthesiologist and get you on the list. It may be an hour or so before she can get up here."

Jessica felt tears of desperation prick her eyes, and Tucker's hand came down on hers, squeezing in a way that said, "I'm here. I'm with you." She grimaced appreciatively before relaxing back into her pillows, already exhausted. "An hour? Won't that be too late?"

The nurse's brow smoothed in sudden comprehension and her mouth quirked up on one side. "You're dilated to six. From your intake forms, it sounds like you labored at home for several hours, but it could be a while yet before you're ready to push. Let's just take this one step at a time. I'll go page Doctor Linbaum and get your epidural moving."

"This sucks," Jess grumbled as she wiped damp tendrils of hair from her face. "Next time we want to do tequila shots and hook up afterward, let's make sure we're at least sober enough to remember contraception."

Tucker rolled his eyes. "Oh yeah, because I definitely have a second unplanned pregnancy on my bucket list."

"Yèsica, cariña!" A rich, warm voice, dripping in a strong Puerto Rican accent, came from the doorway accompanied by Force of Nature, Ivanna Morales.

"Tita." A brilliant smile lit Jess's face at her grandmother's appearance. Five feet tall with abundant curves, sparkling eyes the color of Guinness, and dark charcoal hair that glittered with strands of silver, her grandmother was a sight for sore eyes.

Ivanna wrapped her strong arms around her granddaughter and squeezed until Jess felt like her ribs might crack. "How are you?" She leaned back and swept a few strands of damp hair from Jess's face, glossing over the dark circles under Jess's eyes with the pad of her thumb. "You look tired."

Jess gave her a wan smile. "I've been up all night. I didn't realize I was in labor until my water broke."

"That is what happened to me with your mother. I said

I was fine—worked all day cleaning houses and when I got home, your grandfather insisted I put my feet up. 'Trabajas demasiado, Ivanna. Descanso, mi amor.' But before I could get to the sofa, my waters broke. No hay descanso para nosotros."

Jess let out a small giggle before reaching out for Tucker. "No, I don't suppose we'll have any rest tonight either."

"You should sleep while you can." Ivanna wagged her finger at the young couple. "Take advantage of the nurses. Once el bebé comes home…" Her arms widened and she shrugged her shoulders to encompass the limitless possibilities of parenthood.

After experiencing the modern miracle of medicine, a la epidural, she was resting easier and drifting off into a nice cat nap when Tucker's phone rang. She waited for him to answer it, before wrenching open her eyes to glare at him. His handsome face was completely relaxed in sleep and, for a moment, she saw the innocence of their unborn son in the set of his eyes and the smooth expanse of his brow. It took the edge off her frustration, and she leaned over to grab his phone off the tray table.

Alaina's face was pulsing on the screen and Jess's heart leaped. She swiped the illuminated bar at the bottom of the screen and answered. "Hello?"

"Hey! I saw Tuck tried to call. We just made it through customs at JFK. What's up?" Jess could hear the drone of a crowd, announcements from gate agents, and automated messages about unaccompanied baggage on the other end.

"I—" Jess's voice caught in her throat. They were in New York. There was no way they would make it back in time. "My water broke. We're at the hospital. Tuck tried to call, but you were already in the air."

The line was silent for a moment and she could feel her friend's panic vibrating through the invisible thread between their phones. "But you're not due for another week."

"Well, I don't think your nephew has any sort of calendar in there."

"But, I won't—" Her voice cut off and she could hear Alaina speaking to her fiancé off to the side. "We won't be back in Indy until four."

Jess was quiet, remembering her last cervical check and her doctor's smile when he had told her she was at nine centimeters and could probably start pushing in the next hour or so. She glanced up at the digital clock on the wall opposite her. It was noon now. "I don't think you'll make it, Lainie." Jess's voice was choked, and she fought back the tears welling in her eyes.

"But I—" The tears in her friend's desperate words cut through her like a knife.

"I know," Jess whispered. "But he'll be here waiting for you when you get back." She tried to put her best optimistic spin on the situation and put a smile into her words.

"Give Tuck a hug for me."

"I will," Jess murmured, making eye contact with her boyfriend. "Do you want to talk to him? He's awake now."

With a word of assent, Jess handed the phone off to Tucker and wiped the tears from her eyes. It broke her heart not having her best friend here with her. She'd always imagined they would go through this part together. Even when it was uncertain whether Tucker would want to be involved in their son's life, she had never doubted Alaina would be there by her side—until now.

Jess ran a hand through her hair, combing it back and up to place in a high, messy bun. She drew a deep breath into her lungs and held it until she thought they would burst, then let it back out. She had to let go of her expectations for today. It was what it was. Alaina wasn't here, but Tucker was. No longer hearing the quiet rumble of his voice as he spoke with his sister, Jess hazarded a glance at her boyfriend. He sat on the bench seat he'd been using as a bed, hands hanging between his slightly parted thighs, eyes distant.

"It'll be okay," Jess murmured, wishing she could get up and go to him.

His eyes gained some focus, and he gazed at her with a watery smile. "I know. I just…it's not what I expected to happen. That's for sure."

Jess reached a hand toward him, and he rose, coming to sit on the bed with her. "If you want your mom in the room since Alaina can't be here—"

"No." He shook his head, gently tracing her cheekbone and jaw with his thumb. "I think…I think maybe it should just be us."

Jessica saw something in him then, a silent strength, a quiet knowing that put even her slightest fears at ease. If he was by her side, that was all she needed. "Just us then," she agreed, stroking his face in the same tender way he had touched hers.

He gave her a single nod, his eyes blue in the gleam of sunshine peeking through the blinds. He leaned in and rested his forehead against hers before tilting his head to the right and kissing her with a sense of conviction she desperately needed to bolster her spirits.

"Tuck, I—" She paused for a moment, wondering if this was the right time to bring up such a request before plunging forward anyway. "I've been thinking a lot lately about…about what would happen to Parker if something happened to us. I don't want him to be alone."

Tucker's brow furrowed, his eyes growing dark with worry. "Jess…"

"I spent most of my childhood in and out of CPS. I just want there to be a plan if…if something were to happen."

Tucker opened his mouth to object again, but Jessica tightened her grip on his hand. "Please, just let me get this out." She took another stab at it. "I want Alaina and Grayson to be his godparents—his legal guardians if both of us are no longer living or incapable of taking care of him."

Tucker was quiet for a moment, studying her with concern and confusion. "What brought this on?"

"You're in the Airforce. You could get deployed again. I'm not stupid enough to think it's sunshine and roses over there, Tucker." She took a shaky breath and looked up at him. The deep furrows in his brow made him look so much older than his twenty-two years and she felt the smallest pang of guilt for the lines of worry and stress she was single-handedly etching into his face. "As for me…well, no, I don't *plan* on anything happening, but…look at what happened to Alaina. My life could be snubbed out by someone else's bad decisions and then where would we be? Where would Parker be? If the worst should happen—God forbid—I want our son to be protected. Okay?" Jess shuffled her gaze side to side, pleading with him to agree.

Slowly he nodded, as if suddenly understanding on a deeper level what it meant to be a parent. It was more than financial accountability or moral responsibility. It was about putting someone else's life before your own. Always.

Four

Ten Fingers, Ten Toes

Her eyes were so heavy she couldn't keep them open. She had been up for nearly forty-eight hours except for a couple ten-minute snoozes when she could catch them. Between nurses checking in, doctor's rounds, and phone calls from nosy family members—which hadn't been often—her body felt like a twenty-year-old computer server trying to calculate a Facebook algorithm.

It had been a hard labor, and Jess had pushed for nearly two hours before little Parker decided to join the world. His prolonged entry also cost Jess ten stitches across three tears to her lady parts, but when she looked down at her precious little boy, it made it all worth it. There was something so natural and connective about skin-to-skin time, and she didn't want to give it up. So with her head constantly lolling to one side and her eyelids too heavy to keep propped open with toothpicks, she held her sweet little bundle to her breast and dozed.

She felt Tucker's hands combing her hair out of her face and his lips on her forehead. Then, as if he'd been doing it for years, he pulled the drowsy baby, drunk on milk, from her chest. Jess couldn't force her brain to function enough for a verbal response, but slit her eyes just enough to see Tucker placing Parker in his bassinet before falling headlong into blissful unconsciousness.

Jess woke to the rumble of low voices, and for a split second, she wondered where she was, what day it was, and why every inch of her body from her breasts to her hoo-ha ached in all sorts of unpleasant ways.

But then it all came rushing back.

Hospital. Baby.

She took a deep breath, hoping a sudden intake of oxygen would make her more alert, and pried her eyes open.

"Where's Parker?" Jess croaked, easing herself to a sitting position. Her legs still felt like lead sinkers and her ass hurt, like someone had ripped it open and sewn it back together.

Well...that's not too far from the truth.

The bed pad she was sitting on crackled, but her focus remained on her baby, who was not in the room. Her eyes finally focused on Tucker, who was standing near the door speaking with two guests: Alaina and Grayson.

Tears sprung to Jess's eyes and her best friend ran to her. "You're here," she sobbed, unable to stop her emotions as they barreled down the track.

"I'm here." Alaina wrapped her arms around Jess, squeezing for all she was worth. "It's so good to see you," she murmured, rocking back and forth as her friend sobbed into her shoulder. It had been two long months since they'd last seen each other.

After several minutes of going to pieces, Jess pulled back, using the heel of her palms to wipe the excess moisture from her face. "I'm-m-m s-ssorry."

"It's okay," Alaina murmured tenderly, as she tucked her friend's messy hair behind her ear. "You're tired and your hormones are all over the place. You're allowed to cry."

Jess gave her friend a wobbly smile, feeling tears prick her eyes again. "Where's Parker? Have you seen him?"

Alaina glanced back at Grayson with a smile. "No, we just got here. Tuck said the nurses took him for some tests and to get all of his measurements. They should be back shortly."

"He's perfect, Lainie. He has the most beautiful round face. And tiny little ears like Tuck."

Her best friend smiled. "I can't wait to see him. I'm so sorry I wasn't here." It was Alaina's turn to get emotional, and Jess felt her eyes well in sympathy. "It's okay. Really. Everything turned out fine. Don't let it ruin your engagement bliss. Let me see that ring!" Jess tugged on her friend's hand, pulling it closer for inspection. "This is gorgeous! Grayson did a fantastic job."

"Didn't he?" Alaina's cheeks glowed with a rosy blush as she stared at her engagement ring, wiggling her fingers in absolute joy as she watched the stone shimmer. "You know, if you'd told me last April that within a year you would have a new baby and I would be engaged, I would have laughed in your face."

"Laughed in my face? Hell, I would have willingly gone to the loony bin thinking I'd lost my last marble."

The two young women giggled quietly. "I've missed you so much."

"Alright, Mama. Someone is awake and hungry." A nurse

Jess hadn't met before came through the doorway wheeling Parker in his mobile bassinet. He was letting out quiet mewling noises that held the promise of a full-out squall if he wasn't given sustenance immediately.

Jess peered around Alaina toward her inbound child, feeling the tingle of her breasts as he drew nearer. Her milk hadn't let down yet, but the primal urge to feed her child was there in spades. She reached over for the Boppy Nursing Pillow on the side table and wrapped it around her midsection while pulling at the snap-buttoned top of her hospital gown to let it down.

Grayson shifted awkwardly by the door. "I'll umm…wait outside…give you some privacy."

"I'm not gonna be shy about it if you aren't," Jess spoke in a blunt tone. "I think everyone within a mile radius of this hospital has seen my vagina today. My pseudo-brother-in-law seeing my boobs is at the bottom of the list of things I care about right now."

Alaina glanced up at Grayson with a slight, challenging smirk. His natural modesty was a constant inside joke between the women, and they were about to find out just how far that modesty extended. Grayson's cheeks flushed a deep cherry, and his neck took on the blotchy quality of someone who had a bad case of poison ivy.

Finally, Alaina burst into peals of laughter. "Just go. I'll come get you when it's safe."

Without turning back, he fled from the room like he was in desperate need of a bathroom. "Okaaay," the nurse cooed, holding the tiny baby out in front of her to give to Jess once she was settled. "Here we go."

As soon as little Parker was nestled in his mom's arms,

he was rooting around for a nipple to latch onto. "Well, he knows what he's looking for, doesn't he?" The nurse chuckled. "I'm so glad you got a good feeder. Some moms get a first baby that refuses to latch, and it's such a frustrating experience. Doesn't look like we're going to have that kind of trouble from this little guy, though."

Jess let out a slight gasp as her baby's mouth found her tender nipple and attached himself with a ferocity that belied his tiny stature. She'd fed him once before and had jerked in startlement. This time, her reaction was due more to sensation than actual surprise. It was such a foreign feeling, having something attached to your body like a leech. But after the initial shock, she was able to settle him comfortably in her arms and glance up at Alaina, who was enthralled by her new nephew.

"He's so tiny," she whispered, pulling back his swaddle to see his vernix-covered fingers.

Jess smiled down at Parker and then up at Alaina. "Trust me, he didn't feel so small when he was coming out of me."

"Well no, I wouldn't think so." Alaina snorted. "Could you really feel it, though? I thought you had an epidural."

"No, I couldn't feel *him*. I could just feel an insane amount of pressure. That and the fact that it took me two hours of pushing to get him out. But I tell you what, labor I was prepared for. What I wasn't prepared for—"

"Uterine massage? I've heard horrible things about that." Alaina grimaced.

Jess raised her brow and tilted her head from side to side. "Well, no, that's not fun either, but nothing can prepare you for a nurse coming in at 3:00 a.m. and shoving her entire hand up your vag to check your cervix."

Alaina winced. "Wow, this all sounds so pleasant."

"Oh yeah, it's a good time."

Tucker chuckled from his position over in the window seat as he watched his sister and girlfriend chat.

"Just you wait. I'm sure it will be your turn soon."

Alaina gave a wistful smile and gently stroked the downy wisps of black hair on top of Parker's head. "Maybe."

Jess's stomach did an embarrassed flip-flop as she realized her error. Potential infertility was one of the many repercussions of Alaina's accident seven months earlier, and a major source of grief for her best friend. "Sorry. I didn't mean—"

"No, it's okay," Alaina whispered, not upset by the blunder. "Grayson and I talked about it on the way home. We want to start trying right after the wedding. Hopefully, it will happen naturally, but if it doesn't, I think we're going to ask for a fertility specialist referral." She had healed well from her severely fractured pelvis, but there were still a lot of unknowns regarding the impact on her reproductive organs and overall ability to carry a pregnancy to term. "Doctor Marks says everything looks good, and I haven't had any complications. My cycles are normal and I haven't had any"—she glanced at her brother, who was discreetly ignoring their conversation—"discomfort."

"That's great, Lainie." Jess rested her unoccupied hand on Alaina's thigh and squeezed. "I'm sure it will all work out."

Alaina smiled and nodded. "I hope so. I'm not sure what options we have if something ends up being wrong with me."

Jess's hand squeezed harder. "We'll cross that bridge if we get to it."

Parker's mouth slackened as he fell into a contented stupor and Jess pulled him away from her breast, placing him on her shoulder to burp. He squeaked in protest at the change in position, and Jess shushed him gently as she patted until she got a quiet belch.

"I'll go get Grayson if you two want to keep catching up," Tucker offered, rising to his feet and pocketing his cell phone. "I need to take a walk anyway."

Jessica looked up at him gratefully and watched as he left the room. "He's been so amazing. I could not have gotten through all of this without him."

Alaina gave her a contented smile that sparkled in her hazel eyes. "I'm glad. He's a sweet guy."

Her eyes lingered on the baby with intense yearning, and Jess smiled in return. "Do you want to hold him?"

Alaina's eyes flickered up to her friend's, and she nodded vigorously, as if she couldn't get her hands on him fast enough. As Jess transferred her son to his auntie's waiting arms, she whispered, "Parker, this is your Aunt Alaina, and I'm sure she's going to spoil you rotten."

Alaina nodded, enraptured by his tiny, angelic face. "Hi, buddy." She leaned forward and laid a gentle kiss on his forehead. "You are so precious..." Her quiet voice barely reached Jess, who sat only a couple feet away. The longing in Alaina's body was palpable. She wanted a baby, and Jess hoped her friend would be able to conceive without difficulty. "Have you decided on a middle name?" Alaina asked, finally pulling her gaze off Parker long enough to make conversation.

"Tuck suggested Blane, and I loved it. I expected our name conversation to be a long, drawn-out war, but it turns out we have similar tastes. We only went back and forth for about fifteen minutes before we settled on something we both liked."

"Wow…that's impressive. I think Grayson and I will probably go around the whole nine months before we settle on something we both like."

Movement in the doorway caught Jess's eye, and she gave a nod of acknowledgment as Tucker and Grayson re-entered the room. The strong, confident lines of Grayson's face softened at the sight of his fiancé with an infant in her arms, and Jess's heart stuttered in her chest. If Alaina longed for a baby, Grayson had baby fever. Or maybe it was just the want of their own little family—that they loved each other so much, they wanted to grow that love and give some of it to a little boy or girl of their creation.

She took a deep breath and caught Tucker's eye. He smiled and winked at her, giving her the go-ahead. With a small clearing of her throat, she drew the attention of the room and smiled at her friend. "Tucker and I have talked, and um…" She grabbed Alaina's hand and squeezed before looking at Grayson. "You two will make amazing parents, and…with what happened to you this summer, Lainie, it just got me thinking."

Alaina furrowed her brow and glanced up at Grayson, who gave a slight shrug.

Jess let out a sigh and laughed. "Tuck and I would like you to be Parker's godparents."

Alaina's mouth popped open in shock and she looked back down to the pink-faced cherub she held swaddled in front of her.

"Of course." Grayson was the first of the two to speak, and his chocolate eyes shone with emotion as he knelt in front of Alaina to get a closer look at the star of the show. He gently cupped Parker's head and stroked the top of it with his thumb. "No one knows what could happen to any of us and, if the worst should happen, of course, we would care for him as if he were our own."

"Always," Alaina whispered through the tears streaming down her cheeks. "Thank you for trusting us."

Alaina's emotion brought tears to Jess's own eyes, and she smiled. "Always."

Jess's exhaustion lingered in the room like a cloud, and after a few more minutes of visiting and a promise to return the following day, Grayson and Alaina took their leave to go home and unpack. After returning from their European adventure, it was time to get back to business. Alaina had new employees to train and several weddings to work on, and Grayson would be gone for the next several weekends testing in Florida and California. They seemed to have it all planned out.

Well, that's two of us at least...

Jess scrolled through the pictures Alaina had taken before she left. Most were candid pictures of herself, Tucker, and their new son. The hat Parker was wearing was a soft baby blue, and so big it swallowed his forehead. She smiled and snickered softly. There were a few more pictures of Jess, nearly asleep, holding Parker to her bare chest. She must have dozed off for that one. She didn't remember taking it. And there was one of Tucker, gazing contently down at his tiny son, who lay sleeping in his plastic bassinet. She quickly posted all of them to social media with a brief description.

*"Earlier today we welcomed our son
Parker Blane Montgomery into the world.*

He was 7 lbs, 11 oz, and 20.5 inches long.
We love him so much it hurts. Welcome
to the world, little guy!"

She moved to put her phone away for the evening, but hesitated. With all the text messages and phone calls she'd sent and received, there was one person she hadn't heard from today.

She glanced over at Tucker, who was out like a light, dozing on his back with his hands resting on his chest. She sighed and scrolled through her pictures once again before selecting her favorite, the one of her and Parker, sleeping together, skin-to-skin. Her thumbs hesitated over the screen, wondering if she would regret the photograph and five words she was about to send, but then she sighed, hit the send button, and hoped for the best.

Ten fingers and ten toes.

Her heart hammered with nervous energy for five heartbeats, and then the phone vibrated with a reply.

Congratulations Mama.
He's beautiful.

She hadn't been sure Jack would answer her message, but he had supported her through the early days of her pregnancy. He had known the truth when no one else had and helped her carry the burden. It only seemed right he should get to see the end result. As she went to place her phone on the side table and get some rest, her phone went off again.

**Gonna be in Indy next month.
Maybe we could catch up?**

There it was. The kicker. She and Jack had a connection all those months ago. She'd craved his friendship more than anything. She missed him, and clearly, he missed her. But was it right for her to meet with him? Could she honestly say it was ethical to make plans with an ex-boyfriend while she was involved in a serious relationship with another man?

I'd like that.

And she would, more than she could express. Her foot was just stuck in the metaphorical quicksand of morality. The harder she tried to free herself, the more forcefully it pulled her down.

Five

Shades of Baby Blue

J ess barely felt the scalding dishwater as she took the bottle brush and swabbed Dreft dish soap into the bottle she was holding. The quiet hiss of popping bubbles and trickle of the faucet provided a quiet accompaniment to the constant commentary in her head. She couldn't turn it off. She needed to finish the bottles, fold the laundry in the dryer, and think of something to fix for dinner. Tita made her famous camarones enchilados when they brought Parker home, and they'd been eating off that for the last few days. She supposed they could always dig into the frozen pan of lasagna Maura put together for them, or the soup Alaina had prepared and placed in individual serving-sized bowls to stock the refrigerator.

God, she was exhausted. The adage "sleep when the baby sleeps" was a joke. That was the only time you could get anything done. Tucker was doing his best to help—doing the laundry, running the sweeper, taking Layla out for her walks three times a day. He was great, but his being so great, only made her feel worse.

She wanted to spend time with her son, but with the constant parade of visitors and endless housework, she was feeling more and more like a jug of milk than a mother. Her head fell forward with fatigue and she closed her eyes, swaying on her feet.

"Jesus," Tucker muttered, catching her as she stumbled. He reached around her and shut the water off before plucking the bottle out of her hands and placing it back in the sink. "You're asleep on your feet. Come on. Let's go lay down." His voice was gentle as he wrapped his arm around her to help her over to the couch.

She pushed at him. "I'm fine."

"No. You're not." He looked her over with a critical eye as he took in her disheveled hair, spit-up-stained T-shirt, and the dark circles under her eyes. "Did you sleep at all last night? You need your rest, Jess. I can do the dishes."

"I can do the goddamned dishes, Tucker!" she growled, her eyes flashing.

He put his hands up. "Of course, you can. I just...I'm trying to make things easier for you."

Tears suddenly welled in her eyes and spilled over. She knew he was trying to help, but as he took more off her plate, it only gave her time to dwell on the increasing desolation threatening to crash down on her with the force of a hormonal tsunami. "I know you are. I'm sorry. I just..." Her breath hitched, and she put the back of her hand to her mouth to stifle the emotions clawing at her insides. The dam finally broke. "I'm a terrible mom," she cried, a sob racking her body so hard her chest ached with the force of it. "I don't spend enough time with him. He doesn't think I love him. I'm useless. I can't…can't—"

The blank astonishment on Tucker's face would have been comical had she not been in such dire need of reassurance.

"I barely hold him, and when I do, all he does is cry or… or…"

"Jess, no." Tucker wrapped his arms around her and squeezed her tight in a hug that she desperately needed. God, did she need it: human contact, affection, comfort. "He's a baby, Jess. All he does is eat, sleep, pee, poop, repeat. He doesn't know any different. I promise you, he's fine. You're fine. You're doing great."

"But I'm n-not…" She sobbed. "All I am to him is a boob."

Tucker snorted quietly. "I think that says more about him than you."

When he didn't get even a hint of a smile, he sighed and pulled her back to him, resting his chin on top of her head. "I love you."

Jess stiffened in his arms.

What the f—

"Tuck…" She tried to resist him, but he held on in silent objection.

"I know. I know you don't feel that way. I just…I wanted you to know. You're an amazing mom. Parker will have his whole life to tell you that, but until he can, somebody else should."

Her stomach flip-flopped. Even if she didn't fully believe what he was saying, hearing the words made her feel marginally better. It wasn't that she didn't love him. She just wasn't *in* love with him. "I do love you, Tucker," she murmured, pulling back to look up at him.

His mouth quirked. "I know." The emotion in his turbulent irises told her everything she needed to know though. He recognized the difference between his words and hers.

Would it ever be different for them? Would she ever get there? Would it be enough to watch him be a great father and love their son like no other man could? Could she find contentment in that?

"Why don't you go take a shower? I'll finish the dishes." His low voice rumbled, vibrating through her senses down to her bones.

She sighed, and rubbed the heel of her palm over her bleary eyes, too exhausted to argue. "Okay. I might lay down for a bit too." Dazed, she trudged toward the bathroom, flicking the light on, excited to indulge in her favorite lemon verbena shampoo and shea butter body wash.

The feel of hot water across her tired body went a long way toward numbing the confusion in Jess's muddled brain. As her muscles relaxed and the heat seeped through her thick black hair into her scalp, down her neck, and across her shoulders, she let out a deep breath and closed her eyes, drowning in the miraculous sensation of cleanliness. The sweet, citrus and herbal notes of her shampoo lulled her into a drowsy fog of repletion as she massaged the shampoo and then conditioner into her scalp and down to the ends of her hair. She'd always kept her hair shorter, but a mix of laziness and prenatal vitamins had caused her hair to grow past her collarbone in ebony waves.

She took her time washing with the shea butter body wash and even went so far as to shave her legs. It was the first time since Parker's birth she felt slightly like herself. For days now, she'd been trudging through a thicket of fatigue, hormones, and unrealistic expectations. Unable to find the desire to turn the water off, she simply stood in the stream, letting the steam sink into her pores as she braced herself against the wall where the shower head was mounted.

Her body was screaming for TLC, and she hated to admit Tucker was so damn right. She'd always been prone to pushing herself beyond her physical limits, and no one understood that better than Tuck—maybe Alaina, but she was so guilty of it herself, she would never chastise Jess about it. The truth was, she needed someone in her life that would force her to slow down, that cared about her enough to recognize her exhaustion and take the weight off her shoulders before her knees gave out under her. Tucker would be that person for her. She just had to let him. But could she? Could she allow herself to lean on him? Lord knew she couldn't ask for a better human being. He was everything she'd ever thought to ask for in a man: tender, loving, intelligent, and even a bit rugged with that military edge. He was handsome and sexy and an amazing father. So, what the hell was wrong with her? Why couldn't she find completion in someone like that?

She turned the knob on the shower and pulled the curtain back with the zing of curtain rings against the metal rod. The cool bathroom air hit her damp skin and caused goosebumps to ripple across her chilled flesh. She reached for her towel on the rack and wrapped it around her body before wrapping her head in a hair towel and stepping over to the sink. She swiped her hand across the condensation on the mirror and caught a glimpse of herself for the first time in days. She looked like she needed a week of uninterrupted sleep.

Her breasts ached and felt hard in her palm as she massaged one absently, wondering when that sensation would go away. Many had offered their advice on the subject of breastfeeding—that and everything else. It was probably one of the worst parts of having a child, everyone putting their two cents in on how to properly raise a baby. Breastfeed for at least the first eight weeks, three months, six months, a year. Always sleep with the baby in their crib, in a bassinet, co-sleep, don't sleep. Huggies, Pampers, Luvs, et cetera are the best. It was maddening. She wanted to scream, "He's my son and I'll do what I want!" But of course, she just smiled and nodded, making them feel as if their opinions mattered.

She rubbed moisturizer into her face slowly and then let her hair out of its towel, pinching the water out of the ends before spritzing it with detangler and brushing it out with methodical flicks of her wrist. With each swipe of the brush, she could feel the stars realigning. It wasn't that she felt like her old self, but she felt more capable, more in control than she had in days.

The gleam of precious metal from the small jewelry dish she kept on the sink caught her eye as she sat her brush on the countertop: a simple silver ring encrusted with five small pearls across the band. She'd seen it in the window of a jewelry store one night while she and Jack were walking through the open-air mall not too far from her house. She'd stared longingly at it for a long moment before catching the price on the display and reluctantly turning away.

Jack had surprised her with that ring a week later.

"You deserve to have something for yourself, with everything you've been through lately," he'd said with that crooked, sexy smile she loved so much.

She'd put it on that night and hadn't taken it off—not even after their breakup. It was her way of reminding herself she deserved to be happy, even if the idea was easier to preach than to practice. Six weeks ago, with her fingers swelling like sausages, she'd finally pried the thing from her finger, feeling as though she were prying a piece of herself off along with it. She pinched it delicately between her thumb and forefinger now recalling the man who had given it to her.

With a sigh, she let it clink back into the dish.

Six

Mommy Dearest

J ess paced in the corridor between the outer and inner doors of Recovery Centers of America, gnawing on her thumbnail and trying to breathe. On a nicer day, she would have paced outside while she fought her inner demons, but the wind chill was below zero and even the short walk from the parking lot to the building had left her cheeks stinging. Tita had called several days ago to let Jess know her mother was now allowed visitors, and Jess had struggled with whether she wanted to visit. On her sober days, María Morales was usually bearable, not kind or loving, but tolerable. On her bad days when she hadn't gone more than an hour without a drink and popped opiates like Hot Tamales, she was downright despicable: rude, ungrateful, and mean.

Jess hissed through her teeth and popped her knuckles. The receptionist in the main atrium craned her neck to get a better look and wrinkled her brow in concern before looking back down at her computer.

Yeah lady, mind your own business. Nothing to see here. Just your average emotionally abused daughter clinging to her last shred of self-respect.

She had to do this, if not for herself, then for Parker. She had to know if her mother was actually making an effort or if her stint in rehab was simply a way to appease Tita.

The windows in the double doors leading outside were fogging up as Jess's body heat increased the temperature in the small entryway. She was going to have to make a decision. No more screwing around. She wrapped her fingers around the cold metal handle on the door for a split second, blew out another breath as her chest tightened with anxiety, and yanked before she could change her mind.

The curious receptionist's eyebrows rose as she made eye contact with Jess, and then she smiled. "Is there something I can help you with?"

Jess gave a nervous laugh. "Sorry, you probably think I'm crazy."

"It's not my place to judge. Besides, you'd be surprised how many of our inpatients do the very same thing. I'm just glad you decided to open the door."

Jess's mouth popped open in shock. "Oh no. I'm not—" She shook her head, mortified. "I mean…" She took another deep breath. "I'm here to see my mother. María Morales?"

The woman blinked rapidly then cleared her throat. "Oh. Of course. I'm sorry. I didn't mean to imply—"

Jess shook her head again. "It's fine." There was movement down one hallway and she looked over to see a member of the cleaning staff pushing a mop bucket their way. Not wishing to have witnesses, she pushed on with the conversation. "Can I see her?"

The woman, whose nametag read Sheri, clacked on her keyboard and dragged her finger along the screen. "It looks like she just got out of her morning therapy session."

Jess glanced over her shoulder toward the encroaching cleaning crew and then back at Sheri. "Yeah, I know. I spoke with someone yesterday and they said she would be free for visitors after one." Her tone was abrasive, but damn it, she didn't want to be here! "Can you just tell me where to go? Please?" She tacked on the last word as an afterthought, hoping to take the edge off her demand.

"She should be in her room: 110. Take the hallway off to your right and turn left at the recreation room. It's the third door on the left."

Jess gave a tight smile and gripped the leather strap of her crossbody tighter. "Thank you."

Sheri gave a tense smile in return, and Jess felt her eyes on her until she turned at the dead end as instructed.

Nosey little busybody.

She would have paused in doubt again at the door to her mother's room, but the door was already open. Her mother paused—on her way out as Jess rounded the corner. "Jessica." Her deep brown eyes widened in shock at the sight of her daughter.

Jess charged forward with the conversation before she could turn tail and run. "Tita told me you were allowed visitors."

Her mother's delicate pink lips turned up in an amused smile. "Of course. I was just going to meet some friends in the rec room, but…" She glanced over her shoulder toward the room and then gestured for her daughter to come in.

There was a wingback chair nestled in the corner next to a small table, and Jess lowered herself down as María took a seat across from her on the corner of her neatly made bed. "How are you?" Her mother squeezed her hands together tightly in her lap, one thumb nail picking absently at the torn cuticle of another.

"I'm…okay." The word seemed like an accurate enough allowance. "It's been hard the past few weeks. I haven't felt much like myself, but having a sense of normalcy helps. I'm just trying to get into a routine—manage my time better."

Her mother nodded along. "And the baby? Your abuela told me his name is…Parker?" She said the name hesitantly as if she didn't exactly remember what it was Tita had told her.

Jessica nodded in return. "Parker Blane Montgomery."

"Montgomery, huh? After the father that couldn't keep his *pene* in his pants long enough to—"

"Enough." Jessica cut her off violently and glared at her. "The Montgomerys were more of a family to me than you were growing up. I certainly wasn't going to give him your name. It's bad enough I have it."

María glared at her daughter, dark eyes the color of dried cocoa beans blazing with fury. "How dare you!"

"How dare I?" Jessica's voice was an astonished whisper. "How dare I what? Speak out of turn? Offend your fragile sense of self-worth? Defend the father of my child?" Jessica shot up out of her chair and swiped her purse off the table. "I shouldn't have come."

"Sit down," her mother demanded.

Jess whirled on her, steam coming out of her ears. "*Excuse me?"*

"I said, 'Sit. Down.'" When she didn't move from her position, María let out a breath and continued to speak. "The only reason I'm in this place is because your abuela insisted I sober up and think about my priorities."

"Not because it's the right thing to do? Or maybe because you were washing your life down the sink with a bottle of tequila and a few hydrocodone?" Jessica snorted and rolled her eyes. She'd figured as much, but hearing it from her mother's lips was infuriating.

"I didn't ask for my life to turn out the way it has," María whispered after a moment of silence. "One stupid decision I made when I was seventeen created a downward spiral I was never able to recover from."

"Didn't *want* to recover from," Jess muttered under her breath.

María pointedly ignored her daughter's jab and continued. "I thought at least you were smart enough to learn from my mistakes. The biggest regret of my life was letting my mother talk me out of an abortion."

Jessica felt like she'd been punched in the gut. Her mouth popped open, but there were no words to speak—nothing that could vocalize the shock she felt.

"You would erase me? Just like that?" Her voice sounded small and fragile, and she hated it. "I knew you were cold-hearted, but I never thought you could kill your own child."

"At that point, you were nothing more than a nuisance—the reason I couldn't go to Juilliard."

"And you've never stopped resenting me for it."

María gazed at her daughter. They looked so much alike, with their sharp cheekbones, black hair, and petite noses.

Jess's green eyes though, those had come from her father. At least she assumed they had. No one on her mother's side had eyes like that. "No. I never stopped resenting you for it."

"My son may not have been planned, but I love him with everything that I am. He has changed my life irrevocably, but I could *never* resent him for that—and neither would his father."

"Of course his father would—and does! Just because he hides it from you doesn't mean those feelings aren't there."

Jessica stared at her mother, dumbfounded. "No. Tuck wanted to be involved. He loves Parker."

"Being a good man slices both ways, mija." The cynicism dripping off María's words curdled Jess's stomach. "Just because he feels obligated to raise his child doesn't mean it's the life he wanted."

Jess thought she might throw up. When she'd first realized she was pregnant, she'd told herself the same thing. It had taken her entire pregnancy to suffocate those doubts, and after these last two weeks with their son, she'd finally convinced herself being a father really *was* what Tucker wanted.

"I gave him the chance to get out, no strings attached, and he chose to stay." Jess's arguments were becoming more feeble as doubt and fear crept under her skin. Her mother was good at that—making her feel like she was no better than a piece of bubble gum stuck to her shoe: a nuisance she tolerated because she couldn't go back in time and avoid stepping in it.

"Chose to stay," she scoffed and rolled her eyes. "You mean those parents of his made him feel guilty for choosing himself. Just like your father's parents would have if I had told him about you!"

Jessica's world uprooted itself and flipped over. "I'm sorry. Did you just say my father doesn't know I *exist*?"

María peered at her daughter from under furrowed brows, affronted. "I loved him. Why on earth would I ruin his life too? He was getting out. He had an Ivy League scholarship. My life was over, but his didn't have to be, and I knew if I told him, his parents would find out and they would insist we get married. Neither one of us would ever live our dreams. We would just be stuck in the same stupid small town, living miserable, ordinary lives, and I didn't want that—for either of us."

Reeling with shock, Jess stumbled back into the chair she'd so hastily jumped from. The one selfless thing María had ever done kept Jessica from half of her family, trapping her in a pattern of emotional abuse and depression she'd fought against most of her life. In Jessica's book, that was unforgivable.

After a long moment, she pierced her mother with a stare and spoke. "What's his name?"

"What?" her mother asked incredulously.

"My father. I want his name."

"It's been twenty-five years. He probably doesn't even remember—"

"Give me his *fucking* name!" Jessica screamed.

Her mother's eyes widened, and she stared up at her daughter, shocked at her outburst. Jess had never experienced a fraction of the rage boiling in her blood. Her pulse hammered in her ears and the corners of her vision blurred with each throb of her heart.

Finally, María sighed. "Julian."

Gripping her purse to steady herself at the sound of her father's name—*Julian*—she dashed a hand across her cheek to catch a stray tear and straightened. "Last name?" Her voice was clipped, but under control again. Barely.

María gazed at her daughter, her dark eyes surveying Jess with smug calculation, jaw set in a stubborn line that made it clear she wasn't saying another word.

White hot anger bubbling back toward the surface, Jess took a shaky breath and leveled her mother with a steely glare. She tightened her death grip on her purse strap and fought for every ounce of self-control she could muster.

You don't want to play ball? Fine.

Like everything else in her life, she'd do this on her own. "This is the last time you and I will ever speak."

Jess slammed the door to her mother's room behind her so hard, the generic landscape prints dotting the walls rattled in their frames. She stumbled blearily back to the lobby, knocking against the walls unsteadily as she fled, her hand her only guide through her blurred vision. Weak-kneed with the aftershocks of life-altering news, she had only been able to sink to the curb outside the main entrance of the rehab center and stare off into space, shaking like a leaf in a windstorm. The ringing of her phone an hour later had pulled her out of the fog long enough for her to stumble to her feet and get in her car—her joints so stiff with cold she was barely able to grasp the door handle.

With her teeth chattering so hard, she thought she might bite through her tongue, she managed a plea for help that sent Alaina to the rescue, driving to pick her up at the rehab center without a single word of explanation. For some crazy reason, Jess felt ashamed, and the last thing she wanted was to explain that her mother—María, she corrected herself; any woman so cruel didn't deserve the title of mother—had admitted she wished Jess had never been born.

"Let me get this straight." Alaina's hazel eyes flashed angrily, her back straightening into impeccable posture from her stooped position as she rummaged through the cupboard for sugar to add to the cup of Hibiscus tea she'd made Jess. Vibrant patches of bright pink stained the apples of her cheeks, and Jess could see the pulse jumping in her neck. "You went to see your mother in rehab, and instead of bonding over her new grandson, she proceeded to tell you she never wanted you, you ruined her life, and subsequently, by not aborting your child, ruined your own life?" Alaina rubbed her temples, wincing. Apparently, her high blood pressure was bringing on a migraine.

"Pretty much," Jess answered—trying to sound casual and failing miserably. A glimpse of movement in her periphery caught her attention, and she shifted her gaze to Tucker, who was leaning against the kitchen sink with his arms crossed in front of him, tapping his index finger against his forearm in agitation. "But that's not…what set me off."

Granted, it loaded the gun, but it hadn't pulled the trigger.

Tucker and Alaina's eyes were plastered to her, waiting.

"She told me…that…" Jess swallowed hard, her heart thumping uncontrollably in her chest at the mere thought of her conversation with María. "She never told my father about me. He doesn't know I exist."

"What?" the Montgomery siblings shouted in unison.

Strong arms folded around her as she went to pieces, and she buried her face in Tucker's broad chest, as if he could shelter her from the cruelty of the world. Jess's early years could have been worse, but that didn't mean they had been a cakewalk. She couldn't help but wonder how different her life would have been if her father had been in the picture.

"Here," Alaina murmured, handing her the hot tea as Tucker helped her sit on the couch.

The warmth from the mug felt amazing as it leached into her frozen fingers. She hadn't realized how cold she still was, despite the long ride home with the heat on high.

From the back of her mind, she heard her son's shrill cry and started, but she felt Tucker's warm hand on her shoulder pressing her back down onto the sofa. "I'll get him. You stay here. Get warm."

Wisps of steam rolled off the cup in her hands and she stared absently into the aromatic liquid, watching small ripples roll across the surface as her hands shook. "Why does my mom hate me?" she whispered without lifting her eyes from her drink.

"Some people just shouldn't be parents." The couch dipped under Alaina's weight and Jess leaned her head against her friend's shoulder, a lone tear streaming down her cheek. Alaina wrapped her arm around Jess's petite shoulders and tried to chafe some warmth back into her. "Do you think your father would be any better? If you found him, I mean."

There was a long silence. Tuck's quiet, deep murmurs came from the next room as he soothed their son and then the soft sound of a melodic song floated to them between the susurrus of the furnace and the thumping of the washing machine. He was everything she wished her own father would be, but she, of all people, knew the world wasn't an idyllic place.

* * *

A light knock at the door roused Jess out of an exhausted doze. She wasn't sure what *day* it was, let alone the hour. Her eyes rasped under her sandpaper lids, and all she wanted was to dive back down under her blankets. Layla, now having been roused to full alert, was barking incessantly at the door.

Where the hell is Tucker?

Then she remembered. He'd gone to grab coffee and catch up with some of his old high school buddies before heading back to Texas next week. She was flying solo. She rose from the couch and glanced at the baby monitor, sighing when she saw that Parker was still fast asleep in his crib.

Another knock sounded. More yapping ensued, and she picked up her pace toward the door, wanting to open it before the racket woke the baby. She turned the deadbolt and pulled the door open to find Maura standing on the stoop, casserole dish in hand. The scents of boiled chicken and melted cheese filled her nostrils and her stomach growled, reminding her she hadn't eaten today. She grinned and took the casserole from Maura. "Hi! Tuck didn't mention you were coming today."

"Well, he didn't know," Maura admitted with a warm grin. "I figured my son doesn't need to know every time I come over to check on you and my grandson. He might get a complex."

Jess sniggered. "Well, it's good to see you. Come in before you catch a cold." She turned to retreat further into the house, taking the casserole with her.

Layla wove herself round and round Maura's legs, begging for pets, and Maura obliged by tentatively stroking the dog's head before following Jess's retreating form. Catching sight of Jess's nest of blankets on the couch, Maura sighed. "I'm sorry. You were sleeping. I should have called first."

"No, it's okay," Jess said with another yawn, beginning to feel more clearheaded as she made her way back to consciousness. "What have you been up to today?"

"Oh, I had the day off and was all caught up on laundry, so I thought I'd come over and see how you were *really* doing—since my son isn't here to interject his opinions." Maura raised an eyebrow and pulled out the barstool at the island to take a seat.

Jess felt like a bug under a microscope and looked down at the casserole to avoid Maura's unnerving gray gaze. "Do you mind if I have some of this? I'm starving."

Maura smiled and gestured to the pan. "Be my guest. That's what it's for."

Jess pulled a spoon out of the utensil drawer and scooped a serving of casserole onto a dish before grabbing a fork and digging in, so hungry she didn't even pause to ask what she was eating. It was delicious, whatever it was.

"Can I get you anything to drink?" she asked as she turned to the refrigerator and pulled out a can of soda.

"Ice water is fine. Thanks. And don't think I don't see you avoiding my question." She thrummed her neatly manicured nails on the granite countertop and continued to study her adoptive daughter.

Jess took a bite of the steaming food in front of her and chewed meditatively as she filled a glass of water and sat it down in front of her guest. "I don't even know how to sort through it all to answer your question. That's the problem."

The faintest of smiles curled at the corners of Maura's

mouth and she shifted in her chair. "Well, how about you start at the beginning, and we can try to puzzle through it together?"

The more Jess filled her stomach with home cooked food, the more alert and capable she felt, and it was easier to articulate her feelings. "I just feel like no matter how hard I work, or how little I sleep, I'm never going to get caught up. I'm never going to be doing enough."

"Honey, that's motherhood. The first year or two is the hardest—not to say that the rest is easy. That little boy will try your patience in ways you didn't know possible, but this part, the lack of sleep—for me at least—was the hardest. It was like taking the most exhausted I'd ever felt and multiplying it by ten."

Jess nodded as she sipped at her soda. "Exactly. Even when I do sleep, it's not relaxing. Sometimes when I wake up, I feel even more exhausted than I did before."

Maura nodded in sympathy. "I'm not going to stand here and preach about taking care of yourself. I know you have that coming from a million different directions, and likely, one of the loudest voices is my son. No doubt he means well, but he can be a bit..."

"Overbearing?" Jess offered.

Maura snorted. "He gets it honest. Him and Alaina both, God bless them. Nate wants what's best for all of us, but it's hard for him to differentiate between taking care of his family and taking away the ability for us to make our own decisions."

"Sounds familiar," Jess muttered. "I love him to pieces, Maura. You know that. But sometimes, I just need some space. Being a new mom is hard enough without being made to feel incompetent."

Maura straightened, now on red alert. "If he's done something—"

"No." Jess reached out across the counter to envelope Maura's hand with hers. "It's not his fault. He just sees how overwhelmed I am, and he's trying to make things easier on me." She sighed. "I've been struggling...emotionally. It's been hard."

Maura stayed silent, but turned her hand over to squeeze Jess's.

"Nobody ever warns you about that part. They say motherhood is great, that the love you'll feel for your child outweighs any other feeling you've ever had, that you would kill for them—and it's true. All of it. But they don't warn you about the grief, the guilt, the...torment of uncertainty and doubt. It's awful. Sometimes I feel like I'll never be able to shut it off. I feel so helpless and...alone." Tears were running down her cheeks unchecked, and she hiccuped, trying to suck in air between her words.

Maura stood and stepped around the island to envelop Jess, wrapping her strong arms around her like a vise. She shushed her in low, consoling waves as she cried. "You are *never* alone, Jessica. Never."

When Jess finally composed herself, Maura pushed her to arms' length and helped wipe the tears from her face. "I don't know if *every* woman experiences it, but I know I certainly did. A lot of women do. They call it the baby blues." Maura slowly walked over to the couch and picked up the blanket Jess had been using, folding it methodically as she spoke. "Motherhood wasn't ever meant to be easy. It's normal to have doubts and fears. Nobody talks about the depression or the anxiety because society tells us we just need to suck it up. To be honest, women talk about it a lot more than they used to. This isn't a conversation I could ever have with my mother or grandmother. That's for sure."

Jess nodded and let out the breath she'd been holding. "I just don't know how to make it stop." Strong emotion was chipping away at her hard-won composure, and she took another deep breath.

"It's only natural. Your body is going through a lot right now as it shifts from growing a baby to coming back down to its normal self. But I'm always here to lend an ear if you need it, and if it becomes too much for you, talk to your doctor, hon. Like I said, it's normal. They'll have some suggestions on how to deal with it, and maybe even medication if it gets beyond bearing. But don't let it go just because you feel like you're weak if you admit it's a problem. Okay?"

Jess nodded, her eyes growing misty again as she took in the love and warmth radiating from Maura.

"And if that son of mine is in need of an attitude adjustment, I'd be happy to give it to him. You just say the word."

Jess snorted, feeling loads better simply by knowing she wasn't alone. "You have raised two wonderful, thoughtful children. But their need to fix things is borderline oppressive."

Maura gave an ironic chortle. "I suppose I should apologize for that."

Jess let out a soft chuckle in return. "Nah, just a little back up the next time you see them trying to railroad me."

Maura smiled and raised her glass of ice water in salute. "Deal."

Mag Mile Mirage

The sun streamed between the high-rise buildings of downtown Chicago like a *very* unwelcoming alarm clock, and Jack groaned, pulling his pillow over his head and burrowing down into the refuge of his thick comforter. He had to be honest, he couldn't party it up like he used to. He'd been dragged kicking and screaming into his thirties, and his new age bracket would not go quietly into the night. A nine-beer hangover in his twenties now felt more like three well-timed Manhattans. While his taste in alcohol may have improved with age, his tolerance for it certainly hadn't.

His head was pounding like a tricked-out subwoofer, and his mouth was dry as the Sahara. He groaned again and tried to fall back into unconsciousness, but the pounding continued. And then with a start, he realized the pounding wasn't inside his skull, but at his door. He sat up quickly and groaned, pressing his hand to his head to keep it from falling off. Slowly, with eyes squinting against the intense morning light ricocheting off the surrounding skyscrapers, he wobbled over to the door of his hotel room on the ninth floor of the Hilton Chicago–Magnificent Mile, and hauled it open to find his brother Chris—face red with barely suppressed fury.

"What the fuck are you doing? We have to be at Lakeshore HQ in twenty minutes!"

Jack rubbed his bloodshot eyes and squinted at his brother. "I thought our meeting wasn't until noon."

Chris puffed up to his full five feet ten and glared, one dark brow raised. "It is."

Adrenaline zinged through Jack's veins and his head cleared slightly, pushing the aching, pulsing, pounding to the back of his consciousness. "Shit. I'll be down in five. Meet you in the lobby."

Chris wrinkled his nose. "Take ten and shower. You smell like a distillery."

"Gee thanks," he grumbled and slammed the door in his brother's face, instantly regretting it when the sound echoed through his brain like a malevolent boomerang.

His older brother-slash-PR representative-slash-agent had always had an affinity for contract negotiations and could pour on the charm like nobody's business. It's why he'd hired him, and if the current status of his hangover was a barometer on how this day was gonna go, he would need every bit of his brother's talent to get him through.

He didn't remember last night with extreme clarity, but he seemed to recall a woman, or rather several women, buying him and Chris drinks at the hotel bar—though he hadn't woken up with any of them in his bed. So, he supposed that was a sign of growth in his old age. Or a sign of how much he was still wallowing over his breakup with Jessica.

How long had it been?

Who was he kidding? He knew exactly how long it had been: six months, two weeks, five days and eighteen miserable hours of trying to keep his head above water. He'd tried to hide his struggles from his family. They could be overprotective, and he didn't want them to hate Jess. But he also had to admit he'd been in no state to hide anything from anyone, and he wasn't stupid enough to think he'd done a good job of keeping his heartbreak on the DL. He'd moped through the last few races of the season and then locked himself up in his parent's cabin in Colorado, avoiding the world and everyone in it as best he could. This trip to Chicago was his first trip anywhere other than the ski slopes in months.

If anyone had asked Jack what he was looking for in a woman a year ago, he sure as shit wouldn't have had "pregnant" or "kids" on the list, and yet, one look at Jessica Morales strutting down pit lane like it was a runway in Milan, and he'd been a goner. It didn't matter she had a past. Hell, so did he. She was who she was, and he was who he was. And the two of them together? Well, to quote his favorite movie, they were like peas and carrots. The end. Case closed.

Until it wasn't.

Since then, he'd spent at least an hour every day wondering what he could have done differently, imagining how things would have ended if it had been his child she carried. No matter how many times he'd rewound the clock, he'd arrived at the same conclusion, which reduced the guilt if not the grief. She'd done what she thought was best for her son and for herself. Who was he to tell her any different, let alone blame her for it? It was all just piss-poor timing, for him and for her.

Today, however, was not the day to walk down memory lane. Today was the day he would seal his ride for next season. Maybe. With a little luck. And some help from his brother.

Ten minutes later, Jack emerged from the elevator and into the lobby, weak hotel room coffee in hand to ward off the hangover. He'd chosen his second-best suit for the occasion—the best suit would be for the contract signing, fingers crossed. His dark hair, still damp from the shower and desperately in need of a good trim, was sculpted and combed off his forehead.

Chris, lounging in one of the chairs across from the lobby fireplace, looked up from his phone, and catching sight of his brother, stood, tucking his phone into his inside jacket pocket. "We're gonna have to hoof it. It'll be faster on foot with the traffic."

Jack didn't relish the idea of wading through the crush of businessmen and women, tourists, and shoppers flooding the sidewalks along Michigan Avenue, but it was his fault they were walking, so he'd grin and bear it. He took another hearty gulp of something that barely passed for coffee and nodded. "Lead the way."

As it turned out, the lunch crowd wasn't as bad as the morning rush, and their commute was spent dodging the occasional person glued to their phone screen, rather than shoving through a sea of elbows and briefcases. Jack drained the rest of his coffee and threw it into a nearby trashcan before dashing across the street after Chris to an accompaniment of horns and middle fingers. He was willing to risk it though. "I got hit by a car jaywalking," seemed like a more valid excuse for being late to contract negotiations than "I didn't hear my alarm because I was sleeping off a hangover."

After four city blocks, Jack checked his watch—11:58 p.m.—and looked ahead to see if any of the buildings looked familiar. Then, like a mirage emerging from the haze on the horizon of a hot day, he saw her. From across the street and half a block away, it was hard to know for sure, but the curve of her hips, the jet black of her hair cascading down her back, the slight angle of her chin…

His step faltered, and he froze to the sidewalk, unable to look away as she continued toward him. As he turned to watch her walk past, he became vaguely aware of his "creep factor" but ignored it.

From the rearview, what had been a "possibly" was turning into a "probably not."

"Watch it, dumb ass," a man grumbled as Jack stumbled into him.

"Sorry," Jack mumbled, but when he looked back up the street, the woman had disappeared in a throng of passersby.

Chris clamped a hand around his upper arm and jerked him out of foot traffic before he collided with a messenger bike buzzing toward them. "Come *on*. You can window shop later," he hissed and shoved his younger brother into the revolving door of the office building next to them.

He blindly followed his brother down hallways and onto elevators, unable to shake the feeling he'd been walloped over the head with a blunt object.

It couldn't be her. Why would she be in Chicago, of all places? She'd just had a baby, for Christ's sake.

There was no way it was her. It didn't make any sense, and he needed to get a grip. If he started hallucinating now, he might as well throw in the towel.

It was time to get his game face on.

Eight

Fit-and-Flare

The high-pitched screech of worn brakes and the obnoxious honking of city traffic was enough to wear on anyone's nerves—especially a sleep-deprived, hormonal new mother, separated from her baby for the first time. She could feel the impulse to scream clawing in her throat as sensory overload slowly boiled her brain. She walked ten paces behind Alaina and Maura as they chatted animatedly about the reason for their presence in the big city—the Windy City to be more precise—wedding dress shopping. She loved both women dearly, but if she had to add their incessant chipper dialogue to the cacophony of the city streets, she might well and truly lose it.

Then she caught a glimpse of something, a passing reflection, that silenced the world as though someone had put noise canceling headphones over her ears. Against the obnoxious, cheery glare of the sun on the storefront to her left, she caught the passing shape of two men, dressed in business suits and walking at a clipped pace that said they were in a hurry to be somewhere and to get the hell out of their way. The first man, narrow through the shoulder and hips, but with an understated grace, looked dressed to kill in his crisp black suit and aviators.

But it was the second man, being towed along by the first, that caught her eye. *Jack.* Some part of her brain had instinctively drawn the connection between the fashionably dressed, dark-haired man of medium height with the man who'd stalked her dreams for months.

For a moment, time seemed to stand still as she gazed in the window, her heart racing as she stared at the distorted image. She wanted to whirl around, to shout his name, to run to him, but she couldn't. Sure, the man shared a striking resemblance to her ex, but without being on the same side of the street and able to look up into his face, she couldn't know for certain.

Suddenly, the fear of looking like an absolute lunática was squashed beneath the overwhelming need to *see* him, and she turned, but by the time the crowd around her parted, they were gone. She stared longingly across the street for a few seconds more before Alaina pushed back through the revolving door on the storefront of Mira Couture.

"Coming?"

Jess turned reluctantly, still searching the crowd. "Yeah. Coming."

A warm gust of air greeted her as she ducked into one of the door slots and pushed into the boutique—giving Jess the strange sensation that she'd stumbled out of a swirling tornado and landed in Oz. Only, instead of a land of vibrant colors and munchkins, it was a land of Swarovski crystals and Chantilly lace.

"Oh, I love this ruching!" Alaina squeaked as she fingered the soft eggshell chiffon of a display piece nearby.

Jess quirked her lips and snorted. "You've been training your whole life for this moment, haven't you?" Being in the wedding business was a girlie girl's dream, and Alaina had been up in the clouds since the day they flipped their shop sign to "open." Thinking up place settings, floral arrangements, and color palettes was foreplay for her. Add in a beautiful wedding dress and she was putty in your hands.

"It's not about the dress, or the reception menu, or the decorations. It's about the man I'm marrying," Alaina replied in a haughty, sing-song voice, sounding so much like Maura that Jess had to stifle a laugh.

"But a pretty dress doesn't hurt?"

Alaina glanced back over her shoulder with a mischievous twinkle in her eye. "But a pretty dress doesn't hurt."

Jess gave up on her sensibilities and snorted as she turned toward the rack nearest her and ran her fingers over a gorgeous ivory satin number with geometric cutouts. Not that she was in the market, but if she was…

"I'm so glad you decided to come." Sincerity coated Alaina's warm contralto voice, and her hazel eyes sparkled with glee. She had come home from Paris with a plan. The engagement would be short—only four months—and there was no time to waste. So, on the fourth Saturday of the new year, Jess was dragged kicking and screaming from her cozy den and hauled up to Chicago for a weekend full of "girl time."

Tucker had been no help, damn him. He'd practically put a dent in her backside as he kicked her out the door. He was convinced she needed to get out and have fun. Since he was leaving Monday, he was more than willing to care for Parker while she was gone for one night. Besides, it gave the boys a little bonding time—at least that's what she kept telling herself. The new mother in her had other anxiety-riddled ideas, and she was struggling not to give them credence.

Intrusive thoughts were her bread and butter these days, and her disastrous meeting with María hadn't helped. She had expected to get some backlash about the baby. That was a touchy subject on María's best day, but thoughts of her father, the fact that María never even told Julian she was pregnant, and the thing that haunted her the most...*My life was over, but his didn't have to be.*

How different would her life have been if María hadn't picked *that* moment to be selfless? What if she'd grown up with a father?

If María and Julian had given up their dreams for her, would it have been a happily ever after? Or would they have grown to resent her and each other? They likely would have ended up divorced, and she'd have gone through an even messier version of the nightmare Alaina and Tucker had endured when their parents split.

Was that what she wanted for herself? Was that what she wanted for *Parker*?

Because she couldn't help but feel like that was the road her and Tucker were headed down—trying to do the right thing for all the wrong reasons with no happy ending in sight. She sighed heavily as she tried to reel her anxiety back in and live in the moment.

Alaina was fizzing with glee as she gently thumbed through the racks, and all Jess wanted was to bask in her glow. It was good to see Alaina happy. Being home with the baby over the past few weeks had given her a lot of time to dwell on the less pleasant aspects of her life. So, maybe a day of wedding dress shopping was exactly what she needed to take her mind off things.

Alaina ran her fingers over a few more dresses before coming to a stop a few feet away. "Ball gown?" She tugged on a mass of creamy skirts fit to cover the state of Rhode Island and grinned.

"Oh my god, you have *got* to try that on—just to get a picture if nothing else." She could slowly but surely feel the tension leaving her body. Separation from María had been healing. She'd almost forgotten what it was like to be treated like a piece of garbage.

"You've got that look on your face again," Alaina chastised, but before she could ask, a bridal consultant approached them and whisked her away to a changing room talking about silhouettes and fabrics.

With a quiet smile on her face, Jess turned and made her way to the other side of the room, where Maura was perusing the sale racks. Grayson was footing the bill for the whole wedding and had given Alaina carte blanche to choose whatever her heart desired, but by the bug-eyed sticker shock on Maura's face, Jess could tell Alaina would have a battle on her hands with her penny pinching mother.

She would shit a brick if she knew how much some of our clients spent on their weddings.

Three boutiques and fifteen dresses later, the trio of women walked out onto the bustling streets of the Magnificent Mile, grinning from ear to ear. They had found a winner. A gorgeous, A-line beauty with charming periwinkle lace accents. The second Alaina had stepped out of the dressing room and onto the pedestal, Jess had known it was the one.

"It's perfect, Lainie," Maura whispered in half-choked benediction as she took in the flushed rose of her daughter's giddy face. Of course, that hadn't been the end of it. Alaina had also walked out of her final appointment with a receipt for a chapel-length veil accented with tiny cherry blossoms, periwinkle satin stilettos, and a set of amethyst teardrop earrings, complete with a matching necklace.

Jess, much to her chagrin, had not been able to escape the clutches of a bride on a mission and had been thrown into a dressing room with several bridesmaid's gowns. "But I'm not even out of my maternity pants yet!" Jess moaned, self-consciously thinking of her less-than-desirable postpartum figure. "Give me at least another month before I try on any dresses."

But her pleas fell on deaf ears. Alaina had given her a no-nonsense tilt of the head. "They'll alter it to fit, Jess. I'm not driving back up here until we come up for alterations and this is the only boutique with the color that matches the lace in my dress." This had been followed by a gentle shove between her shoulder blades that propelled her into the open dressing room.

Her consultant smiled kindly. "You just had a baby? You look *amazing*."

Jess gave her a watered-down smile as she looked at the young woman, no older than herself via their reflections in the three-paneled mirror. "Thanks. He'll be a month old on the twenty-fourth." The image of Jess's saggy abdominal skin and the livid stretch marks across her thighs, love handles, and belly made her tear up.

How could anyone ever find this sexy?

Her happy helper placed the dress down on the floor for her to step into and then pulled it up, fastening her in with a quick zip. "Now, this is a size six. I wouldn't recommend going any smaller than this because if you lose weight, they can always take it in."

Jess toyed with the clingy fabric, pinching it between her thumb and forefinger absently. The dress clung to Jess's figure in a display of hills and valleys that shriveled what little self-confidence she had left. She rubbed her stomach absently as the sting of tears threatened to break loose. "The bride gets what the bride wants, right?" she asked, sniffling.

"You're not the first bridesmaid I've seen steamrolled," the consultant replied in a dramatic whisper that made Jess laugh. "Let's get this over with, shall we?"

Alaina clasped her hands together, beaming with approval as Jess exited the dressing room, uncertainty written all over her face. Noticing Jess's discontent, Alaina's enthusiasm lessened. "You don't like it?"

Jess bit her bottom lip and glanced at Maura, their conversation from a few days ago ringing in her ears. Sympathy gleamed in Maura's eyes and she gave Jess a small nod of encouragement, letting her know she had her back. Jess took a deep breath and closed her eyes.

Dios ayúdame.

"I kind of hate it…" she muttered, looking down at her feet to avoid the basilisk glare she was anticipating.

A quiet snort of approval and amusement came from Maura's general direction, and Jess glanced toward her adoptive mother, who was miserably failing to contain the giggle bubbling against her pursed lips.

"Seriously? Normally you like this kind of thing." Alaina motioned to the article of clothing in question, confused but not angry.

"I just…" She sighed. "I need something a little less formfitting. I don't feel comfortable in this right now."

Some of the tension left Alaina's shoulders. "Well, that's okay. We can find…something…" She glanced at the racks of blush and gold and burgundy dresses searching for another one in the shade she wanted.

Then the consultant stepped in. *God bless her.* "We can order any of those dresses on that rack in the periwinkle you want." Jess's gaze wandered to the far wall where at least thirty styles of dress hung from the rack. The anxiety she'd been feeling lifted in an instant as she took in the different fabrics and cuts. "Why don't we see if we can find something you both like?"

After five more dresses and a little trial and error, they settled on an elegant number with a twist knot and ruching in the front that hid Jess's pooch while still hugging the curve of her hips and the swell of her breasts.

It was the first time in months she felt beautiful.

* * *

Warmth and light seemed to make the entryway of The Drake Hotel in Chicago glow as the three women tumbled through the revolving door and onto the velvety royal blue carpeting. "Are we in the right place?" Jess asked under her breath to Maura as Alaina continued up the stairs toward the main lobby and check-in desk.

Maura's wide gray eyes darted sideways at Jess and then

back at their surroundings as she took in the cream and mauve marble wall panels and intricate coffered ceilings with an ornate crystal chandelier holding court in the middle of the vast room, that somehow felt…homey?

Yeah, maybe if your home was Buckingham Palace…

Alaina had definitely developed a taste for the finer things in life, and she wondered what Grayson thought of that. He seemed so down-to-earth. Was this really how he lived?

Light, classical piano music played on the speaker system, and Jess felt like she needed to go back home and change. An older woman in a Ralph Lauren sweater and smart slacks strode past them next to a dashing gentleman in a Sartorio sports coat with polished Italian loafers. Jess wanted to crawl under the concierge desk and hide in her wrinkly, off-the-rack attire, and she could tell by the way Alaina's mother clutched her shoulder bag, she felt the same way.

Waiting for Alaina to return with the room keys, she stepped into the corner of the room behind a round coffee table with a large centerpiece full of white flowers and greenery, hoping to hide her grungy appearance from most of the hotel's patrons.

Her phone buzzed in her hands, heralding the arrival of a text message—from Anika.

Jessica Morales you are on my SHIT. LIST.

Jess groaned and threw her head back. One of her closest friends from college, Anika Spencer lived in Chicago, and apparently, had gotten word of her arrival. She had been hoping to slide under the radar, just a quick in and out for some wedding dress shopping, no big deal.

Yeah. Fat. Chance.

I know. I know. Sorry?

The slight shuffle of footsteps alerted Jess to Alaina's arrival, key cards fanned out in her hand. "Pick your poison."

Jess selected the middle one and eyed the room number on the envelope underneath the cards. 616. At least they would be high enough to drown out the city below.

**How are you going to make
it up to me?**

*Oh god...*Jess sighed and stuffed her phone in her purse. The last thing she wanted was a night out. This was her first night away from Parker and she just wanted to curl up in her pajamas and enjoy a night to herself.

Yeah, how's that working out for ya?

Her phone buzzed again.

**Drinks at PRYSM. 10.
Be there or be square.**

Jess whimpered and moaned, stomping her feet as they entered the elevator. She recognized it as childish behavior, but who the hell cared? She had a solid nine months before her son started mimicking her, and she planned to take full advantage in the interim.

Alaina raised her eyebrows. "What's wrong with you?"

Jess jabbed the button for the sixth floor and slumped

against the elevator wall, pointing an accusatory finger. "You posted we were dress shopping in Chicago. Didn't you?"

Alaina tilted her head in a slight *And?* gesture. "I'm failing to make a connection between your six-year-old tantrum and my dress shopping post."

"I didn't tell Anika I was coming to Chicago. Now she's trying to get me to go out tonight."

"That sounds like fun!" Maura perked up as the elevator chime rang and the doors sprang open. "You should go. Be with friends. This is your first night out as a new mom. Go have fun!"

"Yeah, but what if I just wanted to lounge in my PJs and watch a movie? Get a full night's sleep? That's kinda my idea of fun these days."

Maura gave Jess a sympathetic smile, but Alaina smirked. "You're twenty-five, Jess. I'm not letting you turn into a grandma. Go hang out with Anika. I'm sure she'll bring some of the girls. You haven't seen each other in almost a year. It'll be fun!"

"What do you mean, 'let me turn into a grandma'? When was the last time you went out to a club with friends? I'll tell you. College. And that was only because I dragged you there," Jess snapped.

Alaina cheeks flushed crimson. "Touchy…"

Jess glared at her friend, barely resisting the urge to throttle her.

Maura, ever the voice of reason, stepped between the girls. "You don't have to be out late. Go. Have a drink and visit for a while. If you're not having a good time, take an Uber and come back to the hotel."

Alaina scanned her card and pushed the door open to a

gorgeous suite with palatial decor: cream-colored satin wing-backed chairs, a bouquet of fresh-cut flowers on the table, and gold damask drapes that framed the floor-to-ceiling windows overlooking Michigan Avenue.

"God, Alaina…have you forgotten how to travel on a budget?" Jess asked, sitting her duffel down on the chaise near the TV.

Alaina snorted. "Grayson and I racked up a ton of loyalty points while we were traveling. I just thought it might be fun to stay somewhere fancy."

So, her friend hadn't come back from Europe a *completely* different person. That was a relief.

Another buzz from her phone.

Jade and Mikayla are in.
See you at 10.

Jess sighed and eyed her bag. Okay, but what was she supposed to wear?

Nine

Goodbye's Been Good to You

The pulsing vibration of rave music could be felt twenty feet from the club entrance where Jess alighted from her Uber chariot. Dread crept up from her stomach to her chest and constricted her airway. She'd been hoping for simplicity tonight, just pizza at Giordano's before heading back to the hotel.

Yeah. Right.

She looked down at the gray sweater dress she'd pulled from the bottom of her duffle, trying to hand-press the wrinkles from the fabric. Packing the garment had been an afterthought, more to ward off bad juju than to actually serve a purpose. She couldn't help but see the irony in *that* thought.

The moment Jess opened the door to the club, the smell of hard liquor, sweat, and bar food smacked her in the face and made her already nervous stomach do a somersault. But before she could turn on her heel and escape into the brisk Chicago night, Anika caught sight of her and squealed. The only blessing to the situation was the music and general air of celebration in the club made Anika's keening barely discernible.

"Girl, you look amazing!" she cried, holding her friend at arm's length to admire her.

"No way you just had an effing baby!" Jade chimed in, swooping in for a hug like a homing pigeon.

Feeling lighter after a few hugs and smiles, Jess allowed herself to be pulled into the massive open space toward the bar where Mikayla stood guarding the drinks and saving seats. "It's so good to see you!" she shouted as she leaned in to kiss Jess on both cheeks. "Where have you *been*? We haven't seen you in ages!"

It *had* been ages. In fact, the last time she'd seen this trio was…the night she'd hooked up with Tucker.

Jess's heart skipped a beat before settling back into its normal rhythm. They'd been in Texas for their sorority sister's bachelorette party when they'd run into Tucker and some of his buddies, enjoying a night off base in Dallas. Several hours of reminiscing and a bottle of tequila later, and, well…she didn't need a reminder of how that night had turned out.

"Oh, you know, just running a business and having a baby," Jess replied as she turned toward the bartender, pretending she hadn't just had a flashback to one of the most pivotal nights of her life. Getting pregnant with Parker had been a wake-up call. It was part of the reason she hadn't seen the girls in so long. They were symbolic of a part of her life that was gone forever—a time when she was young and naïve, when the only person she was responsible for was herself and not even managing that well.

In the recesses of her mind, she liked to tell herself it took two to make a baby, and Tucker was just as responsible for what happened. But she couldn't help but think about María's words: *Just because he hides it from you doesn't mean those feelings aren't there.* Was she right? Did some part of Tucker resent her, resent Parker, for what happened?

No. No way.

"Can I get a gin and tonic with a twist of lime?" she asked the bartender, giving herself a mental shake to rid her mind of María's poison. As she turned back toward her friends, a piece of bling on Anika's finger caught her eye, and she reached out. "What is *this*?" Jess asked, tilting her friend's hand back and forth to let her new accessory sparkle. It was a gorgeous one-carat emerald-cut solitaire diamond in a gold setting.

"Owen finally proposed last night. I was going to text you today, but then I saw you were *here* wedding dress shopping with Alaina."

"Can we take a moment to talk about how lucky that bitch got?" Jade asked, throwing back a shot of tequila. "Seriously, does that fiancé of hers have any single friends? I want a racecar driver. I bet they have fantastic hands."

All the girls sniggered at her innuendo. Well, he did have one particular friend who, as far as Jess knew, was *very* single, but she wasn't about to feed Jack to the wolves. "Alaina and Grayson are perfect for each other. Seriously, they're so sweet. I feel like I've eaten two whole bags of cotton candy when I'm around them."

"Is it true they *literally* ran into each other, and that's how they met?" Mikayla asked, only half attending as she made eyes at the handsome DJ in the corner.

Jess glanced over her shoulder to get an eye full and froze. Her stomach fell into her butt and she saw stars like she'd taken a roundhouse to the jaw. There, in the middle of the dance floor, was a curvaceous, doe-eyed, redhead, swaying seductively to the music with a partner that matched her point for point—broad shoulders tapered into a narrow waist, with a strong jaw, and piercing eyes: Jack Kinney.

Jess felt like she was going to puke. The sight of Jack, there in front of her, had sucked all the air from her lungs, and her stomach was doing somersaults like a sugar-crazed toddler with a case of the Zoomies. The song they were dancing to transitioned to a slower number, and Jack stepped back from the girl with that charming, one-sided grin of his and glanced toward the bar—looking for someone. Suddenly, she wanted to shrink down to the size of a microbe and vanish into the grimy floor. It had been six months, two weeks, and six days, but she remembered the shattered look in his slate-colored eyes as if it were yesterday.

She turned back to her friends, smiling at them as though she were attentively following their conversation and took a sip of her drink, but she felt his gaze lock onto her like a high-powered laser beam burning a hole in the back of her skull, and she turned to meet his eye.

Damn, he looks good, she thought to herself, meeting his steamy gaze for another minute before looking away. She wanted to walk across the dance floor, meld her body with his, and lay a kiss on him that was so passionate the whole room would notice.

But he was here with someone.

What was she talking about? *She* was with someone.

Granted, he wasn't here, but Tucker was a very tangible boyfriend at home with *their son*. She peeled her gaze from Jack and turned to her friends. "I'm gonna go pee. I'll be right back."

She didn't have to pee, but she needed some air. The atmosphere of close bodies, alcohol, and Jack's proximity were suffocating her. She grabbed her clutch off the bar and, with a final swig of her drink, took off for the bathroom before one of the girls got any ideas about tagging along. As she walked up to the one-holer, she ran past the line of women waiting patiently in line and straight into the bathroom, shutting and locking the door behind her to the appalled protestations behind her.

She was hyperventilating, and if she didn't get control of herself soon, she'd fall into a full-blown panic attack. She pressed the palms of her hand into the cold porcelain of the sink and stared at her reflection, focusing on taking slow, methodical breaths…*In and out…In and out…*until her ears were no longer ringing. She turned the knob on the faucet and splashed cold water on her face, letting out one final breath. He would be waiting for her when she opened the door. She knew him well enough to know that.

There was a knock on the door, and she huffed a frustrated sigh. "Be out in a sec!" Taking a handful of paper towels from the dispenser, she dabbed at the water droplets coating her face and tossed them in the trash. She glanced in the mirror one more time before grabbing her clutch and unlocking the door, taking care not to make eye contact with any of the women she'd so rudely cut off in her panic. "Sorry," she murmured to the woman, who pushed past her into the bathroom, clearly about to pee down her leg. She only had a second to feel guilty before she caught sight of Jack hovering nearby, arms crossed in front of him as he waited.

When he caught sight of her, he pushed away from the wall and dropped his arms to his sides, clearly just as nervous as she was. Her feet carried her forward of their own volition, taking no heed of the anxiety humming under her skin like a live wire, and before she knew it, she was standing right in front of him, staring up into the same gorgeous gray eyes she'd dreamed of for months.

He smiled. "Hey, Jess." His voice was husky and tickled her senses in all the right places. She thought her heart might grow wings and fly away at the sound of that vibrating baritone, but then she remembered the perky redhead he'd been dancing with and felt her smile falter. As if divining her thoughts, he looked over his shoulder and then back to her. "She's just a friend."

Jess stiffened and turned to him, arms crossed defensively in front of her. She clamped down on her forearms and forced her shoulders to relax. "It's none of my business." Her shoulders jerked up and down in an awkward motion as she pried her eyes off her devilishly handsome ex and glanced back toward the dance floor. "I didn't know you were in town." She managed through her constricted airway.

"I had a few meetings—there's a team in the area that wants to sign me. Karina works in the front office and invited me out for celebratory drinks with some friends when she heard we agreed to terms this afternoon."

She gave him a genuine smile then, knowing what a new contract meant to him. "That's awesome. Congrats!"

The wattage on his resounding smile was enough to light

up the room. He looked light, unfettered, with a happy glow that radiated quietly from him and warmed her own soul. She hadn't even noticed it until she stepped into his orbit. "You look good," she murmured, her lips quirking in a half-smile.

He straightened and looked her over appreciatively. "So do you." They stood awkwardly for the space of a minute before he gestured to the bar. "Can I buy you a drink?"

She had pumped before she left the hotel. Another drink probably wouldn't hurt.

Another drink with Jack *might hurt...*

She smothered the cynical voice in the back of her head and flashed a tight smile. "Sure."

"Gin and tonic with lime, right?" he asked as they turned and maneuvered their way through the crush of bodies back toward the bar.

She widened her eyes in surprise, realizing what Jack had said. "You remembered."

She could feel the curious glances her friends were shooting her from further down the bar but didn't dare look their way. The last thing she needed was for them to invite themselves over and find out who her companion was.

"When a pretty girl lets me buy her a drink that's not something I forget."

She lowered her gaze to focus on her shoes for a moment as alarm bells sounded in her head. *He's flirting with you. Get out. Now.*

Jack flirts with everybody, another voice reasoned.

She took a sip of the potent drink when the bartender slid it toward her and glanced up at her companion through her dark lashes.

"How has business been?" he asked as he took a sip of his Manhattan.

She watched, enthralled as his Adam's apple bobbed when he swallowed. What was wrong with her? She gritted her teeth and took a deep breath, answering his question without the hesitation she had envisioned to be there. "It's great. After that spread in *Bridal Bliss*, we're fully booked for the spring and summer. We had to hire some help. Of course, I've been on maternity leave, and Alaina was gone from the beginning of October until Christmas. So now Sydney helps handle the books and Marissa is our new designer."

"Alaina and Jessica two-point-oh." Jack surmised with a playful smirk and another swig of his drink.

"Something like that." They both watched the dance floor for a moment, absorbed in their thoughts. "What about you? What have you been up to?"

"Not much—just got back from a ski trip in Tahoe with my brothers."

"That sounds amazing." She was in desperate need of a vacation. She loved her son, and she would cheerfully murder anyone or anything that ever hurt him. But being a mother was hard—harder than she could have ever anticipated—and sometimes, she just wanted a break. "I would love to visit Lake Tahoe. I've never been," she admitted with a wistful note to her voice as she took another pull on her drink.

"I think Gray and Alaina are coming out for Thanksgiving this year. We have a timeshare at one of the resorts. You should come!"

"Oh...I...well...Parker," she said by way of explanation, fiddling with the black plastic straw she had pinched between her fingers.

His face fell for a moment. "Of course. I'm an idiot. Sorry, I should have thought—"

"It's fine." The first drink she'd had in nearly a year had resolved a lot of the tension she'd been feeling. The second drink though…that was getting to her head, and her cheeks were blazing with heat.

With a glance over his shoulder at the dance floor, Jack placed his drink on the bar and offered Jess his hand. "Dance with me?"

"I…" Her breath hitched as she thought about what Tucker would think.

Tucker isn't here.

With a smile, she put her hand in his and let him take her to the dance floor. The pulsing lights had the floor painted in shades of purple, blue, and pink as a song with vibrant Latin undertones morphed into a quick tempo R&B number. Jack pulled her close, his big warm hands pressing into the small of her back with a burning sensation that sent her heart hammering.

"It's good to see you, Sassy," he murmured in a rough voice full of barely leashed emotions.

*Sassy…*She hadn't been called that since…well, since the last time they'd…She felt a blush creep up her neck, but the flush of exertion and the mottled pattern of filtered lights kept her memories from showing in her olive complexion. The sexual energy pulsing off him was enough to melt the panties off any girl in the room and, in her slightly intoxicated state, she wasn't exactly primed to handle his advances. With an impulse impossible to resist, she pressed against him and subtly gyrated her hips so they both swayed in a sensual, magnetic rhythm. His head bent down toward her, and she couldn't help the way her gaze lingered on his soft, kissable lips.

A moan escaped her as his lips pressed to hers, warm and inviting. He pulled her even closer, bowing her body to his as his mouth became more insistent. Something in the back of her head, numbed by alcohol and acute need, stirred.

This isn't right.

She pulled back and tried to ignore her partner in crime who had the stunned look of a man who had just been poleaxed. "I can't," she whispered in desperation before backing away and running off the dance floor.

She barely had time to grab her shit from the bar stool Anika was guarding and make a run for it before he came after her. "Jess!" he cried, chasing her out the front door of the club and into the night.

The wind whipped her dark hair around her face and she wiped a few annoying strands away as they stuck to her glossy lips.

"Jess, wait!" Jack wrapped his hand around her upper arm and pulled her to a stop.

"I'm still with Tucker!" she cried through blurred vision. In her intoxicated confusion, it seemed important that he know that.

And what about Parker?

"I have a son, Jack. I can't be this person anymore."

"What person is that?" he asked, confused as hell. She didn't blame him. She was throwing around mixed signals like it was the flavor of the month.

"The kind of person who hooks up with random guys at bars."

He looked stung. "I didn't think I was some *random guy.*"

They were quiet for an interminable moment. "You know you're more than that." Her voice was husky as she stared deep into his soul.

"More than that, but still not enough." A muscle in his jaw ticked as the words hung in the air between them.

"I told you to let me go. My life is a…train wreck. I don't need to drag you into it with my self-destructive coping mechanisms."

Sympathy and concern saturated his features. "Jessica. Talk to me."

"Talk to you…" She scoffed. "About what? About how scared shitless I am to raise my son alone? About maintaining a long-distance relationship with a man I've known my whole life, and somehow still feels like I don't know at all? About my addict mother, absentee father, or ridiculously fucking perfect best friend? And…" She trailed off before she could finish her thought and do any more damage.

And I can't even be with the guy I want to be with.

A tortured sob ripped out of her throat and she convulsed, wrapping her arms around herself to hold together her shattered bits.

Suddenly Jack was there, helping her pick up the pieces as he wrapped his strong arms around her. "Shhh… You're okay. I've got you," he whispered, squeezing her tight. "I'll always be here for you, Jess. I promise."

Tears sprung up afresh as she resisted his olive branch. "You don't know what you're saying."

"Maybe not, but that doesn't mean I don't mean it." His eyes, black in the meager light of the streetlights, glinted with compassion. He was watching her flounder and trying to offer her a life preserver.

"Take me back inside? I'm freezing."

He glanced over his shoulder at the door of the club, where the music volume abruptly increased and decreased as patrons came and went. "I'll do you one better. How about we get out of here? I know a place."

She stared at the door too, warring with herself for a moment. She didn't want to go back in and pretend everything was fine. She wasn't fine. Life wasn't fine, and the effort of pretense was exhausting. With a deep sigh, she returned her gaze to the man standing in front of her and nodded. "Yeah. Let's get out of here."

Thirty minutes later, tucked away from the arctic chill of the Windy City in the corner booth of a sleepy little retro diner, Jess spilled her guts to a man she hadn't seen in six months.

"So, I'm just trying to sort out whether I want to hire a private investigator." Jess took a sip of her coffee, relishing the feel of its heat as it seeped into her chilled fingers.

Jack, on the other hand, sat frozen in the booth across from her, eyebrows arched so high they nearly merged with his hairline. "Whoa…" Slowly, he leaned forward and rested his forearms on the table between them, trying to get a read on her before commenting further. The clang and crash of dishes from the kitchen startled them both, and they jumped before looking back at each other with sheepish grins. "Well, I was going to say I think you should reach out, but…" He tilted his head and gazed at her. She got the odd sensation he was peeling her skin back and taking a peek at the vulnerable creature underneath. She didn't like it, but couldn't resist either. "You seem scared."

His final assessment singed her around the edges, and

she drew back from his penetrating gaze, crossing her arms across her chest. "I'm not scared." Her molars ground together in frustration as the fingers of her left hand drummed against her right forearm.

"Jess." The way he said her name, silently telling her to cut the crap, had her clamping down on the inside of her cheek. He always knew when she was lying. The difference between him and Tucker was that he didn't try to pry it out of her and give her a chance to go off. He just waited.

The old '50s jukebox in the corner flashed a dazzling display of green, pink, and blue as Elvis crooned through the deserted diner. Besides a bored waitress flipping through a worn copy of *Cosmopolitan* and two sleepy second-shift workers staring at their entrées with clinical interest, they were alone. She dropped her gaze to the table and unfolded her arms to pick at the peeling laminate covering the dingy table.

What *was* she afraid of? Rejection. Humiliation. More questions no one could answer.

She felt tears sting her eyes and inhaled deeply, her breath hitching in her throat. "I don't get happy endings, Jack."

"You know that's not true," he rebutted softly. "Look at all the great things you have in your life!"

A huff of ironic air escaped her lips, and she sat back abruptly, the faux leather of the booth creaking loudly under her. "Exactly! That's how it goes. Everything is fine. Hunkydory. And then—" She pounded her fist into the palm of her opposite hand with a sharp *smack* by way of illustration. She angrily swatted at the extra moisture in her eyes and sniffled. "It's so stupid. I *know* it's stupid. I'm just tired of getting hurt."

Jack gave her a sympathetic smile and squeezed her hand. "What can I do? You want me to beat somebody up? Hire a hitman?"

Jess's eyes widened in alarm, and she glanced over her shoulder. "Jack," she hissed. "You're gonna get us arrested. Would you shut up?"

He gave her a half-cocked grin and sniggered which made her burst into hysterical laughter that *did* get the attention of the diner's other occupants. "What are you hoping for, exactly? If you look for your dad?" Jack's piercing eyes studied her hard, as if he could read her mind.

Maybe he can...

Jess shrugged, toying with the stirrer stick in her coffee. "I don't know. Answers, maybe?" The bell over the door clanged merrily with the admittance of several college-aged youths, laughing quietly among themselves. That kind of carefree existence felt like a lifetime ago for her. "I guess some hopeless romantic part of me has this crazy idea that when I meet my father, maybe the part of me that never made sense...will make sense?"

"You know that's part of being human, don't you? It doesn't mean you're a fish out of water. It's just life." He raised his white ceramic mug to sip at his lukewarm coffee. His full lips brushed the rim of the cup in a tender caress, and with a sudden wave of embarrassment, she realized she was mirroring the flick of his tongue across his lips. Jack's mouth curled in silent amusement, but he passed on the opportunity to comment. "Listen." He clinked his cup back onto its saucer and leaned forward to steal several fries from her plate. Chewing meditatively, he studied her, indecision warring in his expression. "I promised I would be here for you, and I will. If you really want to find this guy—"

"I do." The words came out in a rush of certainty that shocked her. Until that very moment, she hadn't known how badly she needed the blanks filled in. Jess stared down at her hand. It had instinctively shot across the table to grab Jack's, and the current running between them hummed and vibrated. With the same force of will it took to separate two industrial-grade magnets, she lifted her hand and waited for him to elaborate on his proposal.

"My brother, Noah, is a private investigator. He worked for Denver PD as a detective for several years, but there's no money in public service. He had his masters in criminal psychology and decided to put it to use."

"I don't have a lot of money, but if you could send me his contact info, I can reach out and see if he'd be interested in my case."

Jack waved her off. "Stop. I'll talk to him. He owes me one."

Jess raised a quizzical eyebrow, but figured that was a story for another time. It was late, and she needed to get back. "I should go. Alaina will be worried." She reached for her clutch to pay the bill, but Jack was ten steps ahead and threw down more than enough cash to cover their food and a thirty percent tip. "You don't—"

"My treat," he insisted and raised a hand to halt any further protestations. *"Humor me."* He tilted his head and smiled, flashing a mouth full of perfectly straight, pearly whites.

Finally, she rolled her eyes and acquiesced, placing her wallet back in her purse and sliding across the faux leather booth to stand.

It was the gentlemanly thing to do. She knew that.

Still doesn't mean I have to like it.

Ten

Take the L out of Lover

"Go kiss that baby for me!" Maura cried as Jessica tripped out of the back seat of Alaina's CRV laughing. It had been a good day, and she felt light, more like herself than she had since Parker's birth.

"I will," she assured them with a broad grin before grabbing her duffle out of the back seat and slamming the door.

Alaina waved rapidly out the windshield and then turned to back out of the driveway. Jess sighed, thinking about what she had to do next. After her impromptu therapy session with Jack, a few things had become abundantly clear: her relationship with Tucker wasn't working and she needed to find her birth father. But somehow, despite those life-changing revelations, she felt freer to make her own decisions than she had forty-eight hours ago and was empowered by that sentiment.

"Hello?" she called out as she stomped the snow from her

boots and let herself into the house. "Anybody home?"

"In here," Tucker called from the back of the house, near the bedroom. The house was spotless from floor to ceiling, almost as though her boyfriend had been stress cleaning, but she knew that's just how he was. It was a trait the military had instilled in him, more than his natural disposition, but she had to admire his attention to detail. Even the return vent, which she'd been meaning to clean for months, had been wiped down. What got her blood pressure up was the furniture he'd seen fit to move in her absence—no doubt in a bid to "make things easier for her."

She let out a deep breath and tossed her duffle on the couch, throwing her frustrations out with it. She was home, and that was all that mattered. She could move the coffee cabinet back after she dropped Tuck at the airport tomorrow.

Leaning on the doorjamb to the bedroom, she caught sight of Parker first, lying in his Boppy, napping. He looked so sweet and innocent, and she wanted to run and pick him up but resisted. Tucker was standing on the other side of the bed—packing. Guilt stabbed through her. Tomorrow he would have to return to Texas, and she hadn't even bothered to spend his last day at home with him. "I'm sorry I wasn't here this weekend," she apologized, watching him as he placed the last of his clothes in the top of his bag and zipped it.

He looked up at her, brow furrowed. "It's okay. We managed." He reached out and lightly touched Parker's belly, smiling absently to himself. "It was good for us to have some guy time. Besides, you needed a break."

He was right. She had needed a break, but she also didn't need him to tell her that.

Deep breath.

"Alaina found a dress. Well, we all did." She snorted in begrudging amusement and scooped Parker up, unable to resist the temptation to snuggle him any longer.

Tucker snorted back. "Oh, I know…I was with Grayson when he got the fraud alert."

Jessica laughed quietly to herself as she envisioned that interaction. "What did you do yesterday?"

"Just hung out and watched the game with Dad and Grayson. It was fun—good to relax before I head back."

She nodded and looked up at him, her heart cracking a little. If she were honest with herself, the funk she had been in the last few weeks wasn't only about her failures as a mother, but about her failures as a partner. Tucker was sweet, honest, and caring—a great friend. She knew with every fiber of her being that he would be a great father to their son, but when it was all said and done, she didn't feel a spark with him. In fact, his incessant need to take care of her drove her up a frigging wall.

It didn't mean she didn't love him—*god, did she!*—but when he touched her, it wasn't the kind of touch that unleashed waves of fiery passion. It was a warm squeeze of reassurance around her soul. He was a friend, not a life partner, and the last thing she wanted was to waste precious time in an attempt to make something out of nothing.

"Tuck…can we talk?" she asked, her voice quiet but clear.

"What's wrong?" Worry and fear and a host of other emotions clouded his features, and more guilt washed over her. Why couldn't she just let him go back to Texas and be happy?

Because that's not fair to either of you, and you know it.

She placed Parker back in his nest and draped a receiving blanket over him before patting the bed and inviting Tucker to sit alongside her. He took her hand, squeezing it tightly in encouragement as she fought for the right words. "Before I got pregnant, did you ever think about your future? Like, what your ideal life would be like?"

His head tilted slightly toward her as he turned the words over in his mind. "I…" he sighed and turned toward her on the bed. "Where is this coming from?"

She turned in so they were fully facing each other and squeezed his hand. "Just…answer the question. Please."

He sighed and pulled his hand back to run it through his hair. "I don't know, maybe. I mean, what twenty-two-year-old guy thinks about having a family? I guess I figured one day, maybe, I'd settle down, get married, have a couple of kids." He shrugged. "Jess…what's going on?" His voice was soft, concerned, like he could feel the ground shifting beneath his feet and was trying not to panic.

"When I first found out I was pregnant, you avoided me like the plague."

His cheeks blushed a furious red, and he broke eye contact, choosing to stare at his hands rather than meet her gaze.

"You didn't want a serious relationship when you thought that's all I wanted, but when you found out I was pregnant—"

"Obviously, I wanted to do right by you. What man wouldn't?" His back went ramrod straight as he searched her face for any clue to what she was getting at.

She squeezed his hand even tighter as she trudged ahead. "But did you want to do right by me because it's what you wanted or because it's what was expected of you?"

"Jesus," he muttered and jumped to his feet. "Are you

serious? You want to have this conversation *now?* When I'm leaving tomorrow?"

"It's a conversation we should have had months ago, Tucker," Jess insisted as she studied his pacing form. "What do you *really, truly* want?"

"I love my son. I love *you*. Why is that so hard for you to understand?"

"Because I don't believe for a second that you *do* love me, Tuck. Not in the way you think you do, and I have *got* to be honest about that if it fucking kills me. Okay?"

The wrinkles on his forehead deepened as he groped for understanding. And then it clicked. "Is this about me not being around? Because my enlistment is up in July. I can be involved, Jess."

The dull ache in her heart jumped to a sharp throb as she realized what he was saying. The last thing she wanted was for him to blame himself. "No. It's not that. I know you're doing the best you can. I just don't want you to resent us."

"I would never—"

"It's not the life you wanted. I'm not the girl you would have picked to take home to your family. There's no shame in admitting that. I just need you to say it, so we can acknowledge it, and move on," Jess whispered in desperation.

"You may not love me, but I *do* love you." His voice cracked under the emotional strain of their conversation, and she hated herself at that moment. She hated that doing what was best for her meant inflicting pain on someone else. And she *hated* that Tucker—one of her best friends—was her latest victim.

"I think you're in love with the idea of loving me. Or maybe you do love me, but it's the same way I love you—as friends, not as soul mates."

"Not everybody gets that," he argued, hell-bent on changing her mind. But that wasn't going to happen.

"Everyone may not get a happily ever after, but I want the freedom to try to find mine. I've lived my entire life being the consequence of somebody else's mistake, and I refuse to be trapped in this endless cycle of obligation, Tucker. I won't do it to myself. I won't do it to you, and I sure as hell won't do it to Parker. We all deserve to be somebody's first and only choice."

His face was blank with shock, the apples of his cheeks flushed pink with something between embarrassment and horror. "So you want to ride off into the sunset with somebody else and take my son with you?" His voice was louder than he'd intended, and there was panic in the whites of his eyes.

"I would never—*never*—take Parker from you. I know how much you love him. I know how much it's killing you to leave tomorrow. We will figure this out. I promise."

"Promise," he scoffed, wiping the tears from his eyes. "My dad promised to be faithful to my mom too, and you see how that worked out. Excuse me if I'm doubting something as flimsy as a few nice words when I'm forced to live a thousand miles away from my kid." His breath hitched, and he stood up in an explosion of anger and frustration.

There it was.

This wasn't about Jess or their relationship—though there was certainly a little wounded pride there. No, this was about Nate's failures as a father, and outright fear on Tucker's part that he would be forced into a similar failure by circumstance.

"You are not your father, and I am *not* your mother. Listen to yourself," she growled, standing. She'd be damned if she'd take his shitty attitude sitting down, even if she still had to look up to meet his gaze. "You're not even upset about the breakup. You're upset about us not being a family anymore. This is the twenty-first freaking century. Families come in a million different forms. So we had a child out of wedlock. One day when we find the people we're meant to be with, Parker will have stepparents who love him as much as we do. That's not a tragedy, Tucker. That's a blessing!"

He stared out the window of the bedroom into the overcast afternoon, hands on hips, silent. This is exactly what she was hoping *wouldn't* happen. But here they were, and now they had to figure it out.

Tucker's shoulders slumped, and he bowed his head, thinking. "So what are we going to do?" He turned toward her. "I want a plan."

She gave him a soft smile. "I'll bring Parker down to Texas in March or April. With how much Alaina travels, surely we can find some time for me to come down to see you, and we can FaceTime as much as you want. I'm not going to keep him from you. Seriously."

A muscle in his jaw ticked, and his eyes held a murky mix of confusion, grief, and doubt. "I guess I'll have to trust you."

She tilted her head at him, signaling him to cut the crap. Just because this relationship hadn't worked out between them didn't mean she'd ever given him a reason not to trust her. Slowly, she walked around the bed and wrapped her arms around him. "I'm sorry."

For a moment he was as rigid as a tree, the planes of his body stony and unwelcoming beneath her, but under her warm, gentle touch, the tension slowly melted away. He wrapped his arms around her, eventually resting his chin on top of her head. "I really hoped we could make this work." His gravelly voice was thick with emotion, and she heard a faint catch in the words.

"I know," she whispered, hugging him tighter. "But this will be better for both of us."

He was quiet again. She knew he didn't agree with her right now, and that was fine. He would someday, and she could have the patience to wait out his stubborn streak.

Eleven

Band of Brothers

As soon as the ink dried on his contract with Brad Jepson's newly formed Lakeshore Autosport, Jack was itching to jump out of the plush leather conference chair and be on his way. He barely got any sleep the night before, what with the celebratory adrenaline of a full-time ride in IndyCar and the dizzying memory of Jess humming through him. She was every bit as drop-dead gorgeous as he remembered and touching her, kissing her, had given him a buzz—second only to the feeling of hitting top speed down the front stretch at Indy. It was intoxicating.

But a quick reminder from his conscious that she wasn't his wilted him like a cold shower after a wet dream. She was in a different stage of life now: the mother of a tiny baby, and worse, in a committed relationship.

You never should have kissed her.

Yeah, but "*shouldn't* have" sounded a lot better than "wish I *would* have" and he didn't regret it. Not even a little bit.

With a wide grin and a handshake, he posed for a quick picture to go with the press release and exited the conference room, walking so quickly Chris was barely keeping up. "You got somewhere to be?" He huffed as he slid into the elevator beside Jack, barely clearing the doors as they closed.

"We both do if you're heading back to Denver with me. I switched to an earlier flight, but I gotta stop by the hotel to grab my bag first. My flight leaves at four."

Chris looked at his watch as the floor reader clicked down. "As in two hours from now?"

"One hour and fifty-six minutes."

"Shit…" Chris swore and dove out the door as it opened, his brother close on his heels.

As they piled into their hired car, Jack, half-laughing, spoke to the driver. "We need to stop at the Hilton to grab our bags and get to O'Hare for a four o'clock departure. There's a Benjamin in it for you if you can make it happen."

The driver looked at his passengers in the rearview mirror and smiled. "Buckle up."

"Do you ever do anything, you know, the *normal* way?" Chris asked as he clicked his seat belt.

"Where's the fun in that?" Jack laughed as he clicked his seat belt too. They made good time to the hotel and within a couple minutes, they were on their way to the airport.

"I scheduled us for the six o'clock flight. What's the rush?" Chris asked Jack, who was staring silently out the window.

"Noah is leaving town tonight, and I wanted to meet up with him before he's gone for god knows how long."

"And you can't just call or text?" The Kinney brothers had been close growing up, but, in their adult lives, were rarely in the same place at the same time. The youngest of four, Jack traveled the most. By occupation and thus, necessity, he and Chris, the eldest, saw each other the most. Aaron, the second child, had the most normal life of them all: settled, married, and the proud father of two children. Noah, only eleven months older than Jack, was constantly on the move as a private investigator, and the favor he had to ask wasn't something he could ask over the phone.

"No." Jack's tone made it clear he wasn't going to offer further details, so Chris shrugged and stared down at his phone, answering emails in a rare moment of downtime.

Living life in the fast lane was the only way Jack knew how to live, and in the quiet moments when he lay in bed at night or took in the view from the top of the world, he wondered if he would ever be able to slow himself down. It was a juxtaposition if ever he saw one. He operated at warp speed to cram as much into the day as possible, but on the flip side, he also sacrificed happiness, fulfillment, and even a little bit of peace. Maybe it was time for a change. Maybe it had been time for a while.

"How'd you know Ivy was the one? That she was worth making the sacrifice for?" Jack asked quietly.

The phone drooped in Chris's hand as he looked away from the device toward his younger brother. "I'm not sure what you mean by 'sacrifice.' She shuts herself in that office when she's on a deadline. If anybody gets my crazy schedule, she does."

Chris's wife was an investigative journalist by day and a mystery and suspense author by night. When the itch hit, she filled her coffee mug and went to work. In some ways, her life was more hectic than her husband's. He was out of town often, but at least he worked banker's hours.

"Maybe you're the wrong person to ask," Jack muttered and looked back out the window as the city slowly turned into the suburbs. They were nearing the airport. Jack glanced at his watch: two forty-five.

Guess I better get my wallet ready...

Chris gasped in mockery. "Has the infamous ladies' man, Jack Kinney, found himself a woman?"

"'Infamous ladies' man'?" Jack barked a laugh. "Ivy might write mysteries, but are you sure you haven't taken up romance novels?"

Chris would not be deterred though. "Well, go on. Have I met her?"

Jack glanced over with an eyebrow raised as if to say, *"Seriously?"* but then he released his death grip on confidentiality. Who was Chris going to tell anyway?

Well, nobody on purpose.

He did know Grayson, though, and if Gray caught wind of the situation, Jack would be in for an ass-kicking of epic proportions. His phone buzzed in his pocket.

Did you get it inked?

Speak of the devil...

Jack took a deep breath and typed a quick reply to Grayson before continuing his conversation with his brother.

> **All set. You're talking to the newest member of Lake Shore Autosport.**

He clicked the lock button and pocketed the device to give

his companion his undivided attention. "It's Jessica Morales."

Chris gave a low whistle. "Jessica…I thought she dumped your ass."

Jack glared. "She didn't dump me. We mutually decided it was best if she tried to have a relationship with her baby's father."

Chris raised an eyebrow, but let Jack's piddly excuse slide. "Alright, so what? She raises her tail, and you go chasing after her like a bitch in heat?"

"Don't be crude," Jack growled, feeling his hackles rise. The airport was fast approaching, and they would need to make this conversation quick if they had a hope in hell of keeping its contents private. "She's not happy. I could see it on her face last night."

"Last night? Oh, you have *got* to be kidding me. Jack. The last thing you need is to get mixed up with her again."

"Well, I wouldn't call last night 'getting mixed up with her again.' Nothing happened. We went out to a diner, ate crappy food, and talked. Perfectly platonic. No sex." Jack wasn't sure why he felt the need to defend himself. He was a grown ass man.

"You and I both know it's not where you put your dick that concerns me," Chris said, but without heat. After the initial shock, his logical mind was taking over, and Jack could see it picking things up, turning them over, and putting them back down as he thought. "Ivy and I make things work because we realize what we need from each other and reciprocate those needs. She knows when I come home from a long trip I want to lay in bed with her and watch Netflix, and I know after she's had a rough day of interviews she likes a little…extra attention." His brother insinuated with a devilish grin.

Jack winced. "Ugh…I didn't need to know that." Thinking about his brother and sister-in-law's sexual preferences was enough to make him want to roll down the window and puke up his breakfast.

Chris smirked, but kept his train of thought. "What I'm *saying* is, if you don't have that with the person you're dating, then that person probably isn't the one you should marry."

"And you don't think Jess and I have that?" The question was more of a flat and unimpressed statement than a question, but there it was.

Chris put his hands up in surrender. "What I think doesn't matter, Jackson. It's what you know—and what Jessica knows." He shifted his weight against the door and turned to face Jack. "Contrary to popular belief, relationships aren't fifty-fifty all the time. Sometimes you have the day from hell. You're at your wits' end, and you don't have fifty percent to give by the time you get home at night—maybe you only have ten percent left in the tank. The key to making a relationship work is finding a partner that is not only willing to put in ninety percent on those bad days, but is someone you'd be willing to do the same for in return."

Jack thought about that in silence as the car came to a stop at the curb of Chicago-O'Hare International Airport. The brothers hopped out of the vehicle and grabbed their bags out of the hatch as Jack delivered the hundred-dollar tip he had promised for speedy delivery.

Before he could turn and enter the terminal, Chris put a hand on his chest, holding him back. "Philosophical bullshit aside, I hope you know I'm on your side—whether I think it's a good idea or not. We all are."

* * *

A loud cheer erupted all around him as the Broncos scored a touchdown to come within one of the Jacksonville Jaguars in the closing moments of the divisional playoff game. Men everywhere cheered and slapped each other's backs in testosterone-filled embraces. There was something about sports that made the air pop with electricity. It was addicting—the rush of adrenaline that came when your team was close to ruining another team's hopes and dreams. It was a primal feeling, the need to win, to conquer. It was the same feeling he got when he was trailing by less than a car length on the final lap with a good run out of the last turn.

Competition. What would the world be without it?

He felt a hand on his back and turned from the TV where the Broncos had just tied up the game with an extra point to see his brother sliding onto the bar stool next to him. "Sorry I'm late. I got…caught up…"

The wicked grin on Noah's face told Jack all he needed to know, and he rolled his eyes. "You mean that smoke show *friend* you've got didn't want to let you out of bed?"

"Well, it's not all on her. It's hard telling when we'll see each other again." Noah ordered a draft Guinness from the bartender and settled in, turning to study Jack with a practiced eye.

"I'm sure you'll do just fine on your own." Jack smirked and took a long pull on his Blue Moon before setting the bottle back down on the bar and twisting it idly.

"No, I don't screw around when I'm on an assignment. Too easy to get distracted. It's the life of a monk for me until I get this guy tracked down."

Jack raised his eyes, astonished. "You? Celibate?"

Noah rolled his eyes. "Come on, if anybody knows how possible it is to go *six months* without getting laid, it's you."

"Ouch…" Jack winced and went back to his beer, not liking how this conversation was already starting. Aaron and Chris had made their views on Jack's romantic life clear, but they didn't dwell on it. They had their own problems. Noah was different. He and Jack were Irish twins, born on opposite sides of the same year. The first three Kinney boys had been planned. Jack…not so much. But the twins had grown up inseparable in an already close-knit family and were especially tuned in to each other's ups and downs.

"You're still weeping over that girl you met back in Indiana, and it's eating at you. You need to give it up. She's not coming back."

"Hey, I didn't come here to get a lecture. If I wanted one of those, I'd call mom." Jack let his train of thought drift as he watched an attempted onside kick fail.

"So why *did* you come here?" his brother asked as the game rolled into overtime and went to commercial.

"Huh?" Jack asked, signaling for another beer while there was a pause in the action.

"You said you didn't come here for a lecture. So, why *did* you come here?"

This next part would be tricky. Watching Jack flounder for the past six months over his failed shot at love had left the whole family with a bitter taste in their mouths. Getting anyone to do Jess a favor, especially the most overprotective one of the bunch, was not going to be easy. "I need a favor," Jack began.

His companion turned around, so he was leaning with his

back resting against the bar, eyebrows raised in expectation.

"I want to remind you that you owe me."

"You're never going to let that go, are you?" Noah rolled his eyes, cheeks flushing slightly at the reminder of his indiscretion. "I wasn't *actually* her John, you know. I was undercover."

"Yeah, well, you did a hell of a job convincing that vice detective of that."

Three months earlier, on an undercover assignment, Noah had been caught with a known prostitute on Colfax Avenue by a vice detective during a sting operation by the Denver Police Department. Late at night and unable to provide proof of who he was, he'd been arrested with a host of other men and women. The next morning, when his old desk sergeant got in to the station, the solicitation charge was dropped, but that hadn't kept Noah from having to call Jack to be bailed out at 2:00 a.m., and now it was time to collect on the favor.

"Alright, enough. What's the favor?" his brother barked.

"I have a friend that needs a private investigator. They're looking for their birth father."

Noah's cheeks puffed out with a breath as he turned over the proposition. "That's tough. I mean, there are a slew of things that could be tricky. If it's a closed adoption, there's not much I can do, but I suppose I can look into it. What's his name?"

"Who's name?" Jack asked, confused at the question.

"Your friend. Keep up, man."

"Oh…" Jack fiddled with the label on his beer. "Jessica Morales."

Noah's eyes went hard, his mouth pressed into a firm line. "You have got to be fucking—"

"You. Owe. Me."

"I don't owe you this!" Noah shouted, throwing back the rest of his beer and ordering another. "What is wrong with you?" he hissed after catching several dirty looks from nearby spectators. "She has a boyfriend. I am not about to enable you in this stupidity."

"Yes. I know she has a boyfriend. I'm not trying to win her over. I promised I would be there for her. *This* is me living up to that promise."

His brother stared at him, sharp blue eyes studying every movement with uncomfortable intensity. Jack called it his detective stare. "You realize I can see right through your bullshit, right? I've known you a long time. You're not fooling me. You're still in love with her."

God damn it...

Jack sighed. "Okay, I'm in love with her, but it's not like I have a hope in hell of ever being with her. Our paths are on completely different trajectories. I just want to help. That's all."

Noah stared for another long moment and then glanced up at the TV above the bar to watch a couple of plays. He wiped at the condensation on his new glass of beer, contemplating his choices. "I don't like this." He gave Jack a sideways glance.

Jack swallowed and stared hard at his beer bottle, willing his voice into some semblance of calm. "She's going through a hard time. Her mom is an addict, and she just found out her birth father didn't even know she existed." With a sigh, he looked up at his brother. "Look, if you didn't know how things ended between us, you would help her without hesitation, because you're a good guy. You may know me, but I know you too." After a moment with no response, he sighed and rolled his eyes. *"Please?"*

Finally, Noah sighed and ran a hand through his thick brown hair. "Fine. I can look, but God only knows what I'll find. If her mom is into drugs, chances are her dad will be too. What do you want me to do if that's the case?"

Jack bit his tongue, staring at the remnants of crushed peanut shells on the bar as he thought. "Whatever you find, tell me first. If it's bad…I'll break it to her."

"And if it's good, you want to break that to her too?" He snorted and took another swig of beer. The whole room erupted as the Broncos scored a game-winning touchdown, and Noah turned to his brother, shouting above the din. "You're a piece of work. You know that?"

Jack smirked and punched him playfully in the arm. "Yeah. But you love me anyway."

Twelve

Paved with Good Intentions

The drive to the airport had been an awkward one. There was no denying it. Tucker had barely spoken to her the last twenty-four hours. But if Jess was being honest with herself, when you broke up with your baby daddy, things weren't expected to return to normal. She pulled the car to the curb and looked over at Tucker, who stared out the windshield, unmoving.

"I'll text you."

Tucker didn't so much as flinch or bat an eye. He just kept staring at the people exiting vehicles, hugging their loved ones, and wheeling their luggage into the terminal. Finally, he shifted and popped the handle on the car door to get out.

Jess sighed. *Well, so much for cordiality.* She opened her door too and went around to meet him at the hatch. Just as he was reaching to close the rear cargo door, she grabbed his arm. "Are you not going to say anything?" Her quiet voice was full of need for acknowledgment, if not absolution.

"I'm not sure what's left to say." Any emotion he had was sealed away behind a mask of outward calm, and she would have been irritated with him if she hadn't recognized it for the defense mechanism it was.

"I promised I wouldn't keep Parker from you, and that's a promise I *will* keep." More cars were pulling up to the curb, and someone honked their horn impatiently at them as they stood by the curb taking up precious drop-off space.

"Yeah," he replied in a non-committal sort of way. "I gotta go." With one last longing gaze at Parker's pumpkin seat, he slammed the hatch shut and slung his bag over his shoulder.

"Tucker!" Jess yelled after him as he walked away.

"I can't do this, Jess. Not now. I just can't, okay?" He shouted, tears brimming as he looked back over his shoulder. The look of desperation in his eyes nearly cracked her heart as he turned and disappeared through the automatic doors.

Another impatient piece of shit honked at her and she flipped them off before skirting around to the driver's side and slamming her door shut behind her. She hammered the wheel with the heel of her hand. "Damn it!"

Despite the honking of every moron in the greater Indianapolis area, Jess stayed parked at the curb of the airport until she gained enough control to be able to see the road.

Stop it. You wanted this. There's no going back now, the logical part of her brain thought.

The breakup had hurt, but the thought of telling Alaina, Maura, and Nate was like a knife to the gut. She didn't want to see their disappointment or feel their disapproval boring into her like a high-powered drill. This shit was hard enough without their two cents.

But she couldn't drive home. She couldn't bear the thought of her empty house and regrets over Tucker. So instead of heading west toward the suburbs, she headed for the city, the shop, and Alaina.

I must be the biggest masochist alive if I would rather tell my best friend I broke up with her brother than go home and deal with my own conscious...

* * *

"So you just...broke up with him? Just like that?" Alaina arched her brows in incredulity as she stared at her friend. She didn't seem upset, just surprised. She lowered the flowers she'd been preparing to place in a rose-colored vase and studied Jess.

"Yeah. I just...I couldn't keep up the charade anymore. I love him, but—"

"You're not in love with him." Alaina completed Jess's thought with a nod of understanding. "I get it. It's not how any of us wanted this to work out, but we don't want you to be miserable either." She turned and picked the flowers up off the table again. "So what now?"

Jess gave a heavy sigh and looked up at the ceiling of the tiny work room. "Now...I need to find my father."

"That may be difficult." Alaina's voice was full of warning, but Jess had already accepted that. At night, when she was lying in bed, exhausted and praying for sleep, the horrific what-ifs kept running through her brain like a wind-up toy with no off switch.

"I know, but I think this is something I'll kick myself for later if I don't try. I went to my mom's high school, but they couldn't disclose any student records without a subpoena. I tried the newspaper, thinking they might have something from graduation, like a list of graduates or something, but they migrated all their files over to a digital database a couple years ago and they don't have anything on record before 2000." Jess gave a weighty sigh. "I think I'm just going to hire a private investigator and see what they can dig up. I don't have time for a wild goose chase—especially now that Tucker's gone."

Alaina was quiet as she worked, snipping stems for the ten partial floral arrangements on her table. The roses were a deep burgundy the color of good sangria and they paired with the antique vases in an unusual yet pleasing aesthetic. After several moments of silence, her friend stepped back and observed the arrangements at a distance before giving a satisfied nod and turning back to Jess. "Well, I don't know any PIs, but my dad might."

"You don't think I'm bat shit crazy for wanting to do this?" Jess asked as she gnawed on her bottom lip.

"Well, I wouldn't go that far"—Alaina turned to her with a playful smile—"but I also know you're right. You'll never have any peace until you get answers. It was one thing when you thought he didn't want anything to do with you. It's a whole other ball game if he doesn't know you exist."

Jess nodded, looking at the gray and white checked linoleum, trying to make sense of her emotions and find the logic in her cluster of a life.

"What?" Alaina asked, sensing her friend's unease.

Jess inhaled sharply and opened her mouth, but the words escaped her.

Coward...

She'd always been able to tell Alaina everything. It wasn't that she was being cagey now, but Alaina was happy for the first time in a long while, and she didn't want to pop the bubble. Then again, she wasn't sure how lamenting on her problems could ruin the high Alaina was riding, engaged to the man of her dreams—well, everyone's dreams, if she were being honest. Grayson Miles was many things, and dreamy was at the top of the list.

Thoughts of Grayson plunked her down waist deep in the steamy marshes of Jack Kinney's sexy grin. She slammed the door on that thought before it could get her into trouble and cleared her throat.

"Are you planning to tell me what you're thinking or just leave me to make my own assumptions?" Alaina asked with a smirk as she picked a few finished pieces off the table and deposited them with care into a crate for transport.

"That depends. How deep in the gutter are those assumptions?"

Alaina swatted at Jess with a few long-stemmed silk flowers. "Speaking of what happens with your mind in the gutter. Where's my nephew?"

Jess let out a surprised chortle. She wasn't used to this side of Alaina. Being with Grayson had changed her. She was more relaxed, more fulfilled. Happy and carefree, but with a demure sophistication that marked her as a woman who knew what she wanted. "He's out in the office with Sydney and Marissa being spoiled rotten."

Alaina gasped in horror. "You gave him to the girls? Doesn't being an aunt rate me anything?"

Jess rolled her eyes, ignoring her friend's baby fever. "I needed to talk to you, and we both know if I put you in the same room with him, my presence becomes irrelevant."

"Oh shut up," Alaina scoffed with an eye roll. "I'm not that bad."

"Mmhmm."

"Well, if we're done here—"

"I didn't say I was done. You did." There were a million more things she should say. Whether she would have the chance or get up the nerve were entirely different problems.

Alaina crossed her arms in front of her chest and stared Jess down for a three-count. "Listen, if you're just going to let me hang here in suspense, I can think of better uses of my time, like going to see Parks." She placed the wire clippers she'd been holding on the counter and made her way toward the hallway as she spoke, hitting the doorway before Jess stopped her.

"Fine! Fine." Jess's hands were shaking and her heart was beating like a bomba. "When we were in Chicago, I ran into Jack at the bar, where I met up with Anika and the girls."

Alaina's relaxed and carefree posture went rigid, and her knuckles went white as she gripped the door frame. "Did you sleep with him?" The temper flaring in her friend's eyes made Jess take a small step back as Alaina rounded on her.

"What?" The look of complete shock on Jess's face must have convinced Alaina of her friend's innocence because she backed down slightly, not completely losing the defensive, mama bear thing she had going on.

"Please tell me you haven't been talking to him all this time, Jess." The smallest hint of betrayal lurked in her voice, and Jess's heart skittered in her chest.

Somehow, she managed to keep calm as she leaned forward. "I wouldn't do that to Tucker. You know that." Some of the flush left her friend's cheeks at her denial, but Alaina's eyes were still weary. "We ran into each other completely by accident. He was out with a group of friends celebrating his new contract. He could see how out of sorts I was. So, he took me to this little diner nearby where we could get away from all the noise. I talked. He listened. That's it. It turns out one of his brothers is a private investigator. So, Jack is going to ask him to help me out."

"If you're talking about Noah, good luck." Alaina snapped, still struggling with her temper. "I doubt he's feeling generous when it comes to doing you any favors."

Jess raised her brow, affronted. "What? Why? I've never even met the guy."

Alaina raised a single eyebrow, seeming to question whether Jess was actually that dense or just playing dumb. "Grayson says he's hardly talked to Jack since the end of the season. Jack texted him last week to tell him the deal with Lakeshore was getting close, but beyond that, the only reason Gray knew Jack was alive was because he finally got worried enough to call Noah. Noah said Jack shut himself up in some cabin in the Rockies once ski season hit. He pops in once a week or so to check on him. They were finally able to get him out to Tahoe a couple weeks ago, but he hasn't exactly been sociable."

Jess shook her head, confused. "I don't get it. He seemed fine when we talked Saturday."

Alaina rolled her eyes. "Of course he did. He's not going to admit that he's been nursing a broken heart for six months—especially to you. The man still has his pride."

A sinking feeling fell over Jess like a leaky water balloon, deflating her high hopes and smacking her with a fresh wave of guilt. At this rate, she'd bleed to death if she kept cutting herself on the shards of everyone else's broken hearts. She sighed. "I guess if it doesn't work out, you could still reach out to your dad and see if he has any contacts."

Alaina said nothing, but Jess could see something lurking in the backs of her eyes like a shark in murky waters, silent and dangerous. "Tell me you didn't break up with Tucker because you still have feelings for Jack."

Neither of them looked away. "I love Tucker, Alaina. And I'm sure, someday, he'll make some girl a wonderful husband. But he's not my person. I know that in my bones. Does that mean I'm going to run right into Jack's waiting arms? No. Does that mean I'm taking a vow of chastity and swearing I'll never give it another go with him? Absolutely not." After another minute of searing silence, Jess threw up her hands. "I don't know what else you want me to say."

Had her feelings for Jack been the sole reason behind her decision? No. But could she deny that they existed? Also no.

"I'm not stupid, Jess. I know you were in love with him, and probably still are. I just want Tucker to have a chance at mending his broken heart before you throw a happily ever after at him. He deserves a little peace too. You know?"

Honestly, she thought this was coming out of left field. She had zero intention of sleeping with Jack, let alone dating or, god forbid, the M word.

Thirteen

The Knife's Edge

The laptop screen in front of her blurred suddenly, and Jess blinked to clear her vision. It was late. The digital display on the microwave read 12:30 and she sighed, rubbing her sandpaper eyes to draw some life back into them. She was technically on maternity leave until Monday, but if she didn't get these proposals written up, they would be weeks behind the eight ball on their supplier contracts for the new year. It had always been in the books to eventually have their own supply house, and that had never looked more appealing than as she sat reading through the terms and conditions for the use of china, flatware, glassware, linens, light fixtures, blah, blah, blah. Fine print sucked ass, and how she got the job of reading through it when they had underlings now, was beyond her.

She yawned, glanced longingly at her Keurig, and decided a shower was a better use of time. The baby was asleep. The dishwasher was running. The final load of laundry was in the dryer, and she was ready for the sweet oblivion of high thread count sheets. Hopefully, by the time she got her hair dried and did her nightly skincare, Parker would be awake and ready to eat, so she could feed him, rock him, and get some rest of her own.

The night had gone fairly well. For the first time in three weeks, she felt like she was finally getting the hang of the *motherhood* thing. Granted, there wasn't much sleep involved, but as long as she got a couple hours every night, she could get by.

Tonight, Tita had come over to help fix dinner and keep her company—which had been a great distraction from the fact that Tucker hadn't called like he was supposed to. She didn't want to be *that* ex—the one that claimed he didn't care about his child, and if he cared, he'd call on time. She knew that wasn't true. Honestly, the fact he hadn't called flat out concerned her. He never missed a phone call.

For a while, the pure delight of watching her grandmother play with her son was enough to keep the worry at bay. After doing the single mom thing for the past three and a half weeks, having someone to help change diapers and feed the baby had been amazing, but now that the house was quiet, her anxiety was creeping back in.

Tucker was a big boy. He could take care of himself, but that didn't stop her from worrying. Because she wasn't just concerned for his physical wellbeing, but his emotional wellbeing as well. The guilt she felt over their breakup was eating her alive. She just wanted to know he was okay.

Only when the hot water ran out and she was left standing in a stream of icicles could she bear to pull herself out of the shower and dry herself off. The postpartum hair loss was dramatic, and she felt like every few nights when she washed her hair she was scooping a handful of the black strands from the tub and tossing them in the trash. She pumped out a handful of serum and worked it into the ends of her hair.

Taking her time with her nightly routine was the highlight of her day. Every muscle in her exhausted body was relaxed and ready for sleep, but the squawk of the baby monitor alerted her to her son, ready for his late-night snack. Her breasts tingled, and she rushed to his room as she felt her milk let down. The door hinges of the nursery squeaked quietly amid the snuffles and cries of Parker's hunger. "Hello, my little man," she murmured and lifted him, sleep sack and all, into her arms. She hastily changed his wet diaper and settled in the corner rocking chair. With any luck, she could sleep for four or five hours after this.

The buzz of her phone snapped her out of the exhausted thousand-yard stare she had going on with the diaper pale. She glanced down at the table next to the rocker, seeing Tucker's face, and sprung for the phone, blinking rapidly to keep herself awake as she waited for the video call to connect. "Hey," she greeted around a yawn.

The poor guy looked as worn out as she felt, but she wouldn't let it show. The last thing he needed was to be worried about her when he was already missing their son. "Hey," he replied with a tired half grin. "Sorry it's so late. I just got off duty and back to the barracks. Is he asleep?"

"No. Just milk drunk." She flipped the camera around so Tuck could get an eyeful of their baby's cherubic face. Watching Tucker's eyes grow glassy nearly undid her in her fragile state, and she bit her lip hard to keep the tears from flowing. It was hard not to imagine the situation in reverse. If she were separated from Parks for weeks on end, she would go insane. She needed to get down to Texas soon. Maybe she could surprise him for his birthday.

"He's getting so big," Tucker murmured. "I feel like he changes every day."

Jess smiled and turned the camera back around. "Hang on." She shifted the sleeping baby to her other breast, bringing him to full alert in the process, and settled back into the chair. "Sorry. Had to swap sides."

"All good," Tucker replied as he collapsed onto his bed and gazed up at his phone. "Anything new to report?"

She did, but this would be their first milestone moment apart, and she didn't want to upset him.

"You're doing that lip thing. I know you have something to say. Spill it. I'm not gonna shoot the messenger," he said with an exhausted laugh.

She pulled her teeth out of her bottom lip and gave him a small smile. Sometimes she forgot how well he knew her. "He smiled today, and he's started cooing too. It's so cute."

"Maybe he'll smile for me when he's done eating," he suggested with a hopeful cock of his left brow.

Jess smiled. "We'll see what we can do, won't we, big guy?" she murmured to the half-dozing baby in her arms. She shuffled him a bit and he snapped to, ferociously suckling as if he thought this would be his last meal.

She closed her eyes and shook her head slightly to dispel the cobwebs before giving her attention back to Tucker. "Why were you on duty so late?"

"Battalion inspection tomorrow. Everything needed to be gone over with a fine-tooth comb—literally. Fucking hate this shit."

"I know. Have you decided whether you're going to re-up?" Her tone was gentle, and Tucker gave a deep sigh.

"No. They keep throwing reenlistment bonuses at me. It's tempting. It's a lot of money. But part of me wonders what I would do with my life if I got out."

Jess nodded in sympathy. "Whatever you choose, we'll figure it out."

There was a comfortable silence between the two of them and Jess closed her eyes, enjoying the feeling of not having to focus her gaze on anything in particular. "You look exhausted," Tucker whispered with quiet concern.

"Gee, thanks," she quipped back, not moving.

"I worry about you," he reasoned. "Are you getting sleep? I'm sure mom or Alaina wouldn't mind coming over and helping you once or twice a week so you can get some rest."

"Tita came over tonight and I was able to get a nap in," she lied around another yawn. "Park doesn't like to sleep after his one a.m. feeding, so we're working through it."

Tucker nodded and closed his eyes too. Parker had stopped suckling and was now squirming in her arms, a sure sign he was ready to burp. She propped the phone on the side table and hoisted the baby up onto her shoulder, patting his back with soft, methodical thumps until he let out a satisfactory belch. She scooted toward the front of the rocker and laid Parker on the floor before picking the phone up and joining the baby on the plush carpet. She flipped the camera around to face the little blue-eyed boy and spoke in a high voice. "Are we going to show Daddy how we can smile?"

She made funny noises and blew raspberries on his tummy until he smiled and let out a little coo of delight that had

Tucker grinning like an idiot. She rubbed her finger under Parker's chin, tickling him so he smiled again and Tucker laughed. "So damn cute. God, I wish I could just snuggle him."

"I know. I'm hoping to get down to see you soon, but it all depends on work."

"I know," he replied. "I understand if you can't. It's a long way. Just…" He drifted off, torn between what he knew to be logical and what he wanted to be true. "Just let me know when you know for sure."

"Of course. Talk to you Saturday?"

"It's a date. Get some sleep," Tucker said with a barely concealed yawn of his own.

"You too."

Trying to find the energy to heave herself up off the floor, she gathered Parker in her arms and groaned as she pulled herself upright. She hugged him close to her breast, patting his butt as she walked over first to shut the door, and then to the changing table to tap the top of the Egg sound machine. The low rumble of brown noise filled the room, and she resisted the urge to sit in the rocking chair and fall into oblivion. For several minutes, she rocked back and forth on the balls of her feet, lulling him into a contented stupor, praying the peaceful silence from her infant would continue when she sat him down. For several more moments, she paced a circle into the carpet, patting and swaying. When he hadn't stirred for a while, she walked to his crib, careful not to stub a toe or trip over anything in the complete blackness of the room and placed him in his crib.

By the time she made her way to her bedroom and pulled the covers back from her bed, Parker was howling from the nursery. Unable to summon the strength to walk back down the hall, she crawled into her bed and put her pillow over her head to drown out the noise. Maybe he would cry himself back to sleep.

That's a thing, right?

She rolled over on her side, sandwiching her head between the two edges of her pillow and squeezing her eyes shut. If she didn't get some sleep soon, she might have a mental break. In the last three days, she'd slept a grand total of seven hours and the level of exhaustion she felt was unimaginable to the average person. Never had she regretted shooing Tita out the door more than she did right now.

After ten more minutes of her son screaming bloody murder, she hauled herself out of bed and shuffled down the hall, her vision going in and out of focus with fatigue. She opened the door and approached his crib, scooping him up in one deft motion and rocking from side to side to soothe his cries. She fumbled blindly in the crib for his pacifier and found it wedged between the mattress and one of the crib bars. It only soothed Parker's frantic cries for a few seconds before he spit it out and continued to squall.

She patted and swayed and bounced and murmured sweet nothings. She sang lullabies and made funny noises and rocked and swayed some more. But every time she went to lay him down, he would startle and scream as though he were being stabbed with a safety pin.

Finally, at her wits' end, she sank to the floor in a completely debilitated heap, closed her eyes, and drifted to sleep with her son resting peacefully on her chest.

* * *

Monday's alarm came entirely too soon, and before Jess knew it, she was standing in her bathroom, fully dressed, her curling iron letting out soft *pffs* as she waited patiently for it to do its magic. She tapped her toe lightly on the tile of the bathroom floor and stared at her reflection. It was the first time in several weeks she had dolled herself up, but today was a big day. It was her first day back in the office, and they had a day full of suppliers' contracts and staff meetings.

Jess unraveled her hair from the hot iron and grabbed the can of hairspray from the counter, bending over to toss her hair and spray like no tomorrow.

Parker let out a screech, and she stood up, coughing through the fumes. She quickly fixed any flyaways before grabbing her earrings to put on as she made her way into her bedroom where he sat in his bouncer. Her cobalt blue silk blouse and black pencil skirt were a bit snug, but her new shapewear was working wonders on her postpartum figure. She was ready to take on the day. Or, at least, she felt like she was.

"What's the matter, buddy?" she asked as she knelt to pick him up and nuzzle his soft head of black hair. She patted him a few times on the back and walked out into the kitchen to get her toast out of the toaster. It was lukewarm, having popped several minutes earlier, but she could handle cold toast.

What mom gets to eat hot food anyway?

As she cradled her son in one arm and buttered her toast with her free hand, she eyed the clock. "Mierda," she swore under her breath. It was eight thirty, and she hadn't packed the diaper bag yet.

Once again, her toast was relegated to the back burner

as she laid the baby in his bassinet next to the couch and scurried to the nursery. She would have to come up with some sort of meal prep plan for breakfast if she ever wanted to eat again.

Overnight oats? Açaí bowls?

Rummaging through the changing table and dresser drawers, she dug out a day's worth of diapers and wipes, two clean outfits, burp cloths, gripe water, and other odds and ends that came with an infant.

Tita, bless her, had agreed to watch Parker while she was at work.

"Nonsense, cariña! I'm retired. No hay otra manera en la que quisiera pasar mi día."

"¿Estas segura?" Jess had asked, raising her brow. The last thing she wanted was to pawn off her infant son onto a woman well into her seventies who spent most of her days watering the orchids in her greenhouse, watching afternoon telenovelas, and sewing quilts for the local nursing home residents. She knew her grandmother would never tell her she wasn't up for the task. It would be up to Jess to come to that conclusion for herself.

"Yèsica, he's un bebé. He'll nap. We'll go water flowers. He'll eat. We'll watch *El Cuerpo del Deseo* and go for a walk before we both take a nap." Her grandmother gave her a playful wink. "Ningún problema."

Her phone went off with an incoming text message from somewhere in the kitchen and she sighed, shoving the rest of the necessities into the diaper bag. She had enough breast milk in the freezer to last Parker until he was six months old, but remembering to pack it on the other hand... "Diaper cream!" she shouted triumphantly as she swiped it from the changing table and jammed it in the front pocket of the hefty bag. With one last glance around the room, she slung the bag over her shoulder and sped back to the kitchen for her damn toast.

Her phone dinged again, but she ignored it and took a bite out of her breakfast before walking over to the freezer and grabbing five frozen pouches of breast milk to put in the cool pouch. Another bite of toast. She pulled four clean bottles from the dishwasher and crammed them into the diaper bag too. Parker squealed angrily from his bassinet and she plucked his pacifier off the counter to offer him while she swallowed the remnants of her breakfast and glanced around for a clean coffee thermos.

The pacifier did little to *actually* pacify her son, and she scooped him up to take him with her as she went to remote start her car and warm it. "Shhh, buddy…It's alright. You've gotta stop crying though…Mommy's gotta go to work… Shhh…"

The distressed wails quieted abruptly and were followed by the ominous gurgling of spit-up coming down the pipe. But before she could remove him from her shoulder, she felt hot white goop spilling across her shoulder and down her back.

"Parker…" she moaned, throwing her head back in dismay. She didn't have a backup outfit planned, and not only did the coagulated breastmilk soak her shirt, but parts of it had also found its way into her hair. Her already frayed nerves snapped and tears pricked at the backs of her eyes. She was never getting to work now.

Walking into the bedroom, she laid the baby on the bed and peeled her shirt away from her body, taking care to save as much of her hair from the melee as possible. She dabbed at the black strands gingerly with a damp rag while haphazardly, pulling shirts from her closet and holding them up to her. Would any of them even fit? Eventually she decided on a gray cowl neck sweater with buttons up the side and spritzed herself with perfume to stave off the remaining smell of sour milk before charging back into the bedroom, bound and determined to get out of the house if it killed her.

The occasional ding of more text messages was replaced by a cheerful ring. The screen declared the inbound call from Denver, Colorado with SPAM RISK scrawled across the bottom. Something else on the phone caught her attention too. The time.

"Shit!" she shouted and spun around looking for Parker's car seat. This day was not off to a good start.

An hour later, disheveled, exhausted, and at her wits' end, she sat in the driver's seat of her car, staring off into space as cars sped by on the busy city street outside Decadent Designs. The gentle swish of tires on damp pavement was enough to lull her into a stupor. How she was going to make life as a working, single mother work was beyond her. She'd been to the shop a few times throughout her maternity leave, but looking up at the storefront that had begun as the dream of two naïve young college graduates caused the waterworks to start all over again. Four years ago, this had been her dream—to become a successful, career-driven woman.

And now…? Now she could barely get to the grocery store without forgetting why she needed to go in the first place.

Her phone rang again from the same Denver number she'd ignored earlier. She had to admit, two calls from the same spam caller in one day didn't seem likely. So, she took a deep breath and answered the call as she leaned over to gather her purse from the passenger seat. "Hello?"

"Hello. Is this Jessica Morales?"

She paused, her heart stuttering. The man on the other end sounded so much like Jack she stopped breathing.

"Hello?"

"Y-yes. This is her," Jessica stammered, sitting up straight.

"Hey, this is Noah Kinney. Jack's brother."

Jack's brother?

A million questions flung to the forefront of Jess's mind and she couldn't sort through them fast enough. To be honest, she'd given up on hearing from Noah but hadn't had time to reach out to anyone else.

"Hey!" She shut off the car and put the phone to her ear as she grabbed her stuff and headed inside before the ominous-looking clouds cracked open with whatever form of precipitation they had planned.

"Is this a bad time? I called earlier, but it went to voicemail."

"Yeah, sorry about that. My son was having a meltdown and then we had a bit of a spit-up disaster as we were heading out the door."

"Oh. Right. You have a kid. Jack told me, guess I forgot." His voice had settled somewhere between disapproval and embarrassment, and Jess wasn't sure how to take that. She doubted he'd 'forgotten' she had a three-month-old, especially if what Alaina had said about the man was true.

"Yeah, well, he's a lot, but I love him. What can I do for you?" she asked, putting on her best customer service voice as she pulled open the front door of the shop and entered the cozy confines.

"I'm just wrapping up an assignment in Pittsburgh and will

be driving through Indianapolis on my way back to Denver. Jack told me you are searching for your birth father and need a PI. I thought, if you're free this evening, maybe we could get a drink and you could give me a few details?"

Jess's breath caught in her throat and she dropped her stuff on her desk heavily in shock. Was this really happening? Did Jack come through for her?

Of course, he did. He always does.

"Umm. I-I'll have to ask around and see if I can find a sitter, but—"

"Or we can do coffee, if that works better. You can bring the little guy." Something in Noah's voice had changed; it was less judgmental.

"Sure. There's a place not too far from my abuela's. I can send you a pin. Does six o'clock work?"

"Uh…yeah. Sure. I can make that work. Just send me the specifics. I'll talk to you then." The call disconnected abruptly, and Jess stared at the phone in disbelief.

"Who was that?" Marissa asked, bouncing into view with her head full of dark curls. She was a bundle of energy, and Jess wasn't sure she could take her this morning.

"Just a guy. We're making plans to meet up tonight." She didn't feel like advertising her birth father woes and hoped like hell Alaina hadn't felt the need to advertise them either.

"Oooh, a *date*?" Sydney asked as she sauntered over to join the two women at their desks.

Wisps of steam rose from her sparkly teal mug, and Jess inhaled the fragrance like it was the aromatic equivalent to the fountain of youth. She'd run off and forgotten her thermos full of coffee on the kitchen counter and was losing steam fast.

Noticing the yearning on her face, Sydney extended the cup of coffee. "Here. Take mine. I'll make another."

"Bless you," Jess sighed and took the coffee, pouring it down her throat despite the burn. Her first jolt having been consumed, she got back to the original inquiry as she pulled her laptop from her bag and plugged it into her docking station. "And no, it's not a date. It's business. I have some work I need to…contract out, and he's interested."

"Be careful about that. This true crime podcast I listen to just covered a case where a guy was using Help Wanted ads to find victims." Marissa warned in complete sincerity.

Jess tried to swallow her laughter along with her next gulp of coffee, but didn't quite succeed. "I highly doubt he's a serial killer, but I'll take my stun gun, just in case."

Sydney chortled from the coffee station where the Keurig was depositing a new brew. "Who needs a stun gun?" Alaina called from the hallway as she made her way from the storeroom with her iPad in hand.

"Hopefully no one," Sydney said as she added cream and sugar to her coffee and took a sip. "Jess was just telling us she's meeting with some contractor tonight, and Marissa's true crime addiction was showing."

"I'm sure Grayson would go with you if you need a guy."

Jess shook her head. "It's fine. Really. We're meeting at Café Delish at six. He suggested drinks, but when he heard I would have to find a sitter, he switched to coffee."

"At 6:00 p.m.?" Marissa's antenna was twitching.

"I don't know the guy, but I know his brother. He used to be a cop. I'm not worried. Really. He seems perfectly nice." All statements hit a five out of ten or higher on the truth scale. She *did* know his brother. He *did* used to be a cop. The 'perfectly nice' part? Well…

Alaina caught her eye and held her gaze with a cocked brow. Having all the information allowed her to read between the lines, and Jess gave her a slight nod of assent before logging into her computer and tuning back in to what the girls were saying.

"Well, is he cute? I have a thing for cops." Sydney was practically swooning as she leaned in toward Jess.

"I don't know. I've never met him in person," Jess laughed. "But I do know his brother, and since they're all cut from the same cloth, I'd wager my best Kate Spade that he's a looker."

Sydney twirled her finger around a dirty blonde strand of hair and bit her bottom lip in contemplation of what was, no doubt, a chiseled, ripped, uniformed police officer, asking to see her license and registration.

"A-n-y-waaaayyy," Alaina sing-songed. "Let's get this meeting going, shall we?" She perched on the corner of Jess's desk and gazed at her iPad for a moment. The sound of office chair wheels on vinyl whirred closer, and Marissa popped up on Jess's other side. "In the past, Jess and I have always attended the Indiana Bridal Expo at the state fairgrounds. However, since we have an expanded team this year, I was thinking we may want to reach out to other events about a booth."

In theory, the idea seemed valid, but race season was coming up and on the weekends Alaina didn't have a wedding to attend, she would be traveling with her fiancé. Jess wouldn't be able to tote her newborn around to bridal expos, and while she liked Marissa and Sydney, she doubted they had enough experience to run an entire expo booth on their own. Jess opened up her calendar. "What weekends were you thinking?"

"Well, the expo in Tippecanoe would be a good one. That would potentially get us some business from the Chicago market. It's the weekend of April eleventh."

Jess glanced at her calendar. "As in six weeks from now?" Marissa gave Alaina a side eye, and she lowered the iPad to speak directly to her.

"It's fine. I already talked to Marissa about it. We've got a plan in place for the displays and Sydney put together some package options."

Jess's temper was slowly creeping toward a boil at Alaina's audacity. After being gone for *months*, she had waltzed in and started making decisions like Jess didn't even exist. Jess took a deep breath and nodded, not wanting to make a scene in front of the newbies. Instead, she took to clicking the thrust device on her pen so ferociously, she thought she might jam it.

Alaina glanced back at her blasted iPad as if it were the Holy Grail and continued. "Bloomington normally has one. It's at the end of May after the graduation rush from IU disperses. I'd like to try and make that one."

Jess dropped the pen on the desk. "Let me guess. Memorial Day weekend? I can think of at least one person in this room who is booked solid for the entire month of May. Not to mention it's one of our busiest wedding months!"

Sydney had suddenly found the dregs of her coffee extremely fascinating, and Marissa's normally bubbly demeanor was fizzing out like a flat soda. "I thought this meeting was about the Indianapolis expo we do every year. Not adding a bunch of things to our plates we can't handle."

"It is, but—"

"No. Alaina. I can't do it, and neither can you. Stop acting like we don't need sleep or time to balance the freaking checkbooks!" She pushed back from the desk and stormed off to the parlor simply to get out of the office. Today had started off bad and was only getting worse. She thought her best friend, of all people, would understand how overwhelming her life was at the moment. She'd been balancing on the knife's edge of sanity since Parker was born and this sudden decision to double down on the business end seemed not only implausible but downright impossible.

A stack of magazines lay in a haphazard spray across the coffee table and she gathered them together, stacking them so the corners matched and then spreading them in a symmetrical pattern like a deck of cards. She tucked several vendor binders and display books back onto the bookshelf, aligning all the spines together, and wiped at a coat of dust from the sideboard. The door latch clicked, and she raised her head, shoulders going rigid at Alaina's presence.

"Jess…"

She whirled around to meet her friend's call and leaned against the solid piece of cherry furniture behind her. The light coming through the sheer curtains was dull with cloud cover, and the normally cheerful and sophisticated sitting space suddenly seemed drab and dingy. "This place is a wreck. It needs a deep clean." She crossed her arms in front of her chest and glared at her friend.

Alaina placed a hand on the roll-top desk next to the door where they stored brochures, quote forms, and a myriad of other office supplies. "What's going on, Jess? Is it your meeting tonight? If it is…I get it. I'd be freaking out too. Finding your dad…kind of seems like it's happening.

It's normal to be antsy." Her wide, brown eyes, full of compassion, searched Jess's face, looking for answers that weren't there.

"I'm not 'freaking out,' Alaina. I just—I need you to consult me when you're making these decisions. You were gone most of last quarter, and we managed, but I *always* kept you informed. I've been gone *eight weeks* and you've run away with the place. Bridal expos every month? What about the weddings we already have booked? What about race weekends? And I can't be the one to pick up the slack. I have Parker now, and I'm…" Her breath hitched. "I'm barely holding it together as it is. I *can't* add more to my plate right now, and I need my *business partner* to treat me like I'm her business partner and not some ignorant nobody!"

Both women stood in silence for an interminable moment, neither of them knowing what more there was to say. "I'm sorry," Alaina whispered. "I didn't mean to make you feel that way. I was just trying to make things easier on you by not bothering you while you were gone."

Jess slowly meandered to the sofa and plopped down. She propped her ballet flat-clad feet on the coffee table and sighed, closing her eyes. "I know. I'm just exhausted, Lainie. I'm so tired, and I don't know when I'm going to start feeling like a human being again."

Alaina made her way over to the sofa and sat as well, mirroring her friend's lounged position. "Is there anything I can help with?" Her hazel eyes were full of sympathy as she reached across the space between them and gripped her friend's hand.

Jess pried her eyelids open and gazed at the ceiling. "I don't know. I just feel like there's too much to do and not enough hours in the day. Like, I'm meeting Noah after work, and I was supposed to go to the grocery store tonight because Parker's almost out of diapers, but I have to get back to Tita's to pick Parks up so she can go serve at the women's shelter."

Alaina sat up straighter, and Jess could practically see the lightbulb coming on over her friend's head. "Why don't you do delivery? I know it sounds like a pain, but it would save you so much time. You just go on the app for whatever store you shop at and put all your stuff in your cart. Then they drop it off at your front door. It would save you a boatload of time!"

Jess tilted her head from side to side as she contemplated. The delivery fee would be an unplanned expense, but to be honest, it would be worth it just to have one less thing to worry about. "Okay. I'll check it out when I get back to my desk. Any other genius ideas cooking in there?" she asked with a wry twist to her lips.

"I don't know. What kind of problems are you trying to solve?" Alaina smiled, revealing a dimple in her left cheek and Jess smiled back.

"Meal prepped breakfasts?"

Alaina whipped out her phone, her fingers typing rapidly across the screen, and then Jess's phone buzzed with a link: *Ten Quick and Easy Breakfast Ideas.*

"Seriously, who are you?" Jess asked in awe before silently answering her own question.

Super woman, obviously.

Alaina could probably be a single mom to three kids and still have all her shit together.

The two friends sat on the couch in silence for a long moment, eyes closed to enjoy the quiet. "If you don't think we can do the Bloomington Bridal Expo, that's fine. I haven't purchased a booth space. I just thought it would be a good market expansion."

Without opening her eyes, Jess replied. "I think another Memorial Day weekend project is more than any of us can handle. Maybe if Marissa and Sydney are still here next year and confident enough to run point on the project, we can reevaluate."

"Sounds good," Alaina murmured. Another moment of silence passed between them. "Damn, this couch is comfortable."

Jess let out a girlish snicker. "If I sit here much longer, I'm going to fall asleep."

"Well, take a nap if you need to. I don't need the parlor until one." Alaina reached over and patted her friend's thigh. "I'm serious. I know this transition hasn't been easy for you. If you need to work from home or work shorter days, we'll figure it out."

Jess nodded, opening her eyes to stare at the coffered ceiling. It was a beautiful choice—another of Alaina's calls. She really did have an eye for design. "I forgot to ask. Did you get your venue booked?" Weddings were such a part of their everyday lives, it was easy to forget Alaina had her own to plan.

"I did."

Jess didn't need to look at her friend to hear the smile in her voice. She had been dreaming of her wedding since she was ten. The event was as much of a dream come true as marrying Grayson. "The Grainery?"

"Yep. We got lucky. They had a cancellation, so they were able to squeeze us in. We had to narrow the guest list a bit, but that's fine. Neither of us wanted a big wedding anyway. I think it's perfect: elegant but distinctive."

Jess had gone to a client's wedding there last year, and she had to agree. The venue, an old nineteenth century grain storehouse, suited the couple extremely well. Old exposed brick combined with elegant new crystal chandeliers created a perfect fusion of Alaina's sophistication and Grayson's masculine charm. Once it was dressed up with Alaina's magic touch, it had the potential to make magazine spreads from New York to Los Angeles.

Fourteen

Family Ties

The obnoxious screech of a milk steamer radiated through the sleepy coffee shop four blocks from Tita's house on the west side of Indianapolis. Café Delish was a delightful locally-owned bistro with fresh pastries made daily. In the mornings, a line was usually out the door, filled with corporate types picking up boxes of sweet morsels on their way into the office. In the early days, when Decadent Designs was nothing more than an idea with Tita's garage for a mailing address, Jess and Alaina had spent hours in the little coffee shop, taking advantage of the free Wi-Fi and eating an ungodly amount of the shop's famous melt-in-your-mouth glazed donuts.

This time of day, the booths and tables were full of people with laptops doing the exact same thing, and Jess smiled. Of course, there was the occasional group of friends or family chatting animatedly over their steaming coffees, but Jess had an eye out for a lone wolf.

There, in a corner booth, surveying the room with a practiced eye, was a man who could only be described as the "strong and silent" type. His hands were wrapped around the forest green coffee mug on the table, but her eye immediately fell past his hands to his hip, where a handgun rested in an unassuming black holster. Something akin to unease fluttered in her stomach, but she turned back to the counter to order, not wanting to stare.

"Can I help you?"

"Yes, I'd like a flat white, please. And can I get some hot water to warm a bottle?" She paid the barista and tucked a couple of bills into the tip jar before turning back to her companion. Having come to the same conclusion she had, he had pulled a high chair from the corner and turned it upside down to accommodate the car seat. "Noah?" she asked with a smile on her face.

He stood and extended a hand to her. "You must be Jess."

She took the proffered hand and shook it with a warm squeeze before turning to sit the baby down.

"Here. Let me." He gestured and took the carrier from her to place it gently in the frame.

"You seem well-versed. Thanks." She tugged her scarf from her neck and removed her jacket before tossing it into the booth next to her and scooting in.

"My brother Aaron has two little ones," he explained, making small talk as Jess got settled.

"I hope you haven't been waiting long. I tried to get out of my abuela's without getting caught, but she's a talker."

"¿Abuela? ¿Tu familia es de México?" Noah rattled off in perfectly accented Spanish.

Jess did her best not to look shocked and responded, "No, de Puerta Rico. I'm fluent, but I only use it when speaking to my grandmother. I grew up here in the States. You surprised me, though. Isn't your family from Denver?"

"Born and raised," Noah admitted with a nod. "I minored in Spanish, and when I was on the force, I served mostly in District Four. They have a large Hispanic population there—gave me a reason to use it."

"How long have you been out?" she asked, looking up and thanking the barista with a smile as she laid her coffee and a large mug of hot water down in front of her. She reached into the diaper's cool pouch for her last bottle's worth of breast milk and settled it in the cup of hot water to warm before Parker woke up.

"About two years now. It wasn't for me."

Jess tugged the condiment holder over to her and pulled out three packets of sugar. She ripped them open and poured them in before stirring with rapid clinks.

Noah's blue eyes probed her, an amused half-smile tugging at his lips. "What?" she asked, glancing over at Parker, still asleep in his carrier. She reached over and tucked his blanket more securely around him and then sipped on her coffee.

"If you're going to put so much sugar in a simple drink, why not just order something more complex?"

"Because it doesn't taste the same," Jess replied. She raised one arched brow in question and took a sip of her drink.

Noah shook his head and picked up his cup of unsurprisingly black coffee. "So. Tell me about this father of yours. What do you know about him?"

"Not much, honestly. Until a few weeks ago, I thought he was some low-life who didn't want a daughter and never bothered to be in my life, but…"

"But?" Noah asked as he pulled a small notepad and pen out of his jacket pocket and started jotting down notes.

Jess sighed and took a heavy swig of her coffee as if it were a shot of tequila and set her cup down. "Look, I'm going to be honest with you, because I feel like you need to know what you're getting into."

Noah looked up from his notes, meeting her gaze without blinking. She could easily imagine it being the same look he had while questioning witnesses at a crime scene—straightforward and to the point. She felt as though he could see through her; it gave her the urge to squirm in her seat.

"My mom is a piece of work." Jess fiddled with the spoon resting on the saucer next to her cup and sniffed. "Six weeks ago, I went to see her in rehab. That's when she let it slip that my father didn't know about me. She also told me she would have rather had an abortion—that I ruined her life. So…" She sighed and looked up at him through misty eyes. "You won't get any help from her. That much I know."

He lowered his pen slowly and furrowed his brow. "I'm sorry. That's…"

Jess shook her head and cleared her eyes with a few blinks. "I'm not looking for your sympathy. I just thought you should know who you're dealing with."

Parker let out a breathy grunt and stretched in his seat, blinking with squinty eyes at the lights overhead. His face turned bright red in sudden anger at the intrusion and he drew breath to screech, but Jess quickly unbelted him and pulled him to her, doing her best to head off his discontent. In a move perfected over several weeks of single parenting, she took the pouch of heated breast milk and poured it into the empty bottle waiting on the tabletop before popping it into Parker's searching mouth.

"Impressive," Noah remarked with another one of those patented smirks. She never quite knew if he was being sincere or sarcastic and was beginning to find that specific trait more frustrating than endearing.

"Yeah, well, it comes with the 'single mom' territory. If I don't get him fed before he starts howling, my boobs start leaking like Old Faithful, and there's no coming back from that." She let out a small laugh, but was mostly taking the measure of his sense of humor. If they didn't get off on the right foot, this would be a very painful process.

The unflappable private detective's cheeks pinked, but when he realized she had meant to embarrass him, smiled and chuckled. "I can see why my brother likes you. You're a pistol." He glanced over her shoulder at several men who had entered the shop, hoods raised against the rain outside and sat up straighter in his chair, keeping a wary eye on them as they approached the counter. But when they ordered and took their seats near the electric fireplace in the corner, he relaxed and went back to his notepad. "So, I take it you don't have his name on your birth certificate if you just found out the full story a few weeks ago?"

"No. Just my mom's name."

"What can you tell me about *him*? Anything?"

"His name is Julian. I know he went to the same high school as my mother—Lakeland High School. She said he had a scholarship to an Ivy League. That's why she didn't tell him about me. She didn't want to hold him back."

The scratching of pen on paper stopped abruptly. "That doesn't mesh with the woman you've told me about so far."

"Yeah." Jess gave an ironic laugh. "Apparently she had a soul once upon a time." She switched Parker to her opposite arm and resettled herself. "She resents me for keeping her from living the life she should have had." She shrugged. "Don't ask me how that works, because I can't figure it out either."

She gazed down at the peaceful and content face of her son. Her heart swelled seeing the healthy flush of pink in his cheeks and the small trickle of milk down his chin. His eyes glowed with the same iridescent green/blue that belonged to his father, and the downy softness of his hair stood on end with the same cowlick she fought every morning. "How anyone could resent their child is beyond me. I just…" She gazed up at Noah. "I love him so much it hurts. He wasn't planned either, but I can't fathom feeling the level of hatred toward him that my mother feels for me."

The once stern plains of Noah's brow and chin had softened in a sympathetic expression that reminded her of Jack. When she had initially sat down across from him, she barely saw any similarities between the brothers, other than the angular shape of their faces. Where Jack's eyes were a dark shade of gray, Noah's were a vibrant blue. Jack's face was always open, honest, and congenial, while Noah's brow hovered over his eyes like an angry storm cloud, an air of suspicion tinting every part of his personality. But now, as he gazed at her from across the table, his guard lowered, she saw similarities in the set of their shoulders, the curve of their lips, and the shape of their noses.

For a moment, the two of them sat in silence, gazing at the child in Jess's arms. Finally, Noah stirred and flipped his notebook closed, tucking it back in his pocket before draining the rest of his coffee. "I do have one more question."

Jess gave him a small smile. "What's that?"

He studied her, gauging her reaction before even asking the question. "When I find him—"

"If," Jess corrected with a smile that said *God, you're cocky*.

"No. I'm damn good at my job. I'll find him, and when I do, do you want me to approach him?" He let another moment pass before he amped up the pressure. "Do you want me to tell him who hired me and why? Do you want to meet him?"

Her heart thundered in her ears and bursts of fireworks went off behind her eyes as she struggled to steady her breathing. The café, now nearly empty, seemed to be flooded with light and noise. Did she want Julian to know he had a daughter he'd lived in complete ignorance of for twenty-five years?

"If he wants to, I would love to meet him," she whispered, finding her eyes firmly focused on the bald spot near Parker's temple. "But…I guess I would understand if he doesn't."

Noah gave her a curt nod and pressed his hands flat to the table, making to rise.

She scooted out of the booth and stood to meet him, gripping Parker tight in one arm to take Noah's hand in another handshake.

"It was good to meet you, Jess. I'll be in touch."

She nodded and smiled as he walked away, but quickly spun to call after him. "Noah?"

He stopped with his hand on the door of the shop. "Yeah?"

"Thank you."

He gave her a genuine smile and nodded. "Of course." He shoved the door open to the frigid, wailing gusts of an early February rain storm and disappeared.

Fifteen

Black Diamond

The illusive February sun shone down over the Rockies, ricocheting off the snow in blinding rainbows. Coming to the end of his run, Jack jumped sideways and skidded to a stop with a spray of downy powder. It was the last time he would ski before it was back to business. Tonight, he would pack up the rest of his boxes and head for Chicago in the morning. He raised his goggles and tilted his face up to the sun. The rays soaked into his skin and sent vibrations of energy through every cell in his body, rejuvenating his soul. Nothing excited his senses quite like the alpine region of his home state, and he always hated leaving, whether he was on a six-month offseason or a three-day hiatus.

With the greatest of reluctance, he had to admit it was time to go. The slopes closed at four, and the sun was already sinking toward the peaks of the mountains, making them glow in amber light. Taking one more deep lungful of pine-scented air, he turned toward the lift and got in line for the ride back up to the lodge. The slopes were covered with people of all ages festooned in brightly colored outerwear, but one particular family caught his attention as he sat down on the chairlift. A young girl, maybe five, was sliding slowly down the slope with her skis pointed cautiously inward. Her older brother, a foot taller, and more adventurous, was hurtling down the hill with his dad chasing after him while the mother shouted encouragements at her daughter, clapping in elation at the girl's success.

So much of his childhood had been spent on the slopes with his brothers and parents. He'd learned a lot there—the boundary between bravery and stupidity chief among them.

Tucked away in the shaded tree line of a cat trail, a man and woman stood tucked up against a towering Ponderosa pine. He had his arms around her, draped low so his hands rested at the small of her back. She had her hands on his chest and was laughing hysterically at something he was saying. Her dark hair flowed out from beneath her toboggan and her pink-tinted goggles rested on top of her head. For the briefest of seconds, he saw Jess in the brilliance of her smile, but a quick blink cleared the mirage. He thought about her at least once in every hour of the day. It had about killed him to not call her after their run-in, but it was the right thing to do. He might be head over heels for her, but he also intended to respect her relationship with Tucker. Grudgingly.

Fifteen minutes later, with a cup of hot chocolate from the refreshment cart in hand, he clicked the key fob and raised the lift gate of his Acura MDX. With care, so as not to whack his skis on the side of the SUV, he placed them diagonally in the cargo compartment and pressed the button to close the rear door. He hopped in the driver's seat, already nice and warm, thanks to his heated seats and took another sip of his hot chocolate before rubbing his frozen hands together to warm them, ready to make the twenty-minute drive back to his parent's cabin near Boulder.

They had bought the property decades before the area had become the playground of the rich and famous. Now, real estate tycoons were constantly knocking on their door, making offers for the thirty-acre patch of land overlooking Lost Gulch. But there were too many memories there—memories of Christmases when his grandparents were still alive. They used to haul two weeks' worth of groceries and supplies up the mountain to snowshoe, ski, and spend time as a family every Christmas break. Now they kept the cabin mostly for Jack to occupy in the offseason, though Aaron occasionally brought his family up for a long weekend.

Just as he slowed the vehicle to turn up the snow-covered lane toward the cabin, his phone rang over the Bluetooth loudspeaker, giving him a start as he carefully maneuvered the slick and narrow driving surface. He glanced at the touchscreen display on his dash. His brother's crossed-eye face, tongue out in a moment of drunken dishevelment plastered itself to the display and Jack hit the accept button on the steering wheel.

"Yello," he answered, squinting as a ray of the setting sun peeked between two large pine trees and smacked him in the face.

"Hey," Noah greeted. "You still in Denver?"

"Just getting back from my last day on the slopes. I head east tomorrow. What about you? Are you still in Pittsburgh?"

"No, actually. I got what we needed, so I'm already on my way back. I stopped off in western Indiana last night and got going early this morning. I'm almost to Hays, Kansas, and I'm thinking about stopping somewhere soon. God, Kansas is such a terrible state to drive across." The last sentence was all but a moan, and Jack smiled.

He maneuvered his car into the parking spot near the side porch of the cabin, placing it in park and taking in the view from the top of the ridge as he helped ease some of Noah's boredom. "I'm surprised it only took you three weeks. Normally it takes longer."

"Yeah, well, what can I say? The guy's a dumbass. It shouldn't be too hard for my client to win their case."

Jack tossed his head back with a roar of laughter and leaned against the headrest. "Sucks we're gonna miss each other. I'll wave as I drive past."

Noah was silent for a moment. Road noise filtered through the stereo as a muffled whir, the only proof the call hadn't dropped. "Maybe we could meet up for breakfast near the border. What time are you heading out?"

"I'm not sure. I'd like to get a good start in the morning, but then again, I also like my sleep." A reddish blur caught his attention from the corner of his eye and his gaze darted to the right where a fluffy pine squirrel hopped across the snow, making divots in the fresh powder as it headed for the recently cleared deck and a nice warm spot to eat his winter snack. The light was fading behind the mountains, leaving the valley in violet shadow far below. If he wanted to get his boxes loaded up before dark, he would have to hurry.

Only half attending to what his brother was saying, a familiar name caught his attention and he tuned back in.

"Sorry. What were you saying?"

"I said I met Jess last night."

"Way to bury the lede," he growled. "Why didn't you tell me you were meeting with her?"

"Well…to be honest, I didn't know if I was going to reach out. If I worked pro bono on every need your ex-girlfriends had, I'd never make enough money to eat."

Jack snorted and rolled his eyes. "Ha ha. Very funny. So? What did you think?"

"She's…" He drifted off, and Jack could envision the way he squinted one eye when he was trying to think of the best way to describe something or someone. "I can see why you like her," he finally said in the most politically correct comment he'd ever heard any of his brothers make.

"Shut the fuck up. Tell me what you think. I want to know." Jack leaned forward, gripping the leather-upholstered steering wheel in desperation.

Noah snorted. "She's beautiful. I mean, *obviously*. You do have a type."

"If I have a type, so do you. What else?" He was not about to get sidetracked with such fresh information about the woman who haunted his dreams within reach.

"She's more down-to-earth than I expected. All the girls you've dated before were in it for sex or money—nothing serious, just fun. Jess…she has a kid. She wants a good life for herself, but also for her little boy. I admire that. I think it's been hard for her, adjusting to a lifestyle she never anticipated, but from what I've seen, she's doing great."

Hearing high marks from someone with a patent level of skepticism was encouraging. Jack's lips quirked absently. He was so proud of Jess. When she'd found out she was pregnant, she'd been terrified, and he'd done what he could to be a sounding board for her, but at the end of the day, her accomplishments were her own.

"She's had a rough life. I know you told me some of the basics, but hearing it from her…I'm shocked at what she's made of herself. You know? She had no leg up, no gimmes, and look at her. I'd have to be one cold-hearted bastard to not want to help."

Jack felt like he was floating. It was as though every thought and feeling he'd had over the past few weeks had released its death grip on him and they were now flying away like untethered balloons. "You think you can find him?" Jack turned off the car and put his phone up to his ear as he popped the lever on his car door and pushed it open. The snow crunched under his waterproof boots as he walked around to the back hatch and pulled his gear from the car.

"Oh, without a doubt. I did some preliminary searches. That high school they graduated from only has, like, a hundred and twenty kids in each graduating class. She knows he went to an Ivy League. That's a start. The lucky thing is—if you can call a broken home with no father luck—there was no adoption paperwork. No sealed documents. No red tape. I just have to find the guy."

He smiled, able to feel his brother's enthusiasm through the phone. "Well, I hope it's a short search. Let me know what you find."

Noah snorted. "Oh I will. Don't worry. You can ride in like the conquering hero. I'll even let you borrow my noble steed."

Jack laughed. "Well, until she gets off the commitment train, I'm stranded in no-man's-land. It's probably best if you deliver the news. I'll just be happy to know the outcome."

Silence filled the space between them once more. "What?" Jack asked as he pushed the door to the side porch open and propped his skis next to the door.

"Ummm," Noah was clearly mulling over something of magnitude, and if Jack could reach through the phone and shake the words out of him like dirt out of a clogged vacuum cleaner, he would. "I don't know. I got the impression things with her and Tucker aren't the best...I think they may have broken up."

Jack's heart skipped and stuttered to a halt before jolting into a thundering stampede. "She told you that?" he croaked, unable to say more for the vice-like grip adrenaline had on his larynx.

"Not exactly. But she did elude to being a single mother last night. Tucker is definitely back in Texas. Other than that, I can't say for sure. It's just a vibe."

Jack rolled his eyes and leaned back on the wall of the porch, thumping his head lightly against the cedar siding. "Any chance that *vibe* could find a buddy and give me a sure thing?" A cedar waxwing landed on one of the aspen trees growing in the side yard and puffed up his smooth gray plumage before letting out a high-pitched whistle that rose and fell with the tuft on his head. His black mask nearly hid the large orbs of his eyes and his bright yellow tail feathers wiggled up and down as he sang.

"Sorry, buddy. For now, all I've got is my radar. I'll let you know if I come up with something more concrete." The *click-click, click-click* of a turn signal snapped Jack out of his reverie and he twisted the doorknob to let himself into the house. Boxes were scattered across the living room floor, down the hall, and into the bedroom. Other than a few clothing items, he was ready to go. Moving every racing season made him an expert in packing the essentials. Nothing more, nothing less. The rest went into storage. Unfortunately, that meant a trip to Indianapolis and the unit he had rented before heading home for the fall and winter.

Or maybe not unfortunately.

Heading south gave him an excuse to check in on Jess—maybe meet for dinner.

"I can hear the gears turning. What are you up to?" Noah asked in a voice that said, "*Whatever you're about to do, don't.*"

"Nothing," Jack denied as he stooped to pick up a stack of boxes and moved them to the porch for easy access later. "Just thinking."

"Yeah, well, you and I know how dangerous that can be—especially when a woman is involved." Jack couldn't remember the last time Noah had a serious girlfriend. He was the serial dater of the family. Well, he couldn't lay that title solely at his brother's feet. Before Jess, Jack hadn't been looking for anything serious either. But for every rule, there seemed to be an exception these days. Noah sighed. "Listen. You're my little brother. So, I feel like I can tell you this and not completely piss you off. And somebody has to be honest here."

"Oh God…" Jack moaned and popped a squat on the porch stairs to enjoy the last remnants of sunlight as they filtered across the barren peaks of the Rockies.

"You're never going to be satisfied with being her friend. I'm sure you have the best of intentions, and so does she, but at the end of the day, you two have history, and neither of you is going to forget that."

"Well, thanks for that stunning revelation." Jack rolled his eyes. "Does this Yoda-quality advice have a point?"

"Yeah. Shit or get off the pot. If you want to be with her, tell her. Otherwise, cut it with the dramatics. I'll find her father because that's my job, but if you don't have a dog in the fight, stay the hell out of it."

"Sorry, I asked," Jack muttered as he knocked the snow from the top step with the tip of his shoe.

"You don't pay me to sugarcoat things, and it's not my style anyway."

"I don't pay you at all." Jack heaved himself up and went back into the house to get more boxes and throw some pizza rolls in the air fryer. "It makes me wonder how you ever make a living. Don't you have to have some sort of bedside manner when you're digging into people's deepest, darkest secrets?"

"It's not a requirement. Sometimes I'm feeling generous though and throw it in for free." Silence filled the space between the brothers. Then they both snorted with mirth and cracked up. He missed the days of being with his brothers and parents, all living under one roof. It had been madness at times, four teenage boys constantly in and out of the house, sneaking out of second-story windows and covering for each other when one got a little too high at their classmate's party or fell asleep at their girlfriend's house and missed curfew. Life had been simpler then.

"Well, next time you're in Chicago, maybe you could shower me with some of your leftover generosity and take me out for a beer."

"You're the one with the fancy new driver contract. I think you should be taking *me* out for a beer. The ink's not even dry on it yet, and you're already mooching off your family? You can't tell me that loft took *all* of your advance."

"You been checking up on me?" Jack asked, knowing he hadn't told his brother about his new Uptown digs.

"Deductive reasoning is my job, you dork. I know what you like. Besides, I have friends in high places."

Jack shook his head, but couldn't help the smile that crept over his face. He may only see Noah every few months, but it felt good to know he was still looking out for him—even from a distance.

Maybe one of these days, life would slow down enough for them to enjoy a football game or have a poker night. At thirty years old, Jack felt his time in the racing industry slowly coming to a close. Grayson was a driver that success would follow well into his forties. He had the talent, sponsorship, and manufacturer backing to make it happen, but not every driver was that lucky. And while Jack's contract with Lakeshore was new and shiny, it was only for a year with a year option if performance met expectations.

Maintaining his career would be heavy sledding in the years to come and all the conditions would have to be just right before Jack would consider clicking on his skis and heading down a black diamond slope with no idea where the run ended. Then again, the right conditions may lead him to a cushy commentator gig where he could spend the majority of his time at home with the wife and kids he one day hoped to have.

Sixteen

Battle Plans

"Hey Jess, did you get the orders put in for those vases on the Lewis Wedding?" Alaina asked, whooshing into the store like she was riding the east wind.

"Good morning to you too." She chuckled, not looking up from her screen. "Had to get that off your chest, did you?" She took a sip from her turquoise *Decadent Designs* mug and glanced up at her best friend with amusement.

"Well, did you? Because they're on back order and if we don't get them ordered now, it's going to be a tight squeeze to get them by July."

"I did it, Alaina. Jess asked me to place the order before I left yesterday," Sydney said. The light tap of her wedged feet broke the stressed silence from Alaina, and she smiled as she picked up her mug of fresh coffee from the Keurig and bent down to retrieve her creamer from the mini fridge.

Alaina glanced down at Jess with an eyebrow raised, and

Jess put her chin in her hands, giving her business partner her undivided attention. "Lainie, I heard what you were going on about before you ran out of the office at half-past two yesterday to meet with your caterer. We have it under control. Is there anything else I can do for you?"

The request wasn't snarky, but a genuine question. The friends had both been stressed lately and while Jess's catalyst was an ongoing war with Parker that required daily battle plan revisions, Alaina's panic over her upcoming nuptials was slowly but surely morphing her friend into the thing they hated most—a bridezilla. Alaina flounced down at her desk, tears in her eyes. "No. It's just a lot right now," Alaina whispered, her cheeks flushed with embarrassment at her outburst in front of her employees.

Jess took her hand and squeezed. "Trust me, I know, but I think the rest of us are all caught up. Marissa put together the test pieces for the Indy Bridal Expo, and Sydney got the linen orders put in for the May weddings we have booked. So if you need us to help, we can move some stuff around. You don't have to do it alone."

Alaina looked over her shoulder at the two younger girls, who were both standing behind her with open smiles of encouragement and sympathy. "I have to admit, I never planned on putting my entire wedding together in four months. It's a lot."

"Well, let me help," Sydney murmured, swiping her laptop up off her desk and rolling over to huddle with the other girls at Jess's desk. "I made this nifty little spreadsheet that has a timeline of everything a typical wedding requires, and when we need to have orders placed, locations booked, caterer meetings…" She flipped it around and showed her creative genius. "So, let's go through this and see what you already have done. It will give you a better idea of where you stand."

Jess gave a wide grin. "Oh my god, I had no idea you were working on this. This is amazing. We should put this in all of our event files!"

"Absolutely," Alaina agreed as she scrolled through the checklist broken down by each month and week leading up to the big day. "Oh." She pointed at the screen. "That reminds me. I need to go over to Happily Ever After to look at a few linen options. Marissa, do you want to tag along? I can introduce you to the event planners there. You can do some networking and give me your thoughts?"

"I would, but I have to finish up the bouquets for the Ramirez wedding. River is coming in to pick them up at three."

"I can go," Jess offered. "I have a few things to figure out with this time clock thing, but it shouldn't take too much longer—if you need somebody to go with you."

Alaina nodded, her forehead smoothing slightly in relief. "Thanks. That'd be great. I'd just like to get someone's opinion."

Jess snorted quietly to herself. Alaina designed weddings for a living. The idea that she needed Jess's opinion on anything was laughable. She was just going for moral support, and that was fine by her. She didn't need any more accountability thrown on her shoulders.

As Alaina and Marissa began hammering out the Ramirez wedding logistics, Jess tuned back into the week's payroll, which she had been trying to organize through an automated system that worked off the new time clock they had installed last week. Once the automation was synced up, all she would have to do was verify the software calculations set up with the federal and state income tax elections per the girls' W-9s each week. It would take a load off and free up time to work on her next project—real estate. She hadn't talked to Alaina about it yet, but she doubted her friend would object to the expansion of their own warehouse. A lot of the pieces they put together were purchased back from the client at a fraction of the assembly cost for use on other events. As a result, their store rooms in the back were packed to the gills with boxes of silk flowers, chargers, vases, glassware, and a ton of other bits and bobs.

The bell over the door rang cheerfully, but Jess didn't think much of it, concluding she had missed an appointment with a client on the day's schedule. It wasn't until she heard the astonished greeting from Alaina two desks away that her head shot up. "Jack. What are you doing here?"

Jess spun around to see her ex hovering in the doorway like a fish out of water, hands shoved in his pockets against the chill outside. "Hey, Alaina. I was just, um…is Jess around?"

Jess hazarded a glance at Sydney and Marissa who were so tuned in to the sudden appearance of a sexy man in their storefront they might as well have a bucket of popcorn between the two of them. Rolling her eyes, Jess popped up from her desk and made a beeline for Jack before he caught sight of the gawkers. "What are you doing here? I thought you were in Chicago?" she asked, deftly wedging herself between him and Alaina, whose eyes were darkening with suspicion and outrage.

Jack was shorter than Tucker by at least four inches, but still a good bit taller than Jess's petite five foot two. The slate color of his eyes seemed to warm to a rich charcoal at the sight of her, and she couldn't help the pleasant flush that crept up her neck and excited her senses. He smelled of fresh rain and rich leather, and she could stand there with her nose buried in his chiseled jaw all day, imagining the way he would kiss the hollow under her ear.

She cleared her throat. The important thing now was to get him out of the shop before Alaina went off with a bang. "Umm…coffee?" she asked, looking for something, anything to say or suggest. "We should get coffee." She spun around on her heel and swiped her purse from her desk before clamping down on his arm and dragging him from the office.

The day outside was blustery but cloudless and the sun beat down in a vibrating wave of vitamin D. Jess tilted her face up to the sun, eyes closed in ecstasy, and leaned into Jack, her arm wrapped around his as they walked toward the Starbucks on the corner of Capitol and Washington. "Not that it's not great to see you, but do you plan to tell me what you're doing here?"

"Well, mostly, I needed to get my stuff out of storage to move to my new apartment."

Jess darted a glance sideways at him. "New digs…where at this time?"

"Uptown. Not too far from the shop. I only leased it for a year. I have a one-year option on my contract if they decide to keep me around, but I didn't want to commit to anything lengthy."

"For your contract?" she asked, trying to puzzle through what sense that made. What she knew of the racing industry was through osmosis. Being Alaina Montgomery soon-to-be Miles's best friend had some advantages, or drawbacks depending on the day, and twenty years of close contact with a racing nerd had afforded at least a basic knowledge of the sport. That being said, she was fairly certain it was beneficial to have as long of a contract as possible, and a term length of one season didn't seem like either party had much confidence in the deal.

"No, not the contract. The lease." Jack chuckled and pulled her closer to his side. The physical contact between them had been more friendly than romantic, but the way he drew her in made it clear he was enjoying the feel of her hand on his arm as they strolled down the sidewalk. "I usually stay out west with my family during the offseason. So I probably won't be using the space past September or October."

"Well, I'll keep that in mind if Alaina and I need a girl's weekend and a place to stay next winter." They slowed their pace as they approached the door to the café. Jack tugged on the door and held it open for her while she entered. The aroma of freshly ground coffee beans, sugar, and baked goods assaulted her senses.

Once they both had their drinks in hand, they found a quiet table out of the way of other patrons waiting for their lattes and Frappuccinos. "So. Spill. What *really* brings you here? I doubt your storage unit is next door to Decadent Designs."

Jack's eyes danced and sparkled with amusement as he watched her over the rim of his coffee cup, sipping tentatively at the contents. "What, I can't just stop in to see a friend?"

She matched him look for look over her cold brew and replied, "When that friend is also your ex? No. Not really."

He rolled his eyes and shook his head, leaning back in his chair to give the impression of aloofness, but she wasn't fooled. He had nervous energy radiating from his pores. "I talked to Noah."

She nodded and leaned forward with her forearms on the table, pinching her bottom lip between her teeth. "I figured you would eventually. He's an interesting cat, your brother. Not at all like I imagined."

A wicked grin tugged at the corner of his mouth, begging to be unleashed. "Oh yeah? And how is that?"

Jess spun her cup on the tabletop, creating wet figure eights on the tacky surface. "I don't know. He's so…serious."

Jack couldn't contain the laugh that bubbled out of him like spring water. The rich sound of it warmed Jess's insides and relaxed some of her tension. "He is serious, but get a couple of beers in him and he loosens up pretty quickly."

"He seems confident he can find Julian. I'm just trying not to get my hopes up. That's the last thing I need right now—somebody crushing my hopes and dreams." She put her coffee to her mouth and took another swig as she leaned back and crossed her legs.

"I know, but if anybody can do it, he can. He wouldn't tell you he could if he had doubts."

Jess nodded as she gazed over his shoulder, lost in the hundreds of scenarios running through her head. Her phone buzzed on the table, and she glanced down to look at the display.

How long are you going to be?

Jess clicked the screen off, ignoring Alaina's message. Jack glanced down at the phone and back up at her, but let it go.

"He asked me…Did I want to meet him—Julian? Did I want him to approach him and tell him he had a daughter? And I…" Jess gazed down at her coffee, swallowing hard. She picked at the rim of the plastic lid as she tried to formulate words for the emotions roiling around inside her. The question had put the fear of God in her. Until that point, Julian had been a name floated out into the universe by her mother in a moment of weakness. Now someone was actively looking for him, and the thought of coming face to face with him… "What if he's a horrible person? Or…what if he doesn't want anything to do with me?" she whispered.

Jack's hand, warm and steady, took hers and squeezed. "If he doesn't want to meet you, he'll be missing the biggest opportunity of his life. And that would be a damn shame… because his daughter is pretty amazing."

Her mouth popped open, but words were useless as she gazed up into eyes filled with so much love it robbed the breath from her lungs. Her phone buzzed again.

Stop ignoring me.

She gritted her teeth and flipped the phone face down on the table. Every text from her best friend was like a red hot poker to the bottom of her foot, reminding her of Tucker's broken heart.

Which was obviously the goal here...

It wasn't fair—the guilt. Her failed relationship with Tuck had been an inevitability, and Jack was hardly some random guy she met on Tinder.

She turned over the hand he was still holding and threaded her fingers through his, squeezing back. "I miss you," she whispered, gazing at their entwined fingers and wishing it was their naked bodies. She was a physical being; intimacy was as vital as breathing to her. Without it, she often felt adrift in a vast ocean of uncertainty. In the arms of a man was one place she felt safe, for however long that moment lasted.

He let out a shaky breath. "You know I miss you too." Reaching across the table, he lifted her chin to look her in the eye. "I was out of line—when I kissed you. I won't do it again."

She gave him a small smile and squeezed the hand she was still holding. "In all fairness, I let you." She stared at him for a long beat, wanting, all at once, to raise every defense she could manage and collapse every wall she'd ever built. After years of being broken down time and time again, her armor stuck to her like glue. Vulnerability didn't come naturally, but she felt like maybe, just maybe, she could be vulnerable with Jack. "Tita has euchre tonight with some of the ladies from her women's group, so I have to pick Parker up by six."

He gazed at her, waiting for her to complete her thought and giving her room to back out of what she was insinuating at the same time. This move would be hers and hers alone.

With a deep breath, she trudged forward. "Come over?"

His Adam's apple bobbed as he swallowed. "What about Tucker?" His voice was low and steely, as if the mere thought of her with another man drove him to unspeakable jealousy.

She took a small, shaky breath. "Tuck and I broke up."

A flash of something, not quite shock, passed through his dark eyes.

"You don't seem surprised."

His lips twitched. "No. Not surprised."

She furrowed her brow, half-offended. "What, you didn't think I could stick it out?"

His forehead smoothed in bafflement. "No. That's not—

I…" He sighed and rolled his eyes heavenward. "You're tough as nails, Jess. I've known that from the moment I met you. And I knew you would choose Tucker if you believed that choice would give Parker his best shot in life. I just kept hoping that one day you would see it."

"See what?" Jess asked, resisting the urge to pull her hand from his and raise the drawbridge she'd so cautiously lowered over the mote around her heart.

"Families aren't made from a sense of obligation."

The words smacked her in the face, and she pulled her hand from his. "Wow."

He reached out and pulled her hand back across the table, enveloping it in both of his. "Please don't do that."

"Do what?" Tears brimmed her eyes, and she swiped at them, annoyed at how much his words hurt her.

"Get mad at me for telling it like it is. I've always been honest with you, and I don't plan to stop now."

"There's a difference between honesty and knowing when to keep your mouth shut, Jackson," she growled, glaring at him with the full force of her jade eyes. She didn't need another man in her life who thought he knew what was best for her.

"You're right," he ceded with a bow of his head. "And I kept my mouth shut for six months, praying someday your heart would catch up to that logical brain of yours, and you would realize it's possible for someone to love and support you because they *want* to, not because of some misplaced sense of responsibility."

Silence filled the space between them as she glared at him. Inch by inch, she could feel her temper receding until she surrendered with a huff. "You couldn't have told me that six months ago?"

He smirked in relief at the suspension of hostilities. "Would you have believed me six months ago?"

She rolled her eyes. "Probably not." There was something about Jack, his personality, his approach to life, that was oddly refreshing. He had the ability to light her fuse like a stick of dynamite but could also snuff it out like a single-wick candle in a stiff breeze. So weird, and yet, so right. "So," she sighed. "Are you coming over tonight or not?"

He chuckled and grinned. "I wouldn't miss it."

Seventeen

The Spice of Life

The rich scent of cumin, coriander, and turmeric wafted in the air as Jess pulled the lid from the pot to inspect her handy work. Parker was down for a nap, the naan was in the oven, and the rice was nice and tender. Now all she needed was her dinner date. She did a spin around the open-concept floor plan of her house, inspecting the state of things before rising on her tiptoes and grabbing plates and glasses out of the cupboard to place on the table.

"Alexa, turn the music up to five," she commanded as she set the table with care and swayed her hips to the beat of an R&B number streaming from her Echo Dot. She took the remaining dirty bottles in the sink and rinsed them with hot water before placing them in the dishwasher and then spun to grab a serving bowl from the storage space in the island for the chicken tikka. As she was scraping the last remnants of the dish into the bowl, a knock sounded at the main door.

Layla, who had been dozing under the bar, jerked awake, barking in manic confusion as she came to full alert. "Hush," Jess hissed. She placed the bowl on the counter and wiped her hands on her sage green half-apron. As she approached the door, she paused for a moment, taking a deep breath to calm her racing heart. Why was she so nervous? It was just Jack. *Right.* Just *Jack.* That was the equivalent of saying Whitney Houston was *just* a singer. It was incongruous. She rolled her eyes, tossed her hair over her left shoulder, and opened the door before she chickened out and pretended she wasn't home.

He was wearing the same black leather jacket and worn blue jeans he'd been wearing earlier, but something about him, framed in the light of the setting sun with a brilliant smile and a bouquet of hyacinths in his hand, froze her where she stood, speechless. "Hi," he greeted in a tone that, if she hadn't known better, would have been considered shy.

"Hi," she squeaked, reaching out to take the fragrant flowers. Layla weaved herself between Jess's legs and nearly tripped her in her elation. The scent of the flowers in her hands made her giddy, and she had to blink to clear her tilting vision.

He remembered my favorite flower.

What else did he remember? She opened the door further to let him into the house, trying for all she was worth to gain her footing.

He bent to pay his respects to the black and white blur at his feet, rubbing the scruff of her neck and patting her head before standing up and continuing further into the house. "It smells amazing in here." His cologne mingled with the hyacinths in an erotic mix of feminine and masculine scents.

Struck speechless by an influx of hormones to her brain, she gestured for him to make himself at home and followed him toward the kitchen. "I uh, I made chicken tikka. It's one of my go-to's when it's cold outside. You can always count on a little bit of spice to warm you up."

"I've never had it," he admitted as he casually placed his palms on the island and gazed into the serving bowl, curious. She gave him a small smile before donning a pair of oven mitts and stooping to remove the naan from the oven. Her stomach rumbled at the heady smell of baking bread, and saliva pooled in her mouth. With Jack showing up so unexpectedly this afternoon and then the meeting with Alaina once she got back, she hadn't had time to eat.

She transferred the plate to a potholder on the table and then added the bowl of tikka as well before standing back and surveying the spread, hands on hips. What was she forgetting?

Drinks!

"Can I get you something to drink?" she asked as she reached around to untie her apron. She looked up at him briefly as she struggled with the knot and paused. Jack was watching her with amusement, the hint of a smile curling the corners of his mouth.

"What?" she asked as she finally freed herself and tossed the apron onto the counter.

He shook his head and let the smile come all the way through as he followed her to the refrigerator. "Nothing."

"I have Coke, root beer, ginger ale, beer, wine…"

"I'll take a beer." He shrugged off his jacket and draped it on the back of one of the table chairs as she pulled the drinks out of the refrigerator and kicked the door closed with her foot. "Where's the little guy? I figured he'd be here," he asked as he took the beer and pulled out a chair for her.

"He is." Jess took a swig of her water. "He's napping. He'll be up in an hour or so." The house was silent aside from the clink of utensils on plates and the soft, constant shush of Parker's sound machine. Jess finally took a breath, tired of the awkward silence, and asked, "So, how long are you in Indy?"

"Just for the day. I really did have to pick my stuff up from the storage unit—believe it or not." He put a forkful in his mouth and chewed thoughtfully. He pointed to his plate with his fork. "This is amazing."

Jess smiled. "Thanks. I got the recipe off Pinterest forever ago." They ate in comfortable silence for a few more moments before Jess spoke again. "So what have you been up to?"

Jack took a swig of his beer and sat back a bit. "Not much. Skiing, spending time with my niece and nephew. We had a few test days at Thermal last week, but other than that, not a whole lot. What about you? Besides, ya know, motherhood."

"Oh besides that?" she asked in a joking tone as she forked another piece of chicken. "Not a whole lot. Just work. It's been an adjustment having Alaina back. There for a while, it was one or the other. She was gone with Grayson and then I was gone on maternity leave. It's been…interesting."

"Oh, so that's what that was this afternoon." He nodded as if he completely understood Alaina's sudden disdain for him. "I almost took it personally."

Jess rolled her eyes and snorted. "No. That wasn't work. That was something else." Alaina had been livid when Jess returned from her impromptu coffee date, and in an effort not to poke the already *very* angry bear, Jess had been amenable toward her friend for the rest of the afternoon. But she was still annoyed.

Jack raised an eyebrow at her, urging her to continue, but she changed tactics.

"Did you tell Grayson we were having dinner tonight?"

Jack shifted in his seat and quirked an eyebrow. "No…but I don't really see where that would be any of his business."

"Exactly," Jess affirmed, flinging her hands up in a *thank-you* gesture. "She feels protective of her brother. I get it. But Tucker is a thousand miles away. Besides, we broke up. What am I supposed to do? Become a nun?"

"Well, that wouldn't do." Jack suppressed his amusement as much as possible and crossed his arms over his chest. His biceps bulged and rippled beneath the cuffs of his worn red T-shirt, and it took every ounce of willpower Jess could find not to stare. She felt an insane urge to giggle at his mischievous innuendo, but picked her fork back up and pushed the food around her plate instead. "She's just so freaking judgy."

"I wouldn't say Grayson is 'judgy,' but he definitely has a defined sense of right and wrong. Don't get me wrong, he'd tell me his opinion if I asked for it. But as a general rule, we stay out of each other's business."

"Must be nice," Jess grumbled. After another moment of stewing silence, she dropped the fork on her plate with a loud clink and sighed. "She literally seethed the whole afternoon. I think she thinks I'm lying to her or something. She practically had a conniption when I told her we ran into each other in Chicago." She ran her hands through her slightly tangled hair and stared at the table for a long moment before taking a deep breath. "I mean, I get it. I don't want to hurt Tuck either, but *damn…*" She took several dishes to the sink and deposited them with a series of rattles and clinks.

"I'm sorry," Jack sighed. "I didn't mean to cause problems by showing up today."

Jess blew out a breath and turned to face him again, her back resting on the counter. "It's not your fault. And I was glad to see you today. Alaina's just…" She rolled her eyes, leaving her thought unfinished as she meandered back to the table. "Do you think I'm being unreasonable?" she asked, her voice little more than a whisper.

He laughed, relieving some of the tension between them. "Like I would say you were being unreasonable." He rolled his dark gray eyes and pushed to his feet. "I think, objectively speaking, I can understand why Alaina is upset. I can even understand where you're at with this whole thing. Even if he's not your boyfriend, Tucker is still your friend. You've known him since you were kids." He slowly approached until he was standing in front of her and placed his warm hands on her shoulders. The heat of him seeped through her thin sweater and relaxed her tense muscles as she looked up into his tender gaze. "But, honestly, it's hard for me to be objective when it comes to you."

Their lips were only inches apart. If she stood on her toes, she could connect the distance between them in a millisecond. Her breath caught in her throat as she thought about pressing into him, feeling the whole length of him against her. "And what is your not-so-objective opinion?" she murmured, struggling not to be washed away in the tidal wave of testosterone rolling off him.

"I think"—he was so close to her now she could feel the whisper of his breath across her cheek—"you should do what feels right."

Her heart was pounding so quickly she thought it might burst from her chest. With a sudden breath of anticipation, she tilted her chin up toward him and connected their lips in a spark so hot it could have burned the house down around them. He gripped her love handles and pulled her closer, pressing her against him as their lips melded together in a sinfully long exchange. He tilted her head back, opening her to him in urgent need and slipping his tongue deep within her mouth. There was a spicy blend of want and need in his exploration.

She pressed into him further, her sensitive breasts aching as they grazed his chest. She moaned at the exquisite onslaught of sensations assaulting her body. He smelled of oakmoss and crisp night air with a hint of the beer he'd had with dinner, and she wanted more. More of his hands. More of his tongue.

He ran his hands up through the dark tendrils of her hair and gripped the roots to bend her head back and expose her throat. Her insides hummed as he played a tantalizing game of catch and release with his lips, setting her on fire as he reeled her in, only to abandon the chase and move on. Every cell in her body pulsed, and she let out a frustrated gasp as he continued to tease her. "If I don't have you inside me in the next thirty seconds, I'm going to scream."

She felt the breath of a chuckle against her cheek and goosebumps rose across her arms and down her legs.

"God, I've missed you, Sassy," he murmured back as he grazed her earlobe with his teeth. She fought for traction as she reached to fumble with the button of his jeans, but a loud squawk from the baby monitor put an end to any hopes they had. She closed her eyes, and deflated with a sigh, dropping her hands from his pants and stepping back out of his embrace. His lips quirked in a reluctant grin, and he let her pass unchallenged to tend to her son.

Five minutes later, appeased with his pacifier and a clean diaper, mom and baby bounced down the hallway in an enthusiastic reveal. "Ho-ly shit. You actually have a baby." He inspected the squirming bundle in Jess's arms with a slightly stunned expression, but then smiled.

"Trust me, I think that *at least* five times a day."

Jack reached out and tickled the little boy under the chin, which got him a quiet coo. "You're a cutie, aren't ya? You gonna be a ladies' man?"

"God, I hope not. I don't even want to think about him being a hormone-crazed teenager." She bent down and kissed the top of his head. "You're just my sweet boy. You're never gonna grow up, right?" She nuzzled his ear affectionately and straightened, offering the baby to Jack. "You want to hold him?"

"Sure," he agreed with enthusiasm. A twinge of desire flooded through her at the sight of him holding Parker, and she had to admit, to a single mom, a man who loved babies was just as sexy as any six-pack.

Feeling confident her son was in good hands, Jess made her way over to the freezer and pulled out a pouch of frozen breast milk to heat for his dinner. She'd decided to stop breastfeeding earlier in the week, but being near her baby, or any baby, when they were crying caused her breasts to ache. So, in addition to feeling like she was carrying two cantaloupes on her chest, she was also leaking at regular intervals like a dairy cow.

After talking to her doctor at her six-week appointment, she'd learned breastfeeding could contribute to her hormone production, and likewise, her baby blues. Dr. Adler had encouraged Jess to do what was best for her. Her breast milk would be good for up to a year when kept frozen, and she had enough to last Parker at least the next four months without switching to formula. Coming to terms with what was best for her had been a two-week-long road, but in the end, she had decided if Parker could get the nutrients he needed through her frozen breast milk and formula, there was really no reason to continue this craziness.

"Do you want to feed him?" she asked as she took a seat on the couch next to Jack and offered him the bottle.

Jack raised a skeptical brow and handed her the baby. "Let's take this one step at a time. Shall we?"

She laughed and expertly cradled the baby in one hand while popping the bottle in his mouth with the other. The couch creaked slightly beneath her shifting weight as she got comfortable and leaned her head back against the cushions. Jack caressed the side of her face with the backs of his fingers and she turned to kiss his hand with tender affection.

"You seem to be doing better with everything." His voice was intimate as he stroked her, and the sound of it sent a small thrill through her. For months, she'd been yearning for something she never thought she'd have again. And now here he was, sitting right next to her.

She turned his observation over in her head for a moment, thinking about how things were now versus the overwhelming flood of hormones, fatigue, and sensory overload she had been experiencing the last time she saw him. "Yeah. It's a little better. I still don't get a lot of sleep, but the day-to-day is easier." She dropped her gaze to the baby in her arms. His face was perfectly content, eyes closed as he suckled. She had worried that after eight weeks of breastfeeding, he might not take to the bottle, but it had been a smooth transition—thank god.

"I'm glad," he murmured as he curled a loose tendril of her hair around one finger. "I've worried about you." He moved his hand to her shoulders and neck, gently kneading her muscles.

"Why didn't you call?" she asked, gazing up into his warm eyes. The lead weight of her son in her arms made her unaccountably tired, and she closed her eyes against his gentle ministrations.

"Because…when we met in Chicago, you made it clear we couldn't be anything." He was quiet for a moment and she opened her eyes to gaze up at him, desperate to know what emotion was bubbling under the surface. "It's too hard to watch you be with somebody else, Jess." His voice was rough with emotion, and if she hadn't been holding a two-month-old in her arms, she would have picked up that thread right where they left it in the kitchen.

God, he drove her crazy in the best way.

The faint buzzing of a phone called them both out of the lock they had on each other. Jess glanced at the digital clock on the microwave and swore under her breath. "It's probably Tucker. He usually calls at this time to see Park before he goes to bed."

"Do you need me to leave?" Jack asked, shifting to get up.

"No. No." She reached over with her spare hand and pressed down on his thigh to keep him on the couch. I'll just go into Parker's room and take the call. Please. Stay." She gave him a pleading look which, she hoped, communicated how badly she wanted him there and rose from the couch to find her phone before the call disconnected. She found it on the island and hurried toward the nursery as she clicked the accept button.

By the time the call connected and Tucker's anxious face popped up on the screen, she was seated comfortably in the nursery rocking chair as if she'd been there for hours. "Hey!" she greeted, propping the bottle up with her cheek so she could hold the phone.

Tucker grinned. "You're getting pretty good at that."

"Yeah, well, when necessity meets creativity. Did you just get back to the barracks?"

"Yeah. I'm meeting the guys off base for a drink in a few, so I figured I'd call and wish little guy good night."

Jess tilted the phone so Tucker could see Parker. Parker wasn't completely focused on the screen, but he recognized his father's voice and was more alert tonight than he had been for the past several phone calls. He popped the nipple out of his mouth and smiled at the phone.

"Hey, baby boy," Tuck murmured. "Daddy misses you."

Jess tilted the screen back up. "I'm hoping to get tickets booked by the end of the week. We'll be able to fly into Dallas-Fort Worth and stay for the weekend."

Tucker's face lit up. "Really? When are you coming?"

Jess smiled at Tuck's enthusiasm. It had been a while since she'd seen him that happy. Actually, the last time she'd seen that smile was the day Parker was born. Guilt instantly washed over her, but she shoved it into a mental closet and locked the door. "Next weekend. I talked to Alaina about it, and if I fly out late Friday afternoon and come back Sunday,

I shouldn't miss much."

"That's awesome. God, Jess, you have no idea how excited I am."

"I know how much you miss him." She laid a tender kiss on Parker's head before lifting him into a sitting position on her lap and placing the nearly empty bottle on the table next to the chair. "I wanted you to see him at least once before the wedding. And if I could get away from the shop, why not hop down to Dallas for a few days?"

"Absolutely. I'm not sure what kind of stuff you want to do while you're here, but I can look into—"

"Tucker," she interrupted with a patient grin. "Having someone else to help take care of the baby so I can relax for a bit sounds like heaven."

He gave her one of his patented grins that brought out the dimple on his cheek. "Okay. But at least let me take you out for Tex-Mex."

She snorted. "You've got yourself a deal."

Tucker looked off-camera and then back down. "Hey, I've got to go, but text me your flight information? I'll talk to Wes. I'm sure it wouldn't be a big deal for you guys to stay at their place."

"Sure thing—"

"And kiss Park for me, okay?"

"Always."

"I'll talk to you later." He gave a quick wave and then the call disconnected.

She furrowed her brow in thought and glanced down at Parker. "What was that about?"

It would be nice if she could stay with Wes and Cassidy on base instead of getting a hotel. Wes and Tucker had been best buds since basic training. He and his wife had a baby girl a few months older than Parker. Cassidy had been pregnant with her the last time she'd seen them—the night Parker was conceived.

The baby boy in question kicked Jess's stomach, and she made a playful *oof* sound. "Are you kicking Mama? That's not nice. No. That's not nice." She buried her face in his stomach and snarled. He gasped in return and let out little gurgling noises. Her heart was so full she thought it might explode.

Parks might be a lot of work, but he was worth every second.

* * *

With an exhausted sigh, Jess let her head fall back, eyes closed, and stood outside Parker's door, waiting to see if he would cry. The muffled *shhhh* of his sound machine was the only thing that came through the door. Did she dare to hope tonight would be a good night? Slowly, she shuffled out to the living room, biding her time in case he decided he didn't *actually* want to sleep, but the silence from his bedroom continued.

The sight in the living room though, brought a smile to her face. All the toys were put away, the dinner dishes were washed and drying on a towel next to the sink. Soft jazz was playing on the sound system, and there, relaxing on the couch, was the man responsible for it all. "You are a godsend." She plopped down next to him and curled her legs underneath her while burrowing into his shoulder.

He clicked his phone closed and tossed it on the coffee

table as he wrapped his other arm around her, pulling her into his side and kissing the top of her head. "I thought you might appreciate a little help."

That's an understatement.

As turned on as she had been earlier, it was nothing compared to the fire burning in her now at the sight of a clean house. She weaved her fingers with his and kissed the inside of his elbow tenderly. He took a deep breath, and Jess could feel the play of his muscles flexing under her as she leaned into him. God, she wanted him so bad it was hard to think about anything else. Not giving herself time to overanalyze her actions, she twisted around and grabbed fistfuls of his shirt, pulling him to her so she could reward his thoughtfulness with a kiss.

Their lips collided with a combustible spark that quickly spread from her mouth down her spine to her nether regions and back up. She leaned back onto the couch, pulling him down with her as Jack angled his head to deepen the kiss. Her tongue met his in a seductive twist—the taste of him tangy and salty. He slipped a hand underneath the hem of her shirt and his hot fingertips left a trail of blazing skin in their wake.

With each touch, he was winding her up like an over-tuned guitar string, and any moment now, she would snap. She gave a needy moan and squirmed under him, urging him to stop toying with her. The fabric of his T-shirt slid like smooth silk under her hands as she roamed over his pecks, across his shoulders, and up his neck. Stopping there, she rippled her fingers against his nape, sending involuntarily shudders through him. She wasn't sure why, but feathering that spot had always made him more eager.

Tit for tat, Mr. Kinney.

Sweat was beading on her forehead as he cranked up her internal temperature yet again, pulling her against his hard length while sliding the other hand down her hip to her thigh in a sinfully slow move that ended with her leg hitched over his hip to press against her hot center.

She was drenched and she could tell by the way he held himself in check he was enjoying every second of this torturous process. Keen on revenge, she decided to take a tip out of his playbook and pressed her toes into the crease of his knee, sliding her foot seductively up his leg.

His dick twitched underneath his rough blue jeans, and he groaned. "God, you turn me on, woman."

She smiled against his hungry lips and pressed further into him. "Then stop being an ass and give me what I want," she growled back.

In a sultry Argentine tango, they rose from the couch and moved toward the bedroom, their lips not leaving each other for anything other than air.

Jack possessively cupped her ass, pulling her with him toward the bed.

"There are condoms in the nightstand drawer," she panted, the words spoken between urgent kisses. The anticipation of having each other was quickly outweighing the need for any sort of foreplay. He ripped her sweater over her head as she fumbled with his belt buckle.

Desperately trying to free her foot from her jeans, Jess hopped from one foot to the other until she eventually collapsed on the bed, laughing hysterically. Her hair stuck to her lip gloss and covered her eyes, momentarily blinding her, and the warm rumble of Jack's laugh amplified the pulsing ache between her thighs. Gently, he picked up her foot and tugged the garment free before laying kisses on the inside of her ankle, up her calf to the inside of her knee, and up her thigh. Her breath came out in ragged pants as she clawed for control of her baser instincts. All she wanted was to launch off the bed and ravish him.

He slid a finger under the edge of her panties and dipped inside her for one exquisite moment before withdrawing and tugging the dainty piece of lace from her hips. Instead of going back for seconds, he hovered over her for another kiss, and she obliged for a millisecond before pressing up and rolling him so she could be in charge for a spell.

She flipped her dark mane over one shoulder and bent down to lay a trail of kisses across his shoulder and down his neck. Air whistled through his teeth in a hiss of surprise as she tweaked his nipple with her teeth, but she continued to nip and lick her way across his midsection. The feel of Jack under her, warm, hard, and needy, created a haze that settled across her brain and halted all higher reasoning. It was only about what felt good now. Anything else was inconsequential.

Her heart pounded in her chest, begging to end this foreplay nonsense and satiate the boiling lava flowing through her veins, but she resisted, knowing the longer they waited, the more sublime the quenching of the fire would feel. She grated her hips against his erection, still imprisoned in his black cotton boxer briefs, aligning their bodies with sweet, sweet friction.

Jack growled and reached up to cup her breasts, his hands so hot they felt as though they might brand her as he worked his strong fingers against the tender flesh. She threw her head back and moaned as he massaged her swollen, achy…

Faster than her foggy brain could comprehend, the floodgates opened and a stream of breast milk gushed from her nipples, freezing them both in place for half a second: Jack in shock, Jess in mortification. She gazed down at him, green eyes wide, her mouth open in a small O as she took in the splatter of milk across his chest and face. He bit his lip, his body shaking until a boisterous laugh ripped out of him. Unable to help herself, she dissolved into laughter too, bending over his body from her position astride him and burying her head in his sparse chest hair.

Jack eventually pushed himself up into a sitting position with her legs wrapped around his back. They gazed at each other, their lips still twitching in amusement as she patted at the splatters of milk across his chest. Gently, he placed his hand over hers, stilling her embarrassed fidgeting, and with one questioning eyebrow arch, he bent and pressed his mouth to her breast, gently suckling.

She rested her elbows on his shoulders and clung to him, cupping the back of his head in benediction. "Goooooood-dddd," she moaned, burying her face in the thick hair atop his head. Her breasts had been so sore over the past few days as she attempted to dry up her supply that even an expression as small as the amount Jack was taking eased the ache considerably. He gave her nipple one final swirl with his tongue before releasing her.

Something bold and brazen filled the depths of his eyes as he lifted his head from her chest. He sensuously ran his hand from the curve of her hips to the slope of her shoulders, allowing his fingers to probe each nob of her spine as he gazed at her. "I love you."

She gazed down at him, tears prickling the backs of her eyes as her heart thrummed in her chest like the wings of a hummingbird.

"I've never loved anyone—gotten close a time or two, but you...you're so much more than I ever thought I needed." She opened her mouth, thinking she'd finally untangled her tongue, but he rushed ahead. "I know we weren't together for very long last year. And I know you probably think I'm crazy for telling you this now, when we aren't even dating, but I know what I want, Jess, and I'm tired of pretending we're just friends."

A beat of silence filled the room and her eyes widened with the adrenaline zinging through her veins. The best kind of helpless terror filled her as she stood on the springboard over the deep end, gazing into the fathomless pool of his gray eyes.

Finally, with a slight gasp, she jumped. "I love you too."

There it was, the roiling ball of tumultuous feelings she'd been trying to keep bottled up inside of her for the better part of a year. It isn't that Tucker wasn't a great man. He just wasn't Jack, and however insane people may claim she was, she was completely and utterly head over heels for him. Always had been and always would be.

She leaned across him to the nightstand and pulled the emergency box of condoms from the drawer. A box that she hadn't used since the last time they had slept together nearly a year ago. She could hardly believe how much her life had changed since then. She shuffled off his lap and slipped her fingers under the elastic waistband of his briefs tugging them free of his hips, letting him stand at full salute. A low hum of desperation and impatience rumbled deep in his throat and she tore the foil wrapper with her teeth, rolling the condom on in a gentle downward thrust that nearly brought him off the bed.

"God, you're killing me, Jess," he hissed.

She laughed. "I suppose we've tortured each other enough for one night. Come get me, cowboy. I'm ready for a ride."

Eighteen

Afterglow

Jess stretched like a cat in a warm patch of sun, enjoying the pocket of warmth under her covers. Last night had been the best night of sleep since the start of her third trimester. She yawned and did a self-assessment within her glowing golden bubble of bliss. She was sore in all the right places and so relaxed, her muscles felt jellied. She dropped her arm in the hollow next to her where Jack had laid most of the night, but the bed was cold now. Coming out of her contented daze with a start, she sat up.

Parker!

She tossed the covers aside and pulled her robe from the bedpost, wrapping it around herself as she yanked open the bedroom door in a rush to ensure her son was still breathing. She froze, clutching her robe around herself as she processed the scene.

Jack was lounging on the couch with Parker sound asleep

on his chest. Layla raised her head from its resting place on her paws and perked her ears with interest at Jess's harried appearance. The dog was enamored with Parker and was never more than twenty feet from him at any given time—even going so far as to sleep outside his door at night. So it came as no surprise that she was lying at the foot of the couch, keeping a weary eye on her little master's recumbent form.

"Good morning," Jack greeted. Male satisfaction stuck to him like Layla's fur on tights fresh from the dryer.

"Good morning," she replied, brow furrowed as she looked back to the bedroom and then to Parker and then down the hall. "I…what…"

Jack smiled. "You looked like an angel, sound asleep. I didn't have the heart to wake you. He started crying about six. So I got up and fixed him a bottle. Just one pouch, right?"

"Well, yeah. But I—"

Jack smiled and rolled his eyes. "It's fine. There's coffee in the pot if you want some."

"Do you make yourself at home in all women's homes, or just mine?" she asked as she shuffled over to the cabinet and pulled a mug down to pour herself some coffee.

"I'm sorry. I just thought—"

She spun around and leaned against the counter, smiling as she sipped the dark brew. "I'm just messing with you." She walked over to the couch and leaned over the back to take in her sleeping baby's sweet face. He was so relaxed with Jack. It was adorable to see them together. "Thank you," she murmured and leaned over to kiss the top of Jack's head.

"Anything for my girl."

"Oh, 'your girl,' is it? We have one great night and all of a sudden you're laying claim to me?" Her lips twitched, and his eyes danced.

"I think I did that last night…more than once."

Her twitching lips turned into a full-on grin as she remembered the tangled sheets, the sultry kisses, the hard planes of his body rubbing against hers…

She bit her bottom lip in delicious reverie and brought her coffee mug to her mouth to give it something to do.

"When do you have to go back to Chicago?" she asked as she gingerly sat on the couch next to him.

"I have to leave today. I want to get everything unpacked before I leave for Sebring. We've got one more test before the season opener and only two weeks until St. Pete."

She nodded. "Right. I forgot."

Jack snickered. "You forgot, or you had no clue to begin with?"

Jess rolled her eyes. "Okay, so I know nothing about IndyCar. Is that a deal breaker?"

"No! I just like to tease you. I can't believe you and Alaina have been friends your whole lives and her fascination never rubbed off on you."

"Yeah, well, a stubborn streak is something we have in common." She tucked her legs up next to her and leaned sideways to gaze at Parker, still snoozing peacefully.

"Do you want him?" Jack asked, watching her watch the baby with a content smile.

Jess snapped her gaze back to Jack, a delayed reaction to the fact that he was speaking to her. She sat up. "No. Actually…" She gazed longingly at her bedroom, thinking of the en suite bathroom. "Would you mind if I took a quick shower?"

He shook his head. "No. Go. I'll just lay back and close my

eyes for a few."

She leaned over and laid a tender kiss on his temple. The soft hair brushed her nose, and she inhaled his scent for a brief moment before coming to her senses and heading toward the bliss of a hot shower.

Sooner than she would have preferred, she left the steamy confines of the bathroom, revitalized. A long shower to deep condition her hair, shave her legs, and bask in the steady stream of hot water, combined with a solid eight hours of sleep, had her feeling like a new woman. She opened the door to the bedroom, pinching at the wet ends of her hair to draw the moisture out as she walked back into the living room. Parker was awake now, lying on his mat in the middle of the floor, doing tummy time with his favorite crinkle cloth book.

"So. I have a question," Jess asked as she continued to methodically dry her hair.

"I *may* have an answer," Jack replied as he popped up from his seat next to the baby.

"It may not be one you want to think about," she warned as she tossed the damp towel across the back of the armchair next to her. The soft click of Layla's claws preceded a high-pitched whine from the patio door as she begged to go outside, and Jess padded over to unlatch the door and let the collie into the fenced backyard. She turned back around toward Jack. "What's the plan now? I think we can both agree we want to have *some* sort of relationship. But what does that look like—with you in Chicago and me here?" She leaned forward and placed both hands flat on the round dining table. The kitschy laminate was bubbled in places and beginning to peel in others.

Jack sighed and hitched a hip on the arm of the sofa as he ran a hand through his messy, dark waves. "I don't know. I mean, yes, I live in Chicago, but during race season, I'll hardly be there. So I don't know that it factors in much. Maybe you could come to a few races?" His words were hopeful, but the tongue fumbling at the inside of his cheek said he knew that wasn't a viable solution.

They were both quiet for a bit, lost in their contemplations.

"What are you going to do about Tucker?" He took a deep breath and met her gaze, determined to brave the minefield ahead of him. "I heard you last night. You're planning on going to Texas." The words were a statement. Not a question. She wasn't sure what that meant.

"Yeah. I promised Tuck I wouldn't keep Parker from him. He can't come home, so I'm going to him." Jess shrugged, making it clear that the trip wasn't a big deal. "Does that bother you?"

Jack sighed, contemplating his next words carefully. "I mean…I get it. I just don't want him getting the wrong idea of what you going down there means."

She sighed too and walked over to wrap her arms around Jack's waist. "Trust me. Tucker knows where I stand. He's just excited to see Parker. He's missed him. I can see it in his eyes every time he calls."

Jack rested his cheek on top of her head and wrapped his arms around her, but didn't say anything.

"Don't be jealous," she murmured playfully, pulling back so she could cup his cheek.

The corner of his mouth quirked up. "It's not jealousy. I just…I want to be able to tell the world that I'm yours and you're mine, and it's not that simple."

She deflated a bit and stepped back. "I know Tuck won't be happy about us, but to be honest, I'm more worried about Alaina. Ever since her accident, she has days where she gets so mad…she eventually comes around, but with the wedding coming up, she's extra stressed. Maybe it's best if we don't say anything for now. Give it a few more weeks, and see how it goes."

"A few weeks?" he groaned. "That's so long!"

She swatted at him. "Shut up."

He chuckled and pulled her in. "You know I'd do anything for you. Right? Except let you go. I'm *never* doing that again." He leaned in for a slow kiss that made her tingle from her scalp to her toes.

She smiled against his lips and gave a low hum in her throat. "So we keep it quiet. Just enjoy each other when we can. If you're in Chicago, I *might* be able to use my girlfriend Anika as an excuse to come see you. If you're down here…I don't know, I'm sure you'll think of something."

"Have that much confidence in me, do you?" he asked with a smirk as he reached out and tickled her.

She giggled and squealed. "Stop! Stop, stop, stop…" She was laughing so hard she nearly peed her pants, but it felt good to laugh. And she knew if she let him, Jack would find ways to make her laugh for the rest of her life.

Nineteen

Good Ol' Days

The bright March sun beat down on the track, creating a mirage effect down pit lane. The roar of high-speed engines with upward of seven hundred horsepower echoed across the testing facility of Sebring International Raceway and vibrated through Jack's blood like an extra strength shot of 5-hour Energy. Each time a car came in, the engineers would hook up the massive cables to download data from the car's computer and analyze it before making minor adjustments to the front wing, rear shocks, camber shims, et cetera, and sending the driver back out.

Jack's car was in the final stages of the initial setup, so he perched on the pit wall, face upturned to the sun, soaking up the rays. On a race weekend, most drivers had so many press and sponsor engagements, they rarely had time to chill. Testing events were undoubtedly the more favorable option with a more leisurely vibe, provided the ride you were testing was yours for the season, and you weren't still trying to convince a team you deserved the seat.

Someone's shadow lingered in front of him, cutting off his sun, and he opened his eyes to glare at the intruder. Grayson smirked down at his best friend. "Working hard or hardly working?"

"Hardly working at the moment. I'll make up for it later though. Don't you worry." Jack said with a smile before scooching over to make room for Grayson on the wall. "What's up?"

"Nothing much. The guys are finishing up, so I figured I'd walk down here and see your new digs." Grayson glanced around the stall, nodding in approval. Lakeshore Autosport was a smaller team than either of them was used to. Compared to Grayson's new home at Apex Racing, a multi-million dollar, four-car team, where everything was top of the line from the shock package to the toilet paper, Jack's new team was mediocre at best. But he was making the best of it, and they both knew that. "I haven't talked to you much lately. How's the move going?"

Jack waited to respond until a pack of cars passed by on the track. He smirked at his best friend, knowing that's not what he really wanted to ask, but he was too polite to come right out with it. Fine. If Gray was going to be like that, he would play along. "It's good. I got the last of my boxes unpacked yesterday and had one night in a clean apartment before flying down here."

Grayson nodded. "I get it. Luckily, Alaina's better about the boxes than I am. She had all my crap unpacked within a couple of days."

Jack snorted. That was Alaina alright—a control freak by

his standards—but Grayson loved her, and if he was happy, Jack was happy for him.

"Jack!" his chief engineer shouted to get his attention. "Ten minutes, man."

Jack nodded and pulled his helmet bag over the wall to get his balaclava and gloves out. Grayson took that as his cue and rose from the wall before moving his Raybans to rest on top of his head. "Where are you guys staying tonight?"

"I don't know. I think the Holiday Inn in town." He dove into his balaclava and tugged it back and forth until he got the right fit. He gazed at his buddy with an expectant raise of the eyebrow. More cars whizzed past on the track and a few kicked off onto pit lane with a low rumble as they approached their pit box and killed the engines.

"You wanna grab a burger tonight? Hang out?" Grayson shuffled his feet. If he'd had pockets, he'd have shoved his hands in them by the looks of it.

Jack smiled and shook his head, trying not to roll his eyes. "Sure, Gray. Just shoot me a pin. I'll meet you there at six." He flicked the chin strap out of the dome of the helmet and slid into its snug embrace, tilting and rocking his head to settle it on before fastening his chin strap. Obviously, Grayson had no idea how he was going to approach asking Jack about Jess. If Jack had to guess, it wasn't even Gray's idea. Guys didn't talk about that kind of crap. He smelled Alaina's influence, and it irritated him.

All he had to say was if she had the nerve to say something snarky to Jess in his presence, he wouldn't hesitate to tell her where she could shove her unsolicited opinion.

But none of that mattered now. He had to clear his mind and focus on the feeling of the car around him, the grip of the wheel under his fingertips, and the pedals under his feet as the miles fell away. Everything else could wait.

* * *

Loud music and the sound of conversation poured out of the main door of Gator Tap House with each open and close of the creaky hinges. The heady smell of fried seafood and good liquor wafted on the chilly breeze as he walked toward the main entrance, tossing his rental car key repeatedly into the air. His stomach rumbled angrily at not having been fed since breakfast, and he had never looked forward to a burger and fries so much in his life. Or maybe he'd get something fresh, like shrimp or grilled snapper. *Definitely* clam chowder. Saliva flooded his mouth at the thought of the rich, creamy elixir hitting his tongue.

He pulled open the door and scanned the crowd for his friend. He wasn't late, but he was willing to bet, Grayson had been here for at least ten minutes. Early is on time and on time is late—or so Grandpa Kinney used to say. He caught sight of Grayson at a corner table near the window overlooking the intracoastal waterway and made his way toward him, sidestepping waitresses with trays full of food and oblivious patrons with their chairs in the middle of the narrow path between tables. Finally, having run the gauntlet without a scratch, he slid into the booth across from his friend.

Gray looked up from his phone and smiled before shoving it into his pocket. Before either of them had a chance to speak, a waitress carrying a tray of food came, took Jack's drink order, and hurried away to deliver her goods to the next table. "How was your test?" Grayson asked as he took a sip of his Pepsi.

"We've got a lot of kinks to iron out, but I think this was a solid run." Jack shifted and leaned back against the booth, slinging his hand along the top. "But tell me about Apex. How's it going?"

Grayson's eyes sparkled with barely suppressed excitement. "I'm a tiny fish in a freaking ocean over there, but it's amazing, man. Anything I could possibly want or need…" he trailed off and looked down at his hands.

"Would you quit that?" Jack kicked his friend under the table. "You're allowed to be excited. It's freaking *Apex*."

Gray's big brown eyes darted up to Jack's and his lips twitched. "I know, and I am. Today was awesome. I just…I missed sharing a wall with you." He shrugged and sat back against the booth, trying to act relaxed and failing miserably. LHR had been Grayson's first ride in IndyCar. They had snapped him up fresh out of the feeder series and didn't let him go until they closed their doors last season. Jack had been the lead driver when Grayson joined the team, but it hadn't taken Gray long to outpace him at every turn. As a competitor, it sucked ass to watch some young hotshot come in and show you up, but for the first time in his life, Jack also had the opportunity to feel like a big brother. Watching Grayson now was like watching a little bird leave the nest, and he wanted nothing but the best for him, even if the day was fast approaching when he would no longer share the track with him.

Jack smiled. "There you go, making me all misty-eyed." Jack sniffled and wiped away a few imaginary tears.

Grayson rolled his eyes at his friend's response, but didn't speak.

"I've been in this league ten years, and I've seen a lot of talent come and go. I have to tell you. I think you may be one of the best, Gray, and"—he paused to thank the waitress as she placed his sweet tea on the table and darted off again—"you deserve every ounce of success you get. You've earned it. Don't let anyone tell you otherwise, and don't let anyone make you feel like you shouldn't enjoy it. I don't have to tell you how brutal this industry can be."

"No. You don't." Grayson twirled his glass in the puddle of condensation beneath it and sighed. "I've heard a couple of guys are thinking about going to IMSA after this season. That's a good gig over there."

"Are you tolling the bell for me before the season even starts?" Jack asked in mock horror.

"No!" Grayson shouted louder than he had intended. He immediately lowered his voice and leaned forward, placing his elbows on the tacky wooden surface. "I just meant it might be a good deal. Longer season. Decent money. And it's racing."

"This contract has an option for another year that they can exercise, but to be honest, Gray…I don't know. I might be done." Jack stared at the lemon wedge bobbing lazily in his drink and poked at it with his straw. There was silence from the other end of the table, and he didn't have the heart to look up and see whatever look Grayson was giving him.

"What?" Grayson finally asked, shock co-mingling with incredulity. "Don't be stupid. You're only thirty. A lot of drivers race well into their forties."

"Yeah, but those are the Scott Dixons and Helio Castroneveses of the world. The guys who are still winning 500s and championships in their forties. Gray, I haven't won a race in three seasons."

"Stop. I don't want to—"

"I know you don't want to hear it, but it doesn't make it any less true. It's okay. I'm good with it." Jack smiled and gave his friend another, more playful, kick under the table.

"So, what? If Lakeshore picks up your option, you'll race another year, and if they don't, you just go quietly into the night?"

Jack took a long pull on his tea to quiet his grumbling stomach, wondering where the hell the waitress was. "Ideally, I'd like to get a broadcasting gig. We'll see where the wind blows me." He shrugged and shifted gears. "But enough about me. What about you? How's the fee-awn-say?"

The smile that filled Grayson's face could only be described as dreamy, and Jack fought the urge to gag at his friend's premarital bliss. "She's good. Trying to put this wedding together in four months is stressing her out. So, her headaches have been worse than usual. But I think she's managing."

"Good," Jack commented to keep the conversation rolling. He raised his hand to try and get their waitress's attention, but she was consumed with putting another table's order into the computer.

Can't a guy get some damn food around here?

"Speaking of Alaina..."

Oh God...don't tell me we're doing this before I get to order. Jack looked up with a raised brow.

"She said you paid a little visit to the shop the other day." *Shit.*

"Yeah. So what?" Every ounce of him wanted to tell his

friend that he was happier than he'd ever been, that he would give up every ounce of success he would ever have for the rest of his career and lay it at the feet of Jessica Morales, but it just wasn't the time. Jess didn't want to throw gasoline on the Tucker fire, and he had to respect her wishes.

"I just found it curious—seeing as you aren't dating the co-owner anymore." Grayson leaned back from the table and crossed his arms, waiting for Jack to confirm or deny the insinuation.

"I don't know what you expect me to say." Jack shook his head and finally caught the waitress's attention.

Thank God.

"What can I get you, gentlemen?" she asked with a beaming grin. Her southern accent had a soft twang that was warm and inviting, and Jack smiled back as he ordered.

"I'll take a bowl of clam chowder, the fried clam strips, grilled mahi on a bed of wild rice, and a baked potato with butter and sour cream. Also, can I please get another glass of sweet tea?"

"Sure thing, honey," she replied as she took his menu and tucked it under her arm.

Grayson ordered his burger and fries without incident and once she walked away, zeroed back in on the issue at hand. "Well…something. I expect you to say *something*."

"She's my friend, Gray! She's going through the damned wringer. I'm not allowed to check in on her? I was in town to get the rest of my stuff out of storage, and I wanted to make sure she was okay. I didn't realize that was a crime."

Grayson's dark, coffee-colored eyes pierced straight into his soul, and Jack took another long pull on his tea to hide from his gaze for a few seconds. "You are so full of shit."

Grayson's voice was low, but amused.

"Anything I tell you now is going straight back to Alaina. Don't think I don't know that." He pointed an accusatory finger at his friend. "If I say nothing, you have plausible deniability."

Grayson shook his head. "This is a terrible idea. You realize that."

"I have no idea what you're talking about."

Grayson probed his back teeth with his tongue, seeming to contemplate whether he, or rather *Alaina*, needed all the salacious details. Apparently satisfied the answer was no, he sighed, took a swig of his soda, and let it go.

Jack had to admit, this battle wasn't the whole war, but winning it would definitely earn him brownie points.

Twenty

Texas Hold'em

There was absolutely nothing worse than being stuck on an airplane with a screaming baby. Studies could be done, conclusions could be drawn, but there would be no changing Jess's mind. It was The. Worst. The flight from Chicago to Dallas-Fort Worth had been two hours and forty minutes of pure, unadulterated hell—to the point where, if Parker had the grace to start screaming before the plane had taken off, Jess would have asked the flight crew to open the door so she could get off. As it was, he had decided to wake up on ascent and screech the rest of the flight. She did her best: pacifier, gas drops, bottle, crinkle books, his favorite rattle. Nothing. Worked.

Judging by the stares she got, the entire plane full of passengers would have cheerfully thrown him out the window if that was the only way to get him to shut up. The situation was enough to make her burst into tears, and by the time they arrived in Texas, they were both exhausted. Parker had cried himself out and was sleeping soundly in his carrier as Jess made her way out of the airport, and she found it hard not to be bitter.

Yeah, enjoy your nap. Now that we're not on a plane with a hundred other people, you little shit.

Thank God Tucker was able to pick them up, because if she'd had to negotiate a rental car counter, she probably would have curled into a ball and given up.

But it wasn't Tucker's Silverado that was waiting for them at the pickup curb. Instead, she caught sight of Cassidy's fiery head of red hair bobbing through the sea of people. She smiled and waved when she caught sight of Jess. "Sorry for the last-minute swap," she said as Jess approached with her luggage cart full of crap. "Tuck got caught up. He said he'll meet us at the house."

Jess felt more tears prick at her eyes. Cassidy's act of kindness was nearly enough to undo her after the afternoon she'd had. "Thanks for not leaving us stranded, Cassidy. I really appreciate it."

"Oh, no problem. Here, let me take that. We have the same car seat base. You can just click him in, and I'll put this one in the back. Oh, and call me Cassie."

Jess watched Cassidy—Cassie—disappear around to the back hatch of her Highlander and then pulled the handle on the rear passenger door. She placed Parker's car seat in the base with a satisfying click and checked his buckles before quietly closing the door and getting into the front seat. She sighed and closed her eyes as she leaned her head against the headrest. When her driver hopped in beside her, she pried open her eyelids and looked over at her.

Cassie was a couple of years younger than Jess, but recognized an exhausted kindred spirit when she saw one. "You want to stop and get coffee on the way? Or a bottle of tequila?"

Jess let out a weary laugh. "Both?"

Cassie giggled quietly and checked her blind spot before pulling away from the curb. "Long flight?"

"It was awful," Jess moaned. "I don't know whether Park's ears needed to pop or what, but he screamed the whole flight."

"Oh man, I'm sorry."

Jess sighed and shrugged. "Thanks. I think this will be the last time we travel by plane for a while."

"I feel that." Her companion sympathized.

Traffic was starting to get heavier as they pulled onto the interstate and headed north. It was a long drive to Sheppard Air Force Base, and Jess desperately hoped Cassie was serious about the offer to stop and get coffee. If she wasn't, Jess would be asleep before they could make it halfway there. The last thing she wanted was to see Tucker again with the fog of exhaustion clouding her brain.

Cassie, God bless her, understood that perfectly, and thirty minutes later, they were on their way to the base, Starbucks in hand, as the sun began to sink toward the horizon.

Feeling the return of her higher reasoning and critical thought, Jess sighed. "I feel weird about asking, but…"

Cassie turned to Jess, appraising her. "You want to know how he's been?"

Jess ran a hand through her hair and shifted in her seat. "Is that wrong? I just hate not knowing. I felt terrible for how things ended, and it's not exactly like I can ask him."

"Why not?" Cassie asked as she merged into the left lane to

pass a semi. "I mean, isn't it just easier to go to the source?"

Jess gave a hard laugh. "Normally, I would say yes, but Tuck was so angry with me… I feel like asking would just rub salt in the wound."

Cassie snorted. "Man, I'm so glad I'm married. Wes and I don't even bother anymore. We just come out with it. Dancing around each other's emotions is exhausting—especially in a military marriage. He's hardly home as it is. The last thing I feel like doing is playing the perfect, 'How was your day, dear?' housewife after dealing with Piper's screaming all day."

Jess laughed in acknowledgment of that truth and stared out the windshield in contemplation, wondering if that's how her life would have turned out had she stuck with Tuck.

"In answer to your question, though, he's fine. He spends a lot of time at our house, and Wes has been a good sounding board for him. He misses both of you, and I think his pride's wounded a little bit, but we're not about to let him wallow. Don't you worry," she said with a wink.

Jess smiled in return and felt her shoulders sag with relief. It was good to hear from someone who had actually spent time with Tucker over the past few weeks. "Thanks. Even if we're not together anymore, he's still one of my oldest friends. I don't want to see him hurting. You know?"

"I know. And he knows that too."

Jess closed her eyes and rested her head on the seat's headrest. "I'm just so tired."

Cassie turned to Jess. "How about we have a girl's day tomorrow? Let the boys have the kids, and we can go get mani-pedis?"

Jess sat up straighter. "Oh my god, that sounds amazing.

You realize how long it's been since I've had a pedicure?"

"Probably at least as long as it's been for me," Cassie said with a tinge of irony in her voice. "It's settled then. I'll make us an appointment at the salon just off base."

* * *

Jess had to admit, there were certainly perks to living in Texas. Back home it was in the upper-thirties with freezing rain, but from the back porch of Cassie and Wes's three-bedroom, it was warm enough to roast marshmallows over a gas-lit fire pit and stargaze.

She tilted her head up, not quite able to see the Milky Way, but able to make out the occasional star in the sky above. It had been a great day. She and Cassie had spent a blissful Saturday at the salon getting pedicures, having their nails done, and venting about the frustrations of motherhood while the guys took care of the babies. Cassie, like her, did most of the child rearing on her own, and it had felt nice to talk to somebody who understood what she was going through. Granted, Cassie had Wes to get up with Piper in the middle of the night, and sometimes help with bath time, but he often had training exercises and worked long hours. So, it wasn't uncommon for her to be on her own.

Cassie and Wes were absolutely adorable. Even though they'd known each other for years, they still looked at each other like the same starstruck teenagers they were when they met. Wes gently reached across and wiped a smear of sticky melted marshmallow from Cassie's lip and she giggled, rocking back to avoid his kiss and smear marshmallow across his cheek in playful rebellion. Jess smiled to herself, warmed by their affection, but feeling a deep yearning for Jack at the same time. She sighed and placed her roasting stick on the edge of the firepit, excusing herself quietly to give them some privacy.

She pulled the sliding glass door to the patio closed behind her and looked up at the staircase, wondering if Tucker needed help putting Parker to bed. He had disappeared up the stairs nearly an hour ago, and she hadn't seen him since. She was twenty-four hours into her visit and had barely spoken with Tucker, past the usual pleasantries. That had been by design, though. The purpose of this trip was to give Tuck time with his son, and if her conscience also benefited from avoiding her ex…well, that was just a bonus.

The clinking of bottles from the kitchen alerted her to Tucker's presence, and she headed in that direction, figuring it wouldn't do to avoid him the *whole* trip. Tuck was twisting the top off a bottle of hard cider when she found him, and he took several hardy gulps to fortify himself, oblivious to her presence.

"That bad, was it?"

Tucker started and sucked cider down the wrong pipe. Coughing and sputtering violently to dislodge the stray liquid, he sat the bottle on the counter and wiped at the spillage down his chin. Finally, wheezing, but past the worst of it, he glared at Jess.

She buried her teeth in her bottom lip, trying for all she was worth not to burst into uncontrollable laughter. "I'm sorry. I didn't mean to startle you. I was just coming to see if you needed help with Parker and heard you in the kitchen."

"I think anybody would need a drink after wrestling a crocodile." Tucker teased and picked his drink back up to take another swig. "That kid has major FOMO. You think he's sound asleep and the second you put him down, he's wide awake again."

Jess smiled and crossed her arms against her chest. Leaning with one hip against the kitchen counter, she gave Tuck an amused look. "Oh, I know. Trust me."

"I suppose I should apologize or something. If that's what you deal with every night…that sucks."

That got a real laugh out of her, and when she managed to smother her chortling to a light giggle, she replied. "Apology accepted." Her mirth had set her slightly more at ease, and she felt a comforting sense of normalcy seep between them. He was still Tucker, and if he could pretend everything was fine, so could she. "I haven't talked to you much. How are you?"

"I'm alright." His voice was rough, almost husky, as he brought his eyes up to meet hers. He wasn't a coward, and he wasn't a lovesick puppy, but the look of hurt deep in those mercurial irises told the full story.

"Did you finally get your leave approved for the wedding?"

He nodded, mirroring her pose of nonchalance with a hip against the opposite counter, arms crossed, but keeping ahold of his drink. "I did. I only got a couple of days, but that's enough. If I have to be around Alaina while she goes full-on bridezilla, it might not be pretty. Probably best if I fly in for the wedding and fly back home."

Jess gave him a sly smile. "Oh, come on, you'd be the chillest person in the room. Not even your sister ruffles your feathers. That's why you get along so well."

Tucker rolled his eyes. "Please. She's my sister. I may not let it show all the time, but she definitely gets on my nerves, and with everything else going on… I just don't need anything to set me off."

Her stomach twisted into a fist-sized knot, and she took a deep breath to steady the wave of guilt threatening to crash down on her. He shifted his weight and took another silent pull on his cider as he glanced out the window at Cassie and Wes, cuddling next to the fire. Clearly, he had something on his mind. She sighed and reached across the narrow galley kitchen to prod him with her flip-flop-clad foot. "Tuck. Tell me."

Even if I don't really want to know.

"I'm just ready to come home." He swallowed hard and tossed back another gulp of alcohol, nearly draining it in his haste to hide the tears glistening in his eyes.

"It's been harder than you thought it would be." She surmised as she hopped up on the counter to face him full-on and let him talk. She could do that—give him a shoulder to lean on. She owed him that much.

"So much harder," he muttered, giving in and leaning against the counter behind him.

"I'm sorry. Is there anything I can do?" she asked, swinging her legs idly in front of her.

He straightened, sniffing. The moment of vulnerability passed. "Nah. It's just going to take some time, I think. What about you? Any news on the bio dad front?" He pushed away from the counter and took two strides toward the trashcan, threw the bottle in, and went back to the refrigerator for seconds.

"My PI's still looking. I'm sure if he finds anything, I'll be the first to know. Kind of hard not to let the anticipation eat at me, though. God, I don't know whether to be excited or terrified." She ran an anxious hand through her hair and gave him a smile. "All my life, I thought my father wanted nothing to do with me. I'm not sure why learning I was right would be devastating now. I just have this nagging feeling it's going to sting twice as much this time."

"Because you've had the taste of hope in your mouth, and disappointment is more bitter than a green raspberry." He was trying hard, but he couldn't quite keep the bitterness out of his voice. Then he sighed and prodded her back with his own foot. "Try not to worry about it. Any decent man would want to know his child. If he doesn't want to know you, he's not good enough for you. Period."

Her eyes stung with unshed tears, and she nodded, swiping at the moisture blurring her vision before it could dribble down her cheeks. "Thank you."

He sighed and stepped across the space between them. "Come here," he murmured, and pulled her into his arms, all the hurt and anger momentarily forgotten.

Relief flooded through her at his embrace. It felt so nice to have Tucker's arms wrapped around her. She'd worried when she broke up with him he'd be unable to get past the betrayal, and she'd missed her friend. Because he *was* her friend, whether he wanted to acknowledge it or not. Yes, having a child together complicated things, but was there anything in life worth having that *wasn't* complicated?

She sniffled and pulled back from him as she wiped at the tear tracks on her cheeks. A hug had been exactly what she needed. Without warning, he leaned in, closing the gap between them once more, and pressed his lips to hers. She stood in stunned silence, lips unresponsive, shock making her brain a complete blank. Finally, her synapses fired, and she put her hand to his chest, pushing him away. "Tuck...I—"

His cheeks flushed bright pink, and he skittered backward until he hit the counter behind him. "I'm sorry. I shouldn't have done that."

She put a hand to her lips for a brief second, carefully avoiding any gesture or words that might set him off. She didn't want to backtrack on the progress they'd made, but she also wanted him to know where she stood. "I really do want us to be friends."

He was silent, but his cloudy green eyes were bursting with a mix of emotions: frustration, hurt, jealousy.

Does he know? Does he sense that I'm with somebody else?

She shook off that thought. Whether Tucker was drawing his own conclusions about her relationship status was irrelevant, and she'd be damned if he made her feel guilty about things she hadn't even said out loud.

Finally, he sighed, prying his eyes from hers and kicking at a rip in the linoleum on the floor. "I know. I want that too. It's just...going to take some time. I'm sorry."

She took two steps forward, not close enough to be intimate, but close enough to squeeze his forearm and offer comfort. "Let's go enjoy the fire."

He nodded, not meeting her eye for a long moment. Then, suddenly, he rolled his shoulders back, took a deep breath and marched toward the patio door as if nothing had happened.

Jess stared after him, stunned. He'd fooled her with his mask—the same mask she'd just watched him put back in place—and she felt like a complete idiot.

The Lies We Tell Ourselves

"What are you thinking?" Jack asked, his chest vibrating under her cheek. The leather of the couch creaked as he shifted his weight to hug her closer, and her whole body sighed.

"Nothing," she murmured, burrowing further into his chest. The couch was barely wide enough to accommodate one person, let alone two, but they were making do. As long as they were together, that was all that mattered. Besides, it wasn't as though they *wanted* personal space, and with Parker currently encamped in the only bedroom, their options were limited.

"Liar," he murmured back sleepily as he nuzzled the top of her head.

She'd actually been vividly recalling the look of astonishment and skepticism on Alaina's face when she'd told her she was flying to Dallas from Chicago and not Indianapolis.

Despite the spiel she'd given her friend about cheaper flights and seeing the girls again, it had been clear that Alaina smelled a rat, and the guilt was beginning to sour Jess's stomach. All she wanted was to be honest with the people she cared about, and instead, she was telling more lies.

"I was just wondering how much it would cost to break your lease and get a bigger place," she said with a quiet laugh. The feel of his coarse chest hair, springy under her cheek tickled her senses, and she wanted to bury her face in it.

"Hey now, don't diss my bachelor pad. I didn't sign the lease agreement thinking I'd be entertaining hoards of women on my weekends off. Besides, you know you like having to squeeze together on this couch. You can't keep your hands off me."

"I didn't say I don't like the couch." Her voice was husky as she shifted onto her stomach, half draped over him as she stared into his gorgeous eyes. They were the color of damp granite, dark and inviting, and she could get lost in them.

"New apartment. Same couch. Got it." He pulled her fully on top of him then and craned his neck to cover her mouth with his, letting his tongue flow lazily across hers in an intoxicating combination of his natural tang and the savory spices of the Chicago-style pizza they'd had for dinner.

Jess moaned against his lips, inhaling his scent like she was suffocating and he was the only air in the room. "I could stay here forever," she whispered, letting her forehead fall forward against his lips.

He kissed her there and tightened his arms around her. "Me too."

"Do you think it's wrong to lie to somebody if you're doing it to protect them?" Jess asked quietly, eyes closed, enjoying the feel of him under her in a dreamlike sort of way. Sometimes she had trouble believing she was really here with Jack. She'd spent so many nights trying to push thoughts of him aside and focus on the family she and Tucker were trying to create. But now that she didn't have to do that anymore, it was as though the anchor line tied around her heart had snapped, and she had floated back to the surface, able to breathe again.

"That depends." Jack shifted and she could feel his gaze hitting her like a million tiny pin pricks on her scalp. "Who are you lying to? And what are you trying to protect them from?"

She sighed and opened her eyes. They wouldn't be able to have this conversation without looking at each other. She shifted and scooched so she was perched on the edge of the couch, looking down at him. "Tucker."

Jack didn't say anything for a long moment. He just reached out to grab her hand, squeezing it in sympathy.

"I'm sorry. I shouldn't be bringing him up to you." She looked away and jolted up from the couch, gathering her hair in a ponytail for lack of anything else to do.

Jack sighed and swung his legs over the side of the couch to sit up. "Jess, stop. Come here."

She yanked on her ponytail to tighten it and turned to face him, heart pounding like a jackhammer. Slowly, as if approaching a ticking time bomb, she stepped back over to him and took his proffered hand. Her teeth were embedded in her lower lip, and if she bit down any harder, she'd likely draw blood.

"Come here," he murmured again, pulling her down onto his lap so he could tuck a stray piece of hair behind her ear.

"I don't care if you want to talk about Tucker or freakin'… quantum physics. Don't ever feel like you can't talk to me. Okay? Never." His eyes were smoldering with earnest energy, and she leaned in to kiss him tenderly at the corner of his mouth.

"Well, I don't know how much of a conversation I can have about quantum physics, but if that's a turn-on for you, I could try…" He chuckled and she giggled back, leaning in to kiss him just under the jaw. "You really don't mind?" She pulled back to look him in the eye, wanting to gauge whether he meant it, or whether he was only trying to be the bigger man.

He gazed up at her, his thick, dark lashes emphasizing the tenderness in his eyes. "I really don't mind."

She sighed and looked around the apartment. "Do you have any wine around here?"

With a brilliant smile, he pulled himself off the couch and walked to the kitchen, where he pulled a chilled bottle of pinot grigio out of the refrigerator. He poured her a glass and slid it across the island to her without comment, before putting the bottle back in the refrigerator. Eyes sparkling, he watched her sip at the wine until she was ready to finish her earlier thought.

"I guess I didn't actually *lie* to him. I don't know. I'm just…feeling guilty, I guess." Jess sighed and took another swig.

Jack stooped to place his forearms on the counter and leaned forward. "Guilty? Why? You didn't do anything wrong."

She didn't respond, just picked at an imperfection in the countertop while she stalled for time and tried to make sense of her own emotions. Was it not normal, that intense need to please, the overwhelming sense of failure she felt when she couldn't make everyone happy? She pressed her palms hard into the counter to stop their shaking and forced herself to meet his eye. "I hate hurting people. I would rather put a sewing needle through my eyeball than hurt Tucker." She put her hands to her face and rubbed her gritty, bloodshot eyes. "This blows."

"You can't lie to people to mask your own happiness," he said with a bucketload of irony in his tone. "But I'm betting you already know that, or you wouldn't have asked." Despite her best efforts, he'd noticed the fine tremors running through her and was staring at her with a mixture of concern and sympathy. "Jess." He pushed himself back from the counter and came around the island to pull her in his arms while she shook. "Shhhh."

She didn't know what had caused it, but for some reason, the dam was breached and she couldn't hold back the flood anymore. "Hey, it's okay," he whispered as he stroked her hair and clung to her while she fought for breath against the restricting pain in her chest.

Panic attack, her brain thought muzzily as she fought to suppress the voice in her head screaming at her to run and hide under the bed like she had when she was a kid.

Finally, when the shudders eased, and she stood, limp against him, exhausted in every muscle, he kissed the top of her head and loosened his grip. "You're running yourself ragged trying to accomplish something that's impossible, Sassy. Trust me."

She sniffled and stepped out of his embrace, feeling behind her for a barstool. The adrenaline she'd been running on was fading fast, and if she didn't sit soon, she'd be on her ass.

"What are you saying?" Her brain was still recovering from whatever the hell had just happened, and she couldn't quite process his train of thought.

"You want to keep Tucker's heart from being broken. You want to take the stress off Alaina's plate. You don't want to be honest with me about what you're really going through because you think I'm not man enough to handle it. But we're all adults. We can look after ourselves." He sighed and leaned against the island, arms crossed as he stared at her. "I know you've never spent a day in your life thinking your wellbeing was important enough to not play second fiddle. But damn it, I'm not letting you do that anymore."

"I don't need anyone telling me what I do or don't need," she growled, fire coming back into her at the idea that she'd simply traded one know-it-all for another.

"No, you don't," he agreed, shocking her into confused silence. "But I'm going to tell you what *I* need. Okay?" He studied her for a second, searching for any sign she was going to interrupt him again before he continued. "I'm in this for the long haul, and if you and I are going to have a chance in hell of making this work, I need you to start making your own wellbeing a priority. Because I know you. And I know you will give and give to everyone who asks, and before you know it, you have nothing left for yourself, and then where does that leave *us*?"

She gazed at the floor, feeling that voice rear its ugly head, the one saying she wasn't made for enduring relationships, that she was too broken to be a committed, loving partner.

Jack pushed off the island and stepped over to her, drawing her face up to meet his eye with one finger under her chin. "I will stand like a rock for you, Jess. I swear I will. But one day, I'm going to need you to be a rock for me too. Does that make sense?"

"I think so," she whispered as she gazed up at him. Her lip wobbled, and she bit down on it hard to keep from sobbing. "I-I've spent my wh-whole life fighting against the p-people who kept telling me, I w-wasn't good enough—that I w-wouldn't amount to anything. I just w-wanted to be g-good enough." Then, she couldn't hold it back anymore and cried.

Jack hugged her to him again, squeezing her so tightly she thought her ribs might crack. It still wasn't tight enough. "You are more than enough for me, Jess. You're everything."

It had always seemed cheesy to Jess, hearing guys pour their hearts out in rom-coms and TV dramas, but that was probably because she'd never been the recipient of those grand romantic gestures. Jack's words didn't undo all the bad things she'd ever been through. It wasn't a magic Band-Aid that healed all the abuse she'd endured, but it did go that extra mile to make her feel worthy of a good life, and she supposed that had been his goal, really—to make her understand how loved she was.

He wanted what was best for her, and her happiness and wellbeing meant more to him than his own ego.

God, she loved him so much it hurt. But it hurt so good.

Twenty-Two

Painful Revelations

By typical investigation standards, it hadn't taken Noah long to find Julian. That didn't mean it had been a walk in the park, either. Jessica had been unable to give him much besides where her dad went to high school, the year he graduated, and a vague approximation of his college plans, but there had been three Julians in María Morales's graduating class. One of them had died in a motorcycle accident just before graduation. So, he could be ruled out. That left two to dig into.

A few days of digging revealed that Julian number two had gone to Indiana University and graduated with a degree in medicine. He now had a family practice in southern Indiana where, as far as Noah could tell from public records, he lived happily with his wife and three kids. The guy hadn't attended an Ivy League, but he had made something of himself. He'd tabled that one for further inspection if every other lead was a dead end.

Julian number three had a unique last name: Van Zuiden, but all a quick google search turned up was a link to the biography for a California state senator, and Noah quickly exited out of the search window. Jess's dad would be in his early forties. He didn't know about California, but on a federal level, the average senator was well into their sixties, making it unlikely that *his* Julian Van Zuiden and *Senator* Julian Van Zuiden were the same man.

Besides, if her mother's life choices were any indication of her tastes in men, he certainly wouldn't be the type to run for public office, let alone win. A quick call to a friend at DPD indicated there were no outstanding arrest warrants or charges filed for a Julian Van Zuiden. So, that had been a dead end too.

María had been confident the man had at least *attended* an Ivy League. That gave Noah a good place to start, but with nearly one hundred and fifty thousand students in any given year, searching for one lone student across eight universities was no simple task.

He knew for a fact a prosecutor he'd worked with during his days at Denver PD graduated from Columbia. A quick call to catch up got him indirect access to their Alumni Directory, but no dice. Not even a Van Zuiden, let alone a Julian Van Zuiden, but he had seven schools left—hardly a dead end.

After turning over some more stones and poking around with a very long stick, he realized he also knew the associate director of donor services at Stanford. A week and a significant bar tab later, he found himself looking at the Stanford University Alumni Association registry portal.

Okay, so inviting a woman out for drinks in exchange

for her registry login *could be* considered underhanded, but he wasn't above flirting to get information out of someone. Investigative success was the ultimate high. After being shot at in dark alleys, taping off crime scenes to gruesome murders, and subduing more strung-out drug addicts than he cared to recall, he could play the private investigator role for the rest of his life and never tire of it. If he ever needed backup, local law enforcement was always helpful, but he wasn't a front-line responder—not anymore.

It had only taken a brief search of the alumni registry to find a match. *The* match.

The search result had nearly caused Noah to choke on the coffee he was sipping: Julian Van Zuiden, *summa cum laude*, Class of 2001. Bachelor of Arts in Political Science. He clicked again, this time on the man's LinkedIn profile link.

"Holy shit," he muttered under his breath. There was no way this was the same Julian Van Zuiden who had grown up in a town of three thousand people and knocked up his high school girlfriend. But when his LinkedIn profile picture loaded, there was no denying the familiar jade-colored eyes looking back at him. "Fuck..." he whispered.

*Senator Van Zuiden graduated summa cum laude
from Stanford University with a Bachelor of Arts
in Political Science before pursuing his Master's
Degree in Government at Johns Hopkins University.
Prior to his appointment to the California State Senate,
the senator served as a professor of Political Science
at the University of California-Berkeley.*

A politician? Seriously?

If one thing made his job infinitely more difficult, it was the red tape of bureaucratic bullshit.

So, it was with that taser to the balls that Noah found himself sitting in his car outside the California State House a week later getting up the nerve to potentially wreck a man's political career and personal life. After all, impregnating your high school girlfriend and abandoning her and your illegitimate child to the fallout of a drug addiction didn't exactly scream Man of the Year. The reality of the situation was a hell of a lot more complicated than that, but that would be the press's interpretation, and what the press thought was all that mattered when you were trying to get elected for a public office.

He'd intentionally ghosted Jess throughout the investigation. Years of dealing in these situations taught him it was best to find out where the parent stood first. The last thing he wanted was to get Jess's hopes up, only to crumple them up like an old receipt.

He glanced down at his black stainless steel Fossil wristwatch, marking the time. It was 11:50. He had ten minutes until his appointment. He rested his head against the headrest of his rental with a light, but jarring, thump and closed his eyes.

Deep breath in...Deep breath out.

He leaned over into the passenger seat and grabbed the file that contained copies of every piece of research he'd been able to gather from birth certificates to public records. "Here we go."

The Renaissance Revival style state house loomed large and in charge of the surrounding landscape. The front columned portico reminded him of the Capitol building in Washington,

DC. It was beautiful, and on any other day, he might have stopped to study the prominent statues and dome, but not now. He had an appointment to keep, and if he was late, that could set his case back weeks. The only reason he'd been able to meet with the senator so soon was because he'd had an appointment cancellation only minutes before Noah called and spoke with his secretary.

Fate? Maybe.

Unable to sit, Noah held his leather-bound folder to his side with one hand and gazed up at the large painting dominating the anteroom of several senators' offices. He wasn't current on California's governors, but it seemed to be a painting of one such man from the late nineteenth century. Neither was Noah a great study of artistic technique, but he thought the artist had done the guy a disservice by painting his nose to scale.

"Mr. Kinney? Senator Van Zuiden will see you now." The senator's secretary, an older woman with graying mouse-brown hair, stood at the door to Julian's office, hands clasped in front of her.

Noah gave her a disarming grin, to which she blushed, and stepped through the doorway into a small but decidedly masculine office. The north wall was full of floor-to-ceiling bookshelves covered in law books. A few were open on the table in the corner with book weights laying on the pages to keep the reader from losing their spot. Behind a large oak desk, in a plush brown leather chair, sat the man of the hour. He looked up from the binder he was studying and immediately stood to greet his guest. He stepped out from around the desk and extended a warm handshake. "Welcome! Mr. Kinney, is it?"

"Mr. Kinney is my father. Please, call me Noah."

"Welcome, Noah. You wouldn't happen to be any relation to Jack Kinney?" Julian quirked an eyebrow in a look that was his daughter to the life and gestured for Noah to take a seat in one of the armchairs in front of the desk as he resumed his seat.

Noah smiled. "I *would* happen to be." He crossed his legs and fiddled with the cuff of his pants briefly. "My brother," he elaborated at the senator's expectant look.

"No kidding! I grew up in Indiana, so I'm a bit of an IndyCar fan myself. Maybe we'll get the chance to discuss it sometime."

"I'd love that, sir."

Julian leaned back in his chair, completely at ease, or at the very least, good at pretending to be at ease. "So, what can I do for you?"

Noah rippled his fingers across the armrest of the leather chair, enjoying the feel of its luxurious cushion under his ass before he was tossed out of the office headfirst—the likelihood of which was increasing with each tick of his watch. He gripped the leather dossier and scooted to the edge of his seat, leaning forward. If he stood, that could be taken as a sign of aggression, and that wasn't the message he wanted to send. He placed a hand on the folder and made eye contact with the older man. He was suddenly struck by the fact that he wasn't old at all. This was an incredibly successful forty-three-year-old man who had been *appointed* to the state senate and was also on sabbatical from his tenured faculty position at UC Berkeley. If Noah was the easily intimidated type, he'd be quaking in his size eleven boots. "I'm here on behalf of my client."

"I don't accept appointments with lobbyists, Mr. Kinney." Julian's voice had an edge to it that wasn't there before, and he sat up straighter in his chair.

"I understand that, sir, but I'm not a lobbyist."

Julian eyed the file in Noah's hands as if it were radioactive. "A process server, then?"

One side of Noah's mouth quirked. "No, sir. I'm just a retired Denver PD detective turned private investigator."

"A private investigator?" The pulse in his throat had slowed slightly at Noah's words, but he was still suspicious as hell. He couldn't blame the guy.

"Yes, sir. I wanted to schedule a time to speak with you privately, rather than doing this in a public setting." He handed over the folder, and Julian opened it, his eyes not leaving Noah's for a long moment, unsure he wanted to see what was inside.

His hand shook as he looked down and picked up the first page of the brief. It was a letter of intent stating who he'd been hired by and what he was looking for. His face went as white as the piece of paper shaking in his hand. He flipped to the next document, a copy of Jessica's birth certificate, and his jaw clenched.

Noah's heart thundered in his ears. God, he wanted this to go well. He didn't want to have to call Jess and tell her Julian wanted nothing to do with her. That would be devastating.

Julian wet his bottom lip and looked up through misty green eyes. "You're saying...this girl—this *woman*—is my daughter?"

Noah swallowed and gave a firm nod.

Julian let out another shaky breath. His thumb caressed María's signature on the bottom of the birth certificate as he counted backward to the birth date listed on the document. "María…" he breathed before lifting the birth certificate to look at the next batch of documents: all the public records Noah had used to track him to this very moment. Jess's documents were in the next batch, all clipped together. He thumbed through them, studying her academic record and her business pursuits. When he got to the pages covering her CPS records, he laid the papers down, rubbing his temples. "My God…"

When he reached the last piece of the folder, his hand hovered over it, before picking up the photo and gazing at it for a long moment. Then, with quiet deliberation, he replaced each piece of evidence into the folder, putting the photo of Jessica on top, and took a deep, shaky breath. The pain in his eyes and the frown lines around his mouth made him look ten years older.

"To be honest, I'm not sure what to say." He closed the folder and tapped the cover before pushing it away a couple of inches. "*If* this is true, why has she never come forward?" His voice was tightly leashed, but his frustration was becoming more evident in his posture.

"The look in your eyes tells me you know it's true, sir." Noah kept his voice level. Excess emotion at a time like this could unfavorably tip the scales. He wanted to seem open and sympathetic while in complete control.

Julian flipped the file back open and picked up the photo of his daughter, gazing at her with soft eyes. He shook his head, digging his teeth into his bottom lip. "Why would María not *tell* me?" he asked, hurt warring with distrust in every facet of his being. "I mean, my God!" He gestured at the mountain of paperwork in front of him.

Noah nodded and scooted closer to the desk. "Jess has permitted me to share any information I have. All you have to do is ask."

Julian raised his brow incredulously. "Consider this me asking."

Noah snorted and scooted back into his chair, crossing his leg again as he settled in. He'd rehearsed this speech a million times, trying to envision what a man may want to know about a child he never knew existed, but despite his preparations, he couldn't bring himself to be clinical about it. "As you probably know, María had a dance scholarship to Julliard after graduation."

"Of course," Julian agreed. "That's why she broke it off. She said she would be in New York and I would be in California, and it could never work long distance between us."

"She deferred for a year, but she never attended. She knew she was pregnant before graduation. If she'd had her way, she would have gotten rid of the baby, but her mother told her if she was adult enough to get pregnant, she was adult enough to be a mother. It's a blow she never recovered from. She tried to get back in good form after the birth, but she tore her Achilles, and by the time she recovered, she was addicted to prescription pain medication. She's been in and out of rehab and jail for the last twenty-five years. Jess spent a lot of time in and out of Child Protective Services until her grandmother stepped in and adopted her.

It wasn't until a couple of months ago when she caught María in a rare sober moment that Jess found out you never knew about her. It was devastating, and it took her a while to process it, but then she decided to try to find you. All she had was your name, the high school you graduated from, and your plans to attend an Ivy League—which wasn't much to go on. Luckily, you weren't a difficult man to find." Noah gave Julian an ironic smile to lighten the mood. It worked.

Julian smiled back and thumbed back through the paperwork. "I have a difficult time believing María never told her mother about me. We dated most of our junior and senior years."

"She never told anyone. She wasn't close to her parents, and being conservative Catholic immigrants, a sexual relationship likely would have resulted in drastic action on their part. When she found out she was pregnant, she refused to tell her parents who you were because she didn't want your parents guilting you into staying."

"To hell with my *parents*! I would have stayed because it was the right thing to do! I can't believe this…" He slammed the folder shut again and buried his face in his hands, rubbing at his eyes with the heels of his palms. When he calmed himself once more, he sniffed and sat up straight, rocking back in his chair with his eyes raised to the ceiling in contemplation. "So where do we go from here? Am I allowed to know how she is?"

"María or Jessica?"

"Jessica, of course. I have no interest in knowing what María is doing with her life—especially after she's hidden the existence of my daughter from me for twenty-five years." The disgust in his voice was clear, and Noah felt the tiniest shred of sympathy for the woman who had acted with only his best interests at heart.

Facing facts, there was no way Julian would have what he had now if he had stayed in a rural Indiana farming community to play baby daddy at the tender age of eighteen.

But Noah's opinion wasn't what mattered here, and while María had made her choice nearly three decades ago, the betrayal was fresh for Julian.

"She's a successful young businesswoman. She graduated from Indiana University with a degree in Business Management and she and her best friend Alaina Montgomery own an event and wedding design start-up."

"Alaina Montgomery? Grayson Miles's fiancé?"

Noah laughed. "One and the same. Anyway, she has a three-month-old son, and they're currently living in Indianapolis."

Julian's eyes grew misty again at the mention of Parker. "I have a grandson?" he asked quietly, as if making sure he'd understood Noah correctly.

Noah nodded an affirmative.

Julian shook his head and shifted his weight. The leather creaked as he resettled himself both in mind and body. "I would love to meet her."

Noah heard a big "but" coming, though, and kept his excitement in check.

"I need to speak with my wife before we go any further with this. It may be a nonissue, but I want to be upfront with her. If she's okay with it, I'll reach out. Does that work?"

Noah nodded and reached into his inside jacket pocket for his business card case. "I completely understand, and I appreciate your honesty." Noah handed him the card. "Please feel free to call me anytime. I'll be in town for a few more days, so if you would like to meet again, call or send me a text."

Julian took the card and gazed at the name and number as if committing it to memory. Then, with a final settling breath, he stood. "Thank you for being discreet with this.

I'm sure I don't have to tell you how catastrophic this could be if it got out to the wrong people."

Noah stood as well and shook the senator's hand. "No, sir, you do not."

Feeling lighter after a successful meeting with Julian, he walked out of the joint offices with a bounce to his step. He could only hope Julian's conversation with Mrs. Van Zuiden would go half as well. Then maybe Jess could finally meet her father.

Twenty-Three

Shock Waves

J ess jumped at the sharp prick of a pin in her side. "Ow," she grumbled at the seamstress's graying head as the woman continued to take in Jess's bridesmaid dress.

"Sorry," the woman murmured in a thick Eastern European accent. Her hand was shaking so badly Jess was concerned she had a palsy. "You like? Can bring in leetle bit, if you don't like."

Jess turned this way and that as she took in the dress in all its sheathed glory. It was a thing of beauty, and buying it in a size up was a good call. Now, they could tailor it to fit like a glove. "I love it. What do you think, Lainie?" she asked over her shoulder.

Alaina glanced up from her phone. "Hmm? Oh. Yes! It looks fantastic!" She stood and walked over to inspect the seamstress's handiwork. "Are you wearing your shoes?"

"Yes," Jess confirmed in a borderline patronizing voice.

"Why?"

"I was just thinking you may want to have the hem taken up another half an inch or so. That way, you don't have to worry about tripping on it if you decide to put flats on during the reception."

Jess gazed at her reflection in the floor-to-ceiling, three-paneled mirror. "That's a good thought." She tilted her head from side to side as she contemplated. She didn't particularly want to wear her heels for six to eight hours, and if she took her shoes off, she didn't want to be tripping over her dress and tearing a hole in the delicate fabric either. She looked down at the seamstress, who was rocking back on her heels patiently waiting for a decision to be made. "Could you bring the hem up another half an inch?"

She gave Jess a thumbs up and went back to work on hands and knees, pinching and pinning the fabric. This was merely an appetizer for the main course; Alaina was next.

In no time flat, the seamstress was done and helping Jess out of the deathtrap of pins and needles so she could get dressed and watch her best friend's wedding dress fitting. She was bursting at the seams—*no pun intended*—with excitement. So, she could only imagine how Alaina was feeling. She'd no more than taken her jacket out of the gray velvet chair and taken her seat when the door to the changing room opened, and Alaina emerged, beaming.

"Oh…Alaina…" Jess whispered.

She was stunning. The dress fit well, despite a lack of alterations, and it wasn't hard to envision how she would look on her wedding day. The top of the gown was a deep V-neck fitted to her breasts and waist before flaring out in a delicate tulle A-line. The white skirt fell in delicate wisps over Alaina's hips, down to the ground, but the pièce de résistance was the white and periwinkle lace flower appliqués sewn onto the bodice and down the skirt.

Alaina smiled back through her tears and dabbed at them delicately before they could stream down her cheeks and ruin her makeup. "I almost forgot what it looked like," she laughed as she got a look at herself in the wall of mirrors. "God, it's just perfect, isn't it?"

Jess nodded and stood to walk around and look at her friend from the side. "It really is. It's not at all what I thought you would pick, but it's gorgeous."

The consultant who had helped Alaina and Jess pick out their dresses poked her head in the door and gasped. "Oh, my word! That looks fabulous!"

Jess smiled and opened her mouth to agree, but the buzzing of her phone on the chair behind her caused a momentary distraction. When she caught sight of the caller ID, her stomach dropped and her blood roared in her ears: Noah. She picked up her phone and took the call in one motion. "Hello?"

"Hey, Jess. Happy Saint Paddy's Day!" Noah greeted.

"Happy Saint Patrick's Day," she responded as she stepped out of the room, avoiding Alaina's concerned gaze as she went.

"How've you been doing? My brother seems to think you're alright."

She blushed a bit from her side of the phone. God only knew what Jack had told Noah. He was discreet, but he also wasn't above a humble brag every now and then. "I'm doing good. My friend is getting her wedding dress fitted today, so I'm with her in Chicago. What's up?" She pushed out of the store and into the unseasonably warm day as she awaited whatever news Noah was about to dump on her. It had only been three weeks since he'd started looking. Had his leads not panned out? Or maybe Julian had been killed in a car accident, his life tragically cut short. The scenarios ran round in her head until they made her dizzy.

"Sounds…fun." He offered in a sarcastic yet sympathetic tone.

She sniggered. If it was one thing she could say for Noah, he was able to walk into a room, literal or metaphorical, and read it instantaneously. She'd been looking forward to her fitting appointment, but keeping things from her best friend didn't sit well, and Noah had somehow picked up on that in a matter of seconds.

"Alright. Are you going to tell me why you called or just awkwardly sit on the other end of the line until the call drops?"

He gave a hard, breathy laugh. "I found him."

Jess's heart leaped into her throat and she suddenly found it hard to breathe.

He found him.

"You…you—"

"I found him," he repeated. "He wants to meet you."

"He—" Tears suddenly took over, and she dropped the phone from her ear. Her breath hitched, and she had to hold her breath to keep some semblance of control over her diaphragm.

"Jess? Are you there?" Noah's muffled voice asked.

"I'm here," she said as she raised the phone back to her ear. Her hand was trembling so badly she wasn't sure she could continue to hold the device. "W-where is he?" she finally managed.

Noah let out an incredulous huff. "Sacramento. His name's Julian Van Zuiden. He's a California state senator."

"A senator?" She was trying for all she was worth to wrap her mind around the idea of the man who had fathered her as a teenage boy being an elected official, a senator for the state of California. "Jesus…" she breathed.

"Put your head between your knees." Her companion suggested from thousands of miles away, sensing her shell shock.

She gave him a partially unhinged giggle as she glanced around the sidewalk and its occupants crammed cheek by jowl, some of them stumbling in intoxication despite the early hour. "Not exactly an option." Her voice was breathless as she struggled to drag in enough air. After another minute of slow, even breaths, she spoke again, this time sounding stronger. "I have one question—very important."

"Okay…" He dragged the word out as if he wasn't sure he wanted to know.

"Is he a Democrat or Republican?"

Noah let out a boisterous laugh full of relief at her joke, but answered readily. "He's a Republican with a reputation for crossing the aisle. I've only spoken with him a couple of times, but he seems like a decent guy."

Jess felt her way backward and leaned against the marble-columned storefront on North Michigan Avenue. Her head felt light as a feather all of a sudden and she was unsteady on her feet.

He seems like a decent guy.

Noah's words echoed around in her skull, and she wasn't sure what to do about them. "Does he…" She swallowed hard against the lump in her throat. "Does he have a family?"

Noah was quiet for a three-count. "I thought you might want to hear the details from him, but yeah. He does. Three kids and a long-term marriage."

Three kids...

The world shifted on its axis, and she wasn't sure which way was up. None of this felt real.

"He said he would come to you, but he would have to wait until this session is over. I'd be more than happy to stay here, though, if you want to come out."

Her immediate reaction to that offer was *Yes, please,* but she decided to sit on it and see how she felt in a couple of days. "When?" Her thoughts were buzzing like a cloud of mosquitos around a street lamp on a balmy July evening, but she managed to organize them enough to at least frame that singular question.

"Whenever. I'm not sure how easily you could get to Sacramento, but I'm sure he'll be amenable to whatever works for you."

Her brain was already crunching numbers. She'd flown to Dallas only a week and a half ago. Could she afford another plane ticket so soon? The answer was clear. If she dug into her savings, yes. But her savings account was for emergencies, and she had very strict policies on what constituted an emergency.

Okay. So this isn't an emergency, but it's meeting your freaking DAD. Bitch, get a grip on your priorities.

She sighed again. "I think I could probably swing it—as long as Alaina is okay with me leaving for a few days and Tita can watch Parker." As much as she was curious about Julian and wanted to meet him, she wasn't willing to risk her son in the process. She would keep him out of it until the situation had been thoroughly vetted.

"Great. Just text me when you make all the arrangements and we'll go from there. Sound good?"

"Um…yeah. Sure. Sounds good."

Noah chuckled. "Are you sure?"

Jess shook herself. "Yeah. I'm sure. Sorry. This is just so crazy."

"I can only imagine." She heard what sounded like a car door opening and closing along with the sounds of street traffic. "Listen. It goes against every instinct in my body to leave a woman to meet a strange man by herself—even if I've met the guy and can vouch that my cop radar didn't ping. So, I've got your back. Alright?"

She smiled. Even though they'd only known each other a few weeks, somehow, Noah felt like the big brother she never had. Maybe his relationship with Jack, and Jack's fondness for her, had bridged a gap between the two of them. She hoped so. There was something so damn likable about the guy, despite his ever-present serious face. "Alright."

By the time she ended the call, calmed herself, and got back inside, Alaina's alterations were nearly complete and she was standing in the mirror swishing the full skirt in a playful twirl that picked up the dress enough to show off her matching periwinkle shoes. When she saw Jess in the mirror's reflection, a look of relief washed over her. "There you are! Is everything okay? I was worried."

"Yeah. Everything's okay." She gave Alaina a nervous but relieved smile. "It was Noah. He found Julian."

Alaina's hazel eyes grew round as silver dollars. "Are you serious?" She whirled around to face her best friend. "He found your birth father? Oh, my god. That's…just…"

"Unbelievable? Crazy? Insane?"

"Where is he?" Alaina asked, turning back around at the seamstress's insistence.

"He lives in Sacramento. Noah said he wants to meet up, but I don't know if I can make it work. I *just* got back from Texas."

"Are you kidding? You *have* to go! You've spent your whole life wanting answers about your dad. This is your chance! And it sounds like he wants to know more about you too. That's more than a lot of people in your situation ever get. Take it."

Alaina was right. Jess knew she was, but the next step was the scariest part. She was about to wade into the deep end without a life preserver and prayed there wasn't a riptide hidden beneath the surface ready to carry her away into the cold unknown.

Twenty-Four

Man Up and Fess Up

"Hola! ¿Tita, donde estas?" She wasn't sure how her grandmother would handle the news that she found her biological father and intended to meet him, but some deep-seated instinct to flee had her heart pounding like that of a nervous door mouse staring into the big yellow eyes of a hungry house cat. She never told her grandmother about María's revelation; she didn't see how it could help a situation that had long since spiraled out of control. Shock was the predictable response—anger would soon follow. The level of anger was the wild card.

Jess meandered through the house, peeking around corners. "¿Tita?"

"Estoy aquí, Yèsica." The whir of a sewing machine should have been the first clue to her grandmother's location—the sewing room. Quilting again, no doubt.

She poked her head into the back room and found her

grandmother sewing quilt squares while Parker lay on the floor doing tummy time with a random scrap of orange fabric. "How's my baby boy?" Jessica crooned as she scooped him off the floor and cradled him with a kiss to the crown of his head. She bent to kiss her grandmother as well, who had not looked up from her sewing. "How was he today?"

"An angel, as always. He's such a good *bebe*." Parker cooed and swatted at his mother's chin.

She smiled and kissed his hovering hand with a burst of maternal affection. Holding him both for comfort and to ward off Tita's anger, she took a deep breath and cleared her throat. "I have something I want to run by you."

"¿Que?" Ivanna asked in a distracted tone as she lifted her foot off the pedal and inspected her handy work.

"Tita, por favor."

Her grandmother turned from her craft session with a raised eyebrow and folded her hands in her lap to show her granddaughter she had her full attention.

"You remember I went to see María right after Parker was born?"

"Sí. You were very upset, but I did not want to pry." The older woman's brow was furrowed in thought as she recalled Jessica's distress.

"She told me…" Jess's mouth had suddenly gone as dry as the Sahara and she swallowed, hoping to force spit over her tongue. "She told me she never told my father about me."

Ivanna sent up a breathy plea for patience to the heavens. "She never told your abuelo and me about him. But I assumed she would at least tell *him*. ¡Que horrible!" She ran her fingers through her gray-streaked hair in an anxious rhythm as she fought back tears. "Lo siento, cariña."

They both sat in silence for a long moment as Jessica gathered her courage. "I found him," she finally blurted, going with the adage, "Better to beg forgiveness than ask permission."

"¿Perdóname?" Confusion mixed with disbelief in her grandmother's voice.

"That day, when I visited María, I refused to leave until she told me his name. I hired a private investigator, and he found him—my father."

"Dios mío." If Ivanna hadn't already been sitting down, she likely would have collapsed, judging from her ashen complexion. "What is his name?" she finally asked.

"Julian. Julian Van Zuiden. He's a state senator in California."

If there was one thing her grandmother thought less of than unplanned pregnancies, it was politicians. Her dark brown eyes bored into her granddaughter as she stewed. "You should stay far away from that man. He'll wrap you in his web, and you'll never get out."

"Don't be dramatic. From what Noah says, he's perfectly nice. He wants to meet me."

Her focus zeroed in on the one element of the story she felt, as a grandmother, she was entitled to—the boy. "Who is this Noah?"

"*Noah*," she emphasized in a patronizing tone, "is my private investigator. He met with Julian a few days ago. Julian wants me to come to California. The Senate is in session for the next few weeks, and he can't leave the state. Noah has agreed to go with me to meet him. If everything goes well, and he wants to meet Parker, I can bring him with me next time, but I think it would be best to leave him home this time."

Ivanna tapped her foot in an irritable tattoo on the fringe carpet. "I don't like it. You don't know this man or what he's capable of, to abandon his daughter—"

"How was he supposed to support me if he didn't know I existed?" It was odd to defend a man she'd never met, but her grandmother was being unfair. "Please, Tita. Can you watch Parker so I can go? If he's a terrible person, I'll put it to bed and never bring him up again, but I *need* to do this. Please."

The older woman eyed her granddaughter speculatively for a long moment. It was her natural inclination to protect Jess at all costs, but sometimes, she didn't need protection, only a little support and some well wishes.

"Okay."

Jess's heart leaped in her throat. "Okay?" she asked, afraid to hope that she'd heard her correctly.

"Sí. Mereces saber la verdad. Ve y encuéntralo, cariña."

Tears pricked at the backs of Jess's eyes, and her breath caught in her throat as she struggled for control of her emotions. The fact that Tita saw how much she needed this— needed the truth—meant more than words could express. She was going to meet her father, and she was going to do it with Tita's blessing.

* * *

"I wish I could come with you," Jack lamented over the airwaves as he and Jess video-chatted later that night.

"I think it's a bit fast for you to be meeting my father. I mean, *I* haven't even met him yet," Jess said with a giggle. She was lying flat on her back with her phone propped on her breasts as she stared up into Jack's face.

He rolled his eyes but couldn't help his cheeky grin. "You know that's not what I meant."

She was quiet for a moment as she smiled up at him, appreciating his handsome face. "I know that's not what you meant." She wanted him with her too. The situation was nerve-racking at best, and she could use his steady hand in hers. "Noah will be with me, though."

"That's the next best thing to being there myself. You're in good hands," he admitted.

"Does it feel weird that your brother met my dad before you?"

"Well, I hadn't given it much thought, but now that you mention it, it *does* feel a little weird." They both chuckled, and she wanted nothing more than to pull him through the screen and kiss him. He was in Chicago this weekend, and it had been so hard to get in the car after the fitting and drive home without seeing him. She had been so close, and on a day like today, she could have used his arms around her, his lips on hers, and the surety that only comes with feeling loved. Sensing her longing, he switched tactics before she could dwell on it. "What did Tucker say when you told him?"

She sighed, thinking back to the look of shock and delight on Tuck's face at her news. "He was thrilled. He's glad I'm going out to California, and he thinks I would have regretted it if I'd stayed."

"As much as I hate agreeing with him on anything, he's right." Jack's words weren't bitter, but joking. He had no animosity toward Tucker. She knew that. "So, when do you leave?"

"I fly out next Friday. I'm only staying a couple of days and then I'll fly back home. I don't want to be away from Parker any longer than that." She sat up from her reclined position and rubbed her eyes before trudging over to the pantry and pulling out a tin of chocolate hazelnut wafer cookies. "Where are you off to next?" she asked around a big yawn.

"We're testing at Barber next week, but we don't have another race until Long Beach."

"Too bad Long Beach isn't next weekend. That would have been too convenient."

"Yeah, if you consider a five and a half hour drive convenient."

She rolled her eyes. "Semantics. At least it's on the same coast…" She crunched down on a cookie, letting the rich, sweet, and nutty flavors rush over her tongue. "It's going to be so hard to focus over the next week. I have so many questions."

The screen tilted sideways as Jack sat up. "Maybe you should start making a list. That way, you'll at least have a solid idea of where to start."

That was a good plan. She'd start making a list tomorrow, but that didn't solve her biggest problem—knowing what to say. "I just don't want to…I don't know," she trailed off, not wanting to sound stupid.

He raised a dark eyebrow at her, prompting her to finish her thought with an air of expectation.

"I want to make a good impression. That's all."

Jack stared at her for a long moment, and her cheeks heated under his accusatory glare. "That is *not* what you were going to say."

Tears pricked her eyes, and she looked away as she struggled to maintain her composure. "I don't want to be a disappointment. He has a successful career. I don't know what his wife does, but I'm sure she's equally amazing, and their kids are probably all over-achievers too. It's hard not to think about it." She'd spent her entire life trying to live up to impossible standards and feeling like a failure when she didn't meet them.

"Jess," he murmured. The gentle tone of his voice urged her eyes back to the screen. "I know you think I'm biased, and I probably am, but get out of your head for a minute. Look at what you have accomplished in your life. You're *not* a disappointment."

She nodded wordlessly, wishing she could bury her face in his chest. "I wish you were here," she whispered through the tears threatening to spill down her face. God, she'd cried more in the past couple of months than she had her entire life, and all she wanted was to make the waterworks stop.

"I know, Sassy. I wish I was there too," he murmured back with a sympathetic smile. "Just think, one day, we won't have to hide from anyone, and I can give you all the hugs and kisses your little heart desires. Sound good?"

She grinned and swiped at the tear tracks on her cheeks. "Sounds good," she sniffed. "I almost told Alaina today. She was in such a great mood after the fitting…" She drifted off, running scenarios round and round in her head, wondering how different things would be if she could just come clean with her best friend.

Something about Jack's face, maybe a faint flush to his cheeks, or the glimmer of feigned innocence in his eyes, alerted her to a thought flickering out of reach, trapped behind his sealed lips. "What?" she asked, a bloodhound on the scent. "I know you're hiding something. Spill it."

"What? Sorry. You're going in and out!" Jack shouted making static crackling noises between sentences.

"Jackson. Don't you *dare* hang up on me! Man up and fess up, buddy."

His eyes widened in complete innocence. "It's no big deal."

"If it's no big deal, you would have told me already. What?"

He sighed, deflating in defeat. "Grayson knows."

"*Jack!*" she shouted, equal parts surprised and perturbed.

"Well…it's not like I told him willingly!" he argued as he leaned closer to the phone and tried to plead his case. "Alaina told him I stopped by the shop, and he made a few logical leaps until he arrived at…" He gestured into the air to communicate exactly which conclusion Grayson had arrived at. "I didn't give him any of the details. I told him he needed to have plausible deniability, and he knows you don't want Alaina to know."

"Right, because Grayson never tells Alaina *anything*," she grumbled with a roll of her eyes. "Jesus, Jack! If Lainie finds out, she's gonna go ballistic. There's no way she and Tuck will believe we haven't been secretly rendezvousing for months!" She ran a frustrated hand through her hair and blew out a huff of air as she contemplated her next move.

"Listen. Knowing Alaina, if she knew, you'd know she knows. You know?"

His rapid and very intentional use of the same word in multiple sentences made her smile, and he grinned back, pleased to have cracked the code of Jess's disgruntlement. He was right, though. Alaina wouldn't have been able to hide her hostility if she knew Jess was keeping things from her. "I wanted to wait until after the wedding, but do you think we should tell her?"

Jack sighed and leaned back into the cushions of his couch, having successfully removed himself from the hot seat. "Well, look at it this way. If she knows, we can have sexy slow dances at the reception. You pressed up against me, me whispering sweet nothings in your ear…"

She smiled at the picture he painted, but sighed, popping his euphoric little bubble. "There is nothing I'd rather do. But even if I tell Alaina, Tucker is a whole other can of worms. He's a mess right now. The last thing he needs is something to set him off, and if I tell him now, when he's stuck down in Texas, I run the risk of him feeling like I'm trying to replace him in Parker's life."

Jack sighed, but it was a patient and understanding sigh, which she appreciated.

"I'm sorry. I know that's not what you want to hear."

He shook his head. "It's complicated. I get that. You don't need to apologize. I promised I'd be patient, and I will."

She hated stringing him along. He wanted to go public with their relationship. Hell, so did she, but it wasn't a good time.

But was there ever a good time to dump a bucket of cold water on somebody?

Woulda Coulda Shoulda

A t one o'clock on the dot, Noah pulled up to the main entrance of Jess's hotel. She climbed into his black Nissan without a word, exhausted. She'd tossed and turned all night, and her brain was buzzing with all the what-ifs. Noah gave her an appraising glance and nodded before putting the car in gear.

"So, what's the plan?"

Noah flicked on his turn signal and made a right out of the parking lot. "Julian thought it might feel weird for you to go to his house, but he wanted to have somewhere you could talk. So, he rented an Airbnb for the day—don't worry—" he interjected, noticing her eyes widen in surprise. "I already scoped it out. It's legit, and I'll be in my car out by the curb if you need me." He winked at her and smiled before putting his eyes back on the road. Some of the tension melted away with the knowledge that Noah wasn't taking any chances.

"It's just gonna be him, right? I don't think I could handle meeting anyone else. I haven't slept in days worrying about this."

"Worrying about what?" Noah asked as he merged onto the highway.

She stared at him as if he'd grown a third head. What was there for her to *not* worry about? "How it will go, what he'll think of me. I want to make a good first impression. You know?"

"Well, if it makes you feel better, I think he's worrying about the same things." They rode for nearly an hour in contemplative silence before he finally added, "Honestly, Jess, I know it's easier said than done, but just try to be yourself."

Ba-da-dum, ba-da-dum. Jess's fingers rippled quietly against her jouncing thigh as Noah pulled into a quaint little subdivision full of unique homes. She pursed her lips and blew out, trying to calm her heart before it exploded out of her chest and ran in the opposite direction.

"Would you quit it?" Noah grumbled as he glanced at her out of the corner of his eye. "You're driving me nuts. I know you're nervous, but Jesus..." he muttered.

With some effort, she stilled her leg and sat on her hands as she gazed out the window. She tried to pick out something she liked on each home: gingerbread architecture, white picket fence, hot pink geraniums, three-tiered birdbath, brick walking path.

Noah slowed and pulled to a stop in front of the house with the brick walking path and she looked over at him, eyes wide with panic. "I can't do this," she whispered. "Take me back. I can't do it."

He reached across to put a hand on her knee and squeezed

with warm reassurance. "You can. Just take a deep breath."

"Come with me," she pleaded, her voice weak with her strangled breathing.

"Jess." Her name was stated with such calm she immediately met his eye. "You. Can. Do. This."

Nodding her head like a bobblehead, she bit her bottom lip and removed her hands from under her to grab her purse from the floorboard. They were shaking like a glass of water with a T-Rex barreling toward it. At that thought, she bit down on her lip to stifle an unhinged giggle and reached for the door handle before she could chicken out again. "You'll be here the whole time?" she asked, looking back over her shoulder just before she pulled the lever.

"The whole time. I promise," Noah murmured with a reassuring nod.

With one long exhale, she popped the door open and rose from the car, taking a long look at the house as she settled herself. The white lace curtains in the window fluttered, as if someone was looking out at her, and her heart gave another nervous skip. "This is insane," she muttered as she gripped her purse strap tighter and trudged forward, concentrating on each step so she couldn't focus on the destination. Then, suddenly, she was at the door, knocking.

She pivoted on her heel and looked back toward the car. Noah was standing on the driver's side, forearms resting on the roof as he stared at her, daring her to retreat.

Deep breath. It will be okay. It will. It will. It will.

Behind her, the door opened.

She whirled around and slammed right into a green-eyed stare. The force of those eyes—the same ones she'd seen in the mirror for twenty-five years—was enough to knock the air out of her lungs, and she simply stood there, dumbstruck.

As the shock wore off and she came back to herself, she widened her lens and took in more of him. He was on the taller side, maybe six feet—a lot taller than her own five feet two inches—and slender, fit for a man in his forties. His dark hair was graying at the temples with a bit of salt sprinkled throughout, but the thing that struck her most was the smile lighting his face: warm, friendly, genuine.

"Jessica," he greeted with a voice like melted butter, rich with feeling.

She gave him a sheepish smile in return and forced her shoulders down from their position, anxiously hunched up by her ears. "I hope that means you're Julian."

He gave a breathy laugh and waved her in. "I certainly am. Come in." He widened the door to let her pass and closed it behind her. "I hope this was okay. I wanted a place that we could talk without being overheard."

Jess stood in the entryway looking around at the cute little house. "It's great. I didn't expect…well, I don't know what I expected," she said with a self-deprecating chuckle.

He laughed back and stepped around her. "Would you like a glass of wine? I wasn't sure what you'd like, so I brought several bottles." His voice was growing fainter as he disappeared down the hall, and she followed him, taking in the art déco style of the hallway with its angular gold furnishings and wall hangings.

"Um, yeah. I like wine. What do you have?" she asked as she followed the sound of bottles and wineglasses clinking together.

"I have a nice cab if you like red. Or I can open a chardonnay." He held a wine bottle in each hand and offered them up for her inspection. To be honest, she'd never paid much attention to a wine label before. She'd never had the money for an expensive wine, and probably wouldn't notice the difference if it bit her in the backside.

She shrugged. "You choose. I'm not picky." She sat her purse on the counter opposite where Julian stood and leaned against it, taking in the room. The backsplash with its black and gray design and the gray velvet, high-back bar stools lining the island were adorable. Maybe she could sneak some pictures for next year's vision board before she left…

Julian went for the chardonnay, and she wished she knew wine well enough to know what that said about him. He cranked the cork screw with practiced ease, and she watched his sure, steady hands with admiration. The counter next to the sink was full of freshly washed vegetables and a cutting board sat on the island with a chef's knife on top.

"Are you making a salad?" She pushed away from her perch to accept the glass of wine he was offering her.

"I bought steaks too. I hope that's okay. You're not a vegetarian, are you?" he asked, his eyes widening in sudden horror at his thoughtlessness.

She snorted. "No. Not even a little bit, though I'm not above a good salad."

"Well, you're in luck then, because I make a mean Cobb." He leaned back against the sink and sipped at his own drink before lowering his glass, looking her over—not in the normal way of male appreciation. This was like a blind man seeing the sunset for the first time, full of wonder and joy. "You look like your mother," he finally said, the words faintly choked off. "Except for—"

"The eyes." She finished his thought with a smile. "I always assumed I got them from you, but it's um…"

"Unsettling?" he asked as he gave her a wry smile and took a larger drink of his wine.

"That's one word for it," she allowed with a hard laugh. It was weird. She'd never met this man before in her life, but somehow felt as if she knew him. There was something familiar about him, the way he cocked his eyebrow when he asked a question, the way his cheeks flushed lightly when he regretted saying something too forward, the dimples that popped out when he smiled. The care Julian had put into every aspect of their meeting and his open-book personality put her at ease quickly and helped her relax into the version of herself Noah had insisted on. The real Jess: no muss, no fuss.

They told stories about their families and jobs. Julian shared his adventures around the world, the story of how he and his wife, Janine, met, and why he picked political science as his field of study. He was affable and intelligent, with a sense of humor that could make the most stalwart politician crack a smile.

She could see why her mother had fallen for him all those years ago. He seemed like a genuine human being—someone she could be proud to claim as her father, but she wasn't the only one who had that honor. He and his wife had three children of their own: seventeen-year-old Maddox, fifteen-year-old Riggs, and ten-year-old Aurora—Rory for short. She had siblings. *Siblings.*

In turn, Jess told him about Parker, her complicated relationship with Tucker, and eventually Jack, enjoying the small jolt of shock when he realized his daughter not only *knew* an IndyCar driver, but was dating one.

Eventually, after a comfortable lapse in silence while he chopped lettuce for their salad, he laid the knife down on the cutting board, leaned on the counter, and met his daughter's gaze evenly. "Tell me about your mother."

Jess had promised herself she wouldn't sugarcoat anything. He deserved the truth, and she would give it to him, but that didn't mean it would be easy. "Noah said he gave you the cliff notes?"

He nodded. "He did, but I'd like to hear it from you. If you don't mind?"

She took a deep breath. "I think I'm going to need another glass of wine if I'm going to tell you that story."

He smiled and took a bottle from the fridge, twisting the cork out and refilling their glasses with the pale yellow liquid. "I honestly don't remember a time when she was sober," Jess began, as she slid onto one of the barstools facing him. "Tita said she tried to get back into dancing shape shortly after she had me, but she got hurt and got addicted to her pain meds during her recovery. I think she knew she would never get it back and that made a bad situation worse. She resented me for all the things she could never have—all the lost opportunities and bad decisions." She shrugged, trying not to cry and failing miserably. She swiped at the tears and trudged on. "Let's just say I'm no stranger to government offices." She shot him an ironic laugh, going for a smile and only getting a look of intense remorse.

"I remember one night when I was probably three or four, Mom was drunk or high—I can't remember which. We were at Walmart, and she said she was just going to close her eyes for a second…she passed out. I couldn't wake her up. It was January, six inches of snow on the ground, subfreezing temperatures. The car was off. She still had the car keys in her hand when a police officer showed up and got me out of the car." She blinked and refocused her gaze as she pulled herself from the memory. "Tita was out of town on a mission trip. So, I got placed with a foster family until she got back. It was a couple more years before she got custody of me."

Tears swam in Julian's eyes as he studied his daughter. "Jessica. If I had known—"

She shook her head. "But you didn't, and I know that. It's not your fault."

"It makes me sick knowing I was out living some grand adventure when my *child*—"

"Stop," she said. "It's done. It happened. We can't change it, and if you had been with me back home, you wouldn't be here making the differences you're making now."

He sniffed and wiped his eyes with his sleeve. "How can you be so calm about all of this? It's horrible." The disgust was clear in his voice, and she understood the level of shock he was feeling. Looking at her CPS paperwork had afforded him a level of clinical detachment. Hearing the atrocities she had experienced firsthand, it was harder to remain objective.

"It's my life," she shrugged. "I survived, and I'm stronger for it. If those things hadn't happened to me when I was little, there is no way I would have survived the things that have happened since. I wouldn't have had the fortitude I needed to be a single mother, and I wouldn't have had the discipline and awareness I needed to do better for my child." She raised her chin, feeling a small sense of pride in knowing she was a better person for the things she had been through. "You can be angry, but please, don't pity me. And don't regret your choices. You were playing against a stacked deck."

He studied her for a long minute, gauging the veracity of her statement, and seeming satisfied, nodded. "Okay." Then a wry smile crossed his thin lips. "I won't pity you. I'll be just as much of a hard ass on you as my other kids."

She laughed. "Bring it on."

As the afternoon sank into the evening, they ventured outside, glasses of wine in hand, to enjoy dinner. The backyard was fenced in on three sides by high-planked fencing and was covered in paver stones to create an even surface for the patio furniture. Potted plants and flowers lined the fence along with a small Buddha statue, a bird bath, and several little bits and bobs of lawn ornamentation to give it a whimsical-boho vibe. The savory smell of roasting meat rolled off the gas grill in clouds of smoke as their steaks cooked, and the large umbrella over the table blocked the most intense rays of afternoon sunshine. It was a sweet setup, and she wished she had something like it for her house.

Julian flipped the steaks and then leaned against the house, sipping from his glass. "Have you ever been to Napa?"

She sipped from her glass too, enjoying the crisp sweetness of their newest bottle, a chilled riesling. "I haven't. Alaina and I have always talked about taking a girls' trip up there, but it's something we never got around to."

"It's gorgeous—especially during the harvest when all the vines are full of their fall foliage. Janine and I try to get up there at least once a year. Friends of ours own a small boutique winery in the valley. We usually stay in their loft above the garage. They've had it converted into a one-bedroom in-law overlooking some of the vineyards. If you're ever interested, I could give them a call. I'm sure they wouldn't mind hosting you and Alaina for a couple of nights."

"That sounds amazing. I might have to take you up on that," she said as she took another sip. Julian opened the grill to get a look at their steaks and decided to take them off before they overcooked. He walked over to the table and placed the steaks down before taking a seat at the head of the table and leaning back in the chair, completely relaxed.

"I have to be honest, I didn't get any sleep last night," he said, gazing up at the blue sky. The day was so perfect it seemed to have been made with them in mind: cloudless and uncomplicated. He finally looked down at her. "When a man shows up at your door and says his client is looking for you, and oh by the way, she's your long-lost daughter...that's hard to wrap your head around."

Jess snorted. "I can imagine. I never wanted to complicate your life. I hope you know that."

His responding smile was filled with a fondness she'd never known before. "I wasn't sure of that at first. How could I be? But I thought, if you were in it to cause trouble, you wouldn't have come to me first. So, Janine and I discussed it, and at the end of the day, she told me I would always regret it if I didn't take the chance." His mouth quirked up in irony. "My wife is rarely wrong about anything, and for once, I don't begrudge her the accuracy."

Jess let out an amused chuckle and reached for the tongs to grab some salad as Julian distributed the steaks to each of their plates.

Gradually, the sun sank down toward the horizon until they were left in reluctant darkness. It had been such a fantastic day that neither of them wanted it to end, but she had an early flight to catch in the morning, and he had a wife to return home to. Standing in the entryway, staring up at him, he smiled with tears in his eyes and pulled her into his arms, hugging her tightly. "I'm sorry I wasn't there for you growing up, but I hope you know I'm here for you now. Whatever you need, it's yours."

She simply stood there for a moment, letting him hold her and enjoying the feel of her father's arms around her. The only time she'd ever felt that safe and loved was in Jack's arms, and she never wanted it to end.

Eventually, he loosened his hold on her and pushed her to arm's length. "My parents still live in Indiana. Maybe after this session ends, I'll pay them a visit."

She beamed up at him. "I think that would be a great idea."

Floating on air, she glided to her waiting chariot and tapped on the window. The locks popped and she slid into the passenger seat with a grin from ear to ear. Noah's gaze was focused out the windshield at an SUV parked along the curb a block down. There was nothing suspicious about it, in her opinion. It was a residential neighborhood. There were all kinds of vehicles parked on both sides of the street.

"Are you surveilling the neighborhood?" she asked with a light snicker as she clicked her seat belt and gave another glance out the window. When Noah didn't move or offer an explanation, she sighed. "Seriously? You're starting to freak me out. What are you looking at? Did somebody put a pipe bomb in a trashcan or something?"

He finally glanced over at her with an eyebrow raised. "Wellllll?"

He shrugged. "That car showed up a couple of hours ago and no one has gotten in or out. They've just been sitting there." His gaze latched back on it and something stirred the dormant butterflies in her stomach.

"What are you saying? Is Julian in danger or something?"

"I don't know." He pulled his phone out and scrolled through it for a few minutes before placing a call to the local police. "This is Detective Noah Kinney, Denver PD, Retired. I'm working a private investigation in Sacramento, and I need to report a suspicious vehicle. Yeah… Sure." He went quiet for a moment and then did an identical spiel for someone else before continuing, "It's a black Chevy Tahoe. California plates. I can't make out the plate number from here. It's on the north side of the road. I'm parked at a residence a block west." He gave the address, and Jess peered closer at the vehicle. She couldn't even see if there was someone in the SUV at this distance, but if Noah's radar was pinging, she would trust it.

"Nah. You're all good. We're gonna get out of here anyway. If you could send a patrol car to check it out though, that'd be great… Copy… Uh-huh. Thanks. You too." He hung up the call and balanced the phone on his thigh. "They're going to send a patrol out to check the vehicle. If they're suspicious, they'll hang out until they leave or are cleared."

She nodded and glanced at the vehicle one more time before Noah put the car in drive and pulled away from the curb. As they drove past the Tahoe, he raised the phone and clicked a photo of the SUV's front plate. "What are you doing?" she hissed. "You're gonna piss them off! What if they have guns?"

He smirked. "So do I."

"Are you serious?" she hissed. "Exactly why did you think you would need a gun for me to meet my birth father?"

"Relax," he soothed. "I always carry a weapon. Force of

habit. But it's not like I'm walking around without a license. I have concealed carry permits for most states."

Jess rolled her eyes, sank a bit lower in her seat, and eyed the side mirror to make sure they weren't being followed.

"They aren't following us," Noah said with a smile. "So, I take it everything went well, seeing as it's been eight hours."

Jess smiled and sat up a little straighter in her seat. "It was amazing. He's awesome. It just makes me sad we missed so much time together, but he seems determined to make up for it. He said he'll come to Indiana after this senate session ends. His parents still live there and he hasn't seen them in a while. Isn't that awesome? I have grandparents that live thirty miles from my house and I had no clue."

"That's amazing, Jess. I'm so happy for you." He reached over and playfully ruffled her hair like she always imagined a big brother would.

"Stop it," she growled, before dissolving into laughter. It would take a lot more than Noah messing up her hair to burst her bubble tonight.

Twenty-Six

Everything and More

By the time Jess picked Parker up from Tita's and returned home, she was ready to lay in bed and pull the covers over her head. Her flight had been delayed for maintenance and she was pulling into her driveway a full three hours later than planned, but seeing Jack's car in the driveway lit a small, warm flame in the pit of her stomach. He'd had a charity event in Indianapolis that afternoon, and rather than return to Chicago as everyone thought he had, he'd been camping out at her house waiting for her to get home.

The front door opened just as she was hopping out to get Parker out of the back seat, and she turned to see Jack striding toward her, all wide open arms and big smiles. She closed the driver's side door and wrapped her arms around his neck, standing on tiptoe to kiss him thoroughly. "Hi."

He wrapped his arms around her waist and pulled her off

the ground in his enthusiasm. She giggled against his lips and kissed him once more before he put her feet back on solid ground. "Hi," he replied back. "Is your suitcase in the back?" He hitched his thumb over his shoulder toward the trunk.

"It's just a duffle, but yeah." Meandering around to the passenger side, she opened Parker's door and tucked his travel blanket more securely around his stout little form before pulling him from the car. Once inside and away from the cold March chill, Jess sat Parker's carrier down on the ground and turned back to Jack for another kiss. "I missed you."

She could feel the resounding smile on his lips, but he only made a satisfied hum in the back of his throat. "I could do this all night, but I'd really like to hear about your trip."

She pushed back from him, jolted into reality. It wasn't that she'd forgotten her time spent with Julian, but it had been relegated to the recesses of her subconscious, what with the flight delay and seeing Jack again. She'd talked to Jack briefly the night before, but after the hour drive back to the hotel, it had been almost two in the morning his time, and neither of them was up for conversation past the basic necessities. Now they had all the time in the world—metaphorically speaking—and she wanted to tell him everything.

Jack shifted her duffle bag strap on his shoulder and walked toward the living room to deposit it onto the couch. Some basketball game was playing on the television and he muted it. "Soooo? I'm dying. I know you said it went well, but—"

"He's incredible, like, everything I could have hoped for." She was practically glowing as she recalled her evening with Julian. "I was pretty much having a panic attack by the time we pulled up to the house. I thought Noah was going to strangle me with his bare hands." She snorted. "I'll be honest, I didn't believe him when he said Julian was just as nervous as me, but I think that was a fair assessment. It's what calmed me down, funnily enough—seeing him just as stressed as I was."

She sat down on the couch next to Jack and curled into his side, holding Parker, who was sleeping soundly despite being removed from his car seat, in the crook of one arm. Jack lifted his arm and pulled her into him, playing idly with a strand of her hair as she told her story. "He's been to *forty-seven* countries! He went to Africa on a few of his summer breaks while he was in college to do aid work and actually got to go on safari while he was in Botswana. God, I could have talked to him for hours just about that trip."

"That's cool," Jack agreed. "Though, I have to admit, I never realized you were an African Safari girlie." He poked her playfully in the side and she giggled.

"It's one of those things I've always wanted to do, but probably never will," she said with a shrug. "How cool would that be to see real wild elephants and lions and giraffes, though?"

"I'll take you one day," he murmured, kissing the top of her head in genuine affection before letting her continue her story.

"He met his wife, Janine, on a trip to Italy. She was studying abroad in Florence, and he was visiting the Accademia Gallery to see Michelangelo's David. She was sitting on a bench, looking at a painting, when he sat next to her and struck up a conversation. He got the shock of his life when he realized she was an American." Her absent grin grew into a full-on smile as she retold the story. "Janine was an undergrad student at UC Berkeley at the time. They were literally living an hour apart back in the States. What were the odds they would meet at a random museum in a country thousands of miles from home? Talk about fate."

Jack tightened his arm around her and nuzzled the top of her head. "That's so crazy. And you said they have kids, right?"

Jess jolted upright as a zing of excitement shot through her veins. Parker let out a disgruntled whine in her arms, and she gave him a gentle, "Shhhh," as she bounced him in her arms to settle him. She had thought he might wake up soon after they arrived home and didn't want to go through the rigamarole of having to put him in his sleep sack in his crib, but since he showed no intention of joining the conscious world, she rose and walked down the hallway to place him in his crib.

"Your phone went off," Jack said, his eyes glued to something on his own phone as she returned to the living room.

She sighed and stepped over to where she'd left her phone on the kitchen counter. It was a text from Julian.

Just wanted to make sure
  you got home okay.

She smiled to herself, feeling a small rosy glow growing inside her. So *this* was what it felt like to have a parent who cared about your safety and wellbeing. She bit the bottom of her lip in contemplation for a few seconds and then sent a message back.

**Yep! Flight was delayed but
I'm home now.**

The couch dipped as she knelt and leaned in to give Jack a long, slow kiss, unhampered by her child's presence. "It's feels nice having you to come home to," she murmured.

He leaned in to kiss her again, this time sucking on her lower lip gently. He was so warm and willing, it was intoxicating, and she felt as though she was three tequila shots deep by the time she pulled back from him.

"Don't you want to hear the rest?" Torn between the desire to rip his clothes off or curl up next to him and tell more stories, it would be up to Jack to tip the scales.

His lips curled into a smile against hers, and his teeth grazed her bottom lip. "Sure, Sassy," he breathed, giving her a quick additional peck before resettling himself into the couch. "So. Kids?" He prompted, as if their little interlude thirty seconds earlier hadn't happened. His brain naturally shifted tracks so quickly it gave her whiplash sometimes, but she had to admit, that was probably a good trait for someone to have when they drove cars at 200 miles per hour for a living.

"Oh my gosh. Yeah. Three! I have two brothers and a sister. Isn't that so freaking crazy?"

Jack nuzzled her ear, emitting a low throaty hum of amusement that vibrated straight through to her bones.

"Are you laughing at me?" she asked with mock indignance.

"Not at all," he murmured, laying a kiss on her temple. "I just didn't realize how much I take it for granted. From the day I was born, I've had three big brothers looking out for me. It's fun to see you discover that for the first time."

"I don't think it's really sunk in yet, if I'm being honest. Right now, they're just ideas out there in the universe. I've never met them, so they don't seem real. But to think that I could have college graduations and weddings and family reunions one day? I could be an *aunt*. It's so exciting!" She was vibrating with barely suppressed excitement, and she turned to face her boyfriend, flinging one arm over the back of the couch as she pivoted. "Maddox, he's the oldest. Julian said he's a brainiac—wants to study aerospace engineering."

"Damn," Jack breathed. "Are all of your siblings that ambitious?"

Jess gave a gleeful chortle. "Well, Riggs is only fifteen. So, I don't think he's really thought about a career, but he loves basketball. He should make the varsity team next year, as a sophomore—which is saying something since he goes to such a big school. And Rory—God, I'm so excited to meet her! Julian says she's a complete girly girl. She's ten and insists on picking out her own clothes when Janine takes her shopping. She just got her ears pierced a few weeks ago and already has like ten different pairs of earrings—even though her ears aren't healed enough for her to wear them yet."

Jack smiled. "Now having a sister *would* be a novelty. We were the rough and tumble type at my house. We all played sports growing up, and if we had a disagreement, we settled it in the backyard. Mom's only rule was, if it came to blows, we had to wear the boxing gloves she kept on a peg in the garage. No bare fists—which, as a rule, worked fairly well, until Aaron and Chris got in a fight over a girl after a party one night—too drunk to think about the gloves until it was too late. Bruised knuckles, black eyes, and no car keys for two months when mom found out what happened."

"They got grounded for *two months*, not for fighting, but for fighting without gloves on?"

"No, they got grounded for underage drinking. The degree of punishment was more severe because of the bruises they left on each other," Jack said with a hard laugh.

Jess snorted at that and let the hand draped over the couch drift up to play with the hair at the nape of Jack's neck. "I would love to meet your other brothers someday. They sound like they know how to have fun."

Jack threw back his head and laughed. "Oh, they do. Though they're both married now, so they've slowed down quite a bit in their old age."

"I'm not sure they would take it sitting down if I told them you called them old." She laughed and tugged playfully on his ear with the hand that had been combing his hair.

"Aaron turns forty next year. So, I'm sure he'd agree with me. Chris? He's still in denial," Jack said with a wink. He shifted, a thought occurring to him. "You've met Chris, though. Last year at the track."

Jess paused to think. The only two days she'd spent at the track last year were qualifying—when she'd had such severe morning sickness, she'd had to leave early—and race day. She turned over faces in her brain, trying to match anyone she'd met with Chris's name. "I don't think so..."

"Yeah. He was with me when we met up at victory lane after the race: tall, blonde, looks nothing like the rest of us." Jack laughed softly. "We used to joke with him that he got dropped off by the mailman, because me, Noah, and Aaron all have the same coloring and dark hair."

At that description, Jess vaguely recalled a taller man in a sport coat hovering behind Jack at victory lane, but she'd been so focused on Grayson's celebration and Alaina's stunned joy that she'd barely been attending—embarrassing as that was to admit. "I *think* I remember him, but honestly, I probably wouldn't know him if I saw him again."

Jack gave an amused smirk but let it bide. "Well, maybe someday soon, you can meet the crew. I'm sure Noah's been giving them the 4-1-1. They're probably dying from curiosity."

Jess shifted, thinking back to what Alaina had said to her about his family being bitter over how she'd ended things with him all those months ago. "You don't think they'll mind? Us being back together, I mean."

Her phone vibrated again, and she glanced down, smiling.

**I'm glad you're safe.
Talk soon?**

"Are you cheating on me?"

Jess's eyes shot up to meet his gaze, wide and befuddled. "What?"

"If that's another guy that's got you all lit up like a Christmas tree, consider me green with envy." He lunged playfully for her phone, and she dodged out of his grasp, laughing.

"Stop it."

Finally, he snatched the phone and glanced at the ID, eyes dancing. "I *suppose* that's acceptable."

"Shut up," she muttered, rolled her eyes, and went back to her text.

**Yes. Talk soon. Let me know
when you can come to town!**

She locked her phone and tossed it on the couch, making a show of giving Jack her full attention. "Now, what were you saying?" She batted her eyelashes in a flirtatious flutter.

Jack leaned in closer, amusement dancing with concern in the depths of his eyes. "I said, 'Why would my family mind us being back together?'"

"Oh." Jess dropped her gaze to pick at lint littering the couch beneath her. "I don't know…Alaina said your family was kind of pissed at me…for…how things ended."

Jack was quiet for a long moment and then sighed. "Sometimes, I really wish Alaina would mind her own damn business."

That got Jess's attention, and she looked up at him, brow furrowed. "What the heck happened between you two? I thought you liked each other."

"Hell if I know," he muttered. "The only thing I can think of that might've pissed her off is something I said to Grayson right after her accident…but I just can't see Gray telling her about it." He shook his head, perplexed.

Jess raised one brow in open curiosity. "What did you say?"

Jack threw his head back. "Okay. Well, look," he said, throwing his hands up in supplication. "In my defense, I didn't know he was serious enough about her at the time to marry her. I was just trying to look out for him."

"Oh God…" Jess sighed.

"It was right after her accident, and Gray was clearly struggling with everything. The stress was affecting his on-track performance, and he wasn't sleeping a lot. I told him nobody would blame him if he broke up with her. That wasn't what he signed up for. But he made it perfectly clear he had no intention of doing that, that he loved her. And that was the end of it. I never said anything else about it."

"I can't imagine a scenario where Grayson would bring that up," Jess mused. "And while I can't see Alaina thrilled at the sentiment, it's also not a crime to look out for your best friend."

Jack sighed and rested his head against the back of the couch. "To be honest, Jess, the more I get to know Alaina, the more I feel like she's kind of a spoiled brat."

Jess stared at him, eyebrows raised. "And I'm sure that attitude is winning you all kinds of brownie points…" she said, sarcasm dripping off her words. "Why would you say that?"

"Look, I get she's been through a lot. I'm not saying she hasn't, but hell. You've been through a lot too, and we don't see you traipsing around making demands and treating people like shit the second they don't agree with you."

Jess stood, crossing her arms and staring down at him, giving him one of those "If looks could kill" expressions. "That's my best friend you're talking about."

Jack sighed and stood too, putting a large, warm hand on each of her shoulders, massaging gently. "I understand that. I'm only saying she seems to be taking advantage of everyone's generosity to get her way with a lot of things."

Her shoulders slumped slightly at his kneading fingers. "She can be a little much, I agree, but…" She was running out of excuses because the truth was, she'd noticed the same kind of behavior coming from Alaina in recent months. Most of the time, she just let her have her way because the decisions Alaina was making didn't directly impact Jess. At a time in Jess's life where she was already dealing with a lot of shit, she didn't think she could be blamed for taking the path of least resistance.

"Look, I think you know me well enough to see I'm pretty easygoing, but I don't like bullies or entitlement—especially when those things are impacting the people I care about. I love you and Grayson like family. I'm protective of you both, and while I'd take a lot sitting down, I won't watch anyone take advantage of either of you."

"I don't see Grayson as the type to let Alaina walk all over him." Jess raised an eyebrow skeptically at Jack and he smirked.

"He's not. But he's also madly in love with her—his tolerance level is skewed. Besides, it's not him I'm worried about. It's you."

"Why? I've lived my whole life with Alaina. I doubt anything she could do now would come as a surprise." Jess snorted and walked over to the kitchen for a glass of water.

"You told me you were worried about how Alaina would take the news about us."

Jess shut the refrigerator and turned to look at Jack, brow furrowed in confusion. "Yeah. What about it?"

"What happens if Alaina stomps her foot and gives you that death ray stare and says you're making a mistake by getting into a relationship with me so soon after your breakup with Tucker? You think she's not going to have some sort of bias there?"

"Of course she'll have bias. I'm not stupid enough to think she could be completely objective. It's Alaina. She's never neutral about anything." Jess went back to the refrigerator and grabbed the pitcher of sweet tea before kicking the door closed behind her.

"And I'm not stupid enough to think her bias is going to

be in my favor," Jack said flatly.

Jess sighed and sat the pitcher down on the counter with a thunk. "Are you sure this is Alaina's issue with you? Because it sounds like it's your issue with her."

Jack pinched the bridge of his nose and inhaled. "I don't want to argue about this."

"I'm not arguing with you. I'm just surprised. That's all."

Jack cautiously made his way over to the kitchen, like a man approaching a rabid wolf. "Surprised?"

"I think those of us in Alaina's orbit are so used to her being…*her*, we don't really notice it anymore, but you're pretty much the last person I expected to have a problem with her."

Jack leaned across the island and gazed at her, eyebrow raised. "And why is that?"

Jess waltzed around the island toward him, smiling flirtatiously, until she was right beside him. "Because I thought maybe your gaze was too fixed on me to notice much else."

A smile twitched at the corner of his mouth as he stood and turned to face her. "Don't try to distract me," he growled playfully, staring at her lips as she leaned closer and closer.

"Let me handle, Alaina. Okay? You just keep your eyes on the prize."

"And what, exactly, are we playing for?" he asked, wrapping his arms around her waist.

"You're looking at it, baby," she whispered and kissed him.

Twenty-Seven

On the Horizon

The world of a working mom never stopped, but Jess had to admit, the days when she could bring Parker to work went a lot smoother. Now that she had the art of meal prep down to a science and kept the diaper bag stocked at all times, her morning routine was a lot less chaotic.

Thank God.

A little forethought went a long way toward alleviating unnecessary stress. She'd had to learn that lesson the hard way. But learn it, she had, and now she was on her way to blue skies and sunshine.

By the time Jess arrived at Decadent Designs, the storefront was already opened up and the lights were on.

Somebody got an early start.

It was seven thirty, and Jess wanted to get as much done as possible while Parker was still in his morning ray-of-sunshine mood. So, she had intentionally packed up and been out of the door over an hour early. She tugged on the front door of the shop in the octopus-like fashion of a mother carrying all her child's accoutrements, her own crap, plus, you know, her kid. Clanging and banging everything she was carrying against the doorjamb as she entered the shop, she was surprised she didn't bring paralegals from the law firm next door in with a baseball bat, thinking somebody was trying to break in.

"Hello?" she shouted to whichever one of the girls was present at this hour. She sat Parker down on her desk and let all the other bags slide off her arms and shoulders to the floor. "Hello?" she asked again, slightly louder as she picked Parker's seat back up and wandered further into the office.

There was a fresh cup of coffee steaming on the coffee bar, but no computers were powered up. "Alaina?" She drifted down the hallway to check the sitting room before continuing on to the storeroom. Rustling was coming from the back, and Jess desperately hoped she was about to scare the living daylights out of her friend rather than interrupt a burglary in progress. She pushed the storage room door ajar and entered an alien world full of synthetic lavender roses and eucalyptus leaves. It looked like a flower shop had thrown up. "My…god…"

Alaina gasped as her hand flew to her chest. "Jesus!" She pulled an Airpod out of her ear and glared at her friend. "Are you trying to kill me?"

Jess giggled. "Okay. In my defense, I yelled for you not once, not twice, but *three* times. What in God's name is all this?" She looked around at the piles of wedding paraphernalia, not even knowing where to begin.

"I woke up at three and couldn't go back to sleep. The wedding is in *eighteen days* and I don't have the centerpieces done. I'm freaking out."

"Lainie. Why don't you hire somebody? It will make your life so much easier."

"Three weeks before? Have you lost your mind? Nobody is going to take that on, and if they're crazy enough to try, they'll probably charge me my firstborn to do it. To make matters worse, the invitation company contacted me last night. A third of the invites got returned because somebody forgot to run them through the fucking postage machine!" Alaina tossed her wire cutters on the table with a violent *clank* and covered her eyes with her hands, kneading the sockets.

Jess sighed. Her friend always got frazzled right before a big wedding, but this was ridiculous. "Is there anything I can do to help?"

Alaina was quiet for a moment, but then slowly removed her hands from her face, revealing bloodshot hazel eyes. "Just manage everything else. Please?" she whispered, tears brimming.

She knew one sure-fire way to make her friend feel better and lifted the baby carrier up for inspection. "Did you forget I brought Parker with me today?"

A smile lit Alaina's face, and before Jess could make a peep of protest, her friend had taken the carrier, removed the baby, and was inhaling his powdery baby scent like an addict snorting her first line of cocaine in six hours.

"So…" Jess allowed, crisis averted. "I was thinking we need to find you a bigger storeroom."

"Oh?" Alaina asked, only half attending as she made googly

eyes at the little boy in her arms.

Jess nodded her head toward the hall, indicating she wanted to move this conversation out to the office, and continued to talk as they walked. "The building manager reached out to me and said the travel agency on the second floor is moving out and wanted to know if we'd be interested in the space."

"For storage? That's a lot of space to just throw a bunch of boxes up there."

"Well, I looked at the numbers and we could comfortably swing it. Besides, if we did that, we could branch out like we've talked about and have a party rental side gig that I could spearhead. Sydney is getting more comfortable with the finance side of things, and with our new software, payroll is a breeze. Of course, I'd still be on deck to help with year-end tax stuff and any questions anyone has."

Alaina shifted Parker and turned to face her friend as she took a seat on Jess's desk. "You've been thinking a lot about this, haven't you?"

"I have," Jess nodded. "I think it's a great idea. There are only a couple of party rental locations in the Indianapolis area. Besides, when we purchase new products for an event, we add to our supplies anyway. If we hit up estate sales and auctions for china and flatware and continue to buy back supplies that brides don't want, we're still making money off the design element while taking the overhead cost out of future events. And if brides and companies are simply looking for the decorative things, but don't need a planner, we can rent out items that aren't slated to be used for another event. We could even have displays prepped ahead of time with preset table designs—like a furniture store." Jess shrugged as she stepped over to the coffeemaker and took the cup Alaina had brewed, but not touched. "Are you gonna drink this?"

Alaina shook her head. "You can have it. I'll brew another one in a little bit. So, in theory, if we did this, how much are we talking about in rent every month? I mean, the space upstairs is twice what we have down here. Are we going to be able to afford the second designer I had talked about adding next year?"

"Not next year, but we could take on an intern and then potentially add a second designer the following year. I know it's a sacrifice, but in the long run, I think it will be worth it."

Alaina nodded, but her eyes were far away, running through ideas and scenarios that Jess had already calculated and recalculated over the last few weeks. "Can I think about it? When does he need to know?"

"The agency is in the space until the end of May. After that, he's going to put it up for lease and see if he gets any bites."

Alaina let out a contemplative sigh. "Okay. I'll look at the calendar and the numbers and try to get back to you before the wedding." Jess nodded but didn't comment further. It would *have* to be before the wedding. She and Grayson were going to Aruba for a week-long honeymoon and when she came back, it would be wedding central for the next six months. They wouldn't have time to discuss a business expansion again until November. By then, it would be too late, and Alaina knew that. So, she would let it bide for now. "But enough about all this stuff. Tell me about this weekend. How was it? How was *he*?"

"He's *amazing*." Jess bubbled over with excitement at the idea of sharing her father with her best friend. "You would love him. He's traveled the whole world and done the most amazing things. The man is a titan. I seriously don't know how he balances everything. He's on leave from the poli-sci department at Berkeley while he serves his term, but he has full intentions of going back to teaching. His oldest son, Maddox, is graduating from high school this year and has been accepted into the engineering program at Stanford."

"What's his wife do?" Alaina asked as she made her way over to the Keurig and popped in another dark roast K-pod.

"She's in real estate. I guess she brokers those high-end deals on mansions."

"Ooooh cool. Like on Selling Sunset?"

"Well, yeah, but in San Fran, Sacramento, and Lake Tahoe."

"Daaamn," Alaina commented. "You need to get in good with her."

They both laughed at that, and Jess popped down into her desk chair to pull her laptop from her bag and log into the system. It was eight o'clock now and Sydney and Marissa would be arriving shortly. "Well, if you like that, you're going to love this."

"Oh?" Alaina asked as she handed Parker to Jess so she could retrieve her cup from the coffee bar.

"Julian and Janine spend a week every fall up in Napa at their friend's winery, and Julian said he could hook us up with a place to stay if you wanted to go. I was thinking I might go out with you to Long Beach next weekend and then maybe we could go to Napa for a couple of days as your bachelorette thing."

Alaina's eyes sparkled as she sipped at her coffee. "That would be amazing. I've always wanted to get up there! What winery? Did he say?"

"He did, but I can't remember. He loves IndyCar though, so if I end up going to Long Beach, I'll give him a heads-up and he'll probably come down for the race—if you want."

"Are you kidding? I'd love to meet him! I gotta tell Grayson." She reached over to grab her phone and began texting as she walked back toward the store room.

And she's off.

The bell above the shop door dinged, and Marissa entered, all bubbly smiles and bouncing curls. As she turned to greet her vivacious employee, something caught her attention—a black SUV with heavily tinted windows parked across the street from the shop.

In the city, it wasn't unusual to see any and every type of car parked along the storefronts, but after the incident with Noah in Sacramento, she was on edge. Never in her life had she paid attention to patterns in vehicles or people, but since she'd arrived home from her trip, she couldn't shake the hair-raising feeling someone was watching her. A man in dark jeans and a black leather jacket leaned on the hood of the SUV as he spoke into his phone. The man himself was nondescript except for a scar running down his left cheek.

She didn't like him. Everything about him screamed *danger*.

The quiet melodic tune of her ringtone saturated through the worry and she quickly turned toward her desk, rummaging through her purse with her free hand until she found her phone. "Hello?" she answered quickly before it could go to voicemail.

"Jessica? Hey it's your—It's…um…Julian."

She gave a silent chuckle at his lack of confidence and glanced at the clock on the back wall. "Hey. It's a little early for you, isn't it?" she asked.

"Nah. I just got back from a run, and I'm about to head into the office, but I wanted to let you know I talked to Trevor—my buddy that owns the winery up in Napa. He said you and Alaina are more than welcome to take the loft after Long Beach next weekend if you want it."

Jess was stunned, her mind reeling. "I…"

Words. Use your words.

She hugged Parker tighter, readjusting her grip while she fumbled for something, *anything,* to say.

Misinterpreting her silence, Julian charged ahead. "There're no strings attached. I just thought if you were going to be back out here anyway, you might—"

"No!" Jess shouted, maybe too enthusiastically. She softened her voice. "No. That's not it. I would love to stay in Napa for a few days. It will just depend on if Alaina can get away for that long."

"Of course," her father replied, his voice slightly disappointed, but understanding.

Not wanting to seem ungrateful, she extended an olive branch. "Are you busy next weekend?"

"I don't think so." She heard some papers shuffling on the other end of the phone. "It looks like Maddox has a Scholastic Decathlon on Saturday morning, but that should only last a couple hours. Why?"

"Well, Jack could probably swing a couple of suite passes to the race—if you wanted to come." She hastily added the last part, not wanting to sound presumptuous.

"Absolutely!" he said without hesitation. "That sounds great. I'd love to come."

Jess beamed with delight. "Great! I'll…uh…I'll text you when I hear about the passes. I'm sure we can at least swing some general admission tickets, if nothing else."

"That sounds great. I'll tell Janine. She can't wait to meet you." The warmth in Julian's voice at the mention of his wife made Jess think of Jack, and her smile broadened.

"I can't wait to meet her either. We'll see you in a few days, then."

"Sounds good. Have a great week," her father added in farewell, bringing the unexpected prickle of tears to her eyes. Being a father clearly came as second nature to him, but having that protective love aimed toward her made her feel like she was finally in the orbit of the sun after so many years trapped in the chilled oblivion of a black hole.

"You too," she said by way of farewell and clicked off the phone, glancing back out toward the street.

Scar Face was gone.

Twenty-Eight

Waking Nightmare

The creepy amber light from the lamps lining both sides of the subdivision street raised the hairs on the back of Jack's neck as he made his way through the winding layout toward Jess's house. He remembered the first time he'd driven there, babying the accelerator like his first quarter midget. When a sexy woman invites you back to her house after a fantastic date, you don't hesitate. God, he had been in such a hurry that night.

But this night was different. Very. Different.

The sense of urgency now had little to do with a steamy hookup and a hell of a lot more to do with the woman he loved.

"Hey, it's Jess. Leave me a message. Or don't." The line beeped, and he disconnected the call. Panic had him in a firm grip now, and his stomach writhed like a coil of snakes.

It had been a long day full of fake smiles and endless

patience, and he'd been looking forward to their dinner date, but was running late and had called to tell her as much.

"That's okay. Tita's running behind too," Jess said with a sigh. "Hang on, somebody's at the door."

"I can't believe you actually answer," Jack smirked. "I just pretend I'm not home."

"Yeah well." Jess laughed, and he heard the door open on the other end. "Can I help you?"

Then all hell broke loose. The phone clattered to the floor in a racket of clanks and bangs echoing through his sound system. Shattering glass. Splintering wood. Aggressive voices—men's voices. "Jess?" he called, gripping the steering wheel and leaning forward in his seat in a vain struggle to clear the confusion on the other end of the line. "Jess?" he called louder, his heart leaping into his throat. Jess's cry of pain and pleading voice was the last thing he needed to hear before he hung up and mashed down on the accelerator.

9-1-1 had been his first call as he sped recklessly toward the house. He didn't know who would get there first, himself or the police, but they were all on their way. Jess would have help soon, and while it did little to alleviate his fears, it did make him feel a tad better to know people with guns would be arriving shortly to deal with the mayhem.

The phone rang over his Bluetooth sound system as he tried to call her yet again. "Hey, it's Jess—" He disconnected the call and squealed around the corner onto her street without stopping at the four-way. He could see her house now.

He flew out of his seat as he hit the steep curb of her driveway and slammed on the brakes. Visually sweeping his surroundings for anything suspicious, he took in her black

Chevy Trailblazer in the drive, an old red Camaro down the street, and a utility van in the drive next door, but he'd seen that before. The man who lived there was a plumber. The car door nearly busted off its hinges when he shoved it open, but he didn't care. He'd shovel out his life's savings in repairs if it meant he could get to Jess any faster.

As he rounded the walk toward the front door, he saw signs of a disturbance. The blue ceramic flower pot full of yellow pansies was tipped over and broken. The front door stood ominously ajar, leaving a slit of light pouring out onto the doorstep. Jack listened intently but heard nothing. Had they taken her?

Oh god…

His stomach did an uncomfortable one-eighty, and he swallowed hard before silently pushing on the door. The house was a disaster. Shards of broken pottery and glass littered the floor. A jagged hole had been punched through the entryway wall and drops of blood spattered the floor. The wail of a baby cracked through the silence like a lightning bolt.

Parker.

He stepped further into the house, but it was clear from the stillness, whoever had been there was gone. "Jess?" he called tentatively, searching the carnage for any sign of his girlfriend. "Jess!" His shoes crunched over bits of debris on the floor, and he bent to push a fallen bar stool out of his path. Layla was pawing frantically at the patio door, her nails screeching across the glass and making an awful noise, but Jack ignored her.

A faint thumping sound caught his attention, and he paused, letting his ears guide him, though he couldn't hear much through the adrenaline-induced ringing. The fusillade came again, muffled, but strong. He followed the sound to the back hall, where it was loudest.

"Jack!" *Thump, thump, thump.* "Jack!" He picked up speed, glancing in the office, the bathroom, and then he saw the chair propped under the hall closet door handle. The frame was slightly cracked from Jess's struggles, and the door bowed under the force of her body weight as she threw herself against it again. "Jack!" she screeched. "I'm in here!"

He pulled the chair out from under the handle and pulled the door open, catching her as she collapsed into his arms, sobbing. Relief flooded him. Hundreds of worst-case scenarios had consumed his thoughts on the drive to her house. Kidnapped? Raped? Murdered? But no. She was here. Alive.

The inside of the closet was completely destroyed. Coats that had been hanging neatly on hangers were ripped from the rack. General clutter that had been stored on the shelves above had all crashed down to the floor. The inside of the door was streaked with blood, and he furrowed his brow, pushing her to arm's length to get a good look at her. "Are you okay? Where are you hurt?"

She pushed away and shook her head, making it clear she was not the priority here. "Where's Parker?" she asked, tears still streaming down her face. She turned and flew down the hallway toward his room leaving Jack questioning her sanity as he stared after her. Then he shook off his shock and followed.

More tears welled to the surface and spilled over Jess's cheeks at the sight of her perfectly healthy child lying in his crib shrieking. She bent over and put her hand lightly on his chest, shushing until his cries quieted to whimpers. Some semblance of calm was returning to her features after being reunited with her son, but the wild look in her eyes wasn't about to retreat any time soon. "Can you pick him up for me?" she asked, cradling her wrist tenderly.

"Of course," he murmured, bending to scoop up the sturdy boy. He gestured her over to the rocking chair in the corner and handed him to her after she sat. Her wrist was clearly bothering her, and he wondered what other injuries she was trying to cover up. Now that she was more settled, he knelt next to her and put one tender finger under her chin to tilt her face up to the light. He swallowed hard against the wave of hatred and disgust bubbling in his gut. A sizable bruise was turning her face blue from temple to jaw, and her left eye was swelling shut.

She had a deep gash across her left palm, and her wrist and forearm were swollen, probably where she had fallen—or been pushed—into the broken glass on the floor. He pulled the handkerchief out of his sport coat breast pocket and tied it around her hand with a swift tug. She made a small grunting noise, but otherwise, remained still.

"Brownsburg Police Department!" An officer shouted from the front door.

"Back here!" Jack yelled, squeezing Jess's uninjured hand.

The noisy approach of several emergency responders preceded their appearance in the doorway, guns drawn, but pointed slightly down. "I'm Jack Kinney. I made the call. This is my girlfriend, Jessica Morales. It's her house."

The officer holstered his weapon. "Are you okay? We've got an ambulance outside if you need medical attention."

Jess cradled Parker protectively as she struggled for a

coherent response through her post-adrenaline fog. "I think…my hand…"

"It's okay," Jack murmured, running a hand over her head, to reassure himself as much as her. He turned to the police officers. "Would it be possible to have the EMTs come in here to assess her? It's cold outside."

The officer at the head of the group nodded. "Of course. We'll get someone in here to take a look at her." He turned to the other officers and started giving them orders: to call CSI, to tape off the scene…

Jack tuned them out and put all his focus back on Jess. "Are you okay?" he asked, running a hand back and forth across her thigh. She was shivering and clinging to the baby like a grim death. He stood and grabbed the Afghan draped over the side of Parker's crib to wrap it around her shoulders.

"Thank you," she whispered, her teeth clacking together as she shuddered. His heart was cracking into a million tiny pieces at the sight of her. If he found those sons of bitches in a dark alley, nothing would stop him from taking matters into his own hands.

While the police questioned Jess about what happened, Jack took Parker and retreated toward the quiet sanctuary of Jess's bedroom, seemingly untouched in the melee. He picked his way across the carnage in the living room and entryway, taking care to disturb as little as possible before the crime scene investigators could do their job. The drawers in the living room writing desk had all been removed, upended, and carelessly tossed across the room, taking a gouge out of the drywall on the west wall. This wasn't some insignificant breaking and entering. This was a full-blown home invasion.

He shook his head and held the sleeping baby in his arms

a little tighter. Thank God he was safe.

The red and blue lights of the police cruisers in the driveway and along the street refracted off neighboring houses, and people were beginning to notice. From the window in Jess's room, Jack could see her neighbors peeking out their front windows and standing on their front porches. An officer was standing off to one side, taking a statement from Jess's next-door neighbor, the plumber, who looked bewildered but was cooperating. Then he caught sight of another officer calmly gesturing for the person in front of him to calm down as he spoke with—

"Shit." He turned toward the door and made his way back through the destroyed hall and living room, trying to keep from disturbing Parker as he ran toward the driveway where Jessica's frantic grandmother was screaming in Spanish at the top of her lungs.

"It's okay," Jack assured the officer, who was obviously out of his depth and not used to being yelled at, let alone in a foreign language. "It's okay. She's Jessica's grandmother. I'll take her."

The officer nodded at Jack, still at a loss, but compliant. "Mrs. Morales?" he asked, trying to get her attention without receiving both barrels. "I'm Jack, Jess's boyfriend."

"Yèsica, does not have a…novio." Ivanna's dark brown eyes narrowed as she looked Jack over and then realized he was holding her great grandson in his arms.

"¿De dónde es ella?" she asked, stepping into Jack's space with enough force to back him up a pace.

His Spanish was rudimentary—on par with that of a fourth grader—but he thought she'd asked where Jessica was. "She's in the house. The EMT said she needs to go—"

Ivanna blew past him toward the house, screeching "¡Yèsica!" over and over again.

"To the hospital." Jack groaned as Ivanna disappeared through the front door. With a flustered shake of his head at the officer, who was staring after Ivanna with raised brows, Jack followed, hugging Parker tighter against the cold.

An EMT was finishing his evaluation when Jack walked back into the nursery, and the officer she'd been speaking with was gone. "You're gonna need stitches in that palm, and I don't think an X-ray would hurt either."

Ivanna was standing at her granddaughter's side, murmuring things to her in soft Spanish. Jess looked up at Jack helplessly as he entered, and he widened his eyes, trying to communicate that he'd done his best to keep the whirlwind at bay.

"Mrs. Morales? Would you mind taking the baby for a bit? I think he needs his diaper changed," he said, feigning male ignorance at how to change a dirty diaper.

Ivanna glanced down at her granddaughter, stroking her cheek with a single finger, and Jess nodded in reassurance. Satisfied Jess wasn't in immediate danger, she turned and scooped the baby out of Jack's arms, disappearing in search of a quieter venue to change Parker's diaper.

Jess winced as the EMT tightened the bandage around her hand and wrist and used a clip to pin the end of the fabric to the rest of the wrap. "We can give you a ride to the hospital if you need it," the EMT continued. "How's the head? Tylenol kicking in yet?"

"A little bit better," Jess allowed, gently probing her abused cheekbone and temple. "I think I'm alright though. Jack can take me to the hospital for X-rays."

Jack nodded and stepped closer to place a comforting hand on her shoulder. "Whenever you're ready."

Squeezing his hand for a long moment, she finally sighed and hauled herself to her feet, wobbling unsteadily as she rose. Jack seized her around the waist before she could fall, and her mouth curled up on one side with a sheepish grin. "Sorry. Just a little woozy…"

The EMT eyed her suspiciously. "You could have a concussion. Have them check that while you're at the hospital too. In the meantime, try not to take any naps, okay?"

She nodded in acknowledgment and stepped forward out of Jack's embrace. "Just let me make sure Tita's okay before we leave."

Jack got the distinct impression Ivanna Morales had a backbone made of reinforced steel, but if Jess needed the peace of mind of seeing her son safe into her grandmother's care, he would not object.

* * *

The antiseptic smell identified as "hospital" in Jack's sensory library permeated his nasal membranes and soaked through his pores to the point where he thought he'd need to shower three times to even touch the stench. Okay, maybe stench was too harsh a word, but Jack didn't like hospitals on his best day, let alone a day like today. Jess had been taken back for X-rays and a CT scan, leaving Jack to his own devices until she got back to the little room she'd been assigned. He blinked rapidly to clear his vision and gave a jaw-cracking yawn before leaning back in his chair to rest his head on the wall. He'd just begun to doze off when his phone vibrated with an incoming call.

He picked it up from the small counter next to him and immediately swiped to accept the call without paying much mind to who was calling. "Hello?" he asked around another yawn, glancing at the clock on the wall. It was almost midnight. No wonder he was tired.

"Dude. What the hell is going on out there?" Jack blinked, trying to compute the words coming through the speaker with the voice. "Hello?" The voice asked again. "Jack?"

"I'm here," he replied, blinking and shaking his head to clear the cobwebs. "But unless you've developed ESP, why in the hell are you calling me at midnight?"

"It's only ten my time," Noah said in a verbal shrug before continuing. "A buddy of mine at DPD keeps a notification for me when 'Kinney' pings in the RMS—"

"I'm not even going to ask." Jack rolled his eyes and waited for his brother to continue.

"Good, 'cuz I'm the one asking questions. Why the hell is your name popping up in connection to a home invasion in Brownsburg, Indiana?"

Jack stood up and glanced out into the emergency department before partially shutting the door to the exam room where he was encamped. "Jess's place got broken into tonight."

The overhead speaker squawked. "Doctor Lingelser, call 496. Doctor Lingelser, 496."

"Are you in a *hospital*? Shit. Okay. I'm hopping on the next flight."

"Shut up and sit your ass down. Yes. I'm at a hospital. Jess got pretty banged up and they're running some tests. When we left a couple of hours ago, CSI was just getting there and they said they'd likely still be there when we got back."

"You said Jess was banged up. What happened?" There was nothing but immutable calm in his brother's voice, and it helped quell Jack's unease.

"I haven't had a chance to talk to her about it. She was pretty shaken up on the way here, and after she was admitted, hospital staff were constantly coming in and out. From what I can gather, the assholes broke into her house looking for something. They whacked her pretty good across the face and locked her in the hall closet while they ran roughshod over the entire house: holes in walls, furniture smashed."

"Anything missing?"

"I couldn't tell. The only thing we noticed was Jess's wallet. It wasn't in her purse when we got to the hospital. I'm sure we'll have a better idea once she can go through everything."

"I don't like this, Jack." There was an edge to Noah's voice that sent unease skittering up Jack's spine.

"And you think I do? There are a million other places I'd rather be than in the hospital with my battered girlfriend."

"What about the baby?"

"He's fine. The assholes didn't touch him. Thank God." Jack plopped down in his chair again and absently prodded the empty hospital bed with his foot.

"That's good." Jack could hear the gears turning in Noah's brain as he calculated and recalculated. "Wait. If Jess got the shit beat out of her, and they didn't touch Parker, where were you? How did you get there so quickly?"

"I was already on my way. Jess and I were supposed to have dinner tonight. I was actually on the phone with her when the—" He gritted his teeth against his rising rage and took a deep breath. "—When it happened."

Noah was quiet on the other end. "The police got there quickly, if they were already there when you arrived. That's good. The perps couldn't have gone far."

"The cops got there after I did, but whoever it was was already gone when I arrived."

Steely silence floated through the speaker like a lead weight through pond water. "Do. Not. Tell me you went in that house with a possible active home invasion unarmed and without backup."

"Fine. I won't tell you that," Jack replied with complete angelic innocence.

"I oughta kick your ass to Timbuktu," Noah growled. "You could have been killed!"

Jack jumped up from his seat and began pacing. "You think I don't know that? What was I supposed to do, for Christ's sake? My girlfriend was inside and for all I knew she could have been lying on the floor bleeding out. You would have done the exact same thing, so spare me the lecture." All the pent-up fear and rage he'd been denying over the past few hours needed an outlet, and he suddenly felt an uncontrollable urge to hit something.

"No, I wouldn't have, because I would have had a *gun*. God, for somebody so smart, you can be *really* stupid."

There was a knock on the door proceeded by a hospital attendant pushing Jess in a wheelchair. Her left eye was swollen completely shut now, and the swelling had extended to her cheekbone. Whatever they hit her with, it had been done with calculated force, meant to subdue, not kill.

His heart twisted in his chest at the sight of her. "Jess's back. I gotta go."

"I'm getting on the first flight in the morning. I'll be there around ten thirty, and I'm gonna need more details than what you've given me so far."

"This isn't your investigation. Stay the hell out of it."

"See you soon," Noah said and disconnected the call.

Jack growled in frustration and glared at the phone as if it were personally responsible for his brother's blatant disrespect.

"Was that Noah?" Jess asked. Her voice was quiet, almost… hopeful?

A stab of jealousy shot through Jack, but he put a pin in it. "It was. But we can talk about his pseudo-stalking behavior later. What did you find out?"

"The ER doc is waiting for the on-call radiologist to read the scans. He'll come in and give you the results once he has them in hand," the attendant said as he helped Jess back into the bed and tucked a heated blanket around her legs. "Anything else I can get you?"

"No. I think I'm okay. Thanks."

The assistant left the room with a quiet click of the door, and Jack leaned over the rail of her hospital bed to grab her hand and squeeze some warmth back into it. "That feels nice," she hummed as he lifted it to his lips and kissed her knuckles.

"How are you feeling?" he asked in a low voice as he sandwiched the frozen fingers of her undamaged hand between his two larger ones. Her other hand was cradled protectively against her chest. He hoped it wasn't broken. It would be nearly impossible to care for Parker on her own with a broken wrist. That, and she would have a cast for the wedding in two weeks. She'd be pissed about that.

"I'm alright." Her eyes were closed as she rested her head

on the back of the bed. He was tempted to let her sleep, but the EMT had been clear. No naps. "Just tired. I want to go home."

"I know," he murmured back as he tucked a stray lock of hair behind her ear. "Once you get released, I'll take you home. Then I'll go back to the hotel so you can get some sleep."

"Please stay," she whispered. "I don't want to be alone tonight."

The last vestiges of Jack's bravado crumbled, but luckily, a quick rap on the door saved him the indignity of bursting into tears.

"Knock-knock," the emergency room doctor called as he peeked around the door. "Well Jess, I've got some good news." He entered the room and shut the door behind him, leaning against it so he could face his patient in the close space. "The radiologist looked at your scans. You've got a severe sprain on that wrist. Make sure to ice it well and practice your range of motion on it once the swelling goes down in a few days. You should be back to normal in a few weeks. The CT scan didn't reveal any major anomalies. You've got a mild concussion. So no contact sports or rollercoasters for a couple of weeks." He gave her a friendly wink in jest. "Other than that, we'll get that palm stitched up and get you on your way."

It took longer for the lidocaine to take effect than for the three stitches Jess had put in, and before they knew it, they were signing discharge paperwork and walking out into the frosty night air. It wasn't a long drive back to Jess's house, but Jack would rather have driven four hours than face what was waiting for them.

He'd understood Jess completely when she said she didn't want to be alone tonight. Hell, he wouldn't want to be alone either.

311

Twenty-Nine

Bewitched, Bothered, and Bewildered

"Jesus Christ…" Noah said as he and Jack stepped over the threshold of Jess's house eleven hours later.

By the time the police had wrapped up their investigation and cleared out, Jack had only slept a couple of hours before picking his brother up from the airport. The ride had been mostly silent. Both men were still peeved from their heated conversation the night before.

"Is this how you found it?" Noah asked, squatting to look at a few drops of dried blood on the laminate floor.

"More or less." Jack looked around the room for things that were different from his recollection. "I think the glass is a bit more crunched up and some stuff has been moved, but nothing notable."

Noah nodded and continued his slow but steady progress toward the living room and hallway. He stopped at the closet door, still open with the light on. Bloody smears patterned the inside of the white door. "This is where you found her last night?"

"Yeah…she looked like a fox with her foot caught in a trap. It was awful."

His brother showed little emotion as he walked the space, taking occasional pictures of things he wanted to look at later. "Did CSI take anything?"

"They gave me a list—a picture frame, some documents—nothing major." Jack shrugged and turned to follow Noah back down the hall.

"And you said they didn't bother the baby at all?" He walked toward the nursery, examining the doorjamb and knob before doing a slow turn around the room, evidently finding nothing of note in his observations.

"Not that I could tell. His door was closed, and he was screaming bloody murder from his crib when I got here."

Noah sighed and shook his head. "Where's Jess now?"

Jack hiked a thumb over his shoulder. "In her room. She hasn't really left it since we got back last night. I don't want to push her, but I'm worried."

Noah nodded. "It's not uncommon. If she has a place she feels safe right now, just let her stay there. We'll get a security system installed before I leave, and hopefully that will give her some peace of mind."

"Hello?" Alaina called from the front door.

Jack threw his head back and pinched the bridge of his nose. He didn't have the patience for her today—not on two hours of sleep. But he would give it the old college try. For Jess. Noah gave his brother a side eye, but made no comment as they walked back into the living room to meet their guests.

Alaina froze in her tracks as the two groups converged in the living room, shocked. "Jack…"

"Hey, Alaina." He greeted her with a faint curl to the corner of his mouth. "Long time no see."

"What…are you doing here?" she asked hesitantly, as her gaze flitted between Jack, Noah, then Grayson, and back to Jack.

Jess chose that moment to emerge from her den, and all traces of anger and betrayal vanished from Alaina's face as she caught sight of her friend. A few hours hadn't done anything to improve her appearance. The entire left side of Jess's face was mottled with blue and purple, and livid red fingerprints were popping up on her neck.

"Son of a bitch…" Noah choked out under his breath.

"Oh my God," Alaina cried, as she rushed to her, raising a hand to her face, but not quite touching her. "Are you okay?" she asked with tears in her eyes as she pulled her friend into her embrace. Alaina wasn't tall, but her five feet six inches dwarfed Jess, especially as curled in on herself as she was. There was no hint of the confident woman he'd fallen for in this girl.

Grayson caught Jack's eye, his brow furrowed in a mixture of compassion, shock, horror, and something else Jack couldn't quite read. "It looks like a bomb went off in here," he said with a shake of his head.

"This is awful…" Alaina said as she took in her surroundings. "What could they have possibly wanted?"

Jess shook her head wordlessly, and turned to Jack, her normally penetrating green eyes slightly glassy from trauma and exhaustion.

"Hey…" He gently tucked a few strands of loose hair behind

her ear and gazed down at her, fighting against the wall she was desperately trying to put up. She was biting down hard on her bottom lip. It was a force of habit that might have been cute, could he not see the reasoning behind it: a torrent of tears barely held in check by a dam of sheer stubbornness. He leaned in and kissed her gently on the forehead, holding her until she was ready for him to let go. His dashboard warning light was blinking an ominous red. Whatever she may claim, she was holding on by a thread. "We can handle this if you need to lay down."

She shook her head in harsh determination. "No. I'm fine. I need to see if there's anything I need to report to the insurance company or the police. I can't do that if I lock myself in my room and hide under the bed." Her words were harsh, but when he laced his fingers through hers and squeezed, she let the anger come out of her voice. "I'm sorry. I just—I need to do this."

He nodded and ducked his head closer to speak with a confidential undertone. "If you're going to do your Superwoman thing, then at least let me help?"

She gave him a small smile and nodded back as she stroked his beard stubble with the back of her hand. "Okay."

Jack glanced over Jess's shoulder to Grayson and Alaina, quietly conversing near the kitchen island. Alaina's sharp hazel eyes met his for a split second, and he felt as though she'd skewered him with a large icicle. He couldn't read lips, and after years at the racetrack, his ears were shit, but he could imagine the venom she was spewing.

He rolled his eyes and returned his attention to Jess.

"Thanks for coming," she murmured to Noah, not meeting his eye.

"Of course." His voice was low, almost intimate, and Jack felt the same stab of jealousy creep over him he'd felt last night in the hospital.

Get over yourself, he told the little green monster, trying his damnedest to smother it and refocus on more important matters. Noah made Jess feel safe, and that was a good thing—especially now.

"When you feel up to it, I'd like to go over everything with you. If that's alright?" Noah murmured in a gentle tone. His brother had dealt with his share of battered women during his time on the force and was a good man to have in their corner.

She nodded. "Sure. Can we get everything cleaned up first, though? I'd feel a lot better if all this was gone before I went to bed tonight."

By some unspoken agreement, they all took that as their cue to get to work. "Hey. Can you come help me get the drywall stuff out of the car?" Grayson asked Jack with a nod toward the front door.

"Yeah, sure." Jack took Jess's hand and squeezed. "I'll be right back." He sidestepped Alaina like the ticking time bomb that she was, and glanced over his shoulder back at Jess, but she was distracted for the time being and he elected to leave her to her peace rather than draw attention to her fuming best friend. He just hoped Alaina would get herself under control, or at the very least, take her anger out on him. The last thing Jess needed right now was to get in a pissing match with her best friend.

It was considerably warmer now than it had been the night before, almost balmy by March standards, but a steady breeze kept a touch of the previous night's chill. Birds sang to each other from the highest branches of the blooming crabapple tree in the front yard. Its pink flowers added a pop of color to the relative desolation of plant life. None of the more prominent deciduous trees had begun their slow growth of summer foliage, but the grass was well and truly green after taking in the spring rain of the last few days.

Grayson popped the hatch on his SUV and waited for it to rise before ducking in to remove a bucket of drywall mud and several plastic bags full of patch kits, sanding materials, and other odds and ends. "I didn't know you guys were coming over today." Jack grabbed the remaining sacks and pulled them toward the front of the hatch.

His friend continued rummaging around the back. "Jess called Alaina this morning—told her the house had been broken into and asked if we'd come over to help clean up." His tone was brusque, the words clipped, as he rearranged the surplus of hardware goods he'd accumulated.

Jack furrowed his brow and leaned a hip against the bumper, crossing his arms. "Are you mad at me or something?" He couldn't understand what Gray's attitude was about, and wasn't intending to go back inside until they sorted it out.

Grayson paused and released the handle of the bucket he was holding with a *ka-clink*. He crossed his arms and leaned against the bumper, mirroring Jack's pose as he tried to formulate a response. Finally, he sighed and dropped his arms. "I'm not mad. I just…"

Jack snorted, trying to lighten the mood. "Let me guess. You're not mad, just disappointed?"

Grayson's eyes flashed.

Okay. No humor, then.

"Not disappointed." Gray heaved his tool bag out of the car and slung it over his shoulder. "I just wish you'd told me, is all."

Jack raised an eyebrow and glared at his friend. "Told you what? You knew Jess and I were a thing." He was trying to keep the defensive edge out of his voice and failing miserably.

Grayson sighed and threw back his head. "Yeah, but I thought you were just talking. I thought *maybe* you'd slept together, but not…" He sighed and closed his eyes. "This looks bad, Jack," Grayson muttered, with a slight wince. "What is going on? Are you living together?"

"Damn, Gray. I didn't expect the Spanish Inquisition. Why does it matter? Honestly, it's a damn good thing I *was* here this weekend. Otherwise, Jess could have been locked in that closet for days before somebody noticed. Parker could have died of dehydration!" Jack was fuming at the accusation in his friend's voice. "I really didn't expect this from you of all people."

Grayson threw his shoulders back and clenched his jaw for a moment before saying, "Jack, she has a baby with my future brother-in-law. You are literally putting me in the middle. What did you expect me to do?"

"Be my friend, damn it!" Jack shouted before catching himself and glancing over his shoulder toward the house. "Be happy that I'm happy." Jack furrowed his brow as he studied his friend, who had paled and was studying the ground with rapt attention. "Just…let me and Jess worry about everything else."

"*Are* you worrying about it, though?" Grayson asked, his head suddenly jerking up with a narrow glare.

Jack glared back. "A day doesn't go by when Jess doesn't

worry about Tucker. It's my job to be supportive of her and her decisions. The last thing we need is to get into a pissing match with you and Alaina about how to handle the situation."

"Don't bring Alaina into this." Grayson's hackles were rising, and if Jack didn't right the ship soon, it would capsize and be a complete loss.

"If she has nothing to do with this, then fine. I just have a hard time believing you would have cared what Jess and I chose to do with our relationship a year ago." Jack threw his hands up in the air and backed off.

Grayson finally pushed off the vehicle and turned to face his friend head-on. "Look, I am happy for you. And yeah, a little bit of my *attitude* has more to do with Alaina than because I actually care what you and Jess do. I don't want to see Tucker hurt, but he's a grown man—a grown man that's over six feet and a hundred and eighty-five pounds, by the way. So you better make sure your version of handling Tucker, doesn't involve fisticuffs."

Jack did his best not to let Grayson's jibe ruffle his feathers and sighed. "How about we cross that bridge when we get to it, hmm? You're not putting much stock in our ability to handle this situation like adults."

Grayson snorted. "And you seem to be forgetting how well I know you."

Jack gave an indignant huff, but let it ride, seeing that the argument was over for now. "Alright, let's get this drywall patched." Jack heaved his portion of the gear out of the back and started toward the door, but Grayson called after him. "Hey, can you do me a favor?"

"I don't know, Gray. I'm kinda at my quota for favors

today," he teased as he turned back around.

But Grayson's face was deadly serious. "Try to give Alaina a break. She wants her friend to be happy, but she loves her brother. He's putting on a good show, but this breakup has run him through the wringer. It hasn't been easy for any of them."

Jack had to force himself not to roll his eyes and then followed up that exercise in self-control with a swift kick in the ass. He knew she had health complications from her accident. Add in the stress of planning a wedding and the complete breakdown of her best friend and brother's relationship, and she was dealing with way more than Jack would have liked on his plate. He needed to be gracious and deal with her mood swings like a man instead of the whiny baby he was turning into.

* * *

The day proved to be productive, and by the time Alaina and Grayson left, all the drywall damage had been repaired. The floors had been cleaned, clearing all traces of blood, dirt, and drywall dust, and everything not broken beyond repair was back in its proper place. Suffering no ill effects from the night before, Parker had gone down easily leaving Jess at a loss, used as she was to her nightly brawl with her infant son. Her head was beginning to throb slightly, and she prodded gingerly at her face with the occasional wince as she hit a tender spot on her temple or cheekbone.

She could feel eyes on her as she walked into the kitchen and rummaged through the cabinet for a couple of Tylenol. Noah and Jack were acting like a couple of guard dogs, and she thought with a quiet snort, that if the doorbell rang, they may just start growling. After she consumed the Tylenol along with a glass of water, she turned toward the refrigerator and grabbed the chocolate ice cream from the freezer, mentally saying "fuck it" with the utmost sincerity. If the last twenty-four hours wasn't cause for a tub of Prairie Farms' finest, what was?

She kicked the freezer drawer closed behind her and turned toward the brothers, who were quietly talking among themselves, their low voices creating a pleasant hum like a hive of buzzing bees. She eased herself down onto the couch next to Jack, doing her best not to moan against the soreness in her ribs and shoulders, and drew her feet up under her as she pried the lid off the ice cream tub and dug in. Jack lifted his arm to drape around her shoulders, and she snuggled into his side, feeling at peace for the first time in hours. The ice cream's rich, chocolaty goodness melted across her tongue and breathed some life back into her fuzzy brain.

When she opened her eyes, not fully realizing they'd been closed, she saw Noah's probing blue gaze, full of questions. "Do you feel like you might be up to telling me what happened?"

She felt exposed under that piercing stare, and she wanted to burrow under Jack's arm and hide. But she wasn't going to do that. Not today.

Jess took another spoonful of ice cream and nodded with more confidence than she felt. "Sure. I guess."

Jack tightened his arm around her and leaned over. "If you don't feel up to it—"

"No, it's…it's fine. The more I can remember now, the more it might help later. Right?" she asked Noah with a smile so fake you couldn't sell it on an infomercial.

Noah furrowed his brow, but nodded. "Right." He leaned forward and pulled his phone from his pocket. "Do you mind if I take notes?"

Jess shook her head, not really sure what she was *supposed* to say. If she was going to dump a buttload of trauma on Noah in the interest of finding her attackers, she couldn't very well tell him not to do whatever it took to get the job done.

"Can you tell me what happened? As best as you remember it?" he asked, his gaze intent on hers, but not in an intimidating way. She felt safe with these two men—the Kinney boys—as she was privately beginning to think of them. She knew they had other brothers, but these two, Noah and Jack, were two peas in a pod. It didn't take a genius to figure that out.

Jess took a shaky breath and nodded, glancing quickly up at Jack for reassurance before closing her eyes and pulling her memories to the surface, kicking and screaming.

"I was…on the phone with Jack. He was calling to let me know he was running late. I told him that was fine—Tita was coming over to stay with Parker, but she was running late too. We couldn't leave until Tita got here anyway, so there was no rush." She shook her head and redirected herself back to the task at hand. "Somebody knocked on the door…"

* * *

Someone knocking on the door was odd in her neighborhood. Normally, the delivery drivers just left their packages on the porch and she got an email later stating they'd been delivered.

"I can't believe you actually answer the door." She could hear the playful smirk in Jack's voice and rolled her eyes. "I just pretend I'm not home."

"Yeah well," she sighed in a tone that made it clear how childish she thought that idea was, but loved him despite his antics. She twisted the doorknob and pulled open the door to see two men in front of her, dressed in nondescript black clothing, which she thought was odd attire for a door-to-door salesman. The second man, standing slightly behind the one who had knocked at the door, looked oddly familiar, and her heart gave a tiny stutter of recognition—Scar Face. "Can I help you?" she asked with a smile, assuming casualness.

They didn't wait for an opening, instead taking the brute force approach, and Jess immediately knew she was in deep shit. They forced their way into the house, the front man grabbing her by her shoulders and shoving her backward. Her phone flew out of her hand, and she'd barely gotten the breath of a scream out before the front man bull rushed her. All the knickknacks and paintings lining the hall clattered to the floor in a spray of glass and splintering wood as he pinned her to the wall with a hand over her mouth. The second man checked over his shoulder to ensure no one was watching before he closed the door behind him. With the door closed, even if she screamed, no one would hear, and even if there was a window to escape, would she? What about Parker? She couldn't just leave him.

She screeched against the giant hand covering her mouth. His fingers had such a tight grip on her jaw, she was sure she'd have bruises—if she lived that long. She shoved against him, fighting to get some sort of leverage, but her tiny frame had nothing on a guy well over six feet and built of solid steel. He leaned into her, his rock solid thighs pressing against hers, immobilizing her against the wall. "Now, you just calm down, and nobody has to get hurt," he said in a smooth voice that would have been attractive, had the blue eyes staring down at her not been so cold and unfeeling. "We have a message to deliver, and we can either do that the easy way or the hard way. It'd be a shame to do it the hard way. You're too pretty for that," the man growled in an aggressively sexual innuendo.

What the fuck?

Jess stared up at him, struggling to control her breathing against the hand smashing into her nose as well as clamping down on her jaw. The second man had disappeared into the house, and Jess threw all one hundred and ten pounds of herself against the asshole holding her to the wall.

"Now, if I take my hand away, you have to promise not to scream. Okay? We just want to talk." He sounded almost reasonable. The Velcro on the man's tactical gloves was scraping her cheek, and every fiber in her being was screaming, *"Get him off, get him off!"* She nodded this time and took a gasping breath as he freed her and backed up a couple of feet.

"What do you want?" she asked, her voice raspy, but steady with the adrenaline coursing through her.

"There's a baby back here!" Scar Face shouted, and before Jess had room for a second thought, she was hurtling down the hall toward Parker's room. She'd seen enough true crime documentaries to know the likelihood of her surviving this day was slim, and if she was going to die anyway, she'd spend her dying breath protecting her son, and taking a couple of eyeballs or testicles with her.

"Son of a bitch," the first man grumbled behind her. She didn't make it past the living room before a two-hundred-pound missile slammed into her back and sent her reeling along with the plum-colored vase on the sideboard, which shattered on the floor just moments before she landed there, hands splayed out to catch herself. White hot pain shot up her arm, but she ignored everything—everything except the need to protect her baby. She flipped over, kicking and scratching at the man on top of her. He grabbed desperately at her arms, trying to control her struggles before suddenly lunging over her with his long arms, coming back with a decorative wooden tray that had also fallen off the sideboard and whacked her across the side of the face, knocking her out cold.

* * *

Jack was rigid underneath her as she spoke, and she could feel him straining against the impulse to jump up off the couch and start pacing. Most of what she was saying was news to him, and she'd known he wouldn't like hearing it, but the overwhelming sense of—*What was it? Helplessness? Failure? Anger?*—couldn't be helped no matter how she chose to present the truth. Instead, she ignored Jack and focused on Noah and his questions.

"What did the guys look like? You said they were in tactical gear?"

Jess nodded. "Yeah, all black: cargo pants, long-sleeve shirts, black lace-up cargo boots, vests, and gloves."

"Did they have guns?"

Jess tried to think back to the two men standing on her front stoop. That had been her best view of them, and she didn't remember the front man having a gun, but the other one… "I think one of the guys had one in a hip holster. I don't know. I didn't get a good look at him in the moment."

Noah's eyes shot up from his phone to study her face. "What do you mean, 'in the moment?' Had you seen him before?"

Jess gave Jack a side eye to gauge his reaction. He seemed to have morphed into a marble statue, frozen in contemplation as he stared straight ahead, muscles clenched with anxiety. Then she turned back to his brother. "Yeah. I saw him yesterday morning—out in front of the shop."

Noah's face showed no emotion. He just kept typing on his phone with the pads of his thumb. "Do you guys have cameras on the front of your shop?"

"Yeah. I could pull up the video on my phone. We have an app that monitors all the security cameras on the property."

Noah nodded. "Yeah. Send that to me and to the detective on your case if you haven't already. That should help identify the bastard, or at least give them something to go on."

A fine shiver ran through Jess, and Jack tightened his arm around her, chafing her arm with his hand to force some warmth back into her. She nodded and pulled her phone out to make a reminder to send Noah the file when she had a chance.

"You said they wanted to deliver a message? Did they leave anything or say anything else about this 'message?'"

"No…" she whispered, dropping her gaze. It was hard to think about the attack for a prolonged amount of time, hard to process how close she'd been to being murdered. She'd almost left Parker an orphan. Another shiver ran through her. She'd been such an idiot for answering that door, but she stopped that train of thought cold in its tracks. If those men had wanted in her house, nothing so simple as a door could have stopped them. "When I ran for Parker…they stopped negotiating."

Noah sighed and locked his phone, leaning back slightly in his seat. "I hate to ask, but…when they hit you…is that all that happened?"

Jess took a shaky breath, tears welling in her eyes, but Noah's even gaze, full of strength and poise, steadied her. "It wasn't…I mean, they didn't…" She shook her head and looked back down, shaking her head. There hadn't seemed to be much of a silver lining in the whole situation, but she supposed escaping a violent rape was something to be thankful for at least.

Some of the tension leaked out of Jack like a pinhole in a balloon and his tense shoulders slowly deflated.

"I'm tired," she whispered, looking up at him and then back to Noah. "I'd like to get some rest now, if that's okay?"

Noah nodded. "Of course." He jumped to his feet and gave a jaw-cracking yawn as he reached his hands up toward the ceiling, stretching his back. "I think I'll call an Uber and head back to the hotel—that bed is calling my name."

Jack shook his head. "I'll drive you. Just let me make sure Jess is settled."

Jess sighed, but gently elbowed Jack in the ribs. "I'm not an invalid. Take Noah to the hotel. I'll be fine. Parker will be up soon, and I'll need to get him a bottle anyway."

Jack hesitated, his brow furrowed in concern as he reached out and stroked the undamaged side of her face. "Are you sure?"

"I'm *fine*, Jack," she assured him. "Go. I think we can make it an hour without you, difficult as it may be."

He gave her a lopsided smile full of longing before leaning in to kiss her forehead, and she felt in that gesture everything he'd never say in front of his brother.

She put her hands on his chest, patting gently, and then gave him a little shove. "Go. I'll be here when you get back."

Thirty

Fifty Shades of Fucked Up

"So what's the story with Jess and Alaina?" Noah asked thoughtfully as he stared out the windshield.

Jack furrowed his brow and glanced over at his brother. "What do you mean?" It had been a long day, and he wasn't up for decoding Noah's cryptic messages. The headlights from oncoming traffic washed over the dark interior of the car, illuminating the brothers. Noah's jaw was tight, eyes pensive, as he continued to piece through the evidence stacking up in little invisible piles all around him.

He suddenly shook his head and shrugged. "I don't know. When you and Grayson went outside to get the stuff out of the car, they were hissing like a pair of feral cats in the kitchen. I couldn't really hear what they were saying, but when I peeked in on them, Alaina looked pretty keyed up."

Jack shifted in his seat and gripped the wheel tighter. He had a pretty good idea what that had been about, and the thought of Alaina cornering Jess to emotionally brow beat her after the night she'd had made him want to take the next exit and head for Alaina's apartment just so he could give her a piece of his mind.

"Easy, tiger," Noah joked as he eyed the death grip Jack had on the steering wheel. "It's just a question."

Jack's teeth were clenched so tightly, he thought he might grind right through the enamel on his molars. So, he relaxed his jaw muscles, as best he could, and took a deep breath. "Parker's father is Alaina's brother." Jack's voice was low and careful.

Noah turned in his seat to look at Jack. "Hold up. Your girlfriend is the mother of your best friend's brother-in-law's baby?" Noah's mouth was gaping in shock.

Jack replayed his brother's words, squinting as he manually calculated the veracity of his statement. "Yeah. That about sums it up."

"Jeeeeesus, Jack."

"It's complicated. That's not anything new," Jack grumbled. "But Jess wasn't ready to tell Tucker that we got back together—"

"So naturally she couldn't tell his sister about it either." Noah nodded in understanding as he put two and two together. "But still…Alaina couldn't pick a better time to have it out with her supposed best friend than after her house was broken into and she was beaten within an inch of her life? Kind of a bitch move."

"Yeah."

They managed a full five minutes of silence before the toxic mix of confusion and agitation rolling off Noah unraveled what was left of Jack's fragile self-control.

"*What?*" He hissed as he flicked his turn signal and switched lanes to pass somebody going below the speed limit.

"It just doesn't make any sense," Noah muttered as he looked out the window into the darkness beyond.

"What doesn't?" He was still stuck on the Jess and Alaina kerfuffle and unsuccessfully quelling his rising anger. Jess didn't need him to fight her battles. If that's what she wanted, she would have told him. But that didn't stop him from wanting to do *something* about it. Another asshole drifted in front of him, and he pumped the brakes. "Piece of shit."

"All of it." Noah continued. Like him, Noah had a one-track mind, but when those tracks were going in opposite directions, it made it hard to focus on what the other was saying. Jack was tired of being angry though, so he made the extra effort and jumped the rails to join forces with his brother. "They forcibly entered the house, roughed her up, locked her in the closet, destroyed the house, took her *wallet*, but nothing else, and left the kid like he wasn't even there—and what's this crap about delivering a message? *What* message? And to who?"

Jack gulped. His mind had been circling around that thought like water down a clogged drain, but hearing it from his brother, who was undoubtedly more experienced in this area, cleared the pipes fast. "You think she's still in danger?"

Noah sighed and thumped the back of his head on the headrest. "I don't *think* so. I think whatever they were after, they got it. But just because Jess isn't in their sights anymore doesn't mean this is over. Far from it."

Jack looked over, torn between a desire for answers and the need to protect his brother. When Noah was on a case, he was like a dog with a bone, and sometimes you had to forcibly remove him from the situation to get him to sleep. "Noah."

His brother looked over, unable to ignore the commanding tone in his voice.

"Please, don't worry about this. Let the police do their job. I appreciate your help. So does Jess, but you have your own stuff to worry about. They'll find out who did this. We just have to give them time." A spark of obstinance flared in his blue irises and Jack rolled his eyes. Pulling under the awning of the hotel, he threw the car in park. "I don't need you getting the shit beat out of you too. And I *don't* need to be bailing you out for interfering with a police investigation."

"Now, would I do that?" Noah asked with a smirk as he unclicked his seatbelt and grabbed his duffle from the floorboard.

"I'm serious. Don't dick around with this." Jack did his best impression of a menacing glower, but he was barking up the wrong tree.

"I know you are. I *promise*. I'll be careful. Don't worry about me."

"Right." Jack scoffed. "Now go get some rest. I'll talk to you tomorrow."

As Jack watched his brother walk into the hotel, he couldn't help the unsettling feeling bubbling inside him like a pit full of poisonous gasses. He'd been feeling okay. The guys were gone. Tomorrow they would install a security system for Jess, and he could get back on the road without laying in bed worrying about her every night. Now? Well, let's just say he didn't have the warm and fuzzies about it.

* * *

After a glorious night's rest in a king-sized bed, Noah felt like a new man. He could go without sleep. He'd even become accustomed to the practice when doing stake-outs during his time on the force, but that didn't mean he *liked* it. A venti café mocha with two extra shots of espresso had been enough to keep him going, but he'd stumbled to bed after Jack dropped him off and didn't even remember his head hitting the pillow.

Now refreshed and with a belly full of the best continental breakfast small-town Indiana could offer, he was off to rendezvous with Jack and Jess one more time. He tugged on the zippers of his bag and threw it over his shoulder, but his phone rang before he made it five steps.

"Kinney," he answered.

"Noah? This is Julian Van Zuiden. Have you spoken with my daughter lately? I tried calling her a few times, but it went to voicemail." His voice was layered with stress and panic, and Noah's heart lurched in response.

"Slow down. I'm in Indiana getting ready to meet with her and my brother in a few minutes. What's going on?" He backed up a pace and sat his bag on the luggage rack, catching a glimpse of his rigid posture in the mirror as he did.

"I had an envelope delivered to my house this morning. It wasn't mailed, just had my name written on it. No note. Just one item—Jess's driver's license. Why would someone send me her driver's license? What would they want with her?"

The train whistle screeching off in the distance had materialized into a full-on steam engine barreling down the track. He always trusted his instincts, but that became a thing of unnerving frustration when intuition met a jigsaw puzzle missing a couple of corner pieces. He'd known something was wrong. But this was so much worse than he'd ever imagined. "Sir, with all due respect, you need to hang up with me and call your local FBI office."

"FBI?" Julian shouted. "What the hell is going on?"

"Jess is fine. Her house was broken into a couple of days ago and she was beaten around a bit, but she's okay. The assailants took her wallet though, and if you're telling me you now have possession of the driver's license that was in that wallet, then I believe we are looking at something much bigger than a B and E."

"Oh God..." Noah could only imagine the dread filling him. Jess was only one of his children. Since she lived so far away, that made her the easiest target, but that didn't mean the rest of his family was safe.

"Call the FBI," Noah insisted. "I'll go by the local police department investigating the case and let them know what's going on. I will give them your phone number. You should expect a call from the lead investigator later today."

"But I don't understand. Why would someone do this?"

"In my experience, sir, you either royally pissed off the wrong person, or they're trying to blackmail you. If it's blackmail, you'll probably hear from whoever it is soon. But this has now crossed state lines and involves a state official. The FBI should be notified."

"Jesus," Julian swore. "And you're sure Jessica is safe?"

"As sure as I can be without having her right next to me. My brother is with her, and I'm supposed to meet them any minute now. I'll text you when I make contact."

"Could you..." The older man drifted off, unsure he wanted to complete his thought. "Could you have her call me? Just so I can make sure she's okay."

Noah smiled to himself, feeling an intense sense of gratification at the affection and responsibility he already felt for his long-lost daughter. "Of course. I'll do that."

"Thank you. I'll be in touch." The line clicked and Noah stared at the phone for a long moment before taking a deep breath and picking his duffle back up off the luggage rack.

By the time he made it down to the lobby of the hotel, Jack and Jess were waiting for him under the porte cochere in Jack's navy blue SUV. He opened the door and slid into the back seat next to Parker's car seat. It was so odd—Jack driving around with a kid in the back seat—but he supposed he ought to get used to it. He got the distinct impression Jess was a lengthy, if not permanent, fixture in his brother's life.

"What time's your flight?" Jess asked him as Jack merged back on the highway and headed toward Lowe's. The goal for the day had been to find a comprehensive security system for the best possible price, and Noah had a few products in mind. Unfortunately, they wouldn't have time to look at any of them.

"Five thirty," Noah replied. He would need to be dropped off at the airport by three thirty—four hours from now—a tight squeeze considering their next stop. "Actually, Jack, we need to swing by the Brownsburg Police Department. I need to talk to the detective heading up Jess's case."

Jess swung around in her seat. "Why?" Her voice was saturated with suspicion as her green eyes drilled into him. The swelling had gone down in her face and her right eye was all the way open for the first time in two days. She even seemed to be moving better, some of her soreness having dissipated.

"I have some contacts that reached out to me this morning with additional information, and in the interest of full transparency, I want to tell them what I know."

Jack gazed wearily at him from the rearview mirror. "So, what are your plans when you get back to Colorado?"

"I have a couple of small investigations I have to get back to potential clients about, but nothing major as far as I know—unless we've had someone reach out to us while I've been dealing with this mess."

"Are you coming to Long Beach next weekend?" Jess asked. "Alaina and I are planning on taking Julian up on his offer to stay at his friend's winery in Napa for her bachelorette party. Maybe we could all go out to dinner next Friday night!"

"I hadn't planned on Long Beach," Noah admitted. "I need to be in Denver for a few weeks—especially if I'm going to turn around and come back to Indy for the 500."

"Nobody told me you were planning on coming for the 500," Jack said in indignation.

"I haven't missed a 500 since you got your first IndyCar ride. You think I would snap my streak now?"

Jack snorted. "Yeah, well, I think you might be the only member of the family coming. I haven't heard from Mom and Dad, and Aaron and the fam are starting summer break early with a week in Orlando before the amusement parks get too packed."

"You forgot about our other brother. And Mom and Dad will be there. Don't get all bent out of shape," Noah chastised while rolling his eyes.

So dramatic.

"Chris doesn't count. It's his job to be there."

Jess snickered, but otherwise, kept silent. She seemed content to listen to the good-natured bickering between the brothers. If she found Jack and Noah entertaining, she was in for a treat at the first Kinney Christmas she attended. When all four boys got in the same room, it was nothing short of ball-busting chaos.

Jack pulled up to the Brownsburg Police Department and placed the car in park, giving Noah another suspicious glance in the mirror.

"I'll be right back," Noah said and tugged on the door latch to step out into the brisk spring afternoon. The look of patent disbelief on the desk sergeant's face when he saw Noah open the door and step through was almost comical.

Noah gave him a half grin. "I know. I thought I was leaving too."

He harrumphed and stood from his chair. "What can I do for you, Detective?"

Noah drew himself up straighter. "Is Detective Landry around this morning? I had a call I think he may want to know about."

"He is. Almost missed him. He's due to testify in court at two." The older man picked up the desk phone and spoke in low tones for a few seconds before lowering the receiver and looking back up at Noah. "He'll be out in a couple of minutes. You can take a seat over there." He nodded toward a row of hard vinyl chairs and went back to his work without so much as a "kiss my ass."

Well, that's what you get for sticking your nose in someone else's investigation.

Noah walked over to the waiting area but didn't sit. This police department might not smell like barf and body odor, but he'd be caught dead before sitting in one of those chairs.

The door to the administrative offices popped open and Detective Landry appeared. "Mr. Kinney. How can I help you?" His greeting was tolerant, but not overly excited, and Noah wasn't sure whether that was good or bad.

"Detective, good to see you again," he said with a wry grin as he walked toward the man and extended his hand for a shake. Landry was about ten years older than Noah, middle-aged, and with a dad bod to show for it, but he was a good cop and that mattered more than the man's physical appearance.

"Sergeant Burns said you had something I might like to know?" Landry asked as he escorted Noah back through the secure door and directed him to an office off to the left. It was a quiet department, nothing compared to the buzz of his old precinct, but that was the difference between being on the force in a sleepy suburb versus a district in a major city.

"I know you think I'm just another PI who has nothing better to do than shove his nose where it doesn't belong, but trust me, I wouldn't be coming to you unless I thought this was important."

Landry's tense shoulders relaxed at that, and he signaled for Noah to take a seat as he closed the door.

The chair was hard and unwelcoming, but he didn't plan to be sitting there all day, so it made little difference. "I'm not sure what Jess told you about her personal life, but I just recently helped her get in touch with her birth father—Senator Julian Van Zuiden."

The rigidity came back to the detective's shoulders as he perched on the corner of his desk and glared at his informant.

"He called me this morning—worried about Jess. I thought that was odd considering none of us told him about the break-in. Then he told me about an envelope he received at his home in Sacramento this morning. An envelope with Jess's driver's license inside."

Noah barely had the words out of his mouth before Landry shot up from his desk spewing obscenities. "You could have fucking led with that. Jesus Christ. Son of—"

"I told Julian to reach out to his local FBI office, and I also told him I would give you his number so you could reach out to him."

"Bet your ass," Landry pushed a pad of paper toward Noah as he picked up his phone to make another call. "Yeah. Can you get me the number for Sacramento FBI?"

Noah felt the detective's gaze burning a hole in his scalp as he bent to scrawl Julian's number on the paper. He pushed the pen and pad back toward Landry and returned his unflinching gaze for a long moment before pressing his palms against his thighs and making to rise. Part of him wanted to apologize. He'd just dumped a bucketload of work on the already frazzled detective's desk, and if he had a court appearance today, the last thing he probably wanted was to talk to a bunch of Feds, but Noah wouldn't apologize for protecting Jess, Julian, and their families.

Protect and serve. That was the job. Always.

"I wish I could say it's been a pleasure, Kinney, but I feel like you've whacked me upside the head with a two-by-four."

Noah snorted. "I'm headed back to Colorado. I'll call you if anything else comes up."

"Please do," he said with grudging acquiescence as he picked up his desk phone once more, presumably to call the agent assigned to the case in Sacramento. The look on his face screamed, *Get the hell out of my office,* and Noah happily obliged.

By the time Noah pushed the main door of the police department back open, the wind had picked up into a fierce gust. Not the ideal weather for a leisurely stroll, but he needed to talk to Jess alone. He tapped on her window, leaning closer to be heard as she cracked it. "Can I talk to you for a minute?"

She glanced toward the back seat, probably to ensure Parker was still asleep, before opening the door and joining him in the parking lot. They got about twenty paces from the car before she turned on him, arms braced against the overcast chill. "Noah. Whatever it is, just say it. I'm cold."

Geronimo...

"I got a call from Julian this morning."

Jess furrowed her brow and hugged herself tighter. "Why would he call you?"

"Well, he said he tried to call you and you weren't answering. So, he got worried."

"The guy's known me for like a week. Why would he be worried if I didn't take his call right away?" Jess asked, stepping back to let someone on the sidewalk pass between them. The wind was biting through his thick quarter zip, and he could only imagine how it felt coming through her thinner long-sleeved T-shirt. He needed to speed this along.

"Somebody dropped an envelope at his house this morning with your driver's license inside."

Her face went blank. Then, like a reboot on a computer from the nineties, he saw the blinking green light at the bottom of the screen. Slowly, things began to process. First shock, then horror, then anger, and with each new emotion, more color flushed her cheeks. Her tongue still seemed to be tied, but that would come unstuck soon. If he wanted to get a word in edgewise, he needed to do it now.

"I don't want you to jump to conclusions. I spoke with him.

He had no idea what was happening until I filled him in. I think you caught people's attention last week when you were in Sacramento. Likely, it didn't take much investigating to come to the same conclusion I did."

"That he's my father and now I have a fucking target on my back?"

There it is.

The words were bitter.

"It's not his fault," Noah insisted, managing to keep his voice gentle, but firm, like he was talking to a three-year-old having a temper tantrum. He understood why she was upset, but Julian was a good guy. He didn't deserve her ire. "He likely got on the wrong side of some dirty lobbyist, and they're trying to make a point."

"Noah, look at me. They made their point with a decorative tray to my face. Whoever these people are, I don't want anything to do with them. Period."

"I understand that, but—"

"No." She blew past him and headed back toward the car. How he was going to get through to her was beyond him. He understood her anger, but that didn't mean he agreed with it. "Jess!" he called after her. "He's worried about you. At least let him know you're okay."

She didn't say anything in response. Instead, she jumped in the car and slammed the door behind her, but not before he caught a glimpse of the tears streaming down her face.

Thirty-One

Pixie Dust, If We Must

Six days on from that earth-shattering day in the police department parking lot, Jess still couldn't believe she'd ever been so stupid. Things had been going too well. Her relationship was in a blissful, honeymoon phase. Parker was sleeping through the night. She'd found her birth father who, shock of all shocks, was a good person. She'd been on a major win streak until Noah Kinney, Bubble-Burster-in-Chief, pulled her out into the icy, tropical storm force winds, and dropped a bomb of atomic proportions: the men who attacked her had done so because she was connected to Julian.

And just like that, the angel and devil on her shoulders were back at it.

Should have just let it go. Now you have a black and blue face for Alaina's wedding and we still don't have a father.

By choice. We ghosted him, remember?

That was true. She'd never called him, and she felt guilty about it. Julian had called at least once a day, sometimes twice, for the past week, and his persistence was breaking her heart. All she'd ever wanted was a parent who gave a damn. Well, now she had it, and she was washing it down the drain. That decision wasn't for her benefit though. It was for Parker. She had to keep him safe.

"You're quiet today," Alaina observed as they stepped onto the curb from the crosswalk and made their way toward the reception venue. The wedding was ten days away, and since Grayson and Jack were in California preparing for the weekend's Long Beach Grand Prix, Jess was fulfilling her duties as maid of honor by accompanying the bride to her final walkthrough. Plans for the Great Napa Valley Bachelorette Party had regrettably fallen through when she went incommunicado with Julian, but the girls were still flying into LAX tomorrow morning to support their men. Maybe they could just order room service and champagne and have a low key celebration at the hotel instead? Maybe a spa day on Saturday?

"Just thinking," Jess said with a sigh as she tilted her head up to the sun. It was a beautiful April day in the upper sixties with a light breeze and sunshine peeking through the clouds. The air smelled of flowers, freshly mown grass, and faint car exhaust. Ah, spring in the city.

"Well…I can think of a few things that would have you so contemplative. Let's see." She raised one finger for each item on her list. "Jack, Parker, or the one I'm personally laying money on, Julian."

Jess gave a weighty sigh and shifted her bag on her shoulder. "Am I being completely ridiculous for ignoring his calls? I feel like an ass."

Alaina snorted with poorly concealed mirth and glanced sideways at her best friend. "You're asking the wrong girl. I avoided my father for three years before we finally had our come to Jesus moment. Remember?"

Jess slumped her shoulders, feeling like a complete ditz. *Duh.*

"Okay, but now that you and your dad are on speaking terms again, do you regret all that lost time?"

Alaina wobbled her head back and forth as she weighed the question. "Yeah. I guess. But honestly, it's what I needed at the time. I couldn't handle what he was putting me through, and he was going through too much to be my dad in the way I needed him. It was a completely different situation."

Jess stopped in her tracks, leaving Alaina to skitter to a halt five steps ahead of her. "Different how?" she asked, trying to wrap her head around her friend's words. Both were complete and utter betrayals of trust by their father figures.

Alaina turned to face Jess. "Different because my father wasn't emotionally mature enough to handle being a father at the time. Julian is, and he wants to be there for you. You're shutting him out because you're afraid he's going to hurt you, not because he's a repeat offender."

Jess ground her teeth together in an attempt to avoid defensive behavior. She *had* asked. She couldn't get mad at Alaina for being honest. "You don't think these bruises on my face are reason enough? He *has* hurt me, Alaina."

Alaina raised her eyebrows at her and crossed her arms in front of her chest. "Unless there's a whole lot you're not telling anybody, no. I don't think he's responsible for what those guys did to you. It's not his fault, Jess. It's not like someone asked him if he was okay with it, and he said, 'Sure! Why not? Just go rough her up a bit. I'm sure it will be fine.' If his incessant phone calls are any indication, he was just as appalled as everyone else by what happened."

"I know he didn't *want* this to happen, but it *did* happen. And it happened *because* of my association with him. If it had just been me, I might feel differently, but my son was put in harm's way. If something ever happened to him, I would never forgive myself, Lainie." For an instant, she thought she might puke at the idea, but the nausea eventually passed.

"I know that," Alaina murmured, reaching out across the distance between them to grab her best friend's hand. "But don't you think Julian feels the same way about what happened to you? Don't you think he feels just as guilty knowing people hurt you because of him?"

Tears pricked at Jess's eyes and her breath hitched. "I know he does…" She buried her teeth in her bottom lip and kicked at the sidewalk. "He keeps leaving me voicemails, and I…I can't even listen to them, Lainie. I feel horrible, but I'm just so tired of getting hurt."

Alaina pulled Jess into her side and gave her a big hug, holding her for a long time. "I know. And we'll support you no matter what you choose. I just want to make sure you're not ghosting this guy out of fear. So, just think about it before you do anything drastic. Okay?"

Jess nodded and sniffled, wiping at the tears streaming down her face before they made the short walk to The Grainery. Alaina tugged on the front door of the building, and they were instantly met with the fresh scent of rain and water lilies on the warm breeze of the venue's climate control.

A willowy woman in black pixie pants, a black blazer with cute ballet flats, and a white silk blouse waltzed toward them, iPad in hand. "Alaina, how lovely to see you again!" The woman stooped slightly to air kiss Alaina's cheeks and extended a hand to Jess. "You must be the maid of honor. I'm Chloe, the event manager."

"Jessica," Jess offered as she accepted the woman's warm, firm handshake. "This is a gorgeous space. We've had a couple of weddings here, but I don't think I've ever seen it without an event setup."

"We just had the floors waxed," Chloe explained. "Don't worry, it will be ready to go for the big day."

"I don't doubt it for a second." Alaina was radiant as she took in the space. It was gorgeous with deep cherrywood tones, exposed brick, and industrial-style beam exposure and fixtures.

"Come on in and we can walk it. You can tell me your thoughts," Chloe beckoned them toward the main room. "So, tell me a little bit about the ceremony."

"We're having the ceremony at a cute little church out in the country, not far from where Grayson grew up. It's just big enough to hold our eighty guests. I've made a few flower arrangements for the altar and we're going to put some flowers on the pews to brighten it up a bit, but it's a gorgeous place with several stained-glass windows. It didn't need much attention."

"Oh, that's lovely. So are you using the same color palette and flowers for the ceremony space and the reception space?"

"Yes. I've been meaning to ask you. When can we deliver the centerpieces? I also have glassware, china, and flatware coming from Happily Ever—"

"Yes. I've been in touch with Shawna over there. We've got delivery scheduled for the morning of the fourteenth. We'll get everything all cleaned up and ready to go."

"Fantastic! I'll be by with Marissa the afternoon of the fifteenth to go over everything and introduce you two. She's my event coordinator and will be the go-between for anything you need on the day."

"Great. If you could get me her phone number before you leave, that would be great. Now, how many tables do you need? You said you have eighty guests?"

"Eighty guests confirmed." Alaina nodded her head and walked further into the space. "We're going to do a mix of longs and rounds."

Chloe tapped on her iPad a few times and turned to have the same view as Alaina. Jess was convinced event planners and designers had access to a different part of their brains. Alaina could envision a space and transform it within seconds, swiping through design options in her head like pictures on a smartphone until she got things just so. Then she performed the magical feat of bringing her vision to life. No matter how many times Jess stepped into a venue touched by Alaina's talents, she would always stand in awe of her friend's pixie dust.

"I'm thinking one twenty-top long table on either side of the room and then five staggered eight top rounds to the back. We'll have the DJ setup in the corner over there and create this space for the dance floor. I'll need an additional long table over by the door for gifts and the guest book. Then a small round over there"—Alaina gestured to the opposite corner from the DJ—"for the cake. We'll do cocktails from three to four and then dinner at four fifteen. Grayson and I are going to need a sweetheart table next to the cake. We only have our maid of honor and best man, so we'll just sit them with the rest of the guests—no need for a separate table."

"Yeah, we're not special," Jess interjected with a smile as she walked the space.

"Shut up," Alaina muttered with a good-natured roll of her eyes.

The large crystal chandeliers hanging from the ceiling were magnificent, and Jess knew the contrasted elegance of the chandeliers with the masculine feel of the space had been one of the selling points for her friend. Hearing the two women discuss place settings and centerpieces made Jess ecstatic to see the finished product, and she wanted nothing more than to enjoy the magic of an Alaina Montgomery original in Jack Kinney's arms. But she couldn't do that if they had to walk on eggshells around her ex. She knew it would be a difficult conversation, but the more time she spent with Jack, the more she yearned to bring their relationship out into the light. She loved him, and as difficult as any fallout might be, she was prepared to face it. She knew Tuck was going through a lot, and the last thing she wanted was to set him off, but making herself miserable to protect him was incongruous.

No, she had to tell him. Soon.

* * *

Later that night, with Parker sleeping soundly and Layla lounging under the coffee table, Jess and Alaina sat on the couch, a bowl of popcorn between them. They had an early flight to Los Angeles in the morning, and with both men already in California, it was easiest for the girls to stay together and carpool to the airport.

"This feels like old times." Alaina leaned back against the couch, cupping her glass of wine in her hand as she relaxed with a deep sigh.

"It does, doesn't it?" Jess agreed as she shuffled her fingers around in the popcorn bowl to grab a handful and pop the kernels in her mouth one at a time. "If Copper was here wedging himself between you and the popcorn bowl, it would be total dèjá vu."

Both girls giggled and dug in for more.

"I didn't realize you'd asked Marissa to handle all the wedding logistics. That must be a weight off your shoulders," Jess assessed as she took a sip from her wineglass.

Alaina sighed. "Yeah. I guess," she mumbled.

Jess raised one brow and stared at her friend.

Alaina widened her eyes. "Whaaat? You know I'm a control freak! It just feels wrong to let somebody else take the reins of my own wedding."

Jess rolled her eyes. "Oh my word. Alaina. This is a *good* decision. It was stressing you out. Just give her a chance."

Her friend shifted uncomfortably and grabbed another handful of popcorn. "I know, okay? I know. I just want it all to be perfect, and she's still learning. I'm worried there are things that are getting overlooked."

"Like what?" Jess asked, reaching out to grab her friend's hand. Alaina, overbearing autocrat that she was, already had the heavy lifting done by designing the event space and everything in it, so she wasn't sure what her friend had left to complain about.

"Like, she didn't even know that she needed to send the

song list to the musicians ahead of time. Or that you're supposed to tip the wait staff—even though we paid the caterer in advance. Or that my dress needs steamed at the dry cleaner a week before the wedding. I'm still having to do all this shit!"

Jess squeezed Alaina's hand, which had gone slick with sweat. "Heyyy," she said calmly. "It will all. Be. Fine. It will. She's got the checklist Sydney made—that *you* approved. You hired her for *Decadent Designs* because you know she could do this job. Have a little faith in your own judgment, if nothing else." Jess smiled and nudged her friend playfully, hoping to take the edge off.

Reluctantly, Alaina rolled her eyes and smiled. "Fine. I guess I'll...*try* to not be a such a control freak."

"And you'll *try* to trust Marissa," Jess added with an expectant stare.

"And I'll try to trust Marissa," Alaina repeated. "Now enough about the wedding, let's talk about something else."

Jess snorted. "Okay...Have you given any more thought to renting that storage space?" Jess asked. She'd been trying to give her friend time to think, but the wedding was fast approaching.

"I have..." Alaina admitted with a breathy laugh as she chewed on her popcorn. "You really think it will pay for itself?"

Jess shifted so she was leaning into the couch as she turn to face her friend. "I do. I'm not saying it will right away. We'll likely take a loss the first year as we build up our inventory, but once we get a large supply of reusable flower arrangements, china, linens, glassware, we'll start seeing it pay dividends. Our overhead is going to plummet. We could even give cost incentives to clients who choose to rent things from our warehouse instead of working with our vendors."

"But if we rely on our premade arrangements, what will that leave me with?" Alaina asked, clearly weighing the desire for free time versus giving up a job she loved.

"I think we'll always have high-end brides that want unique pieces. Trust me. If anything, I think this will draw more people to us—brides on a budget. We can be a one-stop shop for them and offer amazing decorations at extremely low prices. And we can offer those low prices because it's not costing us a dime. You get my drift?"

Alaina's mouth twitched, and she sighed. "Yes. I get your drift. You're such a ding dong."

Jess laughed and tossed a piece of popcorn at her friend before taking a couple more for herself. "Plus, I think it would give us plenty of space to set up a display room. You know? For our higher end weddings. We could setup several different table designs for people to do walkthroughs and see samples in real time."

"I like that idea," Alaina murmured, her eyes growing distant as she envisioned the potential of all that extra space. She finally sighed. "Alright. Let's do it."

Jess jerked upright, not expecting such a concrete answer so quickly. "Really?"

Alaina smiled. "Yes. Really. You should call Geoff tomorrow so we can get the paperwork rolling. Maybe if we're lucky, we can get the lease signed and get everything setup before expo season."

Jess nodded and reached for her phone, making a note to call their building manager on Monday after they got back from California.

"So…speaking of things we need to talk about…I have something I want to run by you." Alaina's voice was hesitant, making Jess look up from her phone.

"Oh yeah?" Normally, Alaina came right out with it. The precursor was a dead giveaway that what she had to say was something she didn't think Jess would take lightly. She placed her phone on the coffee table and cradled her injured wrist against her chest. It had improved considerably over the past few days, but still ached—especially after a long day with no ice or anti-inflammatories. She had hoped she could be done with her brace before the wedding, but it wasn't looking promising.

Alaina swirled the deep burgundy wine in her glass with immense concentration as she mulled her words over. "I was talking to Grayson and…we think it might be best if you waited to tell Tucker about you and Jack until after the wedding."

Jess stared at her friend with squinted eyes, trying to understand exactly what this implied. "I think Tucker will get the drift when he sees Jack and I are dancing and sitting next to each other with goo-goo eyes."

Alaina cleared her throat and shifted slightly. "Yeah. About that, um…you and Jack aren't sitting next to each other." She took another larger sip of wine.

Jess felt her blood pressure rising. Her temples pulsed and she fought for every steady breath she could draw in as she clenched her jaw and begged for the patience to deal with this insulting behavior. "What are you talking about?"

Alaina's eyes widened as she met Jess's angry gaze. "Jess. Come on. You know he's not going to take this well. Do you want him to make a scene?"

Jess snorted. "Please, Alaina. Don't pretend this is about anyone but you. I was going to tell Tucker this weekend. He would have a whole week to come to grips before he even comes home and then a few more days of seeing Jack and me to wrap his head around it. You think this is going to go over any better when he finds out we lied to him?"

Alaina sat forward and placed her wineglass on the table with a loud clink that seemed to echo through the quiet house. "I think I know my brother well enough to say this isn't going down smoothly, no matter how it's presented. I would rather the two of you be cordial to each other throughout the rehearsal dinner, wedding, and reception. If you want to tell him after the reception, be my guest."

"So Jack and I are just supposed to, what, not touch each other or so much as *look* at each other the whole weekend? Are you serious?"

"Don't be ridiculous. You're the maid of honor and best man. You have to be together some of the time, and that won't appear suspicious at all." Alaina nervously tucked her hair behind her ear before taking her empty wineglass and rising to go to the kitchen for a refill.

"Right. We'll be in proximity, but God forbid we touch, or kiss, or even smile at each other. He's my *boyfriend*, Alaina. I can't believe you would be that selfish!" Jess hopped up from the couch, fingers balling into fists in sheer fury. Pain shot up her injured wrist, but she didn't care. Steam was coming out of her ears, and she did her best to keep her voice from blowing the roof off the house. If she woke Parker up, she wouldn't be able to get him back to sleep before they had to go to the airport.

Alaina sat the wine bottle she'd just emptied on the counter with a violent clunk. "Would you stop acting like a child? You know I only want what's best for you."

Jess wasn't going to be distracted by the "childlike behavior" jab. Instead, she plowed forward, growling. "I guess I'm failing to see how hiding my relationship from your brother is what's best for me—or hell, even Tucker. So what? I'm just supposed to go to Long Beach this weekend and pretend I don't know Jack?"

"Well, obviously not in front of the cameras. Trust me, the last thing you want is for Tucker to find out about you two like I did. Ya know, without the common courtesy of a *phone call*?"

Jess gave an explosive and exasperated laugh. "I cannot believe you." She sat her wineglass down on the table with enough force to crack the stem, because it was that, or tossing the bright red liquid in her best friend's face. "You want to know why I kept my relationship from you? Because I *knew* you wouldn't be supportive. You can't look beyond your own issues for five seconds to see that Jack and I are happy. That's all that should matter to you, Alaina. Period." She ran a vicious hand through her black waves, shoving it out of her face as she seethed. "But this isn't about me keeping secrets. This is about your incessant need to be the center of attention, and I'm sick of it."

Alaina's hazel eyes were flat and angry, but Jess's own stare was just as fierce. She wouldn't be the one to flinch. Not this time. Finally realizing she'd have to be the one to walk away, Alaina slowly drained her wineglass, placed it on the counter, and grabbed her keys, leaving the house without another word.

The whole situation was ludicrous. Never in her life had

she dreamed she would have such a knock-down, drag-out fight with her best friend over a *boy*. While she'd recognized there was some truth to Jack's case against Alaina, she hadn't been prepared to admit she was a pushover.

The truth hurts.

She growled and flopped on the couch, burying her face in a throw pillow. The thing that pissed Jess off more than the request itself was Alaina's attempt to make this about her concern for her brother. This had nothing to do with Tucker, and it was time for her to take off her rose-colored glasses and accept that.

Thirty-Two

Couples Therapy

Long Beach sparkled as far as the eye could see from the tenth-floor suite of Jess's hotel. The sun had begun its slow and steady descent toward the water, setting the sky on fire with bursts of orange, red, and pink, and the water seemed to glow like lava as it reflected the last vestiges of the day's warmth. Jess sighed and leaned against the window ledge. The Queen Mary loomed off in the distance—a symbol of elegance and finery from a bygone era. She watched as the waves of the harbor lapped in a docile manner against the rocky outcrops of the bay. It was a perfect morphing of imagination and reality as she listened to the sound of ocean waves coming from Parker's sound machine in the next room.

Jack's long arms snaked around her waist, snugging her against his chest as he placed his chin on her shoulder and nuzzled her neck. "I missed you today. I thought you'd come to the track with Alaina."

She leaned her head into his and sighed, closing her eyes against the incredible pull she felt toward him, like the waves toward the shore far below. "I wanted to."

He pressed his lips to her temple. "Was Parker cranky?"

It had been a long twenty-four hours, and she was exhausted, physically and emotionally. Alaina hadn't returned last night, and when she showed up to the gate in the airport, they'd both pretended the other didn't exist. Alaina wanted to be stubborn? Fine. Jess could be stubborn too. All the way to L.A.—a long ass flight when you aren't talking to the person sitting next to you. For that very reason, Jess had avoided the track. She didn't want to add fuel to the fire until she knew where the emergency exits were.

"Your thoughts are so loud you're rattling my eardrums," Jack murmured. His hot breath raised gooseflesh across her entire body as he leaned in to kiss the hollow behind her ear.

"Sorry."

He chuckled and stepped back just enough to turn her toward him. "Don't apologize. Just tell me what's bugging you."

She leaned back so her butt rested against the windowsill and bit her bottom lip as she debated the best way to break news that was going to royally piss him off. "Okay. Here it is." She steepled her hands and gave him a timid "please don't be mad" look. "Alaina and Grayson want us to keep our relationship under wraps until after the wedding."

Jack stared at her, shock emanating from every muscle in his body. "Well, obviously you didn't agree to that…right?"

Jess huffed and crossed her arms, trying to keep her temper from rising. "Well, I wasn't thrilled about it. No."

"Please tell me you told her off, Jess." The muscle in his jaw was ticking slightly, and she could see his pulse hammering in his neck as his glare pinned her to the windowsill.

"I haven't given her an answer yet." Jess kicked the wall below the window with her heel in rhythmic thumps. "I yelled a lot, but we didn't really talk. A car took her to the track from the airport this morning, and Parker and I came here."

Jack crossed his arms in front of his chest, staring at her swinging feet with contempt, before readjusting his gaze to her eyes. "So, what are you going to do?"

"I don't know!" she shouted as she burst from the ledge and started pacing the length of the room. "Damn it, Jack! I don't...I don't know." She closed her eyes and breathed, trying to get a hold on her anger. Aiming it at Jack was unfair. "I'm sorry," she finally sighed.

"You want me to go off on her? 'Cause I will. I'll march down the hall to her room and let her have both barrels," he said, hiking a thumb toward the door.

Her lips twitched. "I have half a mind to let you try. It's just annoying that she would even ask! You know?"

Jack snorted and took two steps to close the gap between them, drawing her back into his arms. "Well, I'd use a stronger word than annoying, but yeah. I get your drift."

"I'm mad at her for being selfish, but I feel like I'm being just as selfish for wanting everyone to know about us." She cupped his cheek, brushing her thumb over his raspy stubble.

"It's not selfishness, Jess. It's just honesty. There's a difference." Jack gazed up at her, the dark pools of his irises swirling with anger, frustration, and need.

"Don't you think I would tell her no and damn the torpedos

if I thought that would be the end of it?" she asked, tightening her hand on the nape of his neck, helpless to make him see what was crippling her. "It doesn't work like that!"

Jack raised his brow at her. "It doesn't work like that because it doesn't work like that or because you've never tried?"

Jess leaped up from her boyfriend's lap and resumed her pacing, angry that he wasn't being helpful. "I don't need a therapy session. I need you to help me find a way out of this—something that doesn't involve shattering my friendship in the process."

Jack sighed and sat forward, dangling his hands limply between his thighs as he searched the blue Berber carpet for answers. "To be honest, Jess, it doesn't seem like Alaina is very interested in a friendship if this is how she treats the people that care about her, but…" He sighed and extended a hand toward her. "If what you need from me is to help you find a way through this bullshit, count me in."

She rolled her eyes in grudging acquiescence as she took his hand and squeezed. "I think we have to give it to her. Trust me, I don't want to, but if it helps lower her stress, I think we have to give her what she wants."

He rolled his eyes, but sighed and nodded. "I'm not gonna lie. This is the first wedding where I actually have a woman I care about on my arm, and I was kind of looking forward to it." His mouth quirked in a semi self-conscious grin as he tugged Jess between his legs and fondled her butt.

"I hate this as much as you do," she said breathlessly as she tunneled her fingers through his thick, silky waves.

"You promise?"

"I promise." Her mouth fitted over his in a smoldering

caress hotter than a pit of glowing coals, and she shuddered from the heat.

There was something about a simple touch from him that set her world ablaze in colors and textures. She came alive in his arms, and the mere idea of denying her connection to him, for even a millisecond, was painful—especially after being so free with him for the past week. It felt like a regression of the worst sort.

Thirty-Three

Life's Great Mysteries

From the Seaside Suites on the back stretch of the Long Beach Grand Prix street course, Jess watched the bright liveries of the twenty-six-car field zip by in blurs of technicolor. The roar of their engines would have been deafening, if not for the thick glass that separated her from the track. For a girl who had grown up in the shadow of the Indianapolis Motor Speedway, she had very little interest in motorsports. Although, she had to admit, attending the Indianapolis 500 with Alaina and watching Grayson win by inches had been an absolute thrill. If all races were that exciting, she could understand the obsession some people had with the sport.

Alaina…

Jess had to admit, a lot of things had suddenly started to make sense when her best friend landed in the arms of IndyCar's biggest star. She'd been preparing her whole life for the role of a racing driver's wife. Where she saw the humor in life's grand design was when she looked at her relationship with Jack. She was by no means a gearhead—never would be—but she would support Jack. Always. In the end, she supposed that was all that mattered.

Parker stared wide-eyed out the window at the people, cars, and boats bandying below like ants on an anthill. He bounced with excitement in her arms as he reached to bang on the glass. The light sparkled off the navy waters of the Pacific Ocean beyond the temporary racing facility and cast a glare that made her squint and reach for her sunglasses. Jack's team caught a favorable wind when they pitted just before a caution flag, and he was now running in third with twelve laps to go. If he could hang on to his position, that would put him in a great points position for Indy—or so Alaina said.

She eyed her friend from across the room, speaking animatedly with Grayson's sister and brother-in-law. A good night's rest had tempered some of her anger, but she was still resentful as hell. She and Jack had come to an agreement the night before. They would give Alaina what she was asking for, but this would be the last time.

A sudden burst of laughter from the cocktail table in the corner had her eyeing a gaggle of beauty queens. They were married to some of the most famous and influential men in the sport: beautiful, classy, and oozing wealth and influence. Alaina called them the "Wives Club." Would she ever fit into that world?

Let's not get ahead of ourselves.

"Excuse me. Are you Jessica Morales?"

Jess turned on her heel and came face to face with a

beautiful woman in her midforties. She had warm olive skin and big brown eyes full of sugar and charm. "That's me," Jess responded, jostling Parker a bit to soothe his disgruntlement at being turned away from the windows. "Do I know you?"

The woman gave a breathless laugh and flipped her thick, wavy brown hair over her shoulder. "Not quite. I'm Janine Van Zuiden."

What the f—

"I'm sorry to ambush you like this, but I thought if you knew I was here you wouldn't speak to me."

Jess was stunned into silence. What on earth would possess this woman to hunt her down *here*? After everything that happened, the tickets Jess had promised to Julian were never sent. She'd been perfectly clear on where she stood with that, and Jack would never go behind her back. But this wasn't some random backyard hootenanny. It was the Long Beach Grand Prix, and it would be easy enough to get suite tickets. Easier still if you could make connections with one traitorous best friend. Jessica's gaze drifted to Alaina, who was side-eyeing the conversation between her and Janine while pretending to be absorbed in a conversation with Grayson's PA, Cami.

She brought the full force of her green eyes to bear on Janine's friendly countenance. "Well, this ought to be good," she replied with more animus than she truly felt. Seeing how taken aback Janine was by her attitude, she instantly wished she could reel it back in. "What can I do for you?"

"I just—" The older woman took a deep breath and squared herself up for the task, determined to speak her piece, even if it wouldn't be well received. "Julian told me what happened. He feels awful about it."

"I'm sure he does, and I'm glad he told you. Nobody's safe until those assholes are caught." Thinking about how easily Parker could have been snatched from his crib while she banged helplessly on that closet door created a rage in her unlike anything she'd ever felt.

"But they arrested them," Janine replied, baffled.

For a moment, Jess's mind went completely blank.

Arrested? No. There's no way.

Jess shook her head, holding Parker a little closer. "I think you're mistaken. Someone would have told me."

"Julian got a call from the Special Agent in Charge in Sacramento. He said they arrested two men in connection to the break-in at your house. They haven't said who they're working for, but they're being charged with extortion in the California court system and then they'll be extradited to Indiana on counts of battery and breaking and entering. They're looking at several years of prison time."

Jess backed up a step, searching for somewhere to sit. The back of her legs found a plush leather chair, and she plopped into it. The nightmare was over. She could sleep soundly now, knowing the men were behind bars. "Why wasn't I notified?" she asked. Her contralto voice was soft, almost inaudible below the constant growl of high horse-powered engines outside.

"The FBI agent planned to call you, but Julian wanted to tell you himself. Then you wouldn't take his calls, and I guess things fell through the cracks."

'Things fell through the cracks.' If that's not the story of my life.

"If Julian wanted to tell me himself, why isn't he here?" Jess asked, trying to focus on one issue at a time instead of trying to herd the dozens of thoughts bouncing around her head like over-caffeinated bunny rabbits.

A gasp from behind them halted the conversation, and Jess's eyes immediately went to the video monitors covering the rest of the track. A bright purple car with white accents was in the tire barrier in Turn 8.

Not Jack's car…

That's as far as her line of consciousness went before she returned her attention to her putative stepmother.

"Julian wanted to come, but when it was all said and done, he couldn't bear to see the disappointment on your face. He said he wasn't feeling well, but I knew the truth. I just wanted to make sure you knew the men were no longer walking around free. As a mother, I would want to know my babies were safe, but as a wife…I wanted to come here and ask—beg if I have to—for you to give Julian another chance. He wants to do right by you, Jessica. You have to know that." Janine's hands were clasped so tightly in front of her, Jess could see the whites of her knuckles beneath her lightly tanned skin.

"You must love him very much to even ask." Jess bent to kiss the top of Parker's head. His wispy black hair tickled her nose, but the scent of him, clean and innocent, calmed her racing heart. It was hard to believe Julian loved her the same way she loved her son. How could he? He didn't know her, and if she couldn't find a sliver of compassion and forgiveness, he never would.

"I love him with my whole heart," Janine affirmed, her dark eyes never leaving Jessica's face. It was the most confident answer she'd ever heard anyone give, and she could only hope she would have that kind of love one day.

"It doesn't bother you that he had a child with another woman?" Jess asked, nonplussed by Janine's relaxed demeanor.

Her eyebrows rose in surprise and her cheeks pinked slightly. "Why would it? I knew he had a serious relationship with his high school girlfriend. He was still a bit heartbroken over it when I met him, but it wasn't something he kept hidden from me. If that were the case, our relationship would have been damaged beyond repair."

"Because of the lies?"

"Because the man I've been married to for the last eighteen years isn't capable of turning his back on his child. If I were ever to find out otherwise, it would mean our whole relationship is based on a lie."

Janine and Julian had a taproot that went back twenty years. Their love withstood the revelation of Jess's parentage as if it were nothing more than a light breeze in a tree's upper branches. Her feelings for Jack were passionate and all-consuming, but the roots were shallow, lacking the complex luxury of time. However, Jess had no doubt the love she and Jack shared would grow into that same kind of solid existence, comforting in its steadfast consistency as the years passed by.

"He seems like he would be a good father." Emotion began to constrict Jess's throat. For the first time since Noah's revelation, she was allowing herself to think about the man who had fathered her—how kind, intelligent, and caring he seemed.

"His work has kept him away more than usual, but when he's working at the university, he rarely misses a ball game or a debate. It kills him to miss things. So much so, I don't think he plans to run for election at the end of the term."

"You mean reelection?" The people around them were all

on their feet at the windows of the suite watching the restart of the race, but Jessica was fully invested in her conversation with Janine. It was interesting to get a glimpse of the man Julian was outside of their fledgling relationship.

"No. Julian was appointed to his position after the senator for our district died of a massive heart attack. It was an opportunity he couldn't turn down, but I think he got more than he bargained for." The look of cold anger on her face was one Jessica recognized well, a mama bear protecting her cubs.

"Do you think he should run?" Jess asked, bouncing Parker up and down on her knee to keep him complacent.

"Julian is an honorable man, and sometimes in politics, that puts you in a tight squeeze. He doesn't hesitate to cross party lines when he feels a situation warrants it, but that doesn't always sit right with his constituents—or their lobbyists." If Jess didn't already know Janine Van Zuiden was a high-end real estate broker, she would have thought *she* was the politician.

"I don't believe I've had the pleasure," Alaina greeted as she sidled up beside Jess and extended her hand.

"Janine Van Zuiden."

Alaina's eyebrows rose and her mouth popped open. "Julian's wife?"

"The one and only," Janine responded with a warm smile and firm handshake.

"Wow. I didn't know you were on the guest list." Alaina gave Jess a single raised eyebrow that silently asked, "You okay?"

Jess nodded once in assent, but couldn't help the confusion now flooding through her. Alaina seemed just as shocked as

Jess felt, and if that was the case, it clearly wasn't her who had invited Julian to the Seaside Suites.

Chalk one up to life's great mysteries.

"I wasn't, but my husband was, and luckily, I was able to use his pass. I doubted I'd ever have a better opportunity to meet my husband's long-lost daughter, and he spoke extremely highly of her after they met."

Jess felt a spark of pride flare up inside her. Julian was an impressive man. For him to find her worth bragging about was the highest compliment anyone could give.

Janine stepped back a pace and made eye contact with Jess once more. "Please think about what I said. You have his number if you change your mind. It was wonderful meeting you, Jess. I do hope I see you again soon."

Jess felt such a pull toward Janine it was hard to let her go. She was everything she'd ever wanted from a mother, and while she knew she couldn't expect her to fill that role, she got the feeling Janine would welcome her into her family with open arms if that's what she chose.

But that was just it. She had to choose.

Janine made her excuses to Alaina and made her way to the exit. Both women watched her go, making sure she was entirely out of sight before turning to each other, wide-eyed and speechless.

"Who in the H-E-double hockey sticks invited her?" Alaina muttered through the corner of her mouth.

"Beats me. I thought it was you."

Cheers went up from the other side of the suite as the checkered flag waved. Jack had earned his first podium of the year, and Jess felt kind of bad for missing it, but big things were happening in her neck of the woods, and she knew he'd understand.

"So…what did she want?" Alaina asked, curiosity burning in her eyes as she helped Jess pack up Parker's diaper bag and make for the exit.

"She wants me to take it easy on Julian. And she wanted to tell me they arrested the guys who broke into my house."

"What?" Alaina's voice blasted through the suite.

Jess waved a hand in timid apology at the annoyed glances they were getting. "Yeah. Julian wanted to deliver the good news, but I ghosted him and things went sideways." Jess rolled her eyes and tugged open the door. They would have to walk back to the hauler from their suite, and she wasn't looking forward to baking in the southern California sun along the way.

"Well, I'm glad they arrested the bastards, but it would have been nice if someone had told you." Alaina's voice was clipped, annoyed, and Jess knew she needed to intervene before her friend worked herself into a tizzy.

"It's my fault. I should have taken Julian's calls, but I was too busy thinking I knew what was best."

"So, you're going to call him?" Alaina asked, carefully watching her step as they descended the aluminum stairs down to street level. The thump and clunk of a hundred other people descending before them was enough of a distraction to allow Jess a reprieve until they got to the bottom.

"I don't know. If I don't, what's my excuse?"

It was so hard to put the life she'd always wanted into perspective compared to the life she had now. Meeting Julian had been amazing. Talking to him and getting to know him had helped her make sense of herself, and it was hard to imagine never completing that journey, never meeting her siblings. When it came down to brass tacks, she wanted that, desperately.

She didn't have to decide now. The problem would keep for a little while longer. Besides, she had other issues—like Alaina seeming to think their issues were resolved after a few days of fuming.

If only it were that simple.

* * *

Noah's bachelor pad in Downtown Denver was a sweet gig, there was no denying it. Jack looked out over the city below and admired the glow of taillights and headlights dotted down Wewatta Street like a merry string of Christmas bulbs. He was still riding a high from the race the day before and hadn't wanted to go home to his lonely Chicago loft. So, he'd made the executive decision to have a seventy-two-hour layover in Denver where he could crash on Noah's couch and reminisce about the good ol' days before he hopped a flight to Indianapolis for Grayson's wedding.

The Long Beach Grand Prix had been his highest finish in five seasons, and for the first time in a long while, he felt relevant again. Despite the highs, there had been one thing to put a damper on everything—the shittiest shit he'd ever witnessed—the edict handed down from the bride and groom. He'd talked to Grayson about it after qualifying on Saturday, and his friend had talked him off the metaphorical ledge, but the truth remained. If Grayson wasn't his best friend, he wouldn't have even considered this whole charade.

But he was. So he supposed it wouldn't kill him to keep up the lone wolf facade for one more weekend.

They were adults and they should be able to control themselves in high-stakes situations, but damn it, what if he didn't want to? He got the girl, and he had a right to be happy about it. Granted, there was a fine line between happiness and gloating. He flirted with it regularly just for the hell of it, but now was not the time. He could accept that.

Round and round the mulberry bush, the monkey chased the weasel...

An elbow nudged his arm, and he glanced over to see his brother with a cold bottle of Sam Adams tilted toward him in offering. Jack nodded his thanks and took the bottle to clink with Noah's. They both took a long pull and took in the view in silence, enjoying the familiar buzz and hum of nightlife below. "Sorry to impose. Feel free to leave me here and go spend the evening with your"—Jack cleared his throat—"Friend."

Noah gave him a doubtful side eye and raised a single dark brow. "Friend? Seriously? Who do you think I am? Fabio?"

"Aren't you still friends with benefiting that girl from Cherry Creek?"

Noah shook his head. "Dude, that hasn't been a thing for over a month."

Jack leaned into his brother with a playful nudge. "Well, damn. Why didn't you say anything?"

"Because it was casual and these things happen in casual dating," he said over a subterranean rumble of amusement. "But what about you? If you don't want to go back to your place, fine. But why are you here sleeping on my pull-out instead of shacking up with your girlfriend? Don't you have a wedding to attend this weekend?"

Jack rolled his eyes. "It's a long story, but Tucker flies in on

Friday, and it would look kind of suspicious if I was sleeping at Jess's house."

"He doesn't know yet?" Noah asked incredulously before taking another drink of his beer. "That sounds like a disaster waiting to happen." He turned and plopped onto the couch, using the coffee table as an ottoman for his sock-clad feet.

"That's what we tried to tell Grayson and Alaina, but they want what they want."

"Oof," Noah groaned. "Speaking of Jess, how did this weekend go?" He reclined so that his head rested on the couch and gazed at Jack.

"Um…good, I think."

"So, Julian showed up? He was iffy about it when I sent him the ticket."

Jack leaned his head back against the window with a quiet thud and smirked. "No. His wife showed up instead. Jess was gobsmacked."

"The *wife*? Damn. That's a plot twist. How did Jess take it?"

"I think she's still trying to decide. She wants him to be a part of her life, but she's trying to be a good mom too."

"She's overthinking it."

"Probably," Jack agreed before lapsing into another comfortable silence. "I still can't believe you roped Grayson into giving you that ticket."

Noah's blue eyes popped open at Jack's sudden proclamation. "Yeah, well, he has a soft spot for father-child relationships. When you wouldn't help, I had to go with plan B." He shrugged and finished his beer before sitting the bottle on the side table with a soft clink.

"I wouldn't help because it's not our place to interfere.

That's her dad, man. It needs to be her decision whether she brings him into her life. It's not like she's had a lot of say in that up to this point."

Noah rose from his seat and went to the refrigerator for another drink. "And I would understand her hesitation if he was a piece of trash, but I'm finding it hard not to think about how he feels. This wasn't his choice—to not know his child for the first twenty-five years of her life. She would have had such a different life if he could have cared for her. Think about how you would feel if you found out you had a twelve-year-old daughter walking around out there living life with your high school prom date like you don't exist."

Jack shuddered. "What a fucking nightmare."

Noah gave a nod and a hand gesture that thanked his brother for making his point for him. "I understood when you didn't want to get involved. There's an integrity in your relationship that you don't want to compromise. I respect that. But damn it, I wasn't going to sit here and watch Jess let her own happiness slip through her fingers. Not again."

If there was one thing to be said about his big brother, it was that he took the bull by the horns. He wasn't brash. He never made a decision without mulling it over. And over. When he made a choice, he made it with confidence and would defend it until his dying breath. It's what made him good at his job, and it's what made him a great sounding board for those on shaky footing. Jack had to be confident in his career field too, but confidence for him meant keeping his foot in it through all four turns at Iowa—not covert handoffs of suite tickets for the Long Beach Grand Prix.

"Are you going to tell her?" Noah finally asked, as he walked back into the living room.

Jack shook his head. "I figured, in ten years, if everything works out, I *might* come clean. Until then, if you want to get it off your chest, more power to you. Leave me the hell out of it."

Noah smirked and clinked the neck of his bottle against Jack's. "Deal. So. Tell me. How'd it feel to stand on the podium yesterday?"

Jack couldn't help the shit-eating grin that crept onto his face as he reminisced. Champagne tasted so much sweeter when you were drinking it after a race. It stung like hell when somebody sprayed it in your eyes, but he wouldn't give it up for anything. "It felt great. Especially in my third race for the team—makes it hard to think about giving it up."

"Giving it up?" Noah was on full alert now as he came up off the couch to an upright position. "Since when?"

Jack shrugged uncomfortably. "I don't know. I've been thinking about it since the end of last season. I thought, if I didn't get a ride this season, then it wasn't meant to be. Now that I'm with Jess…I feel like it might be best to transition into commentating or reporting for one of the bigger networks. I just don't want to be gone all the time."

"Have you told Chris?" Noah's singular raised eyebrow told Jack he already knew the answer to that question.

"No. And I'm not going to. If Lakeshore doesn't pick up the option on my contract, we'll discuss it then."

Noah rolled his eyes and flopped back to his original position with his head lolling on the back of the couch. "That ought to go over well."

Jack snorted and rose from the couch to put his empty beer bottle in the recycle. "Yeah, well, if he and Ivy start having kids, maybe I'll actually get to see them. It would be nice to see you guys more often."

"Well, you might see them more often, but I doubt you'll see me for a while after the 500—even if you don't get your contract extension." Their conversation was interrupted by a quick *rap-tap-tap* on the door that heralded the arrival of their pizza. Jack jumped to the door, his stomach doing a reflexive rumble at the carbs it was about to consume. The hot smells of cheese, oregano, and grease wafted into his face as he opened the door, and saliva rushed to his mouth.

He took the pizza with a grateful smile and tipped the delivery guy before shutting the door with his foot. Not even bothering with the pleasantries of cutlery, he took the pizza to the living room, where they took pieces straight out of the box and consumed them as though their lives depended on it.

"What do you mean you won't be around?" Jack asked as he blew steam out of his mouth full of pizza.

"I got a job in California."

"For how long?" Jack asked, manfully swallowing the piping hot food and chasing it with a gulp of beer from his brother's bottle. He then rose from the couch and made for the refrigerator to get a fresh one.

"Why do you even ask at this point? You know I never know how long I'll be gone."

"Right, but you're gone all the time on jobs, and you never mention it. I get the feeling you think this one's a long one." Jack jammed the bottle against the edge of the countertop and popped the cap off as he waited for his brother's reply. He may not have cop radar, but he had a keen sense of smell, and something was giving off a fishy odor.

Noah had an absent look on his face as he stared at a

nondescript stain on the standard-issue cream-colored living room carpet, and Jack waited patiently for his reply. Noah would tell him when he was damn good and ready, not a minute before. Finally, he took a deep breath and made eye contact with his little brother. "I haven't said anything because I don't want anyone to worry, but Julian's hired me to look into some people. He thinks he may know who's responsible for sending those guys to rough up Jess."

Jack sat his beer bottle on the counter with a loud clunk and took a deep breath to help level off his rising blood pressure. A vein throbbed in his temple and he gritted his teeth against the impulse to go ballistic. "And you didn't think that's something we needed to know?"

"Not really," Noah replied. "Look, the guys were arrested, and whoever sent them isn't going to try pulling a stunt like that again. The FBI is doing its due diligence, but Julian doesn't feel like they're looking in the right places. That's where I come in."

Jack let out a slow, measured breath, counted to ten, and then counted to ten again. Not only was it irritating that his brother was keeping shit from him, it was scary as hell knowing Noah would be directly in the line of fire if this thing went south. "I don't like it," Jack finally muttered. "Have you told anyone else?"

Noah shook his head. "My firm knows I'll be out of pocket and where I'm setting up shop, but as far as the family? No. I'm keeping it on the QT. I don't want anyone connecting dots that are better left alone. The more people who know, the more dangerous the situation gets."

"Well, that just makes me feel all warm and cozy." The cool marble countertop pressed into his back and seeped into his skin, making him shiver.

"You can't tell Jess," Noah insisted. "Julian doesn't want her to know and neither do I. She's just starting to feel like she doesn't have to look over her shoulder every five minutes, and we want to keep it that way."

Jack rolled his eyes. "I'm starting to understand why you're still single."

Noah's cheeks pinked, but he didn't take the bait. Instead, he leveled his brother with a bold, blue gaze. There would be no changing his mind. When people he loved were threatened, he wouldn't back down until the one doing the threatening was either behind bars or six feet under.

Thirty-Four

La Vida Estaría Vacía Sin Ti

The rich smells of chicharones, tostones, fresh garlic, and sautéed onions, along with the warm Latin bounce of a little reggaeton music, had Jess puttering back and forth across the kitchen floor, holding Parker in front of her as she made faces and danced. His smiles and coos were enough to melt her heart, and she'd dance forever if she could freeze this moment in time. Tita stood at the stove swaying to the beat with a little two-step, hip sway combo. Jess laughed again and swirled, eliciting a loud *oog* sound from Parker.

"You're in a good mood." Tita observed as she stirred her green platanos in olive oil for her famous Mofongo. Jess's stomach rumbled in anticipation. She placed Parker in his swing and made her way back into the kitchen as a slower number came on and went back to mashing garlic in the mortar and pestle for the garlic sauce—her usual contribution to the dish she'd been making with Tita for nearly twenty years.

"I am," she said with a smile. "We got the contracts on the second-floor storage space today, and Alaina is officially out of the office until after the honeymoon, so she can stop driving us *nuts*." She sang the words "nuts" in a high falsetto and Tita's laugh, rich as dark molasses, melted into the hazy air of the kitchen.

"¿Donde esta tu novio?" she asked, asking after Jack in an unusual display of interest. Normally, Tita tolerated her boyfriends as temporary inconveniences—not that Jess could blame her. She'd rarely had a boyfriend long enough for Tita to bother.

"Colorado with his brother. He's flying in Thursday." Jess swirled to meet her grandmother eye to eye. "Tita, recuerda, Tucker no sabe de nosotros."

"Si, si." She placated with a wave of her spoon, and Jess breathed a little easier. How they would get through this weekend without somebody spilling the beans was beyond her. What was that old saying? "Three may keep a secret, if two of them are dead?" Well, a lot more than three people knew about *this* secret, and none of them were dead. But she tried not to dwell on that.

Tita turned to her, brandishing her spoon as she looked her granddaughter over. "He makes you happy."

Jess could feel the glow in her cheeks, but kept her eyes carefully on the garlic she was making into a paste. "He does."

"Cariña," her grandmother crooned, asking for her attention with a gentle, verbal nudge. "Solo quiero que seas feliz."

The glow bloomed into a full-on grin at Tita's words and tears of pure joy welled in her eyes. "Gracias," she managed through her constricted airway. It was a novel feeling—happiness. That wasn't to say she didn't still have issues swirling around her like a storm cloud, but for the first time, she felt like she had a sturdy umbrella to keep the worst of the monsoon at bay.

After a beat of comfortable silence, her grandmother spoke. "Tu madre...she called this afternoon." Tita's voice was pitched so low, she barely heard her among the grinding of the pestle and the steady hissing bubble of the olive oil in the pan.

Jess paused in her ministrations, gripping the smooth stone of her pestle like one would bear a cross against evil. Forcing her voice to remain calm, she grabbed a spoon off the counter and scraped the mashed garlic from the mortar.

"She said you would not take her calls." Tita was slowly scooping the fried platanos out of the oil and placing them on a paper towel-lined plate, intentionally keeping her eyes from her granddaughter in the process.

Jess's hands were shaking so hard she had to put down the spoon and instead pressed her hands flat into the cool countertop. Flashbacks to her panic attack in Jack's apartment had her struggling to keep her breaths steady as she reached for the olive oil dispenser and poured a generous amount into the bowl with the mashed garlic. "I blocked her number."

Ivanna sat the platanos down in front of Jess with a frustrated clank. "Did it ever occur to you there was a reason she was calling?"

"She could be dying, and I wouldn't give a damn," Jess growled as she grabbed a few piping hot plantains and tossed them into the mortar.

Ivanna gasped in horror. "Yèsica!"

Jessica tossed her hands in frustration, sending the pestle clanking against the counter. "I told her we would never speak again, and I meant it. I can't keep letting her dictate my life! She didn't want that right twenty-five years ago, and she hasn't wanted it for a second since. So, I took it back."

"Ella es *tu madre*," her grandmother said in a voice that sounded betrayed as well as disappointed.

"And I'm her daughter," Jessica whispered, tears streaming down her cheeks. "Look what that has gotten me." She turned back around and began furiously mashing plantains, garlic sauce, and chicharones with wild abandon, taking her frustration out on the food rather than Tita. After all, she was a mother trying to do right by her child.

"I did my best, cariña," her grandmother murmured, coming to pull her into her arms.

"I know that," Jess whispered into her grandmother's shoulder as they held each other. "I don't blame you for any of it."

"Lo sé," Ivanna murmured. "Te amo." She stroked Jess's hair, holding her until Parker began to fuss in his swing. Then she went to comfort him instead.

Jessica continued to mash in contemplative silence until all the ingredients were mixed into one tightly compacted mortar full of Mofongo, and there was nothing left to do but eat or ask the obvious. "What did she want?" Jessica asked as she took a butter knife and scraped the dish away from the sides of the mortar.

"¿Que?" Tita asked as she bounced up and down, patting Parker on the butt to settle him.

"María. You said I didn't think to ask why she was calling.

So…what did she want?"

Ivanna sighed and eyed her granddaughter wearily. "Your father called her."

Jess stared at her grandmother, her mind completely blank as she tried to piece together what she'd just heard.

Julian? Calling María? How? Why?

"I know you have questions, and to save you the trouble, I don't know. Your mother said she had not spoken to Julian since before you were born and has no idea how he got her information."

Jess certainly had a few guesses as to how Julian got in contact with María. Her best one started with "No" and ended with "ah." "But Julian knows I'm not speaking with María. Why would he call her?"

Parker chose that moment to let out a squawk of frustration and Tita shushed him as she resumed her bouncing. "No sé. Maybe he thought you would listen to me, if not her."

Jess tilted her head, eyeing her grandmother, who was focused intently on the baby in her arms. "Listen. To you." Quite a lot of things about this weren't making sense.

"Sit down, nena," Tita said soothingly as she gestured toward one of the barstools.

Jess's heart was in her throat. She'd gone out of her way to not speak of Julian's involvement in the break-in to her grandmother. She knew it would only complicate matters—Tita having that passionate Latin blood. Ivanna Morales was hot-tempered and could hold a grudge with the best of them, and if Jess was still trying to figure her shit out, the last thing she needed was Tita's unsolicited advice. Her grandmother wanted what was best for her. She knew that, but sometimes her protective streak was too much.

When Jess was finally settled, Tita handed her the baby and then sat on the bar stool facing her so they were knee to knee. "He told your mother he's tried to call you several times since the incident. Is that true?"

"It is," she whispered, squeezing Parker to reassure herself.

Tita reached across and placed her hand on Jess's arm, patting it gently. Her dark brown eyes were shining with sympathy, and the deep lines of her forehead were furrowed with concern. "Yèsica…dime."

So she did. She told Tita about her father's political career, his associations, and how those associations had resulted in the attack in her own home. She told her about her fear for her son and for her own safety, clinging to her baby boy like a life raft through all of it. And when she finished, she simply sat, shaking like a leaf, tears streaming down her face as she stared into her grandmother's warm coffee-colored eyes. They held such love and tenderness; it created at least a small sense of peace within her, and she was finally able to breathe.

"I understand," Ivanna murmured, leaning forward to stroke her granddaughter's face.

"You do?" Jess asked, voice weak and drained after a lifetime's worth of revelations.

Tita sighed and pulled back slightly. "You have always been selfless, cariña. To a fault, even. Giving others everything and expecting nothing in return because you never felt like you were truly worthy of their love or respect. Over the years, that doubt has hardened into this…wall. A wall you build higher and higher until there's no way for anyone to climb over. Yèsica—" Tita leaned forward again, grasping at Jess's free hand as she cradled Parker with the other. "I am so proud of you—for leaving Tucker, for finding your young man, for going after something you *deserve*."

More tears welled in Jess's eyes, and she bent forward to press her lips to her son's soft hair, her tears rolling down her nose and into the soft black down. "I'm so afraid someone is going to come along and take it all away…and I don't know if I could pick myself up again if I lost any of them," she whispered.

"Is that why you are really shutting Julian out?" Tita's voice was quiet, almost like a light breeze blowing through a tree, a breath above silence.

Jess took a jagged breath, struggling to control her words. "I'm shutting him out because…because I don't want to hurt anymore." Her voice was high, distressed, and full of still unshed tears.

Her grandmother stood and pulled Jess into her ample bosom, shushing her as she sobbed. "I don't agree with your decision to shut your mother out, but I can understand it. You have given her more chances than anyone has a right to. But your father…he deserves his chance to *be* a father. You should try to let him in."

"And if I can't?" Jess sniffled, looking down at Parker who was now snoozing obliviously in the crook of her arm.

"Let that be tomorrow's worry, cariña, not today's fear."

So many emotions swirled around inside Jess's body: doubt, anger, sadness, yearning, hope, and fear. She so badly wanted to sort through them, to understand which voice to listen to, because her grandmother was right. Worrying about things that may never come to pass was like sinking a ship before it ever left port.

Thirty-Five

Love and Misery

The ethereal gleam of hundreds of flickering tea lights gave the room a warm glow that paired nicely with the massive crystal chandeliers above. Alaina had outdone herself with the centerpieces and place settings, but Jess expected nothing less from the best event designer she knew. The girl had dreamed about her wedding for half her life. It was only right that it looked like it belonged in a bridal magazine. Centerpieces full of wisteria, lavender, and hyacinths in an array of heights and spreads dotted the long tables on either side of the room. Hurricane glasses filled with water created a mesmerizing reflective surface for the dozens of floating votives casting the room in romantic shadows and refracted light. The heady scents of the flower arrangements commingled with the sugary scent of fondant icing and the savory smells of prime rib and roasted chicken.

But all the gorgeous decorations and fantastic food in the

world couldn't distract Jess from the sight in front of her. She could feel the love radiating from the couple in the middle of the dance floor as they swayed to a contemporary rendition of "I Can't Help Falling in Love with You."

The way Grayson looks at her...

Okay, maybe she was a tiny bit jealous. "Admitting you have a problem is the first step to recovery..." Jess muttered under her breath as she swiped a flute of champagne off a passing tray, her eyes never leaving the happy couple. But how exactly were you supposed to recover from a problem that wasn't of your own making?

Easy. Stop being such a people pleaser.

Right...like that's a thing.

The angel and devil on Jess's shoulders continued to bicker despite the buoyant atmosphere outside of her body. Alaina laid her head on Grayson's shoulder, eyes closed, completely lost in the moment, and his cheek rested on the top of her head. The look of peace and contentment on his face made her stomach clench. His mouth moved as he whispered something in Alaina's ear and a smile broke out on her face as she pulled back to gaze up at him and laugh.

The click of camera shutters and their accompanying brilliant flashes lit up the room as the song drew to a close. Grayson twirled his new bride once and brought her in, dipping her ceremoniously and sealing their dance with a kiss.

Jess took a large sip of her bubbly and sighed. It would be time for toasts soon.

"Makes you wonder, doesn't it?"

Jess whirled at the sound of the voice, champagne splashing out of her glass and running down the back of her hand in a cold trickle before dripping to the floor. With her heart still in her throat, she raised her eyebrow in question. "Wonder if we're ever going to remember this moment and not be bitter?" she asked, turning back around to look at Alaina and her new hubby as they made their way over to the cake table.

"Something like that." Jack gave the breath of a laugh and stepped up next to her, so close she could feel his body heat on her bare shoulder. "How's your day going?"

A small smile tugged at her lips, but she tried to keep it contained in case anyone was watching. "Oh, you know, putting fires out left and right—every maid of honor's path to glory. At least Alaina didn't get cold feet. That would have been too much for my sanity."

"Tell me about it. I'm still trying to figure out how I'm supposed to dance with you later and pretend you don't turn me on."

A blush began to creep up the back of Jess's neck, and she struggled willfully to maintain her composure. They had been given one dance together after begging and pleading, but only under the condition that they act as though it were completely platonic. No. Romance. "You're breaking the rules, Jackson," she muttered under her breath.

He snorted and stepped away. "Yeah, alright. I'll catch you later," he said with a wink and wandered off toward the bar.

Jess took a deep breath and glanced over to where Tucker stood two tables away with their son nestled in the crook of one arm, chatting to guests and completely oblivious to the little *tête-à-tête* that had just taken place. This miserable evening was all for his benefit, and with any luck, he'd never notice the difference.

For the rest of the night, she was so focused on the

three minutes she would be allowed in Jack's presence she barely registered her maid of honor speech—a speech she'd rehearsed so much, she could practically recite it in her sleep.

When the DJ cued up "Kiss Me" by Sixpence None The Richer it was all she could do not to jump out of her seat. Instead, she waited for Jack to approach her, casually twirling her champagne flute on the tablecloth as if she hadn't a care in the world. Couples—Alaina and Grayson, Grayson's grandparents, even Maura and Nate—slowly drifted out on the dance floor to the upbeat nineties' song.

She smiled. Alaina's parents had a not-so-amicable divorce four years ago. Nate had been in a rough place emotionally, but when Alaina had her accident, it had been all the motivation he needed to go to his ex-wife on bended knee and plead for a second chance. They'd been together ever since, and it gave Jess hope that maybe her second chance would work out too.

A light tap on her shoulder brought her out of her reverie and she turned to see her boyfriend standing behind her, hand outstretched, with a mischievous smile on his lips. "May I have this dance?"

Jess's smile equaled his as she took his hand. "You may."

Carefully, they wove through the throngs of people, both seated and standing, to find a small patch of real estate on the dance floor. Jack's warm hand gripped hers and twirled her around in a circle that had her squealing in unexpected glee. She twirled back into him effortlessly and he pulled her close, swaying to the beat. She grinned at him in amusement, surprised by how much he seemed to be enjoying himself. "I never pegged you as a wedding dancer."

He looked down at her with a beatific smile. "Normally,

I'm not, but I was oddly excited for today. I wanted to dance with you—show you off."

More people joined them on the dance floor, making it crowded, but not unbearable. The smell of champagne and draft beer was mixing with the scent of close bodies in an intoxicating aroma that left her head spinning. A girlish giggle bubbled through her lips. "You're always surprising me."

He swung her around again and pulled her back in, amplifying her laughter. "Mom made us all take lessons as kids. It was one of those things we hated at the time but appreciate as grown men." He leaned in to put his lips to her ear. "The ladies love it."

She swatted at him playfully and lost herself in the rhythm, letting him lead her across the floor and between other couples until the closing bars of the song. When the music came to a close and faded into Forest Blakk's "I Choose You," she gave a remorseful sigh and pulled her hands from him. "I suppose we ought to get back to reality."

For a long moment, he held her gaze, and she watched as passion and love, frustration and indignation all flashed through the dark depths of his eyes. And then he pulled her back in and kept dancing. "If I'm going to feel bad about something, it's not going to be about how much I love you," he murmured with his cheek pressed against her temple.

"Jack," she said in passive protest as she tugged at her hand. She could feel the stares of her loved ones branding her back. But somehow, lost as she was in his eyes, she couldn't find the will to care.

"Humor me, Sassy. Just this once."

With a resigned sigh, she pressed her cheek into the smooth

polyester of his tux jacket and let him twirl her around the dance floor, the palm of his hand pressed firmly into the small of her back.

It took every ounce of control she could muster, not to rise on the balls of her feet and kiss him when the song ended. But this wasn't the place or time. With one last lingering look, Jack squeezed her hand, and they parted, destined to spend the rest of the evening in opposite corners of the room.

She bit the inside of her cheek at Alaina's cold expression. They'd deviated from the plan. She knew she would likely get a cussing out later, but it had been worth it. At least, she thought it had been—until she caught a glimpse of the confusion and hurt on Tucker's face.

"Carajo."

Thirty-Six

House of Cards

Quite a few magnums of champagne later, the party was still going strong. It was almost midnight and the younger crowd that was left, mostly friends and family of the bride and groom, were buzzing like a hive of contented bees. Rather than make Tucker and Jess leave the party, Maura had offered to take Parker home. He'd been sleeping well in the arms of his grandparents but would need a diaper change and a bottle soon—better for him to be within a stone's throw of his crib when the bedlam broke out. Jess dug frantically through the layers of wraps and jackets in the coat check closet searching for the diaper bag.

"Jess…" she whirled around, her head spinning as her vision course-corrected through the alcohol-induced wobble of her surroundings.

Shit.

"Not now, Jack." She continued to rifle through silk,

organza, and woolen overcoats.

Wool? Seriously? It's April.

"Did I do something wrong?" His voice was low now, pleading. He stepped toward her and she took a reflexive step back.

"No. I just...I—" She stopped, feeling her resolve weaken. *Stop it. Get the diaper bag and go.*

"Tucker is waiting on me. He's already pissed after... whatever the hell that was." She used her flailing arms to insinuate the massive violation of The Rules. Tucker was jealous. They had counted on that. What they had not counted on was their inability to control themselves in close proximity. Like now.

She crossed her arms defensively over her chest and stared at the floor. Her silver satin heels peeked out from under her full-length lavender skirt, and the rhinestone accents glinted in the pulsing strobe lights from the dance floor in the next room. Her newly manicured nails dug into the tender flesh of her upper arm in an attempt to sober her muzzy brain before she said, or did, something she'd regret. A blast of air from the main door drifted through the room, causing gooseflesh to ripple across her olive skin. "Maura wants to take Parker home. I have to find his diaper bag." Jess crossed the room briskly and began to rootle around under another pile of coat check items.

Jack was still standing behind her. "Would you at least let me help you?" She could feel him there, watchful, like a bird of prey perched above a freshly harvested field, waiting for some unsuspecting field mouse to hesitate a little too long.

Right, like you're a victim here.

She wanted him as badly as he wanted her. She was just

trying to be an adult about it.

"Ha!" she exclaimed as she sighted the gray backpack and pulled it free with a small grunt of effort, causing coats, purses, and long-forgotten wedding gifts to collapse into the void left behind. When she turned back toward the door, he was right behind her, so close that as she turned, she found herself staring directly into his eyes, burning with such passion it made her stomach flop like a landed fish.

"Jess." He breathed her name as though the mere speaking of it caused him pain. Filled with the heady scents of bourbon, sugary icing, and sweat, the space between them was intoxicating, and she leaned in without a conscious thought, their lips crushing together with acute need.

Jack wrapped his arms around her, spreading his fingers to span the width of her shoulder blades. His touch was hot on her cool skin and the pleasant sensation spread quickly, causing her breasts and belly to tingle in anticipation. With each enticing tick of his fingers down the knobs of her spine, her excitement grew more fervent, until she was pulsing with need. So much so, when he dug his fingers into her love handles and pressed her against the rough brick wall behind them, she nearly came undone.

Moaning, she arched up into him and roamed her hands down his chest, under his tuxedo jacket, and around to his back. His arousal pressed against her thigh and her insides quivered. It would be so easy to reach between them and unbutton his fly. She could envision his hurried excitement as he pulled up the layered organza of her skirt in search of what he wanted—what they both wanted. But instead, she pulled her hands out from underneath his jacket and moved them to his hair, busying her fingers with his thick locks, rather than a certain button-zipper combo.

She gave a breathy sigh full of frustrated need and pressed her lips against his strong jaw. The sharp stubble prickled her lips in a tantalizing fashion that only caused the heat between her legs to grow.

"Jack…" she panted. God, she was dripping, and it was like he could smell it.

"I need you," he growled, pressing her harder into the wall, covering her mouth with a kiss that edged passed urgent and went straight to frenzied.

Oh God—

"What the *fuck?*"

Jack leaped back from her so quickly, it was as though the movie Jess had been watching skipped five frames ahead. Tucker stood in the doorway, face purple with rage, cheek muscles bulging under the strain of his clenched jaw.

Jess's chest was heaving from the exertion of her make-out session and she pressed a hand to her breastbone, fighting to control her breathing. "Tuck—"

But Tucker was already across the room, holding Jack by the lapels. "You sneaky son of a bitch."

"What's the matter, Montgomery? Feeling a little bit jealous?" Jack taunted. His white teeth gleamed in the dimly lit room, and Jess's heart stopped.

As if in slow motion, Tucker's fist floated through the air and crashed into Jack's jaw. Jack's eyes glazed for a half second before he snapped back into focus and ran at Tucker, shoulder lowered, taking him at the abdomen and ramming him into the opposite wall. The air rushed out of Tuck's lungs with a loud *whoosh* and Jack gave him a quick one-two in the ribs before Tucker brought an elbow down between Jack's shoulder blades. He let out a sharp grunt and Tucker shoved him off, running at him so they both went sprawling headlong into the pile of outerwear stacked against the window.

"Stop it!" Jess screamed. "Morons! Stop it!"

Her screams brought people running from all directions, and then Grayson was there. He hooked an arm across Tucker's chest, and heaved, but Tucker, deep in the haze of red covering his vision, brought an elbow up sharply and crunched it into Grayson's nose. Grayson cried out and clapped his hand to his face as dark red blood oozed between his fingers.

A sharp whistle split the room, and everyone froze. Tucker's arm was drawn back, poised to land another blow. Nathan Montgomery stood in the doorway, a large blue vein standing out on his forehead, and his face crimson with fury. "Tucker. Take a walk."

The blood still clearly boiling in his veins and itching for a fight, Tucker slowly lowered his arm and clenched his hands at his sides. He drew breath to speak, but Nate didn't give him a chance to get the words out.

"*Now*, Tucker."

The younger Montgomery's jaw twitched, but with one last seething glance at his adversary, he stalked out of the room and slammed the outer door open with enough force to bulldoze through a concrete barrier by sheer force of will.

"Grayson!" Alaina cried, pushing and shoving against the crowd gathered in the doorway to get to her husband who was attempting to stanch the flow of blood from his damaged nose with the sleeve of his shirt.

"Are you okay?" Jess asked Jack in a low aside as she ran

a hand over the side of his head. She lightly traced the blooming blue and purple splotch of a nasty bruise across his jaw with her thumb and winced. She knew how much that would hurt tomorrow.

"I'll leave these two to you, shall I?" Nathan voiced to whoever was left in the room. Jess assumed it was Alaina—possibly Grayson?

There was a beat of silence. Jack gazed up at Jess, his tongue probing the teeth on the side of his face with the bruised jaw gingerly, wincing when he hit a particularly tender spot on the inside of his cheek.

"What the hell is the matter with you?" Grayson's query came through a wad of cloth still pressed to his face. He sounded like he had a bad head cold. She turned to face him, staring in horror at the blood spattered across the clean white linen of his dress shirt. Alaina's brow was scrunched in sympathy as she rubbed his back and reached up to smooth the tufted hair at his temple. Grayson's dark eyes were locked on his best friend, seething. "I fucking warned you about this, Jack. He's not some Jo Schmo you picked a fight with in a bar!"

Jack rubbed his jaw meditatively. "Clearly."

"Do you want me to get you some ice?" Alaina whispered to Grayson, peering up to look at his swollen nose.

He gave her a brief shake of the head, letting his glare rest on Jack for another moment before storming out.

Alaina looked after him, worried, before turning toward the disheveled couple in the hot seats. "Jack, get out, and for God's sake, steer clear of my brother."

Jack's teeth clicked together at her rude tone, but, with a hesitant glance at Jess, did as he was told. He had likely just ruined their wedding night, after all. The least he could do was leave before Alaina kicked him in the balls.

Slowly, Alaina reached for the doorknob and pulled the door shut to give them privacy. "Alaina—"

"Don't," Alaina growled.

Jess swallowed, even though her mouth felt like the Sahara desert, and abruptly sat on the windowsill behind her, staring at her friend with wide eyes.

"I'm not sure whether you've got your head up your ass or what, but I'm gonna need you to get your *shit* together, Jess!" Her voice was at top volume and Jessica flinched. "It was one weekend. That's all I needed. One weekend where we could put this whole mess on hold and I could get married. You said you wouldn't touch each other or so much as fucking *smile* at each other. All. Weekend. So I was nice. I said you could have a dance—which you totally ignored." Alaina was barely taking breaths between sentences, and Jess could feel her own temper rising. "You should have told Tucker."

Thinking she'd misheard her friend in her struggle to keep the lid from blowing off the kettle of her rising anger, she started. "I'm sorry. What did you say?"

"Trying to keep this from Tucker was a terrible idea. You should have told him."

Jess's mouth popped open in incredulity and her blood hit the boil before Alaina even finished her sentence. "Are you seriously trying to fucking *gaslight* me right now?" she screeched. "This was *your* idea! I wanted to tell him two weeks ago! Don't throw it back in my face now after it all went to shit!"

There was a light knock at the door, and both women jumped like a startled covey of quail. It was Maura. "Sorry to bother you girls, but um…did you ever find that diaper bag?"

Propelled into action by deep-seated maternal instinct, Jess lunged toward the pale gray bag that had been kicked into the corner during the melee and promptly handed it to her child's grandmother with a tight smile. "Thanks."

The older woman murmured a few words to her daughter and, after a quick peck on the cheek, closed the door with a quiet click. The sound of her heels tapping on the parquet floor faded as she made her way back toward the main event space, and the girls waited for the sound to disappear completely before continuing their conversation.

"I was trying really hard to put our differences aside until after the wedding, to be a good friend and not add to the stress you were already feeling, but I'm done with that shit. You've been a complete *bitch* for weeks now, and I can't handle it anymore!"

Alaina reared back like she'd been slapped, her eyes sparking. "Tucker catches you half-naked with Jack in a coat closet, and somehow this is *my* fault?"

Jess propelled herself off the windowsill, her skin tingling with the sparks off a burning fuse. "Yes! It is your fault! It was *your* idea to keep Jack and I a secret from Tucker. You're the one who made impossible demands on us! *You're* the one who has been a *terrible* friend, Alaina, and I'm fucking done." She paced up to her friend and put a finger in her chest. "I deserve an apology, and I'm not the only one. Jack, Tucker, Grayson, we all deserve an apology, and until you can get off your high horse long enough to do that, don't talk to me."

Jess sidestepped her friend, who strongly resembled a person who'd been sucker punched, took a deep breath, and threw open the door to the coat closet, feeling freer than she had in months.

Thirty-Seven

Lonely Country Roads

ool spring air bit at Jess's bare shoulders as she walked out into the night in search of Tucker. She hugged herself, chafing her hands against her arms as she walked along the path to the outdoor part of the venue. Large lanterns lined the canal, lending a mystical fairytale element to the property. In the center of the back patio area, a large pergola with a plush set of outdoor furniture underneath stood illuminated by a large fire pit cheerfully flickering away.

Tucker stood near the open fire, flexing his right hand absently as he massaged his fingers. He stared deep into the flames, flickering orange, red, and yellow with the crackling embers.

"Plotting your revenge?" She wanted to give him time to walk away. If she didn't give him a heads-up, he would feel cornered, and that could be dangerous.

His shoulders went rigid, but his eyes stayed locked on the fire for an interminable moment. Then he sighed and looked at her, his mouth twitching. "Are you putting yourself up as the sacrificial lamb?"

She gave him a sad smile. "If it will make you feel better."

He let his gaze drift back to the fire and shoved his hands in his pants pockets. Eventually, he shifted and cleared his throat. "I just…I want to know." He sighed and looked straight at her, no holds barred. "How long? Has it been going on since I went back to Texas?"

She furrowed her brow and stared at her feet. If she didn't say something soon, she might as well not say anything at all. "No," she whispered, wondering how much to divulge. "We didn't get back together until several weeks after you left."

He let out an angry hiss through his teeth and shifted his feet, looking up into the dark, starless night. Then, slowly, he brought the full weight of his gaze to bear on her.

Jess stepped to the fire's edge, reading him as he was reading her. "This is exactly what I was afraid of when you said you wanted to try. I was afraid all we would be left with is the loss of a friendship and awkward special occasions."

"I know," he whispered, squeezing his eyes shut and pinching the bridge of his nose. "I know. Okay? I fucked it up. You don't have to tell me."

Jess furrowed her brow. "I'm not *blaming* you, but you and I both know it wasn't working. I tried Tucker. I really did. But…" Tears dribbled down her cheeks, and she swiped them away quickly, taking a deep breath. "I missed him."

"And you don't miss me." It was a statement full of hurt and anger, and his eyes were dark, turbulent pools of water that would drown her if she wasn't careful. She had known this day would come, ever since that night in the club three months ago, known that hurting Tucker would be unavoidable no matter how it came out.

"Of course I miss you!" She could feel her emotions rocking the boat of resolve back and forth, cresting a wave and plummeting into the trough. Her breath hitched. "I care about you. I never wanted my happiness to come at the expense of yours, but I can't sacrifice myself at the altar of your wants and needs."

He scoffed and rolled his eyes, stepping back from the fire in disbelief. "Can we not turn this around to make it as though I'm the bad guy here? I have a right to be upset." His words weren't loud, but they bit through the distance between them.

"Do you?" She couldn't help the incredulity in her voice. How could he have a right to any sort of emotion other than the slightest hint of jealousy? Hell, they'd been broken up for three months. The only rights he had were where their son was concerned. Those concerns she would listen to, as long as they were expressed in a calm and collected manner. She didn't have time for high school bullshit.

He looked as though she'd slapped him. With a frustrated sigh, he whirled and stalked away, yanking his hands through his hair. "This is so fucking stupid," he hissed. "And damn you for making me feel like this is my fault!" He kicked the sofa in front of him explosively, and it skittered several feet before coming to a stop. "What the hell am I supposed to say that doesn't make me sound like a complete asshole?"

She'd never been the one with the answers, but she supposed she owed him some now. "When I found out I was pregnant, my life turned upside down. I knew you weren't looking for anything serious. Hell, neither was I. But from the get-go, I could tell Jack anything. We barely knew each other, but he could tell I was carrying something heavy." Her voice trembled, and she wiped away a stray tear before blinking hard and continuing.

"He never made me feel like I was something he needed to fix, or like I had something to live up to. And I needed that. I needed it like I needed air to breathe. It was unlike anything I've ever felt before—to be completely honest with someone, never worrying about how he would take it, or how I looked admitting it." She looked up at him then, willing her lungs to inflate so she could get the words out, but he cut her off.

"That's bullshit and you know it." One long pointed finger stabbed the air, pointing at her in accusation. "I treated you like you hung the moon. So don't you *dare*." His voice shook with the same fury that shook his hand. "Don't you *dare* try to make this out to be him treating you better than I did. If you want to say it wasn't working, that it didn't feel right for you, fine. But *do not* act like this is a matter of me treating you like shit and him strutting in like the conquering hero. It's not my fault I live in a different state. It's not my fault I can't help you raise our son. It's not my fault you decided to look somewhere else instead of telling me what you were struggling with."

"No, but it's your fault I broke up with him in the first place!" Even the cacophony of frogs in the canal seemed to silence with the echoes of her explosion, and Tucker stared at her, the anger momentarily stunned off his face. "You had this idealized version of how our lives would go, that we would grow to love one another and raise a family, but I loved Jack. And no matter how hard I tried—no matter how hard *you* tried—I couldn't make it go away!" Jess took a deep cleansing breath and closed her eyes, willing her temper back into the box and clicking the lock shut. "You're the father of my son, and every day when I look into Parker's beautiful eyes, I thank God for you, because…because you gave me the thing I love most in this world. But thinking this could *ever* work between us was a mistake."

Her brow crinkled as she pled for understanding, but the silence stretched between them like a lonely country road: no road signs to guide the way, no lampposts to light up the dark.

Frozen to where he stood, she wasn't sure he'd even been listening, but slowly, he was coming back to life. "Back before Parker was born, you asked me if I thought we would ever have what Grayson and Alaina have. Do you remember that?"

"Of course," she replied, knowing exactly what had prompted that question and feeling slightly guilty about asking.

"I told you I thought that kind of love was few and far between, but it didn't mean there weren't other kinds of happiness." He slowly lowered himself onto the cushy lounge chair behind him and stared at her, hands dangling between his thighs. "I thought maybe, one day, we could be happy— that the three of us could be a family. But you…you knew that whole time, didn't you?" Tears brimmed in his intense green eyes. She'd never seen them look so similar to the hazel of his sister's.

She clenched her teeth. There were fewer things in the world she wanted less than to drive the knife deeper into his stomach, but she had to be honest, even if it killed her. That's the only way they would get through this. "Yes."

He closed his eyes as more pain rippled across his face. He let his head fall into his big hands. "Why didn't you tell me, Jess?" It was a moan, unlike anything she'd ever heard from him. He was Tucker. Happy-go-lucky. Charming. Impulsive. Loving. And she hated herself for what she was doing to him.

"Because I wanted it to work too!" She went to him then, unable to bear the distance separating them. "I wanted to fall in love with you. I wanted to be a happy little family. Don't *ever* think I didn't want that. But I can't stop feeling what I feel. I've tried so hard." The last four words were a desperate breath. She hadn't realized how badly she needed him to understand.

"It's not okay," he finally muttered, glancing at her before staring out into the vast darkness beyond their meager flames.

"I know it's not."

"And I don't want to understand it." He shifted and sat up straighter in his chair, throwing his shoulders back in stubborn disapproval.

"I didn't expect you to." Despite the sentiment, she could feel the tension easing ever so slightly. Her lips twitched as she gave him a sideways glance.

His lips twitched too, unable to hide his sense of humor, even now after so much hurt and betrayal. The crackle and pop of the logs in the fire sent a spray of orange sparks into the night, and they danced for a millisecond before being extinguished by the brisk breeze. "I'm moving back home."

The words seemed to appear out of thin air, and she turned toward him sharply. "What?"

"In July. I decided not to reenlist."

The wind kicked up to a full-blown gust and guttered the fire.

Well, let's hope that's not an omen.

Jess's heart fluttered in her chest at the news. She'd no longer have to worry about where he was, what he was doing, whether he would come home. But it didn't change anything. They both knew that. A sense of uneasiness curdled her stomach, making her queasy. "Tell me you didn't do this for me."

A particularly loud party of wedding guests, drunk and still in the mood to celebrate, were making their way out to the street above. Two men staggered and threw their arms around each other before singing the chorus to "The Death of a Bachelor" at the top of their lungs. Their dates giggled helplessly and trailed behind, swinging their high heels from their fingertips as they walked toward their Uber. It was well past one a.m., and she wondered where Jack was.

"No. I did it for me." His baritone voice was clear and strong in the darkness, and she glanced up at his face. A strong jaw and sharp cheekbones were hidden in shadow along with the rest of him, but she could imagine their determined set.

All she could bring herself to say in that moment was a single word. "Good."

He snorted. "Seriously? You'll be glad to have me back, making a nuisance of myself and constantly cramping your style?"

"Just because I'm not in love with you doesn't mean I don't miss you like crazy. And it will be good for Parker. I never wanted you to be away from him, but I wasn't going to make you feel guilty for it either."

"I've been miserable these past few months without him. I don't want to be an absentee father."

She reached out and covered his hand with her own, squeezing gently, but as she opened her mouth to speak, someone else's voice called out. "Jess?"

She stood to face the venue and the anxious face of Marissa. Alaina's wedding was her first as an event coordinator, and she had held up well under pressure, but judging from her panicked expression, something had snapped her streak of good luck. "What's up?"

"I can't find the checkbook and the caterer and the DJ are packing up—"

"It's in my purse. I'll be right there."

A look of profound relief flooded her doe-eyed features, and she smiled. "Thank you!"

Jess smiled and waited until the younger girl was out of sight before turning back to her…what was he now? Friend? Ex? Baby daddy?

Some twisted mix of all three.

He gave her a weak smile and stood to join her. "Go ahead. You've got important duties to perform."

"This is important too," she insisted, making it clear she wouldn't leave until he was ready for her to leave. He reached out tentatively, putting a big hand on her chilled cheek. Her head naturally leaned into his gentle caress, and she reached up to cup his hand, holding it to her face for a moment longer. Things were about to change, and she wasn't sure she was ready. "I really am sorry, Tuck. For everything."

He took his hand back and leaned in to give her a lingering kiss on the forehead before wrapping his arms around her and pulling her in for a hug. "I'm not going to make promises

I can't keep and say I'm happy for you or that it doesn't hurt like hell to watch you go off into the sunset with someone else, but I do want what's best for you. Even if that's not me." He kissed the top of her head and then pushed her to arm's length. "Just promise me one thing."

She wiped the tears from her eyes and nodded, sucking in her bottom lip to keep it from trembling.

"When you decide to get married—and if he feels for you like you do for him, I know that's only a matter of time—just promise me we'll sit down and discuss how that's going to work. Parker is more important than any of the rest of us, and I want a say in how he's raised."

Jess swallowed a lump in her throat and nodded. "Of course."

He rolled his shoulders back as he took a deep breath. "The minions are beckoning." He gestured over his shoulder with a nod of his head and gave her a watered-down smile that didn't reach his eyes. "You should probably go."

"Yeah…" she whispered. "Thank you, Tucker."

He snorted. "Well, don't thank me yet. You've known me for a long time. I can have the best intentions, but sometimes, the green-eyed monster has other ideas."

Her lips quivered as she tried to contain an unhinged giggle. She *had* known him a long time, and she knew this was more difficult for him than he would ever admit. "Come on, let's go inside. It's freezing out here."

"It's okay." His voice was soft but absent. "You go ahead. I'm gonna…hang out here for a bit. Maybe take a walk."

"Tuck—"

"It's okay. I'm fine. Go." He assured her as he stepped out of the circle of light and started toward the walking path along the canal, humming softly to itself in the distance like a quiet lullaby as the city slept.

Thirty-Eight

Give Me Liberty

Jess stood in the open space of The Grainery, surveying the damage for a moment, before letting out a sigh that ran all the way to her high heel-clad feet and plopping down at one of the tables. She kicked off her shoes, wiggling her toes in pure bliss, and closed her eyes. She was exhausted and couldn't wait for her bed. The clank of dishes and glassware rattled through the large room as staff continued to tear down the event. When she pried her eyelids open again, she saw Marissa across the room, finishing with the DJ. Jess hadn't seen Jack since he'd been dismissed by Alaina earlier and assumed he had gone back to the hotel for the evening. She would text him when she got home to make sure he was okay.

Blinking rapidly to focus her eyes against fatigue and the remnants of champagne, she scrolled through her phone apps. Finding an Uber or a Lyft at this time of night would be nearly impossible, and she was sorely regretting not having a car service to take her back home. She finally found one twenty minutes away and booked it before it disappeared.

The chair next to her scraped against the floor and she froze at the sight of Jack, tux jacket hung over one shoulder by a finger. He looked like he'd had his face slammed against a tree trunk. She wrinkled her brow in sympathy. "Your face."

"Yeah…" He sighed. "I'm sure I'll feel it tomorrow." He eased himself down into the chair and turned to her, tucking a stray curl behind her ear with a small smile.

"Let me see," she murmured, taking his chin gently in hand and tilting his face toward the light. His left eye was nearly swollen shut and his jaw was mottled with purple and blue bruises. Tucker may not have had the last word, but he certainly made his point. "You shouldn't have provoked him like that." She hoped the two men could work out their differences eventually, but she had to admit, they weren't off to the best start.

"Yeah, well, Mr. Johnnie Walker thought it was a good idea. You heading home soon?" Jack asked, turning his face back to look down at her.

"Yes," she sighed with relief. "It's been a long day and I am ready for my bed." He grabbed her chair and slid her closer to him. With a smile, she picked up her legs and draped them over his lap so her unshod feet dangled freely in the cool air conditioning. She leaned in and placed her forehead on his shoulder, feeling his hand come around and stroke her back. Up and down, up and down. She smiled with a hum of contentment, and raised her head to kiss him, but was interrupted by a delicate throat clearing.

Surprised, Jess jumped slightly and turned to find Alaina standing in front of them, shuffling awkwardly from foot to foot. Her hair was falling down around her face, and the hem of her white dress was slightly stained with dust and dirt from the floor, but she still looked beautiful—if a little distressed. "Can I talk to you, Jess?" she asked quietly.

Every muscle in Jess's legs, back, and shoulders was taut as a bowstring, and if it weren't for Jack's warm hand on the small of her back—and sheer exhaustion—she probably would have sprung to her feet. As it was, she just glared. "Whatever you have to say to me, you can say in front of Jack."

A muscle ticked in Alaina's jaw—something Jess had never noticed the Montgomery siblings had in common until today. She wasn't sure what that said about the state of things, but wasn't about to get distracted. Alaina's eyes darted to Jack, her cheeks flushing pink, before she looked down at her hands clasped in front of her. Her neatly manicured French tips dug viciously into her palms, and Jess could see her pulse hammering in her throat.

"I'm sorry," Alaina finally whispered, eyes still fixed on her hands. Then she squared herself to the task and straightened, making eye contact. "It was unreasonable of me to ask you for what I did, and I'm sorry." Her hazel eyes searched Jess for any sign that the lava filling her veins was beginning to cool and tucked a stray wisp of hair behind her ear.

Jess raised a sardonic eyebrow at her friend and crossed her arms. "Sorry for which part? I'm going to need you to be more specific." If Alaina thought she would let her off the hook after so many weeks of pent-up frustration and unrealistic expectations, she had another think coming.

Alaina sighed and shifted her weight to both legs, hands shooting to her hips. "For all of it, okay? I should have been more supportive of you guys." Her eyes left her friend and met Jack's gaze. "You're good for her, and she loves you. That should have been enough. But…I let my selfish streak get in the way." She turned back to Jess. "I've just…I've dreamed my whole life about my wedding. I didn't want anyone to ruin it."

"Oh, that worked out well," Jess muttered with an eye roll. She felt Jack's hand, which had been resting on her back, snake around until his arm was wrapped around her waist, warning her with silent restraint.

Alaina swiped at the tears dribbling down her cheeks and rolled her eyes. "Yeah. I know. You don't have to rub it in." Her cheeks had flushed from a delicate pink to a furious red, and the pulse hammering in her throat had migrated to a vein in her temple. It was costing Alaina a good deal of pride to admit her misgivings and it was hard for Jess to not get a small thrill out of the high and mighty Alaina Montgomery-Miles admitting fault.

"What you did was really shitty."

"I know," Alaina agreed.

Jess dug her nails into the flesh of her palms, mirroring Alaina's behavior while she tried to decide how many more mea culpas would be enough. But therein laid the rub. She wasn't as vindictive as her friend could be. Part of that stemmed from her personality and part of it from the way she had grown up, having very few things to count on besides herself. For those reasons, she simply didn't have it in her to remain angry for long.

"You're never going to do that again." The words weren't

a question, but a statement of fact. She'd had enough of indulging her friend. They were at a crossroads. They could either learn and grow from it, or let it ruin what they'd spent a lifetime building.

Alaina nodded in wordless agreement, unsure what else to say.

Jack's hand squeezed Jess's hip in reassurance, telling her he was satisfied if she was, and she sighed, swinging her legs from his lap to get them under her and rise.

With a rustle of skirts, Jess stepped over to her friend and drew her in for a hug, her earring clinking against Alaina's cheek as they held each other. "I really am sorry about your reception," Jess murmured.

"I know." Alaina sighed and leaned her head against Jess's. After a few solid, relief-filled breaths, Jess sighed too and opened her eyes. Grayson was standing ten feet behind them, nose puffy and red, but relatively undamaged, Alaina's white fur wrap draped over his arm.

"Your husband is waiting for you," Jess murmured in Alaina's ear, a smile in her voice.

Alaina pulled back from Jess, wiping at the tears trailing down her cheeks before glancing over her shoulder at Grayson.

"You ready?" he asked in a low, tender voice.

She nodded and sniffled. "Yeah. I just need a minute," she said with a small smile in his direction.

Jack took that opportunity to rise from his chair and make reparations of his own.

"You look like shit," she heard Grayson say with a smile in his voice before redirecting her attention to Alaina.

"Try to enjoy your honeymoon," she said, as she wiped

another tear from her friend's cheek. "I'll hold down the fort back home. I promise."

Alaina let loose with a noise halfway between a sob and a laugh. "I signed the new lease and left it on your desk."

Jess nodded and looked over at Jack and Grayson who were embracing with a few smacks on each other's backs.

Alaina glanced over her shoulder at the two men and then back at Jess. "It was Grayson," Alaina murmured under her breath. "He's the one that got Janine the suite ticket."

Jess pulled back, slightly startled, and gazed at her friend, too confused to formulate a response. Finally she settled on, "What?"

Alaina reached out and grabbed Jess's hands, grasping them tightly. "Don't be mad," her friend pleaded, pinning Jess in place with her intense gaze. "He knows what it's like not to have a father. He wouldn't wish that on anyone."

Jess let her gaze fall from Alaina to where Grayson was now chatting amiably with Jack. She shook her head, still baffled. "I'm not mad."

"You promise?" Alaina asked with a single, perfectly arched eyebrow.

Jess laughed. How could she be mad at Grayson? He was sweet, and he'd meant well. "I promise!"

Alaina reached across and lightly tugged on her friend's earlobe. "I know I'm running low on luck, but…can I ask a favor?"

Jess raised her mouth in a lopsided smile and rolled her eyes: permission granted.

"Don't let it go to waste—what he did for you. Okay?"

It was Jess's turn for tears to prick her eyes, and she glanced one final time at the two handsome figures silhouetted against the doorway. How was it that two men, another set of best friends, could have changed the trajectory of her and Alaina's lives so irrevocably? "I'll see what I can do," she murmured to Alaina. "Now go. You've got a wedding night to enjoy, and I have a baby to get home to."

Alaina's bridal glow returned, and she leaned in to kiss Jess on the cheek. "I'll see you when I get back."

"Wear sunscreen!" Jess shouted after her with a smile, her heart swelling as she watched Grayson place Alaina's wrap around her shoulders, a look of unutterable tenderness on his face. That boy had it bad.

She let her gaze drift over to Jack, who she expected to be watching the couple as well, but he was watching her, gray eyes soft and full of passion. She blushed and smiled at him before turning to grab her clutch off the table.

It was time to go home.

* * *

The brisk breeze helped to clear the remaining haze from Jess's mind as they pushed open the main doors and stepped into the night. Indianapolis's normal hustle and bustle was nonexistent at this hour, which allowed one to truly appreciate the beauty of the Circle City. She took a deep breath and let her head fall back to look up at the night sky. The clouds were finally starting to clear to reveal the stars above.

Alaina and Grayson's town car had been waiting at the curb, and they were safely tucked away and headed to the hotel before Jess's car arrived. She shivered against the cool air, cursing herself for not bringing a wrap or a jacket. Jack,

416

gallant gentleman that he was, removed his tux jacket and draped it over her shoulders while he waited with her for her chariot. A silver Prius sidled to the curb, and the driver rolled down his window. "Jess?"

She waved at him. "Yep, coming."

Jack turned to her, wrapping his arms around her and giving her a tender kiss. "Sweet dreams, Sassy," he murmured as he leaned in to rub his nose against hers.

She gave him a sad half-smile and nuzzled him back. "Come home with me."

"You think that's a good idea? Maura's there, and I'm sure she's not pleased with me after tonight."

Jess pushed him playfully. "Puh-lease. If Alaina has known about us for two and half weeks, I can guarantee Maura did too." The Uber driver honked impatiently, and the noise traveled through the empty streets, echoing off the nearby buildings. Jess ignored him.

"I was talking about how I started a brawl at her daughter's wedding," Jack elaborated with an amused twitch from the undamaged side of his mouth.

"Oh…I totally forgot about that." The sarcasm dripped off Jess's words, and she shoved him again. "Come home with me."

Jack sighed and glanced past her toward the incensed Uber driver. "Alright, but only because your driver is going to have a conniption if you don't get in the car in the next thirty seconds, and I don't want you walking home."

Jess's heart did a giddy quickstep as Jack pulled her into the backseat. It wasn't the usual thoughts of wild sex or a steamy make-out session that caused the warm glow in her stomach. It was the thought of lying next to the man she loved and feeling the solid warmth of his body next to her as they slept. It was the idea of waking up to the pale dawn light and gazing into his eyes.

She couldn't imagine anything more perfect as she nestled against Jack's shoulder and closed her eyes.

They were finally free.

Thirty-Nine

Icing on the Cake

Sunday morning came more quickly than any sane person would have liked, and Parker, having gone to sleep at a normal time the night before, was up with the sun, bright-eyed and bushy tailed. It took a couple hours and several cups of coffee before Jess started to feel human again, but watching Jack make breakfast for them almost made the early wake up worth it.

Jess shuffled to the coffeepot for her fourth cup to the accompaniment of Parker's ecstatic coos and squeals from the living room. Bacon and eggs sizzled in the frying pan on the stove making Jess's stomach gurgle, and she meandered over to peer into the skillet, sitting her coffee cup on the counter to wrap her arms around Jack's middle and bury her face between his shoulder blades. "A man who can cook is a major turn on," she murmured, nipping playfully at him.

He turned in her arms and arched a brow, a plate full of

eggs in one hand. "Oh really?" His low voice rumbled in his chest, and he leaned down to give her a reciprocal nip on the neck.

They were just finishing their breakfast, cuddled up next to each other at the kitchen table, when there was a light knock at the door. Jess started like she'd been poked with a cattle prod, eyes wide, and Jack, sensing her distress, put a hand on her thigh to quiet her. He kissed her cheek. "Stay here. I'll get it."

She wrapped her shaking hands around her coffee mug, rising slightly to catch a glimpse of Parker, still perfectly content as he swatted at the dangling starfish and dolphins on his play mat mobile. She took another sip of her warm cup of joe, settled herself with a deep breath, and rose to make her way toward the unintelligible voices in the entryway. "Jack?" she asked quietly as she peeked around the corner.

He was standing with his back to her, one hand resting on the partially open front door, blocking whoever it was from view. He turned at the sound of her voice though, revealing the silhouette of a man standing on the front porch.

She froze to the spot, recognizing that tall, slender frame and perfectly groomed hair. Suddenly, she was overwhelmed with the urge to turn and run for the bedroom, maybe even crawl under the bed, but she took another breath, and then another. When she had calmed her racing heart and found her tongue, she stepped toward the door. Toward her father.

Jack turned to her, brow furrowed in concern at her pallor. "I can tell him to leave," he whispered, taking her hand in his to warm her cold fingers.

She shook her head. "No. It's okay. Um…" She glanced at Julian and then back at Jack. "Can you go get Parker?"

Jack nodded, glanced one more time at their unannounced guest, and disappeared back down the hallway, leaving Jess alone with the problem she'd been avoiding for more than two weeks.

She stepped up to the door, placing her hand on the knob and twisting idly. "What are you doing here?" she asked, her voice soft and unassuming.

Julian's green eyes—*God, were her eyes really that beautiful?*—probed her, flicking from the faint yellow tinge of fading bruises on her face, to the brace on her wrist, to the pain in her eyes. "I just…" He gave a heavy sigh and shifted his weight. "I had to know you were okay."

Jess lifted her chin a fraction in mild indignance. "If you wanted to know how I was, why did you call María? You had to know she wouldn't be able to tell you anything. I told you. I cut her off."

He gave an exasperated huff and threw his hands up. "I didn't know what else to do, Jessica. You wouldn't take my calls! Noah wouldn't tell me anything. It took every string I could pull just to get María's phone number."

She looked at the floor, unable to stand the pain stamped all over his face. She'd misjudged him, and that admission stung. A lot.

"Jessica," he whispered, begging her to look at him.

In. Out. Innnnn. Outttt.

She gripped the doorknob tighter to steady her shaking hand, and then lifted her gaze to meet his, unable to hide her tears. "Why do you care?" she asked, her voice so weak a feather could have knocked it over. "I mean…you don't know me."

He furrowed his brow, desperate to make her understand.

"Because you're my daughter." He said the words as though it was the most simple explanation in the world, and something in her broke.

The breath stuttered in her chest, and suddenly he was there, over the threshold, wrapping his arms around her. She sobbed into his chest, desperately gripping at his shirt as she let everything else fall away: the guilt, the grief, the anger, the hurt.

"I'm sorry," he murmured as he held her. "I'm so sorry."

Never in her life had she felt a father's love, or anything even close. The immensity of it, the overwhelming strength and steadfast sense of safety were dizzying. For so long, she'd muddled through on her own, struggling with a sense of doubt so profound, it colored every decision, every thought and action. She had people in her life who cared about her. She'd never doubted that, but this…this feeling of completeness she felt with her father's arms around her? It was unparalleled. It was like after searching high and low for years and never finding answers, she'd finally given up, only to realize she'd never even asked the question. The utter relief she felt at having that answer, the final puzzle piece, was transcendent.

He stroked her hair and quietly shushed her until she was able to pull herself together. Finally, she pulled back and looked up at him, wiping at the tears staining her face. "So I guess you met Jack," she said with a half-laugh, half-sob.

He gave her a lopsided grin, reaching out to help dab the tear tracks on her cheeks. "Well, I'd love for you to introduce us properly."

Jess nodded with a big sniff and smiled. "Come on."

He quietly closed the door behind him and followed her

into the living room where Jack sat with Parker on his knee, bouncing him up and down, making car noises. Parker was eliciting quiet giggles as Jack tilted his leg left and right making braking and accelerating noises. Seeing their approach, Jack hiked Parker into a one-armed hold against his chest and stood.

"Jack, this is my dad, Julian." The word "dad" felt odd on her lips, but somehow completely natural, and Julian didn't flinch either, which she supposed was a good sign.

Jack extended a hand to Julian. "Nice to meet you, sir," he greeted with a warm smile. "Sorry we didn't get off to the best start."

"No apologies necessary. You were just looking out for Jessica. I can't blame you for that." The smile on his face was genuine, but his eyes weren't on Jack at all. They were glued to the baby in his arms. Jess met her boyfriend's gaze and smiled before taking the baby from him.

Her dad looked up, eyebrows raised in silent question. *Could he?*

Her smile grew, and she extended her arms to hand Parker to her father, praying he wouldn't cry. "This is your grandson, Parker."

Julian took the little one in his arms with an expertise born of long experience, automatically bouncing to cajole the befuddled baby, who now found himself staring into the face of a stranger. "Hi there," Julian greeted in his deep, soothing voice. "You're a handsome little guy, aren't you?"

Parker made a small grunt, seeming to be in agreement with his grandfather regarding his devilishly handsome good looks, and Julian chuckled. He seemed to glow from the inside out with his grandson in his arms, and the sight warmed Jessica through to her backbone. Her grandmother had been her one constant, always there to protect her, to love her, and prop her up when no one else could. The idea that she was able to give her son something that important was enough to cut through the final rope tethering her down and send her into the stratosphere, buoyant with joy.

* * *

The day passed by in a blur, and Julian, wanting to visit with his parents while he was in town, had excused himself with a promise to come back before he returned to California. Jess wanted him to meet Tita, and while her grandmother had been in his corner while encouraging Jess to give him a chance, she didn't know how a face-to-face meeting would go between Ivanna Morales and the man who had impregnated her teenage daughter twenty-six years ago.

But there was no rush. Julian wasn't going anywhere, and that knowledge was a massive weight off her shoulders.

She sighed and nuzzled further into Jack's chest. They were laying on the couch, some random TV show playing in the background as they dozed. Parker was napping in his room, the exhaustion from the wedding taking its toll on even the smallest inhabitant of the house.

Jack tightened his arms around her and rubbed his cheek against the top of her head, half asleep. She tilted her head back to look at him. His face was mottled with bruises, but he was still the most handsome man she'd ever seen. He smiled down at her through slit eyes. "What?"

"Just trying to remember how I ended up here," she murmured, not moving or redirecting her gaze.

"I think we took an Uber." His sleepy one-sided grin erupted into a full-on smile, this one full of mischief.

"Shut up. You know what I mean." She chastised him playfully.

He sobered but kept the wistful smile on his face as she looked up at him. "Yeah…I know what you mean."

She tilted her head up further so he could lean down to place a gentle kiss on her lips, afraid to instigate anything physical and aggravate his injuries, but he ran the hand resting on her hip up the length of her body until he cupped her face, finishing what she started. "When do you have to be back?"

Jack snorted, but shifted back so they were facing each other rather than Jess being situated on top of him. "I have to get going soon. The team is hosting a charity event tomorrow. We're testing at Indy this week though, so I'll be back before you know it."

Jess groaned at the prospect of a few days without him and cuddled into his chest, hugging him to her.

"Trust me, I'd rather be here. I don't like leaving you," he argued in reciprocal yearning as he squeezed her around the middle.

She stilled against his chest, her breath hitching for half a second before she blurted, "Then don't."

He snorted in amusement. "Right. I'll just let you explain it all to my team owner then."

"No. I mean…move in with me."

Nothing but the sound of the birds chirping outside and the quiet whoosh of Parker's sound machine filled the air. "What?" Jack finally asked, shifting so he could see her fully, his gray eyes wide and clear as a set of tidal pools.

Fears and doubts crashed around her and threatened to cave in her resolve. Only moments before, she thought it sounded like the best idea she'd ever had.

Impulsive?

Sure.

Crazy?

Maybe.

But now, as she struggled with the reins of a horse threatening to bolt, she was beginning to wonder what the hell was wrong with her. "Move in with me," she whispered. She gently cupped his face, hoping to bridge the divide between them.

"What about Tucker?"

Well, yes, there was Tucker to consider, but after their conversation last night, she knew Tuck viewed any progress in her relationship with Jack as inevitable. "Tuck will be fine. And if he gets pissed off—which he won't—I'll protect you."

Jack raised his brow in mock offense. "Wow…too soon."

She giggled and repeated herself for a third and final time. "Move in with me."

He studied her face for a long moment, and then that gorgeous, devilish smile blossomed on his face, tugging in all the right places, causing his face to glow with uncontainable happiness. "Okay. Let's do it."

They had a lot to figure out, but for the first time in her life, Jess felt like she had a course charted and knew where she was headed. The sensation was unsettling, but only because of its unfamiliarity. It hadn't been that long ago that she had sat on this very couch, scared shitless at the idea of impending motherhood and wondering where her life was headed. She'd learned so much since then, not about anything you could read in a book, but about the things she'd spent her whole life searching for. Family. Friends. Happiness. Love.

Suddenly and without ceremony, those things had been dropped in her lap: a father willing to cross the country for her at a moment's notice, a caring, passionate partner who stood by her when the rising tides threatened to wash everything else away, and a son, precious and innocent, in which to channel every ounce of love she had to give.

And when you had everything you never knew you always wanted, the rest was simply icing on the cake.

Epilogue

"I know you said you wanted whipped icing on the cake, but I'm pretty sure it's buttercream." The cringe on Alaina's face was enough to make Jess fizz with laughter. Her friend's reflection in the mirror was one of stress and confusion as she stroked her six-month baby bump. "I can send it back—"

"Lainie, it's fine. Whipped cream, buttercream, it really doesn't matter to me." She knew most women got some sort of jitters on their wedding day, but she'd never felt more serene. She was in a bulletproof bubble, and nothing, short of someone telling her they couldn't find the groom, was going to pop it. Her head wobbled as the hairdresser tugged on her locks gently to pin them in place, but she continued to study her friend. Impending motherhood looked good on her, and she didn't want her to stress. She and Jack had thought long and hard about what kind of wedding they wanted, and at the end of the day, they decided a few close friends and family at an intimate ceremony were all they needed.

No muss. No fuss.

"How's Jack?"

"Cool as a cucumber," Grayson interjected from the door as he popped his head in. "He says not to worry, and he promises he won't be late."

Jess rolled her eyes but got cut off in her reply.

"He better not be. He's your assignment, mister." Alaina lifted her face to smile at her husband as he sauntered further into the room.

"Hi," he murmured with a resounding smile as he leaned in to kiss her.

Normally, Jess would take the opportunity to make obnoxious cooing noises fit to make Grayson blush, but not today. Today, she planned to make plenty of PDAs herself. "Where's my son?" she asked as she brought her gaze back to her reflection and continued to watch her slow transformation into a bride.

"Last time I checked, Tuck was taking him down to the beach to run off some energy. He wanted to swim, but dream crusher that I am, I told him he couldn't swim until after the wedding," Alaina dutifully informed. Grayson wrapped his arms around her from behind and caressed her belly, to which Alaina hummed, but didn't lean into him, hoping to spare her hairdo. He pecked her on the cheek and said, "Okay, I've delivered my message. Back to the lair I go."

"I'd hardly call the in-law to a multi-million-dollar Malibu beach house a lair." Jess chastised him in a playful tone. Her stepmother, Janine, had been instrumental in securing such a perfect wedding venue. When she'd gotten word that the oceanfront mansion was going on the market, she'd pulled a few strings with her friends in the area and arranged to rent it out for forty-eight hours. The back of the house consisted of a large paved outdoor area, complete with an infinity pool overlooking the Pacific Ocean. Alaina had, of course, added her pixie dust and outfitted the area with a large pergola draped in white gossamer, thick vines of ivy, vibrant sunset roses for a pop of color, and fuchsia orchid petals floating on the pool.

"Yeah, well, until we can come out and socialize with everyone else, it's a lair. You look beautiful, by the way."

"Thank you," she replied with a smile. He was impossible not to like, and he'd been instrumental in smoothing her and Jack's relationship over with Tucker in the months following the wedding. As much as she hated to admit it, she couldn't have done it without him. Well, maybe she could have, but it would have been a torturous process.

An hour later, with hair and makeup complete, Jess found herself standing in front of the glass sliding door to the oceanfront balcony. The flutters in her stomach had started about the time Alaina unzipped the garment bag containing her dress. It wasn't that she was nervous—just excited.

So. Excited.

Carefully, she stepped into her gown, a gorgeous fit-and-flare Randy Fenoli with a V-neck. It was beautiful in its simplicity, but the one flare she'd allowed was the large bow pinned to the low scoop back of the dress that trailed after her in lieu of a train or a veil. She reached up to reassure herself the two sunset roses pinned in her hair were still there and took a deep breath as Tita and Alaina pulled the dress up over her hips, pausing for her to put her arms through the straps. It zipped up like a dream and she sighed with relief. If she'd come close to stressing about anything, it was that her dress may not fit the same way it had in her final alterations appointment two weeks before.

She smiled at her grandmother, who had tears in her eyes as she adorned Jess with the simple teardrop pearl earrings and necklace she'd worn on her wedding day fifty years earlier. When she'd given them to Jess shortly after her engagement, Jess had burst into tears. Her abuelo had given Tita the jewelry on the eve of their wedding, and she'd held on to them ever since.

Until today.

Now they were Jessica's to pass on to her daughter one day. She pinched her matching pearl pendant necklace between her thumb and forefinger and fought back tears as she gazed at her grandmother—the woman who had given her every chance in life.

"Thank you," she whispered, tears spilling over and down her cheeks. "For everything."

"Shhh," her grandmother comforted, patting away the tears before they could take her makeup with them. "No me debes nada, cariña." She drew a shaky breath through her lips, fighting back tears herself, and cupped her granddaughter's cheek. "Estoy tan orgullosa de ti."

Jess wasn't sure what she'd done to deserve such a sweet woman in her life, someone who was proud of her for living her life and doing the best she could. She couldn't have done it without her.

Tita glanced over Jess's shoulder toward the door and gave a knowing smile before stepping out of the way and handing her over into Julian's care. If Jess had been teary with her grandmother, she was a goner now as she stared up into her father's misty eyes.

"You look…" Words failed him. So instead, he moved in to give her a bear hug.

She clung to him as an anchor in the sea of emotion she was experiencing. His presence had the opposite effect of what she expected. It was as if his strength was bleeding into her, and she took a deep breath, hugging him back before releasing him with a smile. "You ready for this?"

He gave her an incredulous look that made her laugh. "Ready? Hell no. It's like giving your two-year-old away in marriage. I just got you, and now I have to give you up?"

She rolled her eyes. "I wish people wouldn't use that term. It's not 'giving up' or 'giving away' anything. Jack and I have been living together for almost two years. The only thing that's changing is my last name."

Julian nodded and smiled. "I hope your marriage brings you as much joy as mine has brought me. And I'm so thankful we could all be here with you today."

She bit her bottom lip in a valiant effort at controlling her emotions and took a deep breath. "Alaina, get me out of here before I have no makeup left on my face."

Everyone in the room smiled and laughed, but shuffled toward the door. Alaina gathered the trailing ribbon of Jess's bow and the hem of her dress so she could better navigate the stairs and followed diligently behind to be of assistance if needed.

"Mama!" Parker shouted from his place by the entrance to the pool area. He looked so handsome in his little tux, and she wanted to scoop him up and leave lipstick stains all over his precious face.

"You look so handsome, baby!" she cried as she squatted to hug him.

"You pwitty, Mama," he proclaimed along with a long stream of other toddler gibberish, wherein she picked up "daddy," "beach," "water" and "bath." Then he gave her a big wet kiss on her cheek and scurried out of her arms over to Tucker, who stood waiting patiently with one hand tucked in his pants pocket by the patio door. The house was a gorgeous mix of modern decor with California beach vibes, and Jess wished she could somehow come up with the three point eight million dollars they were asking for it.

"Nervous?" Tuck asked as he scooped up their son to keep him in one place for more than ten seconds.

"Only the good kind," she responded with a long exhale. She gave him a small smile and turned to take her bouquet of roses and deep purple stocks from Tita. Stepping closer to the door so Alaina could properly fluff her gown one more time, she took the opportunity to speak semi-privately to her ex. "Thank you for coming. I know it wasn't an easy decision."

"Are you kidding? You're one of my oldest friends—not to mention the mother of my son. I wouldn't miss it."

Her hesitant grin turned into a full-blown smile at his sincerity. "I saw your date. Can't wait to hear that story."

His cheeks flushed a delicate pink, and he looked down at his shoes. "It's been a hard year, but we're in a good place."

She reached out and squeezed his forearm, giving him a quiet, knowing smile. "I'm happy for you, Tuck." Then, chucking Parker under the chin one more time for good measure, she stepped aside for Alaina to shoo them to their seats.

Quiet ukulele music played on the sound system in the pool area as everyone hummed with excitement. Jess stood on her tiptoes, peering around the door to catch a glimpse of her fiancé, but he was hidden from view. It was a good thing

Julian was there to hold her back. Otherwise, she'd likely run headlong down the aisle. She wasn't one for pomp and ceremony. She never had been, but she only planned to get married once, and if she was going to do it, she was going to do it right. The music changed from quiet instrumental to the quick strums of Israel Kamakawiwo'ole's "Somewhere Over the Rainbow."

"I think that's our cue," Julian said as he tugged her closer to his side. "You ready?"

Jess let out a steadying breath and nodded. "Ready."

The gentle breeze off the Pacific coast ruffled across her dress and through her hair like the tender caress of a lover as she stepped out onto the terrace, arm in arm with her father. The sun was sinking toward the ocean, sparking the sky with shades of orange, yellow, and scarlet. It was beautiful, and if it weren't for the man waiting at the end of the aisle, she might have stopped to take it all in.

By the time they reached the pergola and its backdrop of sparkling ocean waves, her heart was thrumming in her chest like a hummingbird's wing. Her dad kissed her cheek, and then her hand as he pulled it from his arm and placed it in Jack's waiting grasp. It was moments like these she'd simply never dared to dream of. How did a fatherless young girl without two pennies to rub together end up walking down the aisle with her dad by her side at a multi-million-dollar mansion toward the man of her dreams?

The man of her dreams who had just signed a five-year contract as an autosports commentator for Fox Sports.

The world worked in mysterious ways, and she could go crazy trying to make sense of it all. Instead, she looked up into the sparkling eyes of her soon-to-be husband and smiled.

It wasn't until several hours later, after the celebration had died down, the guests had left for their hotels, and Jack and Jess were left alone, sitting on the edge of the pool, that she let herself go.

"Why are you crying?" Jack murmured as he pulled her in closer to him and nuzzled the top of her head.

Sniffing, she wiped at her tears. "I'm just…today was so…perfect."

He turned and kissed the top of her head. "Yeah. It was."

She sat up and stared at him, tugging his tux jacket tighter around her shoulders. "Do you think Janine can get us a sweet deal on this house?"

Jack let out a hard laugh. "I think your idea and her idea of a 'sweet deal' are about a mile apart, but it was a good thought."

She looked up into the sky, appreciating the way the outside lights displayed the rustic Italianate architecture of the building. Lush greenery bordered the north and south sides of the pool with potted lemon and orange trees which left a great view of the beach to the west, though the terrace itself was high enough above the sand to keep the public from turning into a bunch of peeping Toms. "Well, we have the place for another twelve hours, give or take. What do you say we make use of that gorgeous master suite?"

He waggled his eyebrows at her. "Are you propositioning me?"

"I think propositioning was in the fine print right under 'to love and to cherish.'"

In one smooth move, he pulled his feet out of the water and popped up onto the terrace, pulling her with him. "Shall we?"

He swept her off her feet and she let out a startled shriek before dissolving into uncontrollable giggles.

"Put me down!"

"Sorry, Sassy. Don't you know it's good luck for the groom to carry the bride across the threshold?" He was grinning from ear to ear in the dim glow of the tiki torches lining the patio.

"I think that only signifies if you own the place, and as we just discussed, it's sadly out of our price range, hon." She craned her neck up to kiss him on his jaw and then relaxed and cuddled into his shoulder as he carried her through the kitchen toward the main suite.

"We haven't really talked about it, but uh…what do you think about a baby?" Jack asked. His tone was light, going for another laugh as he laid her across the white duvet dotted with orchid petals.

She bit her bottom lip to hide her grin and looked up at him hovering over her in the dark of the room. The only light between them was the moon reflecting off the ocean in the distance. "I know you're joking, but um…" She practically felt his heart stop and couldn't help the giggles threatening to burst through her lips.

"You're not serious," he said, his voice gravelly with strain.

They had only talked about it a couple times, and while they both agreed they wanted more children, Jess had expressed her desire to wait, at least until Parker's third birthday—but that was several months away, and life, apparently, had other ideas.

"As a heart attack."

He plunked down on the bed next to her, causing her to bounce up off the mattress. "How long have you known?"

His hushed voice was full of incredulity and excitement.

"Just a few days. I thought it would be fun to wait until tonight after everyone left to tell you." She rolled over and propped herself up on one elbow to get a better look at him. "Are you…happy?"

"Are you freaking kidding me? This is…Oh my god, yes. I'm so happy!" He leaned into her and gave her a kiss she wasn't likely to forget, even long after she was dead.

The joy and love and hope radiating from him were contagious, flooding her from head to toe with a pulsing desire to live life to the absolute fullest. She pulled him closer and kissed him back, letting herself get swept away in a future of boundless possibilities.

When I first began writing *Downforce,* I had no intentions of that novel ever becoming a series, but the story of Grayson Miles and Alaina Montgomery is inextricably linked with the stories of their friends and family, and slowly but surely, Jess's voice started to niggle at me. Flashes of a new story began to run through my head. I was staring off into space thinking about this compelling love triangle, when suddenly, a flashbulb went off. These characters I created to support Grayson and Alaina weren't side characters, but main characters in their own right, people who love deeply, have fiery tempers, make bad decisions, and struggle with their pasts.

I think I can safely say I *did not* see Jessica Morales coming. She walloped me over the head at least ten times while I was writing this book—in the best way. She's a person that has experienced more misfortune in her short life than any one person should, and her resilience floored me. She was forced to exude strength from an early age, and as a result, has built a nearly impenetrable wall around herself. She lives to protect others, to build them up, and make them feel good, but she often does it at her own expense. It was important for me to portray that in a very real and vulnerable way. I had a lot of trepidation surrounding the creation of a Latina main character, but I want to thank Lara, Mae and Jazmine for not completely laughing at my toddler-level Spanish, and helping me put a little life and Puerto Rican flair into Jess's story.

Jack and Jess really seemed to hit it off in *Downforce* and I felt mildly bad about pulling them apart at the end of the story, but Jess and Tucker wanted to do right by their child, however misguided, and I respected that. When book two started taking shape, I knew I needed to dissect that separation. We all know the path to hell is paved with good intentions, and I wanted to explore what life looked like when every action a person takes is powered by the need to do the right thing for others. It's emotionally exhausting and physically draining on Jess. It wears on her strongest friendships. It destroyed her relationship with a man she deeply, and truly loved, and impacts her very essence. It's only when Jack comes back into her life and insists upon putting *her* first, that she begins to heal from all the pain and hurt she's endured.

My life could not be more different from the female lead I created in *Riptide*, but we still have our similarities, and writing her truth became therapeutic for me as she learns to deal with her crippling anxiety and her need to constantly prove she's good enough. I want to send out a massive hug and lots of air kisses to my two fabulous alpha readers Jess and Casey. Your constant support, even when I'm sure I was a complete pain in your sides, has been indispensable, and I cannot thank you enough!

When an author finally gets through their story and writes "The End," it's actually only the beginning, and to get a story from its first draft to a product ready for publication takes endless hours, lots of patience, and a boatload of finesse. Luckily, I have the best editor on the face of the earth in my dear friend Lacey. From the beginning stages, coaching me through plot holes and shaky character arcs, to figuring out the one missing piece nobody could crack the code on, it's because of you that *Riptide* has evolved into this story I'm incredibly proud of.

Over the last three years, I've poured my heart and soul into this story, and I really hope you love it as much as I do. If you do, and you are sad to see it end, don't worry! While Jack and Jess may have their happily ever after, there are still a couple of guys out there looking for their lady loves. I leave it to you to speculate on the who, what, and when, but just know, they're always percolating in the back of my mind, and I have something truly spectacular in the works!

Riptide Playlist

True to form, *Riptide* is full of angst, but I also can't write a story without a little bit of laughter and a whole lot of love! Here are a few songs I found myself listening to on loop while writing Jack and Jess's Happily Ever After!

- "How Long Will I Love You" by Ellie Goulding
- "Want to Want Me" by Jason Derulo
- "Issues" by Julia Michaels
- "Hands to Myself" by Selena Gomez
- "Dreams" by NEEDTOBREATHE
- "I Remember" by Forest Blakk
- "Someone to You" by BANNERS
- "One Call Away" by Charlie Puth
- "Mercy" by Brett Young
- "Simple Things" by Teddy Swims
- "Somewhere Over the Rainbow" by Israel Kamakawiwo'ole

Up Next for the Crossroads Series

I'd always planned on Tucker's story being the third—and possibly the last—book in the Crossroads series. So, imagine my surprise when Noah Kinney popped up out of the clear blue sky and brazenly assumed he was getting a book as well. So, three books became four, and suddenly I was struggling with my next move. Who gets to go first: the sweet, single dad with anger issues, or, the Alpha male, ex-cop with a soft side?

How is a girl to choose?

Well, to be honest, it all boiled down to the fact that Tucker was more stubborn—that and I felt bad for making him wait a second longer after the shit show he endured in *Riptide*.

So, while you're patiently waiting for whatever comes next, I thought I'd give you a taste of what you have to look forward to when *Aftershock* makes it's grand entrance.

And now... enjoy the first chapter of Crossroads: Book Three, *Aftershock*.

Why was it, every time he returned home, it either started or ended in disaster? If it wasn't a drunk driver trying to run over his sister, or Jess putting a wrecking ball through the future he envisioned for them, it was him deciding to pour gasoline on an already roaring bonfire.

God, he'd need a week's worth of workouts to even put a dent in the jealousy, betrayal, and rage swarming around him like an angry hornet's nest.

Alaina's wedding had been a disaster, despite his best intentions.

Jess wanted to be friends. He…did not.

And yeah, he'd fucked up royally when she'd brought their son, Parker, down to Sheppard Air Force Base, where he was stationed, for a visit. Kissing her had not been a smart move, but there was just something about her he couldn't resist…or at the very least, didn't *want* to resist. This time, he had been determined to keep himself in check.

He'd shown up to the wedding rehearsal with full intentions of taking the high road, and hopefully, as the weekend went on and things settled between them, talk things out, tell her he had chosen not to reenlist, and develop a game plan to move forward as co-parents once he moved back home.

That had been the plan, anyway.

She'd been cagey from the get-go, avoiding eye contact, conveniently leaving a room as he was entering, and in the rare moments when he could catch her alone, only indulging him with mild, polite conversation that always centered around Parker. He'd thought she was still feeling some sort of way about the kiss, and he'd kicked himself over and over for crossing a line she'd so firmly drawn in the sand. But then, he'd started to notice things: slightly smeared lipstick when she returned from the bathroom, a faint glow to her as she walked down the aisle on her ex's arm, the stolen glances they would share when they thought no one was looking.

He hadn't been sure whether to be appreciative of their discretion, or offended they thought he was that oblivious. But catching them half-naked in the coat closet at the reception had promptly ended any thought he'd had of a gracious retreat back to Texas. He'd completely lost it. No reason. No control. Just blind rage. A rage that still simmered just below the boiling point and fueled his need to beat the living hell out of someone or something.

"Jesus. You weren't kidding when you said you needed to blow off some steam." Wes's raised voice came to him above the constant dull thud of his fists hitting the punching bag in front of him. The smell of chalk dust, sweat, and equipment cleaner normally helped to calm him when he was upset, but not today.

Sweat poured from his brow and dripped to the floor, droplets spraying from his face as he delivered a vicious jab-cross. Putting his hand out to still the bag, he turned to Wes. "And you weren't kidding when you said you have a very punchable face."

Wes raised a brow, but the corner of his lips twitched in amusement. "Ouch. What's got your panties in a wad?"

"Nothing," Tuck grumbled, as he tightened the Velcro on one glove and turned back to the bag. "Did you bring your gloves?"

"Hell no. You know I don't spar with you when you get like this. I'd wind up with a black eye." Wes crossed his arms and leaned against the squat rack next to the station Tucker was occupying.

Jab, jab, cross.

"Damn… you're wired. What the hell happened?"

Tucker gritted his teeth, not ready to talk about it. *Jab, cross, left hook. Jab, jab.*

"Alright… so you don't feel like talking. That's cool. I'll just… let you do your thing."

Jab, jab, cross, left hook. Jab, right hook.

"You know… if this has anything to do with Jess—and I'm guessing it does—"

Cross, left hook, cross. Jab, cross, lead uppercut.

"—you might be better off talking to Cass. I know nothing about women. You know that." Wes snorted, continuing to watch the timeless battle between irresistible force and immovable object.

Right uppercut, left uppercut, left hook. Jab, cross, jab. Left hook, right hook, cross. Tuck continued to pound on the bag with more and more fury, throwing in an MMA style skip knee.

"Alright, I see we've dispensed with just boxing…is that good or bad?" Wes asked, attempting to get some sort of communication out of Tucker.

Jab, right uppercut, left hook. Jab, jab, cross. Cross, left hook, lead uppercut. With one more powerful burst of anger, he swung the entire weight of his body and laid a haymaker on the bag, feeling the reverberation all the way through to the soles of his feet.

He backed away from the heavy bag, which was swinging lazily in a wide arc with the force of his final blow, sucking wind. He pulled on the tabs of his gloves with the rending sound of separating Velcro and tossed them on the weight bench next to him. Wes, sensing he was ready to talk, offered a bottle of water by way of peace offering. Tucker took it, guzzling half of it in one go before running his forearm across his forehead to clear the rivulets of sweat running down his face and stinging his eyes.

Finally, after getting his breath back, he took one more gulp of water and turned to his friend. "I walked in on Jess fucking her ex in the coat closet at Alaina's reception."

Wes let out a low whistle, dark brows raised in shock. "Ouch."

Every muscle in his arm quivered with exhaustion as he lifted the water bottle back to his lips for another long drink. With the bottle completely drained, he tossed it into a nearby trashcan and made for his gym bag and the towel inside. He was still pouring sweat and needed something other than his equally sweaty forearm to staunch the flow.

"I kinda lost it." His words were muffled in the towel as he dabbed at his face, but Wes heard him clearly. When he removed the towel, he saw that his friend had pushed off of his lounging spot and was standing in front of him, caution stamped on his schooled features.

"Define 'kinda.'"

Tucker proceeded to lay out the whole story, bit by agonizing bit, until every unsavory detail was out in the open. It wasn't that he relished reliving the experience, but he needed an objective opinion, and he knew Wes could be counted on to give him that.

"Shit, Tuck…" Wes's face was scrunched up in overwhelmed exasperation, and he ran a hand roughly over it. Finally, he sighed and opened his cool blue eyes, ready to dish out a dose of his best no-nonsense "dad" advice. "You've got to do something about this. It's getting out of control."

Tucker clenched his jaw and stared down at his tennis

shoes, shuffling them from side to side on the rubber mat covering the gym floor. He didn't like it when Wes's opinions echoed the inner voice he'd been trying so hard to ignore. He liked it even less when those opinions shoved a high-powered searchlight into the dark crevices of his soul where he'd shoved his mangled memories of war and death and attempted to plaster over them with a flakey mortar composed of pride and denial. But whether he wanted to acknowledge it or not, it was always there, lurking, waiting for a vulnerable moment in his defenses to stick its head through the crack in the mortar, all red eyes and gnashing teeth.

"I'm handling it," he grumbled as he turned back to his gym bag and shoved the towel and his boxing gloves inside. The zippers whined in protest with his vicious yank.

"Bullshit."

If he mashed his teeth any harder together, his molars would crack. The urge to lash out and hit something was coming back with a vengeance, but instead, he took a deep breath and let it out slowly.

"You really want to go back to your family, to your *son*, like this? Unable to stop yourself from lashing out and hurting someone? You may be able to hide it when you're talking to them on the phone or only seeing them for a few hours at a time, but that only goes so far. You could have been arrested for that stunt at the wedding. You realize that, right?"

"I'm done talking about this. Okay? I don't need to pay somebody to tell me I have issues. I think that's pretty obvious to anyone within earshot." He glanced around at the other men scattered across the gym, nervous at being overheard. Tucker tossed his bag over his shoulder and started toward the exit, careful not to make eye contact with any of the guys they passed as he picked his way around random workout stations.

Wes didn't speak again until they'd made it to the parking lot and were hovering between their vehicles. "You're still able to keep Piper on the tenth, right? Cass made a reservation at some fancy bed and breakfast for our anniversary, and I'd hate to lose the deposit."

Tucker smirked, the emotions roiling around inside him easing slightly at the thought of his adorable little goddaughter. He and Pippy were two peas in a pod. Whether he was using her as a surrogate for his own son, whom he barely saw, or because he was feeling particularly paternal these days, he didn't mind the prospect of a few days with his girl while her parents went and enjoyed some "alone time."

Lord knew, he didn't have anything else to occupy his time. "Yeah. Sure thing. I'm looking forward to it." Tuck tugged open the back seat of his truck and tossed his bag inside, sighing as he pushed it closed and turned back to face his best friend. "I was really excited to move back home. To see Parker again and to spend some time with Lainie and Grayson, but now..."

"Cut it out. You're still excited for all of those things." Wes rolled his eyes and punched Tucker lightly in the shoulder.

He threw his head back and pinched the bridge of his nose, desperate to solve at least one of the thousand problems he had piling up on him like the leave requests in his chief engineer's inbox. "I just hate how fucking awkward this has all become. Ya know?"

"Well, then quit making it awkward," Wes argued with an amused grin as he tossed his keys with one hand.

The lighthearted teasing was working. Tuck could feel the weight that had been suffocating him for two days begin to lift off his chest as they talked. "You make it seem so easy."

"Listen. You're butt hurt. I get it. But this isn't about you. It's about Parker, and he deserves a lot better than what's on offer right now." Tucker jerked his head up like he'd been slapped, and Wes rolled his eyes again. "I know you'd never do anything to hurt him, but you've gotta be the bigger man here, Tuck. Moving back home is like stepping onto foreign soil. You gotta respect the natives."

Tucker gave a low growl, but acquiesced. He knew what Wes was saying, and it made sense. He was just damn tired of taking L's. Everybody deserved a win every now and then. Otherwise, what was the point?

www.ingramcontent.com/pod-product-compliance
Lightning Source LLC
Chambersburg PA
CBHW070304310726
48976CB00005B/1559